RUNAWAY
MURDER

RUNAWAY MURDER

A Carson Stables Mystery

Leigh Hearon

KENSINGTON PUBLISHING CORP.

www.kensingtonbooks.com

KENSINGTON BOOKS are published by

Kensington Publishing Corp.
119 West 40th Street
New York, NY 10018

All Kensington titles, imprints, and distributed lines are available at special quantity discounts for bulk purchases for sales promotions, premiums, fund-raising, educational, or institutional use. Special book excerpts or customized printings can also be created to fit specific needs. For details, write or phone the office of the Kensington sales manager: Kensington Publishing Corp., 119 West 40th Street, New York, NY 10018, attn: Sales Department; phone 1-800-221-2647.

ISBN-13: 978-1-4967-1410-7
ISBN-10: 1-4967-1410-5

First printing: July 2018

10 9 8 7 6 5 4 3 2 1

Printed in the United States of America

First electronic edition: July 2018

ISBN-13: 978-1-4967-1411-4
ISBN-10: 1-4967-1411-3

For Sandy Dengler
Who's responsible for just about everything.

Darby Farms Dressage Show
October 14–15

Entrants	**Trainer**
Liz Faraday *Sammy, Danish Warmblood gelding* *Training level test 1*	Patricia Winters
Lucy Cartwright *Prince, Hanoverian gelding* *Training level test 1*	Melissa Phelps
Amy Litchfield *Schumann, Arab gelding* *Second level test 3*	Melissa Phelps
Tabitha Rawlins *Jackson, Friesian gelding* *Second level test 3*	Harriett Blechstein
Gwendolyn Smythe *Martinique, Dutch Warmblood gelding* *Third level test 2*	Harriett Blechstein
Nicole Anne Forrester *Andy, Andalusian gelding* *Prix St.-Georges*	Who needs a trainer?

Hollis and Miriam Darby, *hosts*
Jean Bennett, *judge*
Margaret Woods, *scribe*
Brianna Bowen, *technical delegate*
Annie Carson, *guest*
Gustav Raymond, *chef*

Chapter One

"Well, I'd say this was a runaway success, wouldn't you?"

A hearty slap on the back nearly knocked Annie over, and she grasped the first object she could find to keep from falling. It was a card table, stacked with appetizers, and for a moment, she thought the carefully crafted trays would crash to the floor along with her.

Annie had spent the past three days hauling fifty horses to the stable in which she was now standing. She was tired. Bone tired, in fact. Her muscles hurt, and apparently now a few more were going to, as well.

Wincing a bit, she looked up into the round, smiling face of Sheriff Dan Stetson, the head of law and order in Suwana County. He looked so pleased with himself, she couldn't help but smile back.

"It sure is, Dan. It's a wonderful party."

Dan nodded smugly and moved his bulky frame toward a row of beer kegs. Annie watched him tap off a local microbrew. Well, he *was* off duty.

Looking around, Annie viewed the festivities, now

in full swing. The stable was festooned with crepe, ribbons, and balloons. A large banner overhead read WELCOME TO ALEX'S PLACE! Guests crowded the appetizer tables and wine bar, and the buzz of animated conversations filled every corner. Judging by the fashionably dressed people surrounding her, the venue could have been Lincoln Center. Instead, it was a brand-spanking-new sixty-stall stable, an immense structure constructed of newly logged and planed Northwest cedar, oak, and Doug fir. Annie still couldn't get over the cold and hot running water taps in each stall. No such amenities existed in her stable. She was used to breaking up icy water in her horses' buckets each winter with a good thwack of a small shovel.

The sharp sound of amp adjustments reminded her a country-and-western band was gearing up to perform. When the band struck its opening chords, Annie knew real conversation would be impossible. The stable's high rafters made conversations float to the ether zone and were hard enough to follow without extraneous noise.

Fortunately, the real tenants were nowhere near the noise. Fifty mares, gelding, foals, and yearlings were in several nearby pastures, contently munching on the last of the autumn grass that hadn't turned dry and brown over the summer. When the party was over, all the horses would be led into their new quarters and put away for the night. She wondered whether they'd realize that they'd fallen into a permanent lap of luxury. Probably not, she decided. They already were used to three square meals a day at her friend Patricia's place, Running Track Farms. But the fact that they'd never again have to worry about their next meal wasn't lost on Annie.

She looked through the crowd and saw the man responsible—well, mostly responsible—for it all, Travis Latham, one of Suwana County's most venerated citizens, who had purchased land once owned by Annie's boyfriend, Marcus Colbert, and turned it into a rescue center for both horses and young boys, all of whom sorely needed help in their lives. Travis had named his nonprofit after his grandson, Alex, who'd died at the hands of young bullies years earlier. His goal was to thwart the too-often-inevitable journey into crime that at-risk boys seemed to embark on and to help them toward a better future. When Annie came across fifty abandoned horses that had been earmarked for the slaughterhouse, the board of Alex's Place unanimously decided to take them on and let the boys participate in the rehabilitation and training process. It was an incredibly ambitious plan, Annie knew, but Travis—and Marcus—had spared no time or expense in getting the property ready for use. It was now early October. By Christmas, Travis hoped the bunkhouse, now under construction, would be fully occupied.

Threading her way through the chattering crowd, she reached Travis, who was just finishing up an interview with Rick Courtier, a reporter from KXTV in Seattle, a short ferry ride away. Annie noticed a tiny microphone clipped to a buttonhole in Travis's wool vest. As usual, he was dressed in tweeds, along with a thick corduroy jacket with elbow patches. No one could surpass his sartorial splendor as the country gentleman, Annie thought, not even Marcus, whose tastes ran toward Armani.

"We believe the boys and horses will learn a great deal from each other," Travis was saying.

Rick slowly nodded. "But isn't it risky to let boys, many of whom have never been around horses before, participate in potentially dangerous activities?"

"Life *is* a risk, man!" Travis was impatient with the question, which Annie suspected he'd heard plenty of times before today. "Every single boy who comes here already is at risk, and in far more troubling ways than taking a fall off a horse. We'll have skilled trainers *and* counselors, who will live with the boys and make sure they're kept safe, as well as a full-time RN on board. But each boy will be responsible for taking care of his own horse. I suspect both student and horse will be teaching each other many important life skills before too long."

Annie was standing next to a pole beam, partially hidden from sight. She had no desire to get caught up in an interview with Rick Courtier, who'd used every single wile he could imagine to wheedle information out of her earlier this year, after she'd come across a dead body. She had to admire Travis, though. He clearly knew how to use a reporter to get his story across.

Country music burst from the stage, and the interview was thankfully brought to a halt. Annie wiggled the last few feet to Travis and gave him a quick hug.

"You were marvelous," she said, her eyes sparkling at him. "No one can deliver the message of Alex's Place better than you."

"Nonsense," Travis said, but he smiled as he said it. "Everyone on the board is a good ambassador. I just get tired of hearing the naysayers. I have full faith in what we're doing."

"As do I," Annie said firmly, and snared a glass of champagne from a roving waiter.

"Where's Marcus?"

"Haven't seen him since he gave his speech. We agreed to wander separately so we could meet and talk to as many prospective donors as possible."

Travis laughed. "Excellent idea! We'll take all the help we can get. I don't know which will be more expensive, feeding fifty horses or fifty teenage boys. Whichever it is, it'll be a bundle."

"No doubt. But I can't believe how beautifully you've designed the stables. Everything is at the boys' fingertips. And a heated blanket room! I should be so lucky. My horses and I are green with envy."

"We tried to implement as much on your dream list of stable amenities as we could, Annie. The less time the boys have to spend doing daily chores, the more time they have to ride, groom, and spend time with their horses."

Annie gave an exaggerated sigh. "Don't I know it."

"But you've got Lisa now to help."

She visibly brightened. "Yes, I do, and I hope she'll never leave. I've told her she can get married and live on my property as long as she wants. I'll even throw in a pony for her kids. She's taken such a load off me, which is great, because I have a new horse to train."

Annie felt her phone vibrating inside her blazer pocket, the cue that someone was trying to reach her.

"Hold on a sec." She pulled out her phone and quickly scanned a text from Leif, a local volunteer fireman with multiple skills, including shearing sheep.

A few weeks before, he'd done just that on Annie's flock. Now he was handling a job usually Annie did herself—breeding the ewes for spring births. She'd been watching the ewes closely, and today on horseback, she'd inspected the flock, now in a pasture a mile from her farmhouse and soon to be moved to their winter home. The ewes were in heat, no doubt about it. And the ideal time to take advantage of their condition was precisely now.

"Getting there," read the text. "20 tagged and 20 to go. How r u doing?"

Good for Leif, Annie thought. It wasn't exactly a picnic herding the right ewe into the pen, tagging it after the deed was done, and extracting it without getting the ram too riled. She answered Leif's subtle query of whether she'd be back in time to help.

"Good man," she texted. "Back around 6."

"Party on" was the brief, somewhat morose reply.

Annie felt a pang of guilt for not assisting in this yearly farm chore. But there simply was no way to predict exactly when the ewes would exhibit their telltale signs. In fact, the ewes were a bit early this year in demonstrating their desire for male companionship. Perhaps that boded a short and mild winter. Annie certainly hoped so.

She felt a hand on her arm and looked up. It was Patricia Winters, operations manager of Running Track Farms, a state-of-the-art rehab farm for hunter jumpers, dressage, and racehorses. Patricia had graciously let the fifty feedlot horses live on the premises while in quarantine after their rescue. Annie would have done anything for this woman. Without Patricia's generous offer to house them during those first critical months, the abandoned horses might not have been saved.

"Annie, I want you to meet Liz Faraday, a student of mine. Liz, this is Annie, the woman I've been telling you so much about."

Annie could feel a blush come over her. She wasn't used to compliments, and she assumed that was what Patricia's remarks meant.

"Nice to meet you, Liz," she said, extending her hand. "Your name sounds a bit familiar. Have we met?"

"Over the phone." Liz's voice was high and pleasant. She was a slim brunette with long hair and was wearing riding breeches, just like Patricia. Annie thought for a moment, trying to recall the prior connection.

"You bought one of Hilda Colbert's horses, didn't you?"

"I sure did! As soon as I knew they were ready for new homes, I was at Running Track in a flash, wasn't I, Patricia?"

"She was, indeed. Liz is one of my dressage students. We've been looking for a good prospect for her, but the pickings are slim around Cape Disconsolate. When I told her about Sammy, she was there in a flash."

"Sammy?" Annie recalled that all of Hilda's horses had much more highbrow names than that.

"Well, his real name is Samson, but you can imagine how long it took before that turned into Sammy," Liz replied.

"Oh, yes." Annie now vaguely recalled the horse, a Danish Warmblood with a pedigree that included a

Grand Prix mare. "Was he the gelding originally touted for his 'elastic back' and 'easy lateral work'?"

"Well, whoever wrote his description was correct," Liz said. "I'm really just a beginner in dressage, but Sammy was trained to third level before coming to Colbert Farms."

"Where he wasn't used for much of anything, as far as I can tell," Patricia chimed in. "But he obviously has a tremendous memory, because Liz is making fantastic progress with him."

"I think it's just the opposite," Liz said, laughing. "Sammy's making fantastic progress with *me*. In fact, we're showing training level in a few weeks down in California."

"Congratulations." Annie voiced the word as warmly as she could muster. All she knew about dressage was that riders stood very straight and tall on large horses and maneuvered them from one marker to another in a big arena. And that they all wore tailcoats and hard hats. It all seemed rather silly. How much fun could going from letter A to letter C really be? Annie had barrel raced when she was a teenager in 4-H. She couldn't imagine any equine sport providing a bigger thrill than that.

Marcus was suddenly at her elbow and gave her waist a discreet squeeze, which she immediately and warmly returned. Annie often wondered how such a large man could appear with such catlike ease. It was uncanny, but by no means unwelcome.

"My keen analytical mind tells me you three women are talking about horses. Am I right?"

"A mere child of three could have come to that

conclusion," Annie said drily. "After all, we are talking in a stable."

"Exactly so. Well, ladies, are you enjoying yourselves?"

"Absolutely." Patricia beamed at Marcus. "I'm so glad the rescue horses are finally here, all on time, and all of them healthy."

"It was a minor miracle," Annie said. "And we couldn't have done it without your help."

"All I did was give you pasture space that was going to waste. You and Jessica did all the work."

Annie knew this was not quite true. Her equine vet, Jessica, had put heart and soul as well as her expertise into ensuring that every rescue horse had received the care it needed for a full recovery from the horrors it had lived through, even though many of those horrors would forever be unknown. But she'd often seen Jessica consulting with the team of rehab vets on staff at Running Track Farms and knew that Patricia had freely volunteered their time and services, as well.

"We were just telling Annie how much we're enjoying working with Sammy, who came from your farm. Liz"—Patricia nodded to the woman beside her—"is soon going to compete him in dressage, and he's doing wonderfully." Patricia was being her usual polite and tactful self. Sammy had once belonged to Marcus's wife, now deceased—murdered on the very land where they now stood.

"I'm delighted to hear that. Tell me, Annie, how many of Hilda's herd are still looking for good homes?"

Annie immediately felt a touch of irritation. Wasn't this a topic that should be discussed in private? But then, Patricia, once more, had been immensely helpful in finding homes for the more than twenty horses Hilda had left behind with her death, and Annie had made sure Marcus knew how invaluable she'd been. He'd hired Annie to do the job, but Patricia had really paved the way in finding the best prospects in the area. Annie was used to finding good trail or roping or ranch horses for her friends and clients. Hilda's horses were out of her league, and deep down, she knew it.

"Only eight left, I believe. Right, Patricia?" She looked toward her friend.

"Yes, and Annie, I believe several of them have some dressage training in their background, just like Sammy. Listen, I've got an idea. Why don't you come down to the dressage show with Liz and me? We'll transport the three or four horses that have had dressage training and show them at the grounds. Plus, you'd get a chance to see how one of your star athletes is doing in person."

Several reasons why this would *not* be a good idea were bubbling on Annie's lips, but Marcus jumped in before she had a chance to voice them.

"Excellent idea! Where is it being held?"

"Southern California, near Thousand Oaks," Liz told him. "It's rather a small show, but in a fabulous setting. Two retired movie actors, a couple who were big in the fifties, own the place, and they apparently draw quite an elite crowd. It *would* be the perfect place to show Hilda's horses, Annie. Why don't you come?"

This was too much. Everyone was telling her what she should do, and anyone who knew the well-regarded

Western horse trainer Annie Carson was fully aware that she didn't cotton much to blunt requests.

"I'm afraid it's impossible, Liz. I'm in the middle of my sheep's breeding season and couldn't possibly get away."

Liz and Patricia's faces showed their disappointment. Annie lamely tried to soften her words.

"But I think it's a great idea. Maybe some other time."

"Unfortunately, it's the last event of the season pretty much everywhere," Patricia said sadly. "The next one won't take place until April."

Marcus groaned. "Don't take this personally, Patricia, but I'm not looking forward to another six months of feeding those beasts. Perhaps we could cut down on the number of pedicures you give them?"

Patricia laughed. "Not a chance, Marcus. Not a chance."

Back at Annie's farmhouse that night, she fumed at Marcus's surprising lack of tact earlier. Unfortunately, there had been no time to tell him how thoughtless he'd been. As soon as the celebratory party had ended, Marcus had left for the airport to fly home to San Jose. Pressing business awaited him in the morning, he reminded Annie, and when he'd prepared her for his hasty departure the day before, he had seemed genuinely disappointed. At least they had had one night together. But it was hardly enough, especially when Annie had so many well-aimed criticisms to throw his way.

Didn't he know that selling horses wasn't like a regular retail business? It was incredibly difficult to link a pedigreed horse with just the right owner. The person's riding skills had to be aligned with the horse's own strengths, plus the prospective owner had to assure Annie and Patricia that the horse would thrive in its new home. Both women were sticklers for checking out the horse's new environment before any deal was struck. So far, every new home found for Hilda's horses had been successful. No horse had been handed back, and Annie had made this a condition of sale. After seeing how easily unwanted horses ended up in feedlots, she was doubly insistent; her new Thoroughbred, Eduardo, had ended up in one through no fault of his own.

She was doing the best she could, and damn it, Marcus should know this by now. She was sorry he would have to continue paying very large boarding fees at Running Track. But she could only do so much in a day, and taking off for a frivolous weekend in Southern California, as well as taking on the expense of transporting several horses to the show, just seemed ludicrous right now. Why couldn't everyone see that? She did.

Annie's cell phone rang, and she picked it up without looking at the number. It was Marcus, who'd just landed. She could hear the echo of airport loudspeakers in the background.

"How's my girl?"

Annie found she was having difficulty making a similarly breezy reply.

"Annie? Are you still upset about Patricia's suggestion about showing Hilda's horses in Southern California?"

The man wasn't stupid, she realized. He'd noticed

her reaction. To her surprise, tears pricked at the corner of her eyes.

"I have a lot to do here, Marcus! I've just spent the last three months caring for the rescues, and I need a break to deal with my own life. Why is that so hard to fathom?"

She could hear Marcus's sigh on the other end of the line.

"I know your plate is more than full, Annie. That's why I thought a relaxing long weekend at a completely different horse venue might be fun. You and Patricia and Liz would have a great time together. You might sell a horse or two. And I'd do everything in my power to join you at least for a day."

Annie considered this. It sounded almost reasonable. In fact, it *was* reasonable. Then she remembered and gave a small groan.

"No, I really can't. Leif finished the breeding today, but we've still got to transport the flock to Johan's. And that's not counting the new horse in my stables I'm supposed to be training."

"One long weekend away can't do that much damage to your training or transportation schedules. Look at it this way. Everyone else will be performing— you get to sit around and watch them all sweat. Your only real job is to make sure any interested buyer is properly feted and vetted. And I'm sure Patricia can help you with that."

Despite her earlier misgivings, Annie was now on the verge of changing her mind. But then Marcus spoke, and inadvertently put his foot squarely in it.

"Besides, I thought that's what Leif was planning on doing today. Couldn't he have just had the ewes breed, then transport them all in one day? That way, you'd have accomplished both jobs at once."

It was too much. Maybe Marcus could put together three mergers in a single day. Maybe he had a huge desk in his office with nothing on it but a large paper clip. Annie could only concentrate on one horse at a time. Her office at home was littered with paper and unread magazines. But the worst part was that he was right.

She ended the call with forced civility, poured herself a small glass of Glenlivet, and picked up her phone once more.

"Patricia? It's Annie. I hope I'm not calling too late. I'd be delighted to come down to Southern California with you and Liz. How soon can we transport the horses?"

A shriek of delight emanated from Patricia's end, followed by rapid conversation. When it stopped, Annie paused, then cautiously asked her friend, "Just one more thing. What exactly should I bring to wear?"

Chapter Two

Annie watched her suitcase slowly swivel onto the slanted conveyer belt and land with a resounding *thunk* on the revolving circle below. Her stomach felt as churned up as her luggage might have been had it been an animate object. Aside from one screaming toddler whose lung capacity rivaled that of an opera singer's, the two-and-a-half-hour flight had been uneventful—but Annie had spent the entire time obsessing about the foolhardiness of the journey she'd agreed to make.

She now yanked her bag off the slowly moving track and sighed. Her qualms about making the trip had started once she acquired her clothes, neatly packed inside the suitcase she now held. In addition to the usual sundries, it currently contained two pairs of English full-seat breeches, several polo shirts, and a navy-blue schooling coat. She had never worn such garments in her life, nor had she ever expected to. And then there were the two—*two!*—adorable little cocktail dresses that somehow had made their way in, as well.

It was all her friends' fault. Thanks to the recent horse-rescue mission, which had required every single one of her equestrian friends, every friend was now on everyone else's contact list. When word got out that Annie would be attending a dressage event in Southern California, they all came to the fore with the same fervor as they had when rescuing horses bound for slaughter.

"Don't be absurd," was Samantha Higgins's blunt response to Annie's innocent remark that she intended to wear her dress cowboy boots and jeans to the event—what else would she wear, for heaven's sake?

Apparently, Sam's opinion was universal, because the next day, Annie found herself bundled into a truck with Sam, Lisa, and several other friends, all determined to shop until they dropped. The first stop was an equine shop that catered to the English riding crowd. Annie had balked at purchasing a pair of dressage boots—the price alone was enough to thwart that idea—but she had let herself be talked into more moderately priced attire. She had to admit she liked how tight breeches with spandex made her long legs and waist appear even longer, and they were actually comfortable, too. She was wearing a pair now, along with a more sensible pair of boots that for reasons that escaped Annie, were called "paddocks." If she'd worn them just once in her own paddock, they'd soon be encrusted with mud and worse.

Purchasing the cocktail dresses was an act of utter insanity as far as Annie was concerned, but her friends had gushed so much over how she looked in the Nordstrom dressing room that her resolve quickly withered. Even the personal shopper Sam had snared seemed impressed with how just a slip of fabric, artfully designed, brought out Annie's slim and very toned figure.

"Which one should I get?" Annie had asked her crowd of admirers, twirling around a bit so she could get the view in back.

"Both." Again, the vote was unanimous, and Annie didn't protest. The truth was, she loved them equally. But when her friend Luann suggested that perhaps she should look for "just one more," Annie put her foot down.

"You'll be there five nights," Luann had protested. "You can't wear the same dress more than twice. It's just not *done*!"

"Watch me," Annie replied.

Now she looked down at the suitcase with all her new clothes and wondered what she had gotten herself into. Hadn't Thoreau once written, "Beware of all enterprises that require new clothes?" Her high-school English teacher would not be impressed by how little she had soaked in that lesson.

A buzz from within her Giani Bernini purse—another unnecessary purchase, in her opinion—broke her reverie. It was Patricia, who'd agreed to pick her up at LAX.

"Are you here? Are you on the ground?" Patricia sounded uncharacteristically bubbly.

"I am, and just snared my bag. Where are you?"

"In a cell phone lot, not too far away. What island are you closest to?"

Annie looked toward the exit doors. It looked gloriously sunny outside. How lovely. She'd left Sea-Tac in a gloomy drizzle.

"I think it's twenty-two. Yes, that's it. Twenty-two."

"Be there in half a tick!"

The line went dead. Annie walked toward the exit and out into the enticing glow of California sunshine. It was very warm. The sky was blue as far as she could see. She stopped for a moment, letting the unexpected heat settle over her as other passengers strode by. A sudden soft breeze caressed her body. She raised her face to catch more of it and realized the overhead sun was very bright, indeed. She fumbled inside her purse for her sunglasses and put them on, feeling like a Hollywood star who wanted to remain incognito. Things were definitely looking up. Although it occurred to Annie that she had no idea what Patricia would be driving.

When a cobalt blue Mercedes-Benz convertible zipped up to the curb five minutes later, she had her answer. Patricia jumped out and gave Annie an enthusiastic hug.

"Very cool sunglasses! How was the flight?" she asked, as she took Annie's bag and placed it in an already popped trunk.

"Fantastic. Thirty minutes in the air and the rain clouds magically melted away."

Patricia's buoyant demeanor amused Annie. Back home, she was the epitome of a proper, well-spoken operations manager of a major-league horse facility. Annie had never seen this side of the Englishwoman.

She liked it. The only thing that hadn't changed was Patricia's attire—breeches, a white blouse, and a navy-blue riding jacket emblazoned with the Running Track Farms crest. Almost exactly what *she* was wearing, Annie realized. They could have been twins.

"Let's go, then. We've got a three o'clock appointment with our first prospective buyer. The word's already out!"

"Wonderful. Wouldn't it be nice to sell one of the horses before the show even started?"

"It would indeed. Buckle up, Annie, this car reminds me of my MG back home. We take corners fast and overtake slow drivers even faster."

Annie laughed. "Just remember to drive on the right side of the road, and you won't hear me complain."

Patricia really was a superb driver. She adroitly steered the convertible through waiting cars and throngs of herd-bound people with ease, and they soon reached the on-ramp to the freeway. Annie had not tried to talk to her friend as she circumnavigated the complexities of getting out of the airport; she knew Patricia needed to pay attention to her driving. But she wondered if conversation would be any better once they were on the freeway. It was difficult to hear oneself speak over the noise of traffic, made even louder in an open vehicle.

She needn't have worried. The convertible came to a screeching halt as soon as it rounded the crest of the ramp. Thirty cars were at a standstill before them, each waiting for the red traffic light to turn green for an infinitesimal second, the official nod that they could join the quagmire of cars that stretched across the six-lane freeway.

"Damn!" Patricia put the car in neutral and sighed. "It's only one o'clock, for heaven's sake. Traffic shouldn't be piled up at this hour."

Annie peered ahead of them. "Maybe there's an accident."

"No, I'm afraid it's just business as usual. It seems LA County just can't build new freeways fast enough."

The lanes were worn and patched, Annie noticed, hardly in great shape for driving.

"Seems like the Department of Transportation could do a better job of keeping the roads paved," she noted.

"Yes, well, there are a lot of them. The idea of giving up one's car never really caught on in this part of the world."

At least the crawl gave the women a chance to talk.

"How are the horses?"

"Tickety-boo. They enjoyed nonstop, air-conditioned rides down here and arrived an hour after Liz and I did. No injuries, no worrisome symptoms. They've settled in very nicely, have had a full day of rest, and are being bathed and groomed as we speak."

"How are the facilities?"

"Incredible. You won't believe them, Annie. The Darbys have made the stables into a virtual palace for equines. It's always been a well-run place, but under their care and thanks to their money, it's become thoroughly modernized. And huge! They've built three competition dressage arenas, one of them indoors, although the event this weekend will just use one. It's absolutely top-of-the-line."

That was a relief. There was nothing worse than visiting a subpar stable and knowing there was nothing you could do about it. In her role with the local Horse Rescue Brigade, she'd come across plenty of those.

"So, tell me about the Darbys. All I know is that they used to be big movie stars."

"Oh, they're wonderful. Hollis and Miriam have completely opened up their home to us and couldn't be more delightful hosts. Miriam must now be in her eighties, but she's still incredibly beautiful. And Hollis is just the sweetest guy. He dotes on his wife as if she's still his blushing bride. They've been married for over fifty years, something of a record among their colleagues."

"Didn't they get some special Academy Award a few years back?"

"Yes, for their lifetime achievements in the postwar movie industry. A lot of their films are now cult classics."

Annie wondered if she'd seen any of them. She seldom went to a movie theater, but she was partial to movie classics, especially on dark and rainy winter nights.

"I take it we're staying on the grounds? You told me not to book a motel, and I took you at your word."

"Oh, didn't I tell you? We're all staying in the house, or mansion, I should say. It's at one end of the property; the stables are at the other, with pastures in between. Miriam and Hollis live in a large wing on the second floor, but the rest of us are very comfortably situated, and a maid comes in every day to do our rooms. We've also got the services of Chef Gustav, a very fussy Frenchman whose sole purpose in life is to make sure we enjoy his food."

Annie was focused on one phrase she'd heard: "the rest of us."

"So, we're not the Darbys' only guests?"

"Oh, heavens no. We're just a small part of the crowd, the Northwest contingent. The Darbys are putting up several other riders, plus their trainers, although the trainers are housed in cottages scattered throughout the property. They're all people Miriam and Hollis have gotten to know over the years. Miriam used to be a dressage rider, did you know that? She still keeps up with the local amateurs and, not surprisingly, she's become good friends with many of them."

Great, Annie thought. Getting to know her hosts, two aging, perhaps slightly eccentric Hollywood celebrities sounded like fun, and she knew that she, Liz, and Patricia would bond over the weekend. But a household full of unknown but undoubtedly snooty dressage equestrians was far less enticing. Annie felt a small knot form in the pit of her stomach. She was very afraid she would be a fish out of water and regretted not booking a room at the local motel instead.

"One of the riders, Lucy, is an old family friend," Patricia continued, oblivious to Annie's concerns. "She's from Boston, and definitely born with a silver spoon in her mouth. Someone told me she attended a boarding school where she could bring her own horse. Then she matriculated at Smith College, where the stables are on campus."

Annie's heart sank. It was just as she feared. She was in for a weekend with women who had more money than she'd ever have and whose life experiences were far different than her own. From her meager experience, rich people weren't particularly warm and friendly toward those beneath their income level. Marcus was the one notable exception. She wished he was with her now, to help her integrate into this rarefied social circle.

Patricia was still talking, and Annie made a concerted effort to stop fretting and pay attention.

"Lucy desperately wanted to come along with me to the airport," Patricia said, deftly moving into another lane where traffic seemed to be incrementally faster. "But I told her she'd have plenty of time at cocktail hour."

Annie was confused. "Why would Lucy want to meet *me*? And what's all this about cocktail hour?"

"It's a Darby tradition. Everyone's expected to attend. Someone rings a gong at six o'clock that means everyone out on the patio. Hollis presides over everything and takes great pride in his skill in concocting exotic drinks. He's also very good at steering the conversation to include everyone."

"Why? Do we have a couple of shrinking violets in the crowd? Besides me, I mean?'

Patricia laughed. "Let's just say there are a few women who tend to dominate if they're not held in check."

"So, what's up with Lucy? I still don't get why she'd want to meet a total stranger."

"Oh, that's just how she is—one of those people for whom money can't buy what they really want, which is a good friend and, to be honest, a good riding seat. Lucy's been taking dressage lessons since she was a child, but unfortunately, hasn't risen in the ranks the way one might expect. She's riding the same test as

Liz, training level, which is really for beginners. And she's easy to make fun of—I've noticed a couple of other guests can give her a hard time, especially one, a woman named Nicole, who knows her from boarding school."

"So, Lucy is hoping that I'll be her new best friend? Someone new?"

"Probably. Don't be surprised if she peppers you with questions when you're introduced. She's thrilled at the prospect of meeting a real cowgirl."

"Somehow, Patricia, I have a feeling that Lucy is the only guest who is."

A hole appeared in the thicket of cars, and Patricia took advantage of it. A few minutes later, the freeway miraculously opened up, and they were soon zooming along a straight stretch of highway at eighty miles an hour. Annie noticed there were few posted speed-limit signs, and even fewer state highway patrol cars lurking near the underpasses. Dan Stetson would have a field day here, she thought. In a few weeks, he'd make enough stops to cover the annual budget for the Suwana County Sheriff's Office.

Their new speed inhibited further conversation, and Annie was impressed to see how expertly Patricia threaded her way through the intricate system that made up California's freeways. Annie soon realized that it was folly to cruise comfortably along in just any one lane because in a mile or two, that lane became the exit for yet another freeway. Patricia switched lanes with great regularity, Annie noticed, just to keep on the same freeway and not be sidelined by a rogue offshoot.

"We're passing Beverly Hills," Patricia shouted over the noise of the engine. "Hollywood's just a bit farther east."

Annie looked appreciatively to her right but saw nothing but an unending line of high-end chain stores.

"I'll take your word for it," she shouted back.

"I'd have liked to have detoured and gone the way of Santa Monica, along the coastline," Patricia yelled. "But with traffic so bad, and our appointment at three, I decided we couldn't spare the time."

Annie nodded, hoping Patricia would catch her in her peripheral vision. Trying to talk at high speeds was a challenge.

Fifteen minutes later, Patricia took an exit leading to U.S. 101N. This was a less congested freeway and a couple of lanes shorter on both sides. Rolling brown hills soon surrounded them, and the unrelenting sight of commercial buildings faded away. Patricia decreased her speed to a sedate seventy, turned to Annie, and smiled.

"We're on the home stretch."

"Good. I feel the need to stretch my legs. Not that your rig isn't roomy enough."

"Nice, isn't it? It's one of the cars Hollis lets us use when we need one."

Annie started. "Really? I'd like to see the ones he doesn't loan out."

"Oh, you probably will. Lamborghinis, Ferraris, Bugattis, he has them all, including my favorite, a vintage Aston Martin. Some built for speed, some built for show. He keeps them in a special garage that's climate controlled and tightly secured. But it doesn't take a lot of wheedling to get him to show off his toys."

"I'm sure they're knockouts. But I have to say, for show *and* speed, I'll take a horse any day of the week."

"You and me both!"

Annie was surprised at the unprepossessing entrance to the "mansion," as Patricia had called it. After exiting the freeway, they'd driven on a country road for a scant mile and turned into what appeared to be a private street, flanked on both sides by citrus trees. The lane quickly turned into a one-lane dirt road that meandered up a small hill and past several small farms. It didn't seem to be leading anywhere.

After Patricia had rounded the last corner, and the entrance to the Darby property was in front of them, the reason for the roundabout access road became clear. The edifice before them resembled a Tuscan palace atop a hillside town, a crowning achievement of the owners' wealth and stature. The only difference was that this structure had a definite Spanish flair. The white-stucco exterior rose two stories high, topped by a red-clay tile roof that was shaded by tall trees that Annie was surprised to see resembled the native cedar in her own backyard. A wrought-iron gate magically swung open as they approached, and, as Patricia slowly drove in, Annie saw a lean, not-so-tall man and a short, plump young woman standing just beyond two heavy carved wood doors.

"That's Hollis," Patricia observed. "The consummate host, waiting to usher us in."

"That can't be Miriam with him? She looks a bit young."

"Heavens, no. That's Lucy. I told you she wanted to meet you."

Waving to their host, Patricia drove past the entrance and into a small parking area on the north side. She expertly pulled into a sliver of a spot, flanked by a hunter-green Jaguar and gold Porsche. Most of the cars in the lot were of similar value, but Annie noticed a VW bug and an ancient Toyota also in their midst.

Patricia caught Annie's questioning look.

"Dressage students come from all kinds of backgrounds," she explained. "The leveling field is in the arena."

The rich, fragrant air of cedar engulfed them as they walked toward the entrance, and Annie breathed in deeply, happy to have one reminder of home close by.

"You must be Annie!" Hollis exclaimed, as he held out both his hands to greet her.

He leaned toward her, a shock of white hair falling over his forehead in the process that gave him a boyish look, despite his obvious age. He was dressed in khakis and a white polo shirt, and Annie could readily see how he must have been a heartthrob a few decades ago, and perhaps still was. He was the first movie star Annie had ever met, and she wasn't sure how she should behave.

"It's very nice to meet you," she said, finding her

mouth had suddenly gone dry. "You're so kind to let me stay in your home."

"Nonsense. We're delighted to have you with us. Any friend of Patricia's is a friend of ours. But where are my manners? Let me introduce you to our other good friend, Lucy Cartwright. I'd hoped my wife would be here to greet you as well, but she's having a bit of a lie down after lunch. You'll meet her later."

Lucy smiled shyly and held out her hand to Annie. It was warm and sweaty, and Annie willed herself not to draw her hand away too soon.

"It's lovely to meet you," Lucy said in a small, little-girl voice. "I've never met a real cowgirl before. Do you rope cattle on your ranch?"

Oh for pity's sake, Annie thought. "I just round up sheep, I'm afraid."

"Super! Patricia says you're also a detective, and that you solve murders, too."

Annie laughed. "Hardly. I've only had the misfortune to be around when a few deaths have occurred, that's all." She decided she would kill Patricia later.

"She's just being modest," her future victim told Lucy. "Annie's single-handedly solved any number of crimes this year."

"Well, let's hope she doesn't have to solve any while she's staying with us. We're looking forward to a nice, relaxing weekend, aren't we, Lucy?"

Annie was grateful for Hollis's deflection in the conversation. Someone had to rein in Lucy's rampant imagination about Annie's so-called cowgirl life. Nor did she want to spend the next several days recounting murder scenes, of which she'd seen enough to last a lifetime, just this year.

The front door swung wide open and a tall, angular

woman strode out. Annie's first impression was that an Amazon had invaded the premises; the woman's stature, short-cropped blond hair and steely-gray eyes gave the impression of a female warrior.

"Oh, there you are, Lucy," the Amazon said in a deprecating voice. "Shouldn't you be at the stables right now? I saw Melissa head down an hour ago."

"She's working with Amy," Lucy said in a slightly quavering voice. "I'm supposed to join them at three."

"Well, it's nearly three now, you ninny. You'd better skedaddle on those short legs of yours, or you'll never get there on time."

Annie watched Hollis put his hand on Lucy's shoulder and give a soft squeeze.

"Gwendolyn," he said pleasantly to the other woman. "Before you and Lucy head for the stables, I'd like you to meet our newest houseguest, Annie Carson. Annie, this is Gwendolyn Smythe. She's from the Bay Area. Annie comes all the way from Washington."

Annie put out her hand, wondering if it would be crushed by the woman's grip. She was shocked to realize that Gwendolyn had no intention of shaking hands at all. She stood on the front step, towering over her, a small, sardonic smile on her lips.

"So, you're Annie. Hello, Annie. I believe we have an acquaintance in common."

"I don't think so." The words were out before she could think.

"I do think so. Are you familiar with someone by the name of Marcus Colbert?"

Annie's mind froze, along with the rest of her body.

"Hasn't he mentioned my name by now? No? Well, no matter. Marcus and I go way back. I was Hilda's best friend, you know. But he seems to be getting over her death. At least, he was when I had dinner with him a few days ago."

At last Annie found her voice again.

"You had dinner with Marcus?" It sounded ridiculous, and she regretted the words as soon as they'd come out of her mouth.

"Oh yes. Just last Monday. We dined with his mother. Such a lovely woman, don't you think?"

Annie didn't think. All she felt was anger surge through her. Followed by a wispy thread of fear.

Chapter Three

"My! Look at the time—it's nearly three. Annie, we really must fly if we hope to get to the stables before our prospective buyer arrives. Too bad the convertible accommodates only two, or we'd offer the rest of you a ride. We'll just have to catch up over cocktails."

And with that, Patricia led Annie by the arm back down the circular path and to the parking lot.

Annie was grateful to her friend for removing her from Gwendolyn's presence. Then she felt anger. As the Mercedes wended the quarter mile to the stables, she scrunched down in her bucket seat and silently fumed. All she could think of was Marcus's persuasive story that he had to be back in San Jose bright and early on Monday morning. Now she'd learned a new reason for his rapid departure. Could he really have been so duplicitous?

Patricia tapped her knee, and Annie whirled around, still glowering.

"Don't let Gwendolyn get to you, Annie. She's just a jealous old cow."

"Then why didn't he tell me about the dinner? With his *mother*, for heaven's sake. You know what that implies."

"If Gwendolyn is simply an old friend of the family, it means absolutely nothing, and I'm sure it was. I'm sure Marcus thought it was all a great bore. Now get out of your funk, Annie. We have a horse to market, and I can't have you scowling at a woman who is dying to give us a large sum of money."

Annie sat up straight. "I hear and obey." She tried to put Gwendolyn's sneering face out of her mind.

She agreed with Patricia's assessment of the stables: They were beautifully and intelligently constructed. The designers had thoughtfully installed wooden tack boxes by each stall, which were open, airy, and inviting. Everything was constructed from a deep, mahogany wood and looked as if it would last a lifetime. As she walked down the broad center aisle separating the stalls, she realized the entire structure was air-conditioned. *It must cost a small fortune,* she thought. The Darbys clearly had amassed one or two during their time in Hollywood.

"Wow," she kept repeating as they approached the stall area set apart for Marcus's horses. It seemed to be the most expressive thing she could say at the moment. Patricia just looked at her and grinned.

The "wow" effect not only extended to the luxuriousness of the stables. Annie had never seen such magnificent horses as she did now on either side of her. They were all huge—a sixteen-hand horse here would have been considered a shrimp—and obviously prime equine athletes, from their top lines to their muscled necks and shoulders to their rounded and firm rumps. Annie had never considered dressage a particularly demanding discipline for horses; after all, they performed in a confined area and, as far as she knew, only politely trotted and cantered. Perhaps there was more to the sport than she'd thought.

The last "wow" to escape her lips was to admire the setup that Patricia had designed for buyers. A butter-cream pop-up canopy at the far end of the wall was the designated place for show-and-tell. Inside was a small oak table holding a laptop computer with an oversized screen. Two cloth patio chairs placed on angles were in front of the big screen, and Annie noticed a small Persian rug in front of that. She walked over to the area. Next to the laptop were folders with color photographs of each horse, along with details of its lineage, accomplishments, and strengths. Annie knew the asking price for all of Hilda's horses, but it never ceased to amaze her how highly valued they were in the equine world. If all three horses sold this weekend, Annie could have retired on the money they would bring in.

Patricia was kneeling by a small white refrigerator next to the table, checking its contents.

"I think we're ready." She looked up at Annie, who was studying the folders she had prepared.

"When did you have time to do all this? I've never seen such elaborate preparation for a horse sale."

"We've been shooting video of the horses in action for the past few months, as soon as they were able to be exercised again. The brochures were easy—I have a template I use and just plug in the photos and specs."

"It looks pretty amazing to me."

"I'm glad you're impressed. Considering the price

tags on all these horses, let's hope our prospective buyer is equally in thrall."

Annie walked over to the stalls, where each horse was quietly munching on a flake of alfalfa. Each horse's mane, she noticed, was perfectly coiffed in a row of tightly braided rosettes. Their coats gleamed, and their tails, cropped to an even length, had been brushed until they shone.

"Fantastic grooming job. I like the mane bobs."

Patricia laughed. "Usually only done for competing. It takes too bloody long to do it every day."

Annie noticed an English saddle perched on a portable stand near each horse's stall door.

"These look different than the ones I've seen."

"What looks different?"

"The English saddles. The flaps look longer."

"They are. It's to help riders keep in close contact with their horse."

"Ah." Annie realized that the number of things she didn't know about dressage would circle the stables if written out in full.

"And you may have noticed that the knee rolls are a bit more pronounced than on a traditional saddle."

"Ah, yes. Of course." Make that two circles around the stable. Annie carefully hefted one of the saddles to chest height. It was surprisingly light. Much lighter than her twenty-seven-pound Tucker saddle at home. One thing was for certain—tacking up a dressage horse was definitely easier on the back.

The barn manager informed them on the stroke of three that a woman named Betsy Gilchrist was waiting in the office to see them.

"Super! Please, send her back," Patricia said, as she made a slight adjustment to the angle of a bottle of Veuve Clicquot, now sitting in an ice bucket on the oak table with the handouts.

Annie was beginning to feel a dress code must be posted on the wrought-iron gates leading into the Darby complex, because like every other woman she'd seen so far, Betsy was attired in breeches, boots, and an equestrian jacket. Her white-blond hair was pulled back in a bun, and she carried a Gucci purse that looked big enough to store all her grooming supplies—or a big wad of cash. Annie noticed the three horses had stopped eating and were now looking at Betsy with undisguised interest.

"How do you do?" Patricia said, smiling, and extended her hand. "I'm Patricia Winters, and this is Annie Carson. We're here to answer any questions you have about the horses we have for sale."

Annie wasn't sure what questions she could possibly answer, but she nodded in agreement and smiled confidently at the elegant woman. She'd already decided her role in this game would be to watch and listen.

"I'm so glad I learned you'd be here this weekend," Betsy exclaimed. "I'm really only interested in your Warmblood Beau Geste. I saw photos of him in *Dressage Today* and just fell in love with him. When I heard you were showing him at the Darbys' event, I couldn't believe my luck."

"You've chosen well," Patricia assured her. "Beau is a very giving horse, one who will go that extra mile for you. What level are you riding now?"

"I just started schooling second level, but unfortunately, am about to retire the horse I've ridden for the past twelve years. He's earned a well-deserved rest in our pastures, and it's been difficult to find someone to replace him."

"As I told you over the phone, we're not quite sure what level Beau has trained for most recently, but I've worked with him in the arena and he does a perfect counter canter, shoulder-in and travers, which makes me think he's appropriate for your level."

"May I meet him?"

"Of course." Patricia made a move toward the stall in which Beau Geste, food forgotten, now gazed at Betsy with what appeared to be true love in his eyes. Annie quickly stepped in front to supersede her friend and reached for Beau's leather halter. Holding the horse for a visual inspection was the least she could do to help promote this sale. So far, stable hand seemed to be the best role to which she was suited.

She watched Betsy expertly run her hands along Beau's back and down his four legs. She critically examined his face, although what this was for, Annie could only guess. Perhaps to visualize future portraits together? Finally, Betsy stepped back and sighed happily.

"Do you have time to let me see him in the ring?"

"Certainly. Let me tack him up, and we'll take him out to our warm-up arena. Annie, would you be kind enough to put on his brushing boots?"

Brushing boots? Annie had no idea what Patricia was talking about. She was handed four felt wraps and heard Patricia murmur in her ear, "Fasten on the outside, front to back." Obviously, the wraps, or brushing boots, went around the fore and back legs. This Annie could do. She was used to wrapping her horses' legs with bandages when they were injured or lame. She managed to attach them without difficulty and, to her relief, without error.

Although she had never seen Patricia astride a horse before, Annie was not at all surprised to see her friend mount with all the assurance of an Olympic equestrian. She and Beau walked around the arena and began performing serpentines at various gaits. Annie had to admit that Beau not only was extremely responsive to Patricia's smallest leg cue, but, incredibly, he seemed to be thoroughly enjoying himself. She couldn't fathom what a horse would find intriguing about making repetitive movements—Annie was convinced her horses' greatest thrill was going on a long trail ride—but she couldn't deny what she was seeing.

Betsy stood by her, enrapt. Occasionally, she'd murmur "Lovely!" or "Just beautiful!" and Annie would make a sympathetic noise in her throat that she hoped implied that she totally agreed. In truth, she hadn't the slightest idea what Betsy had just seen that elicited such an ecstatic response. Beau went from a trot to a canter. So what? Every horse she trained could do that. He changed leads at a walk. Hardly the flying lead changes that Sam, her pinto, could make with just a nudge on his hindquarters. What was the big deal?

Whatever transpired in the ring, Betsy obviously thought it was brilliant. She walked up to Patricia, still on horseback.

"May I have a chance?"

"Of course. But let's check the stirrups. We'll probably have to put them down a few holes. I believe you're longer in the leg than I am."

Betsy did not show quite the quiet confidence that Patricia displayed on Beau's back, but there was no doubt she was a competent rider and that she loved the horse she was riding. Annie was sure it was only the sudden dip of the sun over the mountains after a half hour in the arena that persuaded Betsy to reluctantly bring Beau to a halt. Watching Patricia, Annie could see that her friend was pleased by Betsy's riding skills and her treatment of the horse. The sale, it appeared, would take place.

"I want him. How soon can we have him vetted?"

Annie knew that Betsy was asking when an equine vet could conduct his own examination of the horse. Most of Annie's horses were rescues, and while a prior vet exam wasn't a condition of those sales, the first person the new horse usually saw after meeting Annie was Jessica Flynn, her own vet, shortly followed by her farrier. With a horse this valuable, double-checking the soundness of the animal only made good sense.

"The show vet will be out tomorrow," Patricia responded with a smile. "I believe his name is Dr. Chesterton. I'm not familiar with him, but he's supposed to have a stellar reputation. Will that do?"

"Oh, yes, that's fine. I've had Dr. Chesterton out to my place. He's a superb vet. Has Beau had any issues that you're aware of?"

Annie was curious to know if, in the interest of full disclosure, Patricia would mention Beau's hair-raising rescue from a barn fire back in March and his months of rehab at Running Track. Predictably, Patricia did.

"We've got all his health records from before the fire and, of course, afterward. Perhaps I could e-mail them to Dr. Chesterton tonight so he'll have a chance to review them before he comes out tomorrow morning."

"That would be lovely." *Lovely*, Annie decided, was Betsy's operative word.

Betsy dismounted, and the three women walked back to the stables together.

"We do require a home visit," Patricia told her. "Would that be possible after Dr. Chesterton's visit?"

Betsy nodded. "Absolutely. I'm glad you insist on those. I'll be home all afternoon and so will my husband. Ken's a cardiologist at the local hospital but is out of surgery by noon. He's not quite as interested in dressage as I am, but he does have the good sense to know that it's in his best interests to appear to be."

"Smart man." Annie spoke, thinking of Marcus, who, not too long ago, got astride a mule just to show Annie he could sit in a saddle without falling off. Of course, someone else had been holding the lead rope.

Betsy laughed. "Very smart man."

Patricia and Betsy finished their paperwork while Annie groomed Beau in his stall. *What a lucky guy,* Annie thought. He was going to a great home and would be allowed to do what he liked best, even if the thrill still escaped his groomer.

She heard the sound of boots on concrete and peered out of Beau's stall. A small man in a white tuxedo approached them, carrying a tray with tall glasses filled with a drink with a red tinge.

"Pardon me, Mesdames. Chef Gustav wondered whether you would care for a glass of his raspberry iced tea."

"Perfect," gasped Betsy. "I'm positively parched." Annie and Patricia also reached for a frosted glass.

"And here I'd put a bottle of champagne on ice," Patricia said. "Just in case it was appropriate."

"Thanks, Patricia, but I'd much rather have this. I

have an hour's drive ahead of me, anyhow." Turning to the waiter, Betsy added, "Please tell Chef Gustav *merci beaucoup. C'est magnifique!*"

Her accent was perfect, Annie thought. Perhaps she could teach Beau a few commands in French. After all, dressage horses in Paris must respond to the lingua franca.

"Phew!" Annie and Patricia sprawled out in the patio chairs, sucking down the last of their iced tea.

"That. Went. Perfectly." Annie meant every enounced word. "My hat is off to you, Patricia. You are a true salesperson."

"Beau sold himself. It's usually not that easy. And we're not out of the woods yet. Beau did suffer a bit of lung damage from the fire, and although he's young enough to have made a full recovery, the vet might have a few cautionary words about his future performance because of the inhalation of carbon monoxide."

"I doubt it. And even if he did, I think Betsy is so gaga in love with Beau that she'd take him anyway."

"I hope so. She didn't flinch at the asking price. Didn't even extend a counteroffer. With luck, nothing the vet says tomorrow will change that."

A gong sounded from far away.

"Heavens! It's six o'clock already! Where did the time go?" Patricia scrambled to her feet, and Annie wearily pulled herself out of the chair. She was not looking forward to cocktail hour. At least not if Gwendolyn was present, and she knew she wouldn't be so lucky as to avoid that.

Her bedroom suite was lovely—a big bed, private

patio, and separate bath all to herself. Annie would have loved to have collapsed on the duvet and taken a short power nap, but there was no time. After a quick washup, she wrenched off her breeches and replaced them with silk slacks, a sleeveless blouse, and sandals. There was no time to put on makeup, which Annie seldom used anyway, so she simply pulled a brush through her shoulder-length brown hair and called it good. Squaring her shoulders and telling herself in the mirror that she could do this, she left her bedroom and quietly closed the door behind her.

Sounds of laughter came from below, and Annie walked down the spiral staircase separating the floors slowly and with not a little trepidation. She saw an immense crowd of women out on the patio, draped over lounge chairs near a very long pool. Patricia was already there, standing by Hollis, who appeared to be making her a drink. She counted eight women in all before she reached the sliding glass doors. At the moment, she'd have rather faced eight rearing stallions.

"Annie!" Liz called out to her from her perch on a pink chair, next to the pool. She was waving a glass with an umbrella in it. "Congratulations on your sale!"

Annie smiled. At least it was a face from home, even if Annie had only known Liz since a few Sundays ago.

"Patricia did all the selling. I just watched the master at work."

All eyes, she noticed, were on her, and the conversations that had been in full force now suddenly died down. It was as if everyone expected her to make a speech.

"Annie, I'm so glad to meet you." The voice came

from in front of her, from a small, birdlike woman in a flowing caftan and a martini glass beside her. There was no doubt that this was a woman "of a certain age," but Patricia had been right—Miriam Darby still had all the hallmarks of a great beauty, including the poise and the glamour. Annie suddenly had the distinct feeling that she'd seen her face on the silver screen before, with Paul Newman as the leading man. Could that really be? She vowed to politely ask when the time was right, which, unfortunately, wasn't now.

"Mrs. Darby, I can't thank you enough for opening up your home to me," Annie said, mindful of manners that had been drilled into her when she was still a child.

"Call me Miriam, I insist. And stop with the compliments. They'll just go to Hollis's head and make him insufferable."

"My bride speaks the truth," Hollis commented from the side table that contained an impressive row of bottles. "When people tell me how wonderful I am, I believe them. Been that way all my life. Annie, what would you like to drink?"

Her mind went blank. She couldn't just ask for a nip of Glenlivet, her usual drink, could she? Not when surrounded by all these sophisticated women. Not when Gwendolyn, or "the threat," as she now called her in her mind, was watching her every move.

"I'll have a martini," she said in a clear voice. "No vermouth, please. One olive."

This is what she'd heard Marcus order on one occasion, and she figured she couldn't go wrong with a drink that he endorsed.

"Any particular kind of gin?"

"Beefeater, if you have it." If Hollis asked her one

more question about the drink, she'd be stumped. It was all she remembered.

Miriam and Hollis looked at each other and gave an approving nod.

"Coming right up, Annie," Hollis said, reaching for the bottle.

Miriam leaned toward Annie. "You're having exactly what I'm having. You have excellent taste."

Annie began to relax for the first time that day. She listened to Miriam's question about what kind of horses she owned and deliberately turned her back on Gwendolyn, seated a few feet behind her.

A pounding on the door interrupted Annie's description of how Trooper, her first Thoroughbred, had come to her—the insistent, demanding, noise could not be ignored. Hollis looked up quizzically, then at the group.

"Is anyone expecting a visitor?"

All heads shook no, and Hollis sighed, got up from the wingback chair—the only piece of real furniture on the deck, Annie noticed—dusted his knees absently, and walked toward the entrance. Everyone sat quietly, waiting for him to return. There was no attempt at further conversation. The noise had cast a pallor over the group.

Hollis returned a few minutes later, his face pale. He motioned toward Patricia, and Annie instinctively got up with her. They met Hollis in the dining room adjoining the patio, and Hollis closed the glass doors before gently putting one hand on each of their shoulders.

"Apparently there's been a car accident not far from the front gates. The driver, a woman, has been killed. She ran into a large sequoia before making the turn off the hill and appears to have died instantly. No one else seems to have been involved, and it doesn't look as if she was traveling at a high speed. It's most curious. The police and ambulance are there now, and they've identified her as a Betsy Gilchrist. The barn staff say you were with her earlier today."

Patricia and Annie's eyes met as the horror of Hollis's words sunk in.

"She came to look at Beau. She was going to buy him. Oh, the poor woman!" Patricia put her face in her hands and began to cry softly.

Annie stared at Hollis. She had a sinking feeling that once more, she'd found a murder in a place where one would least expect it. And for some strange reason, she felt somehow to blame.

Chapter Four

"Feeling a bit like Jessica Fletcher?" Hollis looked kindly at her.

"Excuse me?"

"Sorry, probably before your time. Jessica Fletcher was an amateur sleuth in an old TV series called *Murder, She Wrote*. Wherever Jessica went, murder followed. It was a very popular show, although why she had any friends left by the tenth season was beyond me. Then again, she always did solve the crime."

Annie smiled despite her shock over the news. She remembered watching the show with her mother on Sunday evenings.

"I guess I feel a bit like that, yes."

"Fortunately, this doesn't appear to be a murder although the police do want to talk to both you and Patricia. I'll drive you down. Let's take the tuk-tuk."

Annie had no idea what a tuk-tuk was, but she didn't want to show her ignorance by asking. She nodded and followed Patricia and Hollis through the dining room and out the front door. She could feel eight pairs of very curious eyes from the patio following their departure. She willed herself not to turn around.

The tuk-tuk turned out to be a golf cart, kept on one side of the house under a sheltering tree. Annie got in the back, and let Patricia have the front seat with Hollis.

"We call it a tuk-tuk because it reminds us of the real thing in India," Hollis explained as the electric cart noiselessly bumped along the road leading to the estate entrance. "You see them everywhere—little three-wheeled scooters driven by local residents. They also serve as cabs. The drivers are very good at weaving through traffic, which includes the occasional cow."

"What were you doing in India?" Annie hadn't traveled farther than the place she was now.

"Miriam and I were on set, starring in one of Hollywood's early versions of a Bollywood movie. Indian films were just starting to catch on here, and our studio thought it should jump in on the action. I was a Rajasthan warrior who heroically saved the Maharaja's princess daughter from a gang of bandits. Miriam was the princess, of course. It was a dreadful movie. Although we made enough to add another odd lot to our then young estate."

They arrived at the front gate and, to Annie, an all too familiar scene. Ventura County patrol vehicles completely blocked the closed wrought-iron gates and doubled as a barricade to oncoming traffic—not that there was any, Annie noted. The road was devoid of vehicles as far as she could see, not counting the ambulance, fire truck, and EMT vehicle stationed several hundred yards down the road. Perhaps on purpose, they completely blocked her view of the accident. It was just as well. Annie had no desire to see Betsy Gilchrist's car wrapped around a giant tree trunk.

A pleasant-looking deputy approached them, young, blond, blue-eyed, and very fit. He was a lot better looking than any of the deputies she'd recently encountered in eastern Washington. Perhaps a screen test was required as part of the application process down here. If so, Annie heartily approved.

"Mr. Darby," he said by way of greeting. "Thanks for bringing the ladies to us."

"My pleasure. If you appeared at our door, a bevy of other women would have swarmed toward you, and I couldn't be responsible for your safety."

Annie and Patricia glanced at each other. Hollis probably was right.

"Mind if we use the barn office to get their statements?"

"Be my guest. I doubt anyone except the stable hands are on the premises, and I guarantee they won't bother you."

"Great. Shall we go, Ms . . . ?"

"Winters. I'm Patricia Winters. And this is my friend, Annie Carson. We met with Betsy just a few hours ago. She came to view one of our horses."

Patricia's voice broke, and Annie was afraid she'd break down again. So did the deputy. He closed his notebook, and said, "Let's wait until we're all seated, shall we? This shouldn't take long. I can get both of your statements at the same time."

Patricia fumbled in her slack pants, drew out a ragged Kleenex, and blew her nose. She turned two red eyes up at the deputy and nodded. Her mouth trembled a little. Annie had a feeling she'd be doing most of the talking.

* * *

"You mentioned that Gustav sent down a server late this afternoon?" Deputy Collins leaned back in his chair and looked at Annie. She sighed. This was getting tiresome, even with a blond Adonis asking the questions. She'd already described their first two hours with Betsy in excruciating detail, or at least as much as she could remember, and was tired of having every nuance questioned.

"As I've already said, it was just around the time we concluded the paperwork for the sale. About five thirty, I'd guess. Right, Patricia?"

Patricia gave a short nod. Aside from offering her name, address, cell phone number, reason for visiting the Darbys, and confirmation that she'd met Betsy for the first time that day, Patricia hadn't contributed much to the interview, nor had the deputy prodded her for information.

"One of Gustav's kitchen helpers just showed up in the stables. At least, that's how he introduced himself," Annie went on. "I only arrived this afternoon and haven't met any of the kitchen staff. But the guy was dressed in a white tux, held a tray of tall drinks, and said Chef Gustav had sent him. We took him at his word."

"I recognized him," Patricia said softly. "I've seen him on several occasions. Mostly clearing dishes from the buffet, that sort of thing. I'm sure he's had a background check. Gustav wouldn't hire anyone without making sure they were honest."

"I'm sure you're right, Ms. Winters." The deputy nodded at Annie to continue.

"Anyway, the waiter asked if we wanted a glass of

raspberry iced tea, and we did. In fact, we simply devoured them." Annie remembered how refreshing the drink had been. "The tea couldn't have come at a better time."

Deputy Collins nodded. "And what did you do with the empty glasses?"

Annie and Patricia glanced around.

"I think we just put them on the table," Patricia said.

"I remember—we were just finishing them when we heard the gong from the house. Betsy had just left."

"Gong?" Now Deputy Collins seemed surprised.

"To call us back to the house for a preprandial drink," Patricia explained.

"Yes, and we were late. We put the glasses on your table, Patricia, and skedaddled."

"Where was Ms. Gilchrist's glass?"

Annie tried hard to remember.

"I'm—I'm not sure. I don't remember where Betsy left it. Surely, she wouldn't have walked off with it. It was crystal, and belonged to the house. I assume she left it on the table, but I can't be certain."

"Well, there are no glasses on the table now." Deputy Collins looked hard at the women, as if they were somehow responsible for their absence.

Enough of this, Annie thought. The same waiter who'd brought the glasses probably picked them up as soon as they'd left the stables.

"What do you think did cause the accident?" Annie blurted out the question. "Hollis said Betsy wasn't speeding. Do you think she swerved for a car or an animal? Or do you think it was a heart attack?"

The deputy shook his head. "Too early to say. We'll

see if any of the neighbors saw or heard anything, and talk with the other houseguests to see if anyone else knew the deceased." He looked intently at both women. "But just to be clear—there's nothing either of you observed—no sign that Ms. Gilchrist was feeling sick, under the influence, or otherwise impaired? Anything at all that might have affected her driving?"

"Absolutely not. She seemed to be in perfect health. And very happy about acquiring her new horse," Patricia said firmly.

"She did tell us her husband is a cardiologist. Presumably he'll be able to tell you if Betsy had a medical condition." Annie hoped the deputy would take the hint and end the interview. But he just sat there, patiently waiting for one of them to say more.

Annie paused, then decided to speak bluntly. "Is there anything more you need from us or are we free to go?" She'd recently uttered that line more than once in eastern Washington and had hoped she'd never have to say it again.

Deputy Collins grinned at her. "That should do it." He spoke into the tape recorder that had been running for the past forty-five minutes. "This concludes the interview of Patricia Winters and Annie Carson. It is now"—he glanced at his watch—"7:35 P.M." The deputy shut off the machine and put it in his shirt pocket.

"Thanks, ladies. We'll call you if we need anything further, but I doubt we'll have to."

"So, this is just another tragic roadside accident?" Patricia sounded a little bitter, Annie thought.

"Happens every day in Ventura County."

Annie couldn't help thinking about another recent tragedy—the loss of the sale of Beau Geste. She was ashamed to admit she felt this loss almost as keenly as she did for the woman who had been so thrilled to acquire the horse.

The good news was that the other guests had finished dinner by the time they returned to the house, and Gwendolyn was nowhere in sight. The bad news was that Annie was starving. The pretzels on the plane had hardly sufficed as a meal, and aside from Gustav's excellent iced tea, she'd had no other sustenance since six that morning. Patricia begged off exploring the kitchen; the accident had sucked all the life out of her, she told her friend, and she wanted nothing more than to go to bed. She would check in with Liz, but then she was shutting her door.

Annie gave her friend a sympathetic smile and nodded. She watched Patricia trudge up the spiral staircase leading to her suite, her shoulders sagging. Annie hoped a good night's sleep would bring her back to life. That, and immersing herself into Liz's dressage work in the morning.

Considering that seven other guests were staying here, the house seemed far too silent. She wondered where everyone possibly could be. Surely, if they were out by the pool, she'd hear the splash of water or their conversations. All she heard now was the solemn tick-tock of a grandfather clock in the living room. It reminded her of her own Seth Thomas clock at home. Annie found the sound somewhat soothing.

"Oh, there you are, dear," Miriam appeared in the open foyer, a bit breathless. Annie noticed she grasped a cane in one of her small, birdlike hands. "Everyone's gone for the moment. Nicole and Gwendolyn are visiting with Harriett in her cottage, and Amy and Lucy are playing tennis. I don't know where Tabitha is, but probably she's in her room, memorizing her test for the zillionth time. I saw Liz go up earlier."

Annie's uncomprehending stare did not go unnoticed.

"Oh, heavens, you must think I'm stark raving mad. Perhaps I am. You didn't have time to meet the rest of our houseguests, did you, before being whisked off to talk with the local constabulary? Well, you'll have plenty of time to get acquainted with the rest of the gang over breakfast tomorrow. I just wanted to get everyone out of the common areas before you returned. I could see that Patricia was terribly upset by this unexpected accident, and I suspected you didn't want to answer more questions from the girls when you returned."

The Darbys really were the most thoughtful people. Annie smiled broadly and impulsively gave the tiny woman a quick hug.

"You are so right. Patricia was all in and couldn't have handled any more conversation, no matter how well intended."

"Which it wouldn't have been. People are ghouls when it comes to other people's misfortunes. Surely you must have noticed that in your own cases."

Her own cases. Annie had never looked upon the murders she'd helped solve as her own. She was mostly an innocent bystander who'd happened to be caught in the middle of several murderous frays.

"I guess I'm a bit more tough-skinned when it comes to sudden death. Although from what I can tell, Betsy's truly was accidental, and not planned."

"You never know," Miriam said darkly. "If she has been murdered, I'm glad you're here. Patricia told us all about what happened in the Washington desert last summer. I was highly impressed with your detecting abilities."

Annie would never have called eastern Washington a desert although if dry heat, sparse greenery, and brown mountains were desert conditions, then she guessed it might qualify as one. But she wasn't going to contradict her hostess, especially since she was being complimented in such glowing terms.

"You must be starving. Have you had a chance to see the kitchen yet?"

"No, I haven't, but I'm always eager to explore my favorite room in any house."

"Let me show you where Chef Gustav holds court and give you a quick tour at the same time. As you can see, all the common space is on the main floor. The library's the next room over, and you're welcome to peruse our bookshelves any time you wish. People don't use the room as much as they used to, and it's a great pity. If I don't have two or three good books going at any one time, I feel my life is somehow not in sync."

"Me, too. By the way, I love your open-air foyer. It's incredibly inviting."

"Thank you, Annie. Hollis and I used to spend a lot of time in Mexico, and when we were ready to build, I insisted on a traditional Spanish style."

"It's great the way it brings in the scent of the great outdoors, even though I don't know most of your trees. Except for the cedar. That I recognize. We're big on cedar in the Pacific Northwest."

"We call that incense cedar. *Calocedrus* is the official Latin name. It actually comes from the cypress family. We chose it because of its drought tolerance, and believe me, not many other trees have survived what we've been through the past several years."

Annie nodded. They were now walking down a long corridor. Rather than an overhead ceiling, Annie saw glass partitions instead.

"You've really made use of the natural sunlight," she told Miriam.

"We try to. We put in solar panels when most people didn't even know they existed. Thought we were nuts. If they paid our electrical bills, they'd understand."

Annie remembered the central air-conditioning throughout the enormous stable structure.

"You certainly haven't stinted on the horses' comfort."

"No, we haven't. Hollis thinks I'm a bit over the top when it comes to their care, but I pay no attention when he starts to raise his eyebrows. It's just the way I am."

Annie found she liked Miriam more every minute.

"I hear you once were a dressage student yourself."

"Still am, even though I ride very infrequently now. The learning never stops. But that's the way it is in any horse discipline, don't you agree, Annie?"

"I do."

They'd reached the end of the hall, and Annie saw two large swinging doors on the left. Miriam gestured with her one free hand.

"The kitchen's right there. The staff is usually gone by eight, so you're free to rummage the refrigerator and shelves all you want. If Chef Gustav has prepared something for tomorrow, he'll mark it with a

'HANDS-OFF' sign so you'll know not to touch it on pain of death."

"That's good to know."

"Gustav is fiercely proud of what he serves us and does not appreciate it when a ramekin of crème brûlée disappears or a leg of duck confit goes missing. A few of our houseguests have found out the hard way. And they haven't been invited back. I miss one or two of them, but I'd miss Gustav more."

Miriam turned to Annie. Her eyes were a startling blue hue, and quite beautiful. They reminded Annie of another actor who'd had such vibrant eyes, the kind you could get lost in.

"You may think I'm rude," Annie stammered, "but I can't help but ask. Am I right in thinking you starred in a movie with Paul Newman?"

Now the blue eyes twinkled back at her.

"I did, indeed. In many ways, I consider that role the highlight of my career. But don't tell Hollis. He was usually my leading man, especially in the old days."

"I promise."

"I'm going to leave you now, but feel free to explore the rest of the property tomorrow. The tennis court is just over the rise, and next to it, there's an exercise room and small spa. I'll see you at the stables tomorrow. I never miss the chance to see the girls in training before an event. And now, if you'll excuse me, I'll beam myself up to my suite. It was a pleasure talking with you. I look forward to more conversations."

And with that, Miriam touched an almost invisible button on the far wall and two elevator doors silently opened. Annie managed to say good night before the doors noiselessly closed.

She pushed the swinging doors into the kitchen, eager to begin her forage for food. But contrary to Miriam's assurances, she was not alone. At the head of a huge white table sat a small, very plump man with a jet-black goatee. The white chef's coat he wore gave Annie little doubt as to his identity. When she realized he was muttering in French, all doubts disappeared.

"*Merde! Les imbeciles me fatigues! Dégage!*"

Annie had taken enough French in high school to know that the chef thought someone, maybe more than one person, was an idiot. She stood silently by the doors and considered simply leaving. But then, she was really, really hungry.

She cleared her throat. Chef Gustav whirled around in his chair and looked toward the doors. It was a remarkably quick response for a man with such a round girth.

"*Qui est là?* Who comes here?"

Annie responded as blandly as she could.

"Excuse me, Miriam said I could come in and perhaps get a bite to eat. I'm Annie Carson, one of the houseguests, probably the last to arrive."

The chef's change in demeanor was instantaneous.

"But of course! Mademoiselle Carson, come in, come in! I comprehend that you and Mademoiselle Winters were taken off to the gendarmes this evening before you were served dinner, *n'est-ce pas?* Those swine! To deprive you of your evening meal, it is unthinkable! Please, sit down and let me serve you."

The chef heaved himself out of his chair and waddled toward her, his face beaming.

"But let me first introduce myself. I am Chef Gustav, at your service."

Annie held out her hand. "It's very nice to meet you, Chef Gustav."

"*Enchanté.*"

These amenities over, Chef Gustav happily continued his journey to the refrigerator and began pulling out covered dishes.

"Tell me, Mademoiselle Carson, do you have any food restrictions I should know about? You are not, I trust, one of the gluten-free? Or, perhaps, a person who does not care for *boeuf*?"

"Nope," Annie replied, greedily taking in the array of dishes the chef was assembling on the counter. "I eat everything. And I love meat."

Chef Gustav beamed. "Then let me prepare a dinner that will make you curl up like a cat and sleep like a baby. But first, a glass of wine."

Pulling out a wine bottle with a pinkish hue, he delivered a glass of it to Annie and watched carefully as she took a tentative sip. The wine sparkled on her tongue, and she tasted both fruit and a hint of spice. It was heavenly.

"Marvelous!" she told him. "What is it?"

"Ah, mademoiselle, it is a new rosé from the heart of Provence."

"I wonder if I could get this at home."

"*Mais non, mademoiselle!* This is imported especially for the Darbys, and only because the proprietor is my *beau-frère*, or, how you say, my brother-in-law. But I will happily share it with you while you stay here."

"*Merci beaucoup!*"

Over her dinner, Annie learned that she and Patricia were not the only ones who had been subjected to a conversation with the police.

"*Mon Dieu!* They come into my kitchen just as I am serving dinner to the ladies! And they have the *effron-terie* to expect me to drop everything and talk!"

Annie's mouth was full, but she shook her head to express her own displeasure at such rudeness.

"But that is not all! *Non!* Then they ask me to show them the *thé glacé* I serve to the ladies this afternoon. Why? I ask. Are you thirsty? We have very good well water here, and I offer it to them. They will not get my *thé glacé*, I assure you. Not when they disrupt my kitchen and think nothing of it. The waiters are cowering in the corners. They are not doing their job. And my soufflé is in severe danger of falling! No, I say, they shall not have my *création*. Let them drink water. Bah!"

Annie tried very hard to keep a straight face during Chef Gustav's tirade. The best way to accomplish this was to take another bite of food. Fortunately, her dinner companion was far too agitated to notice Annie's attempt to hide her smile.

"And do you know, Mademoiselle Carson, the reason they ask for the *thé glacé*? It is not to slake their thirst. Not at all! It is because they think I have some-how poisoned the woman who dies in the *accident de voiture*! It is unbelievable!"

At this, Annie set down her fork and took another sip of the excellent rosé.

"It is ridiculous," she agreed. "Three of us had your iced tea this afternoon, not just the woman who died. It was marvelous. There wasn't a drop left in any of our glasses. So, you see, you couldn't have poisoned anyone."

Chef Gustav sat back in his chair with a small thump, a satisfied gleam in his shiny black eyes.

"That is what I tell them! But do they believe it? *Bien sûr que non!* They are stupid, incapable of forming a single *idée intelligente.* So I give them what I have left. But if this is how the local gendarmes conduct murder investigations, I fear for all of us!"

Annie put down her fork.

"Murder investigation? I assumed it was an accident. The woman had a seizure or a heart attack . . . or something."

Chef Gustav firmly shook his head and spoke in a conspiratorial whisper.

"*Écoute attentivement,* Mademoiselle Carson! The *accident de voiture,* it looks innocent, but it is not. It is murder most foul, and one of our guests is responsible. There is someone evil staying in this house, I can smell it! And I have a superb nose."

Chapter Five

Annie awakened the next morning to glorious sunshine streaming through her open window. She stretched languidly, sinking into the soft bedding. Then she remembered Betsy Gilchrist's death and flung the sheets away. Chef Gustav's words were still very much on her mind.

She'd tried mightily the previous night to pry more information out of the Frenchman but without success. The only thing she'd managed to pry out of him was a second helping of a lemon tart that had made her whimper with pleasure just looking at it. And that hardly had been a difficult job.

But Chef Gustav had refused to elaborate on his cryptic remark. And there it remained, swirling around in her brain: *There is someone evil staying in this house.* It was a simple statement, completely unsubstantiated and unproven, but to Annie, utterly provocative. Although why anyone would want to kill nice Betsy Gilchrist was beyond her ken.

She intended to find out if it was true. And the only

way to do that was to meet all the guests and start her private examination of each one—Patricia excluded, of course. She knew her friend was beyond reproach. And Liz, she decided. Patricia wouldn't be her friend if she didn't trust her.

She showered quickly and dressed again in breeches, boots, and a polo shirt. Since she had no plans to ride herself, she still considered the attire utterly unnecessary. Still, if looking the part helped her fit in with the other guests, she would do it.

The dining room was full of similarly attired women when Annie entered. Glancing at her watch, she realized she was among a group of early risers. It was only seven thirty, but nearly every seat around the table was taken.

"Good morning," she said cheerily to Hollis, letting her smile encompass the entire assemblage. The attempt to appear both perky and confident took all her courage. She saw everyone except Gwendolyn and a woman seated across from her smile back.

"Good morning back, Annie," Hollis replied genially, and gestured with his napkin to the long table in back of him.

"Help yourself to the buffet. If we're short on anything you'd like, just ring the bell at the end, and one of our staff will replace it."

She gratefully turned to the table, laden with trays of fruit, cheese, breads, breakfast meats, and a variety of yogurts.

"Oh, and ring the bell if you'd like an omelet or crepes. Chef Gustav makes these on order."

"It's the *only* way he makes them," Patricia added to Hollis's last comment. "He calls precooked eggs an abomination."

"He's right." The comment came from the regal woman seated across from Gwendolyn and was delivered in a voice that brooked no dissension. It reminded Annie of Mrs. Whitman, her third-grade teacher, a perpetually grumpy woman who discouraged questions from students and, rumor had it, taught only because she was a widow who needed the income.

The woman's voice had the same timbre as Mrs. Whitman's, but unlike her teacher, she looked as if she'd never had to work a day in her life. Annie couldn't quite put her finger on it since everyone around the breakfast table wore the same equestrian uniform, but somehow, she knew this woman was in a social stratum all her own.

Briefly wondering what the woman's problem was, Annie took her filled plate and sat down between Liz and Patricia, who had thoughtfully saved a welcoming place for her. Annie would have loved a few eggs, but after Chef Gustav's feast last night, she didn't feel it was fair to ask for more special treatment.

"How did you sleep?"

Patricia's question assured Annie her friend was back to her usual, upbeat self.

Curled up like a cat and slept like a baby.

"Fine. Really well, in fact."

"Are you showing?" An anxious-looking woman seated to the left of Hollis stared at her, as if Annie's answer somehow might affect the earth's ability to rotate on its axis. It took Annie a moment to realize she wasn't referring to a nonexistent pregnancy.

"No, just observing."

"Oh." The speaker seemed relieved. Annie guessed the earth would continue to turn.

"Let me introduce you to my friend," Patricia said

firmly, the woman's rudeness obviously rankling her. "Tabitha, this is Annie Carson, a Western horse trainer from the Olympic Peninsula. She's here as my guest. Annie, this is Tabitha Rawlins, who's showing her Friesian this weekend. Like Gwendolyn, she lives in the Bay Area."

"Although that is where our similarities end," Gwendolyn drawled. "Right, Tabitha?"

Tabitha's face abruptly turned ugly, and she glared back at the speaker. "That's right, Gwendolyn." She drew out each syllable of her name. "Aside from dressage, we really don't have much in common."

Gwendolyn turned to Annie. "Tabitha is a tax attorney, if you can believe it, and works in a cubicle reading tax code all day. She also has a cat. I keep telling her she should name the cat Tabby, so they could be twins, but so far, she hasn't taken my suggestion."

"His name is Horace," Tabitha said in a tight voice. "And he's a Siamese, not a tabby."

"See what I mean? I try to be helpful, and yet my ideas are constantly rejected."

Hollis stood up and gave Gwendolyn a pointed look.

"Now, ladies, let's not bore Annie with sundry details of our lives. And let me continue with the introductions. Annie, you met Lucy and Gwendolyn yesterday, and now you know Tabitha. Sitting next to Lucy is Amy Litchfield, a good friend of hers. The two of you met in law school, isn't that right?"

Amy and Lucy both gave small nods. Annie wondered if they weren't talking simply to avoid giving Gwendolyn ammunition.

"Amy and Lucy come from Boston and have stayed with us many times. Miriam and I thoroughly enjoy their company."

Lucy smiled gratefully at Hollis, who smiled back.

"And this is Nicole Anne Forrester," he said, gesturing to the woman who'd given her pronouncement about precooked eggs. "Nicole's a true native, born and raised in Southern California. We met her at a local show several years ago, and she keeps us up to date on all the major dressage events on both coasts. Nicole's a serious student of dressage. I'm sure she can answer any questions you have about what goes on in the arena."

Annie had no intention of asking Nicole anything. There was something very off-putting about the way she held herself, as if she were better than everyone else around the table. Perhaps it was her perfectly coifed mahogany-colored hair and manicured hands. Or the two-carat diamond ring that sparkled on the fourth finger, her left wrist delicately resting on the table so no one could miss it. Even Gwendolyn seemed a bit diminished just being in her vicinity.

"I take it you're not?" Nicole asked.

Annie started. Not what?

"Not a student of dressage?"

Hadn't Patricia just told everyone she trained Western horses?

"No, growing up, I learned Western horsemanship."

"Really? I didn't think there was much to it. Just jump on the horse's back, dig your spurs in, and yell, 'yee-haw.'"

Annie felt blood rush into her face. She counted to three.

"Don't be so bloody narrow-minded, Nicole." Patricia said the words lightly, but Annie knew she meant every one of them. "Surely you must have heard of Dennis Reis, the former professional rodeo cowboy?

Dennis now reschools upper-level dressage horses at his clinics. The women who attend say he's incredibly gifted even though he's had no classical training."

"Do tell. Well, Annie, you'll have to regale us some evening with your own hidden dressage techniques."

"What kind of horses do you have, Annie?" Amy Litchfield spoke up tentatively.

"All kinds—gaited, nongaited, quarter horses. My first horse was a Morgan. And I recently acquired two Thoroughbreds."

"None obviously suited for dressage," Nicole promptly replied. "Particularly the Thoroughbreds. Stiff backs, not supple enough. Do they jump?"

Annie fought the urge to tell Nicole that currently they were herding sheep.

"Time will tell," she said with a tight smile. She got an even tighter smile in return.

Once more, Patricia came to her rescue. "I've seen Annie ride both horses and I think they have tremendous potential as jumpers. All that built-in power, you know."

"Well, I must be off." Nicole clearly was not interested in discussing Annie's herd any further. She flung down her linen napkin, rose from the table, and spoke directly to their host.

"Hollis, I meant to tell you last night, Douglas is taking me out to dinner this evening, so I'll be leaving around five. And I'll probably be back late. Please don't feel you have to wait up."

"Please give my best to Douglas. And let me walk out with you."

Hollis was such a gentleman, Annie thought. To hear Nicole talk, you'd think he was just another one of her vassals rather than a very generous host who allowed her to enjoy the many amenities of a magnificent equestrian estate.

"Who's Douglas?" Annie whispered to Liz after both Nicole and Hollis had left the room. A whiff of perfume still hung in the air where she had walked by.

Tabitha overheard the question.

"Her fiancé. He's an investment banker from the city. They're going to be married in December and honeymoon on the Riviera. But don't worry, she'll return in time for the first spring event in Wellington."

Annie decided not to ask where Wellington was. Tabitha sounded bitter, and more than a tad envious of her colleague.

"I take it she has a job that allows this kind of flexibility?"

Liz was so politic. Annie waited for the answer.

"Real estate, emphasis on equestrian properties. But I think it's just a hobby. Her real job is dressage," Gwendolyn said bluntly. "It's all she's ever done, except for a slight detour to find a husband who can support her habit. Right, Lucy?"

Lucy looked miserable.

"Nicole's always done what she wanted. She was like that at boarding school. When the rest of us had to do homework, Nicole always talked someone into letting her ride."

Annie remembered Patricia telling her that Lucy had attended a private school where students often brought their own horses. She thought it sounded like a dream come true, even if people like Nicole had prowled the school's stables.

"Which probably is why Nicole's riding Prix St.-Georges this weekend and you're still working on your training level. Don't you think, Lucy?"

Gwendolyn's words hung in the air like unseen daggers. Annie was appalled at how quickly the conversation had turned into a display of backbiting barbs. Lucy looked down and didn't reply.

Annie had had enough. She stood up, collected her plate and flatware, and excused herself from the table.

"What are you doing?" Tabitha looked horrified.

"Taking my dishes to the kitchen."

Gwendolyn laughed. "That's what the staff are for. Leave them. It gives them something to do."

Annie stood by her chair, willing herself not to hurl the dishes at the obnoxious woman.

"I think it's a great idea," Patricia said firmly. "The kitchen staff has enough to do. Good heavens, there are eight of us now. That's a lot of dishes to wash."

"I agree." Liz stood up also.

"Me, too." Lucy got up, and Annie noticed that Amy followed suit.

As Annie deposited her dishes in the kitchen sink, she wondered if everyone in the dressage world was this hateful. Well, no, of course not. Liz and Patricia didn't behave like this. Even Lucy, who wore her need to be liked on her sleeve, seemed a kind if fragile human being. And Amy seemed decent enough. Tabitha clearly had issues, but perhaps she was simply socially inept. But Gwendolyn and Nicole were beyond the pale. Talk about evil. As far as ferreting out the person Chef Gustav believed responsible for the *accident de voiture*, she'd already found two who certainly had the mind-set to do the act. All she had to find was the motive.

* * *

Annie begged off walking the short distance to the stables with her friends but assured them she'd be down shortly. She'd yet to connect with Marcus and was anxious to clear the air about his relationship with Gwendolyn. A good night's sleep had brought her around to Patricia's way of thinking. Marcus undoubtedly only tolerated the woman's company because of her past relationship with his deceased wife. After seeing Gwendolyn in action this morning, she became even more convinced this was the case. Who would willingly dine with such an insufferable woman unless absolutely forced to?

Alas, Marcus's phone went straight to voice mail, and Annie was loath to leave a message. Instead, she texted him, telling him she had arrived, was enjoying the sun, and hoped they'd catch up that evening. She waited a few minutes, but no return text appeared on her phone. Well, he was a busy man. And Annie was anxious to examine what she'd been unable to see the previous night. It occurred to her that not one of the women around the breakfast table had brought up the horrific car accident. They must have heard about it by now. Perhaps Hollis had put a lid on the subject. Annie suspected he was the only one who could curtail their gossip, at least while he was within earshot.

It was a lovely time of day to walk the short distance to the main gates, particularly since a mare and month-old foal were grazing in one of the pastures that separated the estate from the stables. The smell of bay and eucalyptus filled the cool morning air and dispelled Annie's lingering distaste for the nastiness served at the breakfast table. She decided that Southern California really was quite beautiful, once the sight of freeways and malls disappeared from view. Who could not love a place where the sun shone in October, and probably all year long?

All the outdoor arenas were in use that morning. Annie first saw Lucy in the warm-up ring, riding a huge Hanoverian gelding. She paused in a willow grove to unobtrusively observe the young woman on horseback. Even from a distance, Annie could sense Lucy's nervousness in the saddle. She noticed Lucy's friend, Amy, perched on the top white stile of the arena's fence line. A tall, slender brunette in the middle of the arena was conversing with Lucy, but Annie couldn't hear the words. Glancing around, she saw Nicole on what appeared to be an Andalusian in another arena, and Tabitha on her Friesian in the third, along with a woman on foot she didn't recognize.

Annie had had enough of all of them for the moment. She walked out from the grove and turned in the opposite direction, onto a footpath toward the wrought-iron entrance gates. She hoped she'd find them unlocked.

They were, and wide open to boot. Annie strolled between them and out to the dusty road toward the place she'd seen the emergency vehicles the night before. She was sure the police had taken measurements, photographs, and whatever else they needed to reconstruct the crash, but she had an overwhelming curiosity to see the scene for herself.

She started by pacing the distance from the gate, figuring one long stride roughly equaled one yard. It was exactly 487 paces to the giant sequoia Betsy's car had encountered, easily identified by the ugly gash that coursed through the lower part of its trunk.

Annie knew it would take a long time for the tree to heal, but it would survive.

She then did a quick calculation in her head. She'd walked a solid quarter mile. If Betsy had been driving a sedate 25 mph, it would have taken thirty-six seconds to reach the tree. Annie hadn't seen any obvious skid marks on her methodical walk to the scene, but now she walked around and away from the tree, looking for signs that showed when—or if—Betsy had applied the brakes. She found none.

The sun was rising in the sky, and Annie plunked down beside the uninjured part of the Sequoia to think. She guessed the distance from the stable parking lot to the front gate to be another quarter mile. That meant Betsy was behind the wheel no more than two minutes before she'd crashed. It occurred to her that she didn't know the make of Betsy's car. If it were an SUV, perhaps Betsy would have survived the crash. If she'd been driving a sporty little convertible and the top had been down, maybe not.

But perhaps it wasn't the impact of the crash that had killed Betsy Gilchrist. Maybe all that had accomplished was to stop the car. If Betsy had suffered a heart attack, she might have been dead even before her car connected with the tree.

Annie sighed, got up, and dusted off the back of her breeches. She had too little information to come to any solid conclusions. She wished her buddy, Sheriff Dan Stetson, were here. He'd have filled her in without blinking, all the while warning her that what he was telling her was strictly between them. She fleetingly considered calling her friend but just as quickly nixed the idea. There was no way Dan could ask for information on an out-of-state case simply because one of his friends was curious. And she certainly didn't want to hear his stentorian voice telling her to let the police do their job.

Starting for the stables, Annie wasn't sure Lucy would appreciate a visitor, so she walked by the warm-up ring as inconspicuously as she could. But Lucy was anxious to make contact. She waved enthusiastically and motioned to her to come over. Annie reluctantly complied.

"Hello!" The tall brunette she'd seen standing in the ring strode up to the fence and extended her hand. "You must be Annie. Lucy's been talking about you nonstop for the past two days. I'm Melissa Phelps, her trainer. You're welcome to stay and watch if you'd like."

Annie had little interest in watching a perpetual neophyte ride but felt she had little choice but to accept.

"Thanks," she told Melissa. "I'm really here to cheer on Liz, but I'd like to watch you and Lucy for a bit if you don't mind."

"Be our guests. Lucy tells me you're a Western trainer, so call out if you have any questions. Although I'm sure you'll see a lot of similarities in what we're trying to do. Which is trying to get the horses to enjoy their job, isn't it?"

Annie grinned. "I couldn't agree more." She walked over to join Amy and felt her chest unclench a bit. Finally, she'd met a dressage person who didn't have her nose in the air *and* respected what she did. Perhaps dressage wasn't as arcane as she'd thought. Or, perhaps she'd learn something new herself.

"Back on the rail, please," Melissa called out to Lucy, who obediently squeezed her calves against the horse's flanks and awkwardly brought him to the rail opposite her spectators.

"Let's see a nice working trot on all four sides. And watch those corners. Remember, Prince has a long back that has to get around, too. Try to go a little deeper this time and remember to bend."

Lucy nodded and after a few false starts urged Prince into a trot. Annie heard Amy sigh next to her.

"What's the problem?"

"She's supposed to transition in three or four strides. They've been working on it all morning."

"Ah."

Lucy finally achieved a consistent trot, and Annie noticed that she was posting.

"I thought dressage riders didn't post." All the dressage riders Annie had seen on televised Olympic exhibitions had been firmly rooted to their saddles.

"That's only in tests at training level. Once Lucy starts schooling first level, she will sit the trot."

"Got it."

As Lucy came to the first corner, she saw Prince's stride imperceptibly shorten. It was a common enough reaction among horses when they approached a corner, and Annie wondered if Lucy was aware that Prince's gait was changing.

Melissa recognized the horse's intent.

"Keep his rhythm up, Lucy! Don't let him slow down!"

Annie watched Lucy nudge the horse's sides and lean forward.

"That's right! Good! But don't lose your center!"

Lucy immediately sat up, and Prince went into a stately walk. She gave a strangled cry.

"I'm trying! But when he slows down at the corner, I always manage to do something that makes him think I want him to walk!"

"You'll get it, Lucy. It's a lot to remember all at once. Walk through the next corner, then pick up the trot again."

Lucy and Prince navigated the next corner much more adeptly. And this time, Prince picked up the trot on cue.

"Unlock your elbows, Lucy! Your hands are going up and down with him. Can you feel him bracing against you?"

Lucy nodded and let her elbows relax.

"That's it! Much better!"

Annie continued to watch Lucy at the trot, then attempt twenty-meter circles at the same gait. This was less successful.

"Use your inside leg, Lucy! Make him bend!"

Prince's head was pointed outside the circle, and Annie could see Lucy frantically trying to collect her left rein to pull his nose in.

"That's right. Use your aids!"

Prince continued to ignore Lucy's attempts and suddenly left the circle and began to trot to the other end of the ring.

"Outside rein!"

Prince continued to trot straight ahead until he reached the end of the arena, where Annie and Amy were watching. Lucy's face was bright red from exertion. She was breathing heavily, and sweat trickled down her cheeks. Of the two, Annie thought, Lucy was working far harder than her horse.

* * *

After thirty minutes, Annie excused herself, told Lucy she was doing great and that she looked forward to seeing everyone at lunch. She managed to walk slowly and calmly away and not break into a dead run. Watching Lucy was torturous, and she felt for both rider and horse. They had a long way to go in their journey toward true partnership, and Annie wondered if they'd ever fully get there. But she had been impressed by Melissa's coaching. Her knowledge of both human and equine physiology and body language was remarkable. And she'd corrected Lucy's many errors in ways that didn't destroy her ego or enthusiasm for trying.

She found Patricia and Liz in the indoor arena, and in the first few seconds could see a significant difference in riders. Sammy was a gorgeous Danish Warmblood who seemed to be thoroughly enjoying himself, as did Liz. Annie watched Sammy do serpentines, circles, and walk, trot, and canter with hardly a blip, and Annie found it fascinating to see how Patricia nudged Liz to improve Sammy's performance. An hour came and went without notice. When Patricia called for a break, Annie was effusive in her praise.

"You know, Melissa assured me our disciplines have a lot in common," she told Patricia. "But after watching both of you, I see how hard you try to keep the horse supple and relaxed while doing all the work. I'm not sure I pay as much attention to that as you do."

"We're all working toward the same goal, and as I mentioned this morning, highly skilled Western riders unconsciously do dressage all the time."

"I suppose. All my horses have to know how to get out of tight corners and be precise. But for me, it's more a safety issue. If I'm riding next to a cliff, I don't want my horse to make a step that I haven't personally endorsed."

Patricia laughed. "That's more in line with the original reason dressage evolved into a training discipline. You do know that it originated around 400 B.C."

"I most certainly did not!"

"It's true. A Greek general named Xenophon believed his army would fight better if cavalrymen and their horses worked in complete harmony with each other. He developed a military style of training that was the basis for the dressage you see performed today."

"Amazing. It looks like such a genteel sport."

"Yes, but remember, many of the riders exhibit the same fierce warrior traits that Xenophon demanded from his own men."

"I believe I met a few of those modern-day warriors this morning."

A gong sounded from afar.

Patricia shielded her eyes from the sun and looked toward the Darbys' home.

"That's our cue that luncheon will be served in fifteen minutes. Ready for battle, Annie?"

"My armor is already on."

Chapter Six

More of Chef Gustav's now legendary raspberry iced tea had been set out in large pitchers on the buffet table, and Annie secured a full glass as soon as she entered. She drained it in one gulp, then realized that perhaps this was not the approved method of slaking one's thirst among her new crowd. Glancing around, she noticed with relief that everyone—Nicole included—was doing the same. The day was hot and everyone was thirsty.

Hollis entered as everyone was finding a place at the table, and Annie noticed with amusement that each guest automatically snared the same spot she'd had at breakfast. It was just like grade school.

"Ladies, may I have your attention for one moment?"

Everyone turned to see what their host had to say.

"I want to let you all know that Judge Jean Bennett will be arriving tomorrow afternoon, along with her scribe, Margaret Woods. Both women will be staying at the Hyatt ten miles away, but they plan to come out tomorrow afternoon to look at the ring and do a bit of setup in the booth. They'll only be here an hour or so, so there isn't much danger of any chance encounters."

"I take it it's not cool to talk to the judge before the event?" Annie whispered to Patricia.

"More than not cool—it's forbidden," Patricia whispered back. "Hollis has room to put the judge and scribe up here, but he deliberately houses them off-site, just to be squeaky clean."

"So, have you met the judge? Ever ridden in front of her?"

"I haven't, but she has quite the reputation. I have no doubt you'll hear the horror stories over the next few days."

Annie wanted to ask Patricia what role the scribe played in the show, but Hollis had not finished speaking.

"Harriett, it's lovely to have you here today. We're delighted you'll be joining us for meals from now on. Annie, perhaps you haven't met our other resident dressage trainer yet. Harriett coaches Gwendolyn and Tabitha and is staying in one of our cottages."

Annie gave a smile in Harriett's direction, which was returned with what she could only describe as anatomical precision. Harriett was a very tall, lean woman with short-cropped brown hair and looked to be roughly Annie's age. She was seated at the end of the table, Gwendolyn on her right. *Talk about twins,* Annie thought. Both were practically identical; the only difference was the hue of their cropped hair.

"We look forward to seeing more of Melissa at mealtimes, as well," Hollis continued, "although Lucy informs me she won't be able to join us until later.

And now, ladies, I must join my bride. Today, we are dining en suite. See you all at six, and enjoy the afternoon, on horseback or otherwise."

A murmur of good-byes followed him out of the room, just as waiters began to appear from the kitchen's swinging doors. They held trays with individual salads, and Annie could see crab legs and shrimp adorning each one. Baskets of crusty French rolls already were on the table. Annie reached for one and sighed happily. Perhaps at this meal, at least, bickering would take a backseat to putting on the feedbag. It was a short-lived hope.

"Where's Melissa?" Harriett asked in the direction of Lucy and Amy.

"She noticed that Prince was a bit lame in his left hind," Amy told her. "She's with the show vet now."

Annie studied Lucy's face, but it didn't show much reaction to this somewhat alarming news. She wondered if dressage coaches routinely addressed horse injuries with medical professionals on behalf of their students, or if Melissa was there at Lucy's request. Annie had no doubt that the trainer was more knowledgeable and better able to deal with a lame or injured horse than her timid student. But it still seemed a bit odd.

"That's too bad, Lucy," Annie told her. "He seemed fine when I watched you in the ring."

Lucy shrugged. "Melissa noticed it at the trot and thought it should be checked out."

Annie wondered why Lucy wouldn't have also noticed that Prince's gait was off since she was on his back, but said nothing.

"Bad luck," Harriett said dismissively.

"Maybe we shouldn't compete." Lucy's words were barely audible.

"He'll be all right," Amy anxiously told her friend. "You've worked so hard, Lucy. It would be terrible if you couldn't ride on Saturday. Anyway, he's still got a whole other day to rest."

Harriett gave an impatient tsk. "One day won't be enough. For all we know, it could be a suspensory ligament injury. If Bennett even suspects he's lame, she'll ring him out for unsoundness. You could be eliminated as soon as you trot into the ring."

It occurred to Annie that in this segment of the equestrian world, most riders probably were familiar with the people who judged their horses' performances.

"I take it you've shown before Judge Bennett before?"

"All of us have," Tabitha told her. "And believe me, she's not one of our favorites."

"I haven't." Gwendolyn gave a nervous giggle. "I've just heard the stories."

"Nor I," Liz said. "I'm not sure I want to hear them."

Nicole ignored Liz's desires. "She's a notoriously low scorer."

Maybe, maybe not, Annie thought. Anyone who got less than what they thought they deserved on a test would say that.

"And her comments are always so critical. She's rude," added Amy.

"I swear she put a hex on my horse the last time I appeared in front of her." Tabitha's eyes were big. "I'd never gone off course before, but I did it twice in front of her."

Gwendolyn gave an almost imperceptible snort.

"We are not going to discuss the attributes of the judge at this table." Harriett's stern edict was met with a sudden hush. For a moment, nothing was heard but the soft clank of silverware on china.

Then Nicole spoke quietly. "You've got more right than any of us to hate Judge Bennett," she told the austere trainer. "Remember what happened last spring."

"*I said silence!*"

Annie had only known Harriett for five minutes, but she already knew that among the three trainers staying at the Darbys', this woman had galloped into the lead position.

Melissa burst into the dining room just as dessert was being served.

"Good news, Lucy!" The trainer was beaming, oblivious to the deathly silence that had prevailed before her entrance.

Lucy now showed the emotional response Annie had been looking for. She leapt out of her chair, nearly knocking it over. "What? What did you find out?"

"The very beginning of an abscess, near the frog. You have been diligent about cleaning his feet, haven't you?"

A quick flush came over Lucy's face. "Pretty much."

"Well, pretty much almost got your horse unable to compete. Fortunately, we've got the farrier working on him right now, and I *think*, if we keep him on Epsom salt baths and wrapped and no riding, he *might* be able to perform on Saturday."

Lucy sat down suddenly. She seemed overwhelmed by what perhaps her less than stellar grooming routine had almost brought on her performance horse.

"Let me grab some lunch, then I'll show you exactly what happened to Prince's hoof. After you've given him a salt bath, find the vet to show you how to wrap his hoof."

Lucy nodded dumbly, but she looked considerably relieved. Annie wondered how much personal care she'd ever given the horses she'd owned. Surely at boarding school she must have attended to quotidian tasks such as the ones Melissa had just described.

Melissa sat down and gratefully dug into the salad that had been placed in front of her by a discreet waiter.

"It's not a surety that Prince will be able to compete, Lucy. But we'll do everything we can to try to make that happen. Prince will tell us how he feels."

Nicole had not uttered a word since Harriett had silenced her. She appeared to be sulking. But Melissa's appearance got conversation flowing again among the other women.

"You will have time to work with me this afternoon, won't you?" Amy's eyes reflected her concern.

"Of course. I'll see you at two o'clock. And let's work on your leg yields. Schumann's left side still needs work."

"Schumann?" Annie couldn't help herself.

Gwendolyn offered up her usual sarcasm.

"It's the name she's bestowed on her little Arab. We're pretty sure she has a St. Bernard named Beethoven back home."

Melissa gave her a sharp glance.

"I didn't see you out in the arena this morning, Gwendolyn."

"We'll be working together this afternoon," Harriett said.

"But I need more work on my ten-meter circles!" Tabitha sounded on the verge of a small hysteria. "I've almost got Jackson to where he should be!"

"You mean where you should be. Jackson needs a rest. We'll work again tomorrow. And I don't want to see you tacking him up for your own private practice. The poor horse has been through enough this morning with you on his back."

Well, Annie thought, *no chance of misinterpreting what Harriett thought of that student's riding skills.* But Tabitha seemed unaffected. The consternation Annie had seen on her face a few seconds ago now settled into a smooth, bland mask.

"All right. I'll just groom him, then. Maybe work on his braids."

"Fine. Just don't apply any of your silly bling. He doesn't need stardust in his mane. Groom him but then turn him out. If you're around him too long, he'll think he needs to work."

No misinterpretation at all.

"Let's catch a few rays, shall we?"

After lunch, Patricia led Liz and Annie toward the patio doors and the brilliant sun outside. It was the hottest time of the day, but Annie didn't care. Lisa, her stalwart stable hand, had sent her a photo of her two Thoroughbreds this morning. It was a lovely portrait, framed with raindrops on the lens.

Flopping into a chaise longue, Annie let the full strength of the midday heat fall on her face.

"So, who trains Nicole?" She'd realized this was the only rider who didn't have a trainer for the show.

"No one," Patricia replied. "At least, not in preparation for this event. She knows it all, didn't you know?"

Annie laughed. For Patricia, this was a rare snarky remark.

"Of course. How silly of me. Although it would take a pretty thick skin to have Harriett critique your riding. Maybe Nicole secretly doesn't want to risk her criticism."

"Perhaps you're right," was Liz's thoughtful remark. "Although Tabitha and Gwendolyn seem to take it pretty well. Of course, I couldn't think of training with anyone but Patricia."

"Thanks, Liz. I appreciate your vote of confidence. But to be fair, Harriett has a lot to be proud of. She trained with Jo Hinneman, you know, and used to name-drop terribly until he started working with a Dutch team. And she made the U.S. Dressage Team at Athens in 2004. She's turned out some excellent students over the years, several of whom have gone on to Grand Prix."

Annie had no idea who Jo Hinneman was but assumed Harriett got all her tough-love training techniques from him. She decided to play devil's advocate.

"Yes, but can't you train just as effectively using your methods—or Melissa's, for that matter? I mean, what good ever came out of constantly criticizing a horse?"

"We're talking about two different animals," Patricia

said firmly. "No comparison. Rewards and punishments are necessarily different."

"I wonder."

The three women jumped. None of them had uttered the two words, which seemed to come from a large palm tree by one corner of the pool. A fabric sunhat emerged in front of it, and Miriam gave a cheery wave.

"I wasn't really eavesdropping," she explained. "I just couldn't help overhearing your conversation."

"Come and join us."

"I shall. Be patient. It takes a bit of time to get me organized these days."

Miriam gathered her many accoutrements and walked the ten steps to where the women had congregated. She was dressed in slacks and a colorful blouse but had stout walking shoes on.

"How can you stand this heat? I had to retreat to the shade almost as soon as I came out."

Liz threw out her arms and raised her face as if to a sun god. "We come from the land of rain. We're storing up your rays to keep us warm when we return. Sort of like the Energizer Bunny."

"Well, you're welcome to them. Frankly, I can't wait for a rainy day. It cleanses the earth and the air."

"So is Harriett really as much of a martinet as she seems?" Annie asked a tad impatiently. Enough about the weather.

"No, not really," Miriam replied, settling into a patio chair. "She just wants results for her students and pushes them as far as they can go. I used to train with her, believe it or not. She was tough, even on me, but I don't think I've ever learned as much as I did in the years I was a disciple of hers."

Annie thought *disciple* probably was the right word.

"But I do see your point, Annie. Harriett once told me I'd be better off taking up knitting. That hurt. With another kind of student such as Lucy, that kind of comment would destroy her. With me, it fueled my determination to do better. I guess we need all kinds of trainers, to fit the many kinds of riders who are drawn to dressage."

"The judge sounds like a mini-Harriett," Liz ventured.

"Oh, she's all right. Jean has judged many of our shows here over the years. The biggest criticism against her, and here I'm being catty, girls, so don't go repeating it, is that she's risen to her position using a variety of different horses to take the tests."

"What's so bad about that?" Once more, Annie was astounded by the intricate rules surrounding the discipline.

"Well, it would hardly be fair to have someone judge you on a level they hadn't already excelled in," Patricia explained.

"Absolutely."

Patricia smiled at Annie and continued. "But generally speaking, riders learn and test at each level on the same horse, to show that the horse has improved incrementally with the rider. Remember how Betsy told us she'd ridden the same horse for the past twelve years? There's no rule that says you can't test on a horse that already performs at a certain level, but when it comes to judges, well, it's just not cricket."

"Ah. That makes sense."

"In her defense, Jean is a very busy lady," Miriam added, looking a bit ashamed at having divulged this bit of gossip. "She teaches English lit at one of the state universities, and her academic schedule is absolutely grueling. Finding time to indulge in her passion for dressage is a real challenge. We're lucky to have her this Saturday."

A round of nods followed this statement. No one was going to argue with their hostess.

"Patricia, I'd like to come and watch you work with Liz this afternoon if I might. Are you ready to go down to the stables?"

"Sure." Patricia glanced at Liz. "It's nearly two o'clock. We really should get going."

Miriam carefully stood up. "Will you join us, Annie?"

"I think I'll first catch a glimpse of Harriett and Gwendolyn in action. That is, if they'll let me."

"There will be more than five hundred people on our grounds in just a few days, Annie. One spectator shouldn't throw either of them off their stride."

Out of deference to Miriam, the tuk-tuk was employed to transport the group to the stables, with Liz at the wheel. Compared to the drive to the Darbys', Liz's motoring was positively sedate—but then, the golf cart's top speed probably was fifteen miles per hour. The lulling ride gave Annie time to think, and it occurred to her that she'd forgotten to ask Miriam about Harriett's previous encounter with Judge Bennett. Perhaps she'd get a quiet moment with her hostess and find out.

Liz vanished to tack up Sammy while Patricia and

Miriam headed in the opposite direction, toward the small turnout pastures where Beau Geste and his two buddies were grazing. Annie entered the stables, where she saw Lucy diligently soaking Prince's left rear foot in a large tub of steaming water, undoubtedly filled with Epsom salts.

"How's he doing?" Annie asked quietly.

Lucy looked up from where she was examining his foot. "I hope he's going to be okay. I feel so bad about not catching it myself."

"Trust me, it's happened to all of us."

"I just hope Prince recovers in time to ride by Saturday."

"Well, if not, there's always the next show."

"Yes. I'd just hoped . . ." Her voice trailed off. "Everyone must think I'm a total loser."

"Don't be ridiculous, Lucy. Things happen to horses, and half the time we don't know why or how it happened. All of our horses could turn up lame, and we'd all be wracking our brains, trying to figure out what we did wrong. The critical thing is the problem was quickly spotted and diagnosed, and now you're treating it. It's the best you can do."

Lucy looked up and gave her a tentative smile.

"Thanks. I really do want to ride on Saturday. I don't want to have to cancel. Even though I was hoping we'd have some other judge than Judge Bennett."

"Is she really that tough?"

"I've shown Prince twice in front of her, and both times she pretty much annihilated me. Of course, I do realize I have a lot to work on. But even Melissa was upset at her last scoring. At this point, I'm kind of afraid to ride in front of her. She has this way of looking at you that just makes you freeze."

Annie wanted to tell her she should be looking at where she wanted to go with her horse, not at the judge. The letter markers in the rings made it pretty clear that should be any rider's focus. But Miriam was right. If she told Lucy what she thought, it would only undermine her further. Besides, coaching Lucy was Melissa's job, and she seemed to be doing a good job of finessing criticism and encouragement to maximum effect.

Although she did wonder for one teeny second if Lucy might have deliberately ignored Prince's incipient lameness to ensure she'd be sidelined from the show. She was ashamed of herself as soon as she thought it. No, that would be too devious. Far too devious for someone as well-meaning and transparent as Lucy.

She strolled outside to find Harriett and Gwendolyn but immediately caught sight of a multicolored horse in her peripheral vision. At least, that's what Annie thought she'd just glimpsed. He seemed to radiate a rainbow of colors, just like a fantasy horse in a kid's movie. Maybe the sun *was* getting to her. She turned around slowly and saw Tabitha's Friesian grazing in one of the front paddocks. The horse was bedecked in what appeared to be brightly colored jewels—a browband adorned with dazzling stones, a flysheet shimmering with multicolored glitter, and over its mane, a long copper-colored leather strap filled with tightly set small stones that clicked every time the horse moved its head. Since Jackson was in a constant search for a new blade of grass, the clicking was constant.

"Isn't he beautiful?" Annie saw Tabitha standing by the paddock fence.

"He's something, all right."

"They're special charms to help us when we compete on Saturday."

Annie nodded and smiled. Dressage people were an interesting bunch, all right.

Chapter Seven

Annie left Tabitha and scoured the three outdoor arenas for signs of Gwendolyn and Harriett. She saw only Nicole, who was riding her Andalusian in the far left ring, the official warm-up area. They were trotting very prettily alongside one long rail, the Andalusian tucking his hind legs one behind each other in a long, diagonal pass. When they reached the end, Annie watched them trot in a small circle and repeat the same trotting diagonal on the opposite side. Despite Nicole's harsh words toward her that morning, Annie felt drawn to observe her on horseback more closely. It was better than hearing about Jackson's magic amulets.

As she approached the ring, Annie noticed how rounded the Andalusian's neck was and how his hind legs seemed to propel his entire body forward. Nicole sat very tall in her dressage saddle, yet, unlike Lucy, she looked relaxed at the same time. Annie saw her occasionally give the Andalusian a quick tap with her boot—which, she noticed, had a spur attached—but other than that swift movement, her legs were practically motionless.

Annie reached the arena without taking her eyes off the horse and rider and unconsciously put one foot on the lowest rung of the white fencing. Nicole's back was now to her. The Andalusian cantered through a corner, then made a small pirouette to the right, all four of its hooves making tiny small steps around an invisible circle. When the pirouette was complete, Nicole loudly slapped the horse on the side of his neck and halted. Then she began a leisurely walk up the center of the ring, and Annie knew from the broad, sardonic grin on Nicole's face that her presence had been detected. Annie also saw the strangest, most complicated bridle she'd ever seen on a horse. She could have sworn he was wearing two bits.

"So, what do you think of all this? Learn anything new?"

The words were thrown out as a definite challenge, but at least they weren't as insulting as her previous remarks about Annie's choice of riding discipline. Annie decided to answer honestly.

"Absolutely. I love the way your horse carries himself. His hind legs and back seem to radiate energy that reaches every part of his body."

"Very good!" Nicole's words had lost her mocking tone, and she looked at Annie with a small modicum of respect in her eyes.

"And I see you wear spurs, as well."

"Knobs. Spiked rowels aren't allowed."

"I've never been a fan of either, to tell you the truth. But I am intrigued by your horse's bridle. Am I imagining it, or do does he have two bits in his mouth?"

"You're seeing right. A curb and a bridoon."

"I'm not familiar with the latter one."

Nicole nimbly dismounted and flung two sets of reins over her horse's head. Well, two bits could require two sets of reins, Annie thought. It made sense. Nicole now was standing by the horse's mouth.

"The second is the double-jointed one. The bridoon's a bit shorter, so they both fit into his mouth. Only riders who have achieved certain levels in dressage use double bridles. I seriously doubt anyone else staying here is."

No, I'm sure they're not. Just as I know you can't help showing off.

"What's the point? I mean, why are two bits better than just the snaffle? Frankly, if I can't get my horses to do what I want with a snaffle, I figure there's something wrong with me, not the horse."

Nicole bestowed a deprecating smile on her.

"Simple. It allows me a more refined use of the aids."

The aids? Melissa had mentioned them, too. What were they talking about? She'd have to ask Patricia later. Annie had no desire to flaunt any more of her ignorance than she already had.

Still smiling, Nicole lightly touched her arm, and Annie tried not to flinch.

"Listen, I want to apologize for my remarks this morning. They really were uncalled for. I'm sure your Thoroughbreds are great athletes, and I suspect you don't have any desire to learn dressage. And I realized after talking with Douglas—my fiancé—this morning that we know someone in common."

Not this again. Annie wanted to groan, but instead smiled back.

"Oh, really?"

"Yes, Douglas said you and Marcus Colbert are quite the item. Marcus has been one of Doug's clients for years, and they've become rather good friends. I understand your . . . boyfriend plans to join us this weekend. It would be super if we could slip away to have dinner one night."

Kill me now. And why does every woman dressed in breeches say "super" all the time? Surely the English language contains more adjectives than that. All Annie wanted to do after Marcus arrived was lock him in her bedroom and only come out to see Liz ride. And for meals, of course.

"Perhaps. Although the real objective of my trip is to find buyers for three dressage horses. I don't suppose you need another one?"

Nicole laughed. "I always need another horse. But this one takes all my time and money . . . at least, right now. Maybe after Doug and I are married, I'll be in the market. A Dutch Warmblood would make a very thoughtful wedding gift, don't you think?"

"Oh, I do. I'll tell Patricia and make sure you get to meet them while you're here." Annie was sweating, and she wasn't sure why. Perhaps it was the nouveau riche side of Nicole that was coming through. Whatever it was, it was making her distinctly uncomfortable.

"Will she be riding any of them?"

"They aren't competing, if that's what you mean. But they've all had some schooling in dressage."

"I hear your first buyer bit the dust a few minutes after leaving here."

Nicole's lack of compassion somehow didn't surprise her.

"Yes, it was a tragic accident. I wondered if all of you had heard the news."

"Hard to miss. First, Hollis comes and collects you and Patricia, then we saw the strobe lights from the patio. The police were there for hours, it seemed. But Hollis made us promise we wouldn't talk about it, at least in front of you."

So much for honoring Hollis's stated wishes. She noticed Nicole's eyes studying hers.

"So, what happened to poor Betsy?" Nicole's words dripped with false sincerity.

"Why, did you know her?"

"I knew *of* her, of course. She competed locally and I saw her at shows. She was pretty much a rank amateur, of course, but did have a lot of determination. I'll give her that much."

"We don't know what happened to Mrs. Gilchrist," Annie replied firmly.

"No stray dog found who'd run into the road? No mysterious oncoming headlights?"

"Why don't you ask Deputy Collins?" Annie was beginning to feel even more heated, and it wasn't just the noonday sun causing her blood to boil.

"I'll do that," Nicole said brightly. "He's asked all of us to give statements. I think I'll deliver mine in person."

She smiled, and Annie intuitively knew that while Douglas's bank account might be bigger, Deputy Collins outranked him in pure good looks.

"Anyway, let me know if you'd like to see any of the horses we've brought." Annie sounded impatient, even to herself, and knew she was not being a particularly good salesperson.

"You should work on Gwendolyn. She's got buckets of money, and I hear she was tight with Marcus's wife before she died, too. But be careful. She's been trying to find a husband for ages and I think she's got herself set on Marcus. Douglas says he's devilishly good-looking."

Not another competitor. Annie wondered uneasily just how many would-be paramours of Marcus Colbert existed between here and San Jose. They probably numbered in the dozens, if not more.

"Well, I must get back to work. Nice talking with you, Annie. Perhaps I'll see you again before I take off on my hot date."

Annie recalled that Nicole wouldn't be at dinner tonight. She reflected that the woman's absence would not bother her in the least. Then the sound of quick, solid footsteps in the dust behind them diverted her attention.

"Where is that woman?" Harriett angrily strode up to the warm-up arena, with Tabitha in tow. "Gwendolyn was supposed to be tacked up and out here by now."

Nicole scanned the stable entrance, a few hundred yards away.

"I think I see her coming now."

"Well, it's about time. What are you working on, Nicole?"

"At the moment, flying lead changes. Although I think Andy has them perfected."

"You should work on them. You have five of them on the diagonal at the canter."

"Yes, Harriett, I know. I've read the test once or twice before."

"Show me what you've been doing."

Nicole stood for a moment, her face a bit flushed. For a moment, Annie thought she might refuse Harriett's demand. Then, her mouth set, Nicole simply said, "All right," and turned to lead the Andalusian to a nearby mounting block.

"*All right?* I'm giving you a gift. I won't even charge you for my time."

Nicole did not reply. She mounted her horse, and once she was seated, instantly began a short, contained canter around the ring. She made one full loop before turning to execute the maneuvers. To Annie, the flying lead changes did look damn near perfect. Using a cue Annie did not see, Nicole had the horse change leads while his four feet were in the air.

She noticed that Tabitha was standing beside her. "She's late," she murmured to Annie in an undertone.

"Really?" Annie murmured back. "Not sure I saw that." Apparently she was of the minority opinion.

"You're late!" Harriett impatiently called out to her. "His hind legs are practically one stride after the front. We need a little more excitement."

As Liz had predicted, Nicole's face showed her displeasure at being criticized, and she urged her horse into a faster gait. Horse and rider made another lap around the ring, then once more up on a diagonal. The flying lead changes came fast—every few strides, it seemed to Annie—but now she saw what Harriett had the first time. The horse's rear legs made the change after the right legs. It wasn't by much, but the timing of the hind change definitely was off.

"Better. But you still need a lot of work. Try riding renvers in canter. Or teach him to pick up the lead from the whip. Anything to stop being so sloppy."

Annie had no idea what Harriett's suggestions meant. But Nicole did. The look she gave Harriett as she cantered by was murderous. Annie glanced at Tabitha. There was a definite smirk on her face.

Gwendolyn rode up and quietly watched the Andalusian's next attempt. He changed leads expertly, but still with the same small-time lag in back.

"I'd give that a four," she drawled after Nicole once more cantered by. "Wasn't that Judge Bennett's score the last time you appeared in front of her?"

Nicole abruptly brought the horse to a halt and jumped off. As she furiously pushed her stirrups up the back of the leathers, she replied, "Oh, I don't think I have to worry about Judge Bennett, Gwendolyn. Not with what I know. It's you who should be worried. First time in front of her, isn't it? It might be your last."

With that, Nicole lifted the latch to the entrance gate and began leading her horse toward the stables without a backward look. Annie knew it would have been hard to thank Harriett for delivering such a severe critique of her riding, but still. Apparently, Nicole didn't have a scintilla of good manners drilled into her.

"Well!" Harriett looked at Nicole's back. She was walking briskly, her shoulders set in a straight line. "That horse will never learn how to change leads if she doesn't listen to my advice." She turned to Gwendolyn. "Neither will you. Are you finally ready to start working? Tabitha, pay attention to what we're doing. You need work on this, too."

After a half hour of watching Gwendolyn on horseback, Annie had seen all she needed to. The woman was a good rider, that was clear, but even Nicole, who was about as egocentric as anyone Annie had ever met, showed more connection with her mount. Gwendolyn, she noted, had to be reminded to pat her horse when it had done a good job. The Dutch Warmblood was a big, beautiful chestnut, and as far as she could tell, had an unending supply of patience and willingness to try the same repetitive movements over and over. But the woman who rode him seemed to treat him more like an exotic sports car. Gwendolyn seemed to think all you had to do was put it in gear, and it would automatically perform.

And, truth be told, Annie was confounded by the terms Harriett used to elicit improvement in horse and rider. She kept asking for "half-halts," a term that completely confused her. How do you half-halt a horse, and more to the point, why would you? Whatever the action was, it happened very quickly. Annie noticed similar responses from the Warmblood after each call for one occurred—he looked more balanced, somehow, although she couldn't have put her finger on exactly why. It was obvious that keeping the horse supple was paramount, and Annie wholeheartedly approved of that. But the attention to the minutest detail was mind-boggling.

She slid off the rail she'd been using as an uncomfortable spectator seat, quietly nodded at Tabitha, and walked off toward the main house. She'd go back later to see how Liz and Patricia were getting on and to privately get answers to the many perplexing terms that she'd heard today, "half-halt" on the top of the list. But now it was time to explore the property, as Miriam had encouraged her to do last evening.

As she walked around the side of the house that flanked the kitchen, she saw Chef Gustav knee-deep in a lush vegetable garden nearby, a straw basket on one arm.

"*Bonjour!*" she called over to him.

"*Ah, salut, Mademoiselle Annie!*"

She was pleased to hear the chef use her first name.

"Lunch was *magnifique! Merci beaucoup!*" Annie could feel her French vocabulary rapidly dwindling.

"You like the *salade de crabe et de crevettes*? It is a fitting repast, *n'est-ce pas*, before your dinner of *magret de canard* tonight."

Annie did not spend a lot of time in her kitchen, unless it was to unwrap mystery packages from her freezer, usually opened long after their original purchase date. But she did recognize the French dish just mentioned as breast of duck. Yum.

"But so much work, Chef Gustav! Would you like some help?"

"Non, *mon amie*, it is not necessary. I have my kitchen staff and will soon have the help of a most charming lady, Mademoiselle Tabitha. And Mademoiselle Amy has promised to come by when she is done with her lesson. So, you see, I have more than enough helpers to make a superb dinner."

"*Très bien!* Then I think I'll look around a bit. *À bientôt!*"

She left him in the garden examining a row of radicchio and headed for the sports pavilion Miriam had earlier referenced. She'd need to acquaint herself with this building if she expected to fit into her Levi's when she returned home from this jaunt.

She found the gym first, an adobe building that melded into the natural flora beautifully. State-of-the-art exercise equipment filled a huge workout room, with mirrors, yoga mats, and rows of white towels strategically placed near each machine. Small HDTVs had been thoughtfully placed in front of several mind-numbing treadmills. Like most private gyms, the machines looked pristine and virtually untouched; although for all she knew, Nicole and Gwendolyn were here every morning, toning their inner thighs and strengthening their cores. She was delighted to find a beverage dispenser with healthful sodas and snacks inside, and which did not require any coinage—she only had to select the product and it popped out. Annie snared a bottle of water and continued her exploration of the compound.

Shower facilities for both sexes were behind the exercise room, along with a sauna, hot tub, and private room for massage. She wondered if the Darbys had their own masseuse or if someone nearby was brought in on demand; she was sure this would be one pastime all guests would enjoy. A door next to the women's showers found Annie looking at squash and pickleball courts. Another exit led her to the outside again, and into a lighted tennis court. A row of racquets neatly lined one wall, and an electronic ball machine at the far end of the court looked as if it had recently been in use.

It was an incredible setup, and Annie wished she'd brought along some sweats to work out in, or at least a swimsuit. Although she wouldn't be surprised that both items would magically appear if she told Miriam of her desire to do something of a physical nature while she was enjoying the Darbys' hospitality. That is, until Marcus arrived.

The Darbys had taken the recent long drought to heart, because Annie found pockets of hardscape gardens along a new, winding path that provided glimpses of small cottages farther in the distance. These must be the guest homes where the trainers were staying, she thought, which made her confident the path she was on would lead her back to the main house. It did, and she saw Lucy, looking hot and tired, coming up the front walkway at the same time.

Annie waved and caught up with her in the circular driveway in front of the house.

"How's Prince doing?"

"Better, I think. He's in his run-in now and doesn't seem to be in pain."

"Good. Well, I guess you'll just have to check him in the morning."

"Melissa said she'd check on him later tonight. And the vet's coming by early tomorrow morning, too."

"Then you're in good hands." Although why the owner of the horse couldn't participate just a tad more in his health care still escaped Annie.

It was tempting to hang out by the pool, but Annie reminded herself that she was here for Patricia and Liz, and besides, the walk back to the stables would be good exercise, especially since she intended to double up on dessert again. Besides, she'd never seen what lay in the back of the stables. She decided to walk the loop around the horse barn to complete her tour of the Darby grounds.

Gwendolyn and Harriett were still at it when she walked by, and she waved but declined to stop. When she came to the far corner of the stables, she saw workmen loading folding stadium tiers onto a small pickup truck. These undoubtedly would be set up to-morrow, in preparation for the show on Saturday. Sprinklers already were in the two unused outdoor arenas although not yet activated. Annie was sure the dust would fly in this hot climate if the footing were not completely doused beforehand. In the back of the barn and under a grove of cottonwood trees, she saw numerous single wide buildings—housing for the stable hands, she guessed. Behind the stables she also found two hot walkers, neither currently in use, and a spacious wash rack with electronic groomers nearby. Turning into the rear entrance, she discovered an im-mense tack room, filled with saddles, bridles, saddle pads, halters, riding whips, and a few equestrian items Annie couldn't identify. A row of tack trunks lined one wall on a floor of bright red ceramic tile, a nice, albeit somewhat extravagant touch.

Once more, Annie appreciated the climate-controlled environment she'd just entered. She'd been walking for the past hour in a temperature seldom felt in her native environment, and the sudden coolness was more than welcome on her skin.

A chopped-off whinny echoed through the stables, and Annie instantly wondered where the horse was pastured. This was a barn where horses were used to staying in stalls and turnouts for long hours at a time, and she knew every horse on the premises always was within eyesight and accounted for. She walked out the rear entrance, scanning her eyes against the bright horizon. She saw nothing except a round structure, approximately thirty feet behind the stables. It had a high, corrugated wall at least twenty feet tall. Wooden stairs had been built by it, culminating in a small stand on top so a person could look inside the structure without entering. She'd missed this building on her way into the stables.

She trotted outside and heard the sound again. It was as if a horse was trying to talk, but its words could not come out. This time, she was sure it came from the direction of the round structure, and it flashed on her that what she was looking at was the Southern California version of a round pen. It was a large one indeed, at least eighty feet across by her estimation. She walked as quietly as she could to the wooden stairs and crept up, then peered over the top.

Nicole was astride her Andalusian, which Annie was horrified to see had its head restrained so that it rested on its chest. Its eyes were pulled so low that the only view it possibly could have had was the ground cover of dirt. Nicole's hands were braced to keep the confinement in place, and a leather strap attached to a girth wound through the horse's bridle and bit and back to the girth again. Annie could see that the strap alone prohibited the horse from moving its head in any direction. The sight sickened her. She tried to tell herself there was a reasonable explanation for what she was seeing and failed. She had been so impressed by the Andalusian's round neck and collected body— but now she wondered if this was the method by which it was achieved. It looked painful and completely un-natural, and she anxiously waited for Nicole to release the pressure and let the Andalusian stretch. After several long minutes, Annie could take the sight of unyielding pressure on the horse's neck and chest no longer. She knew she was a mere novice in the ways dressage was taught, but she did know animal cruelty when she saw it. Trembling with rage, she carefully made her way down the steps and ran lightly into the stables toward the indoor arena.

Patricia, Liz, and Miriam were talking quietly in one corner; Liz had a loose rein on Sammy, who stood patiently by them. The stirrups on Sammy's saddle were run up in back of the leathers, and Annie knew the lesson was over for the day. Annie raced over to the women, and they turned around in surprise.

"Annie! We expected to see you earlier. What happened?"

She shook her head to let them know that how she spent her afternoon was not part of her news.

"I don't know what exactly is going on, but Nicole's got her horse in some kind of stranglehold in the round pen out back," she panted. "He can't move his head at all; it's strapped down to his chest. I don't know how long he's been in that position, but I couldn't take it anymore. What exactly is she doing?"

"Draw reins," both Patricia and Miriam said at once, their voices grim, and then Patricia ran out of the arena. Annie started to follow, but Miriam laid a light hand on her arm.

"Let Patricia handle it, Annie."

"Fine. But will someone tell me what's going on?"

Miriam shook her head sadly.

"It sounds very much like Nicole is abusing draw reins on her horse to achieve rollkur, an extreme form of hyperflexion that's been banned by the FEI."

"FEI's the world governing body for dressage, Annie," Liz added. "The Prix St.-Georges test Nicole is riding is under its banner."

"It's been a controversial technique as long as I can remember," Miriam went on. But it's thoroughly out of favor by the FEI and other dressage organizations because it's considered aggressive force that can cause mental and physical damage. If used incorrectly, it's like putting a razor blade in the hands of a monkey. You have to understand that we all want our horses' necks to be deep and round, but not at the expense of their suffering. What you described goes beyond accepted practices. Nicole knows this very well."

Annie was relieved to know the Andalusian would soon be—if not already—released from its captive stance. The only problem was that once Nicole knew it was Annie who had turned her in, she might direct her malicious intent toward her.

Chapter Eight

The explosion came a few seconds later. The high walls of the hollow round pen reverberated with the screams of one very angry horsewoman, and Annie knew they weren't coming from Patricia. Patricia never lost her temper. Annie wasn't sure her friend even knew how. But the shrill, strident voice of Nicole Anne Forrester came through loud and clear, if not the precise words.

Annie winced. She sneaked a quick look at Miriam, who looked as unsettled as she felt.

"Girls, I think I'd better intervene," she said quickly. "You stay here. Put Sammy away and go up to the house. I'll see you there."

Annie and Liz looked at each other. Neither of them was thrilled at the idea of Miriam's slight frame encountering the wrath of one of her guests, who out-weighed her in size, strength, and clearly lung power. But they merely nodded their assent and watched Miriam walk with her cane toward the rear exit. She looked remarkably determined, and Annie realized that, diminutive as she might be, Miriam Darby could walk into a full-on tornado and emerge unscathed if that was what lay ahead of her.

"Come on, Sammy, you don't need to hear this," Liz told her unruffled horse.

"He certainly doesn't," Annie agreed. The two women left the arena and led Sammy toward the tack-up area, where the echoes of Nicole's unleashed temper no longer could be heard.

It would have been a perfect time to leisurely groom the Warmblood, but both women knew that Nicole could come bursting in at any moment to untack her own horse. So Sammy got a quick brush-down and hoof check and, to his delight, was soon munching on a flake of alfalfa in the sunshine.

"Should we wait for Miriam and Patricia?"

Annie asked the question, unsure of what was best to do. On one hand, she was dying to know how Nicole defended her actions since her tone of voice clearly told her this was the tack she'd chosen. On the other hand, she didn't want to interfere with what the dressage professionals were doing.

"I think we should make ourselves scarce," Liz replied. "Besides, judging by Nicole's initial reaction, I wouldn't be surprised if she came after you with her riding whip. Let's retreat to a safer environment, such as the pool. Besides, Miriam told us to go up to the house. I think we should honor her wishes."

"You're right. By the way, did you think to bring your bathing suit?"

"Briefly. But I figured I wouldn't have time. Now I'm regretting it."

"It didn't even cross my mind."

"Well, we can dangle our feet in the water. Let's just stay in the shallow end and the side facing the patio doors. I don't want to get pushed in by an irate Nicole."

"Good thinking."

Annie could hear the bustle of people active in the kitchen, but the rest of the house was silent and empty, for which she was thankful. Quickly changing her clothes, she snagged a towel from her room and headed for the patio.

Her second-least-favorite rider was already there.

Gwendolyn was lying facedown in one of the chaise longues, one cheek resting on an open magazine. She had on a scant bikini, and obviously was on a serious tanning mission. Her entire body gleamed with oil, while a stretchy headband kept her short blond hair at bay. She looked up briefly, then put down her head again.

"Oh, hello."

"Hi."

Annie crossed over to the area where Gwendolyn was lying and sat by the pool. She'd changed into shorts and a sleeveless blouse and was wearing sandals. She tossed aside the sandals now. She might feel obligated to be in the vicinity of her fellow guest, but she would not be deterred from enjoying the pool, even if only from the ankles down.

"Didn't you bring a bathing suit?"

"No, it slipped my mind."

"I guess that's reasonable, considering where you live."

Gwendolyn was absolutely right. It was reasonable to forget about swimming when short summers deterred most homeowners from building private pools. Still, there was something about the way Gwendolyn had said it that irritated her. Maybe it was the implied put-down of her home territory. Who could be induced to live in the rainy Northwest when all of sunny California was there for the taking?

She heard the patio door slide open. Liz appeared, and Annie was delighted to see her. She was attired the way Annie was, and after nodding hello to Gwendolyn, sat down beside her at the pool's edge and sank her feet in.

"Ah. That feels good."

No response came from the oiled beauty on the chaise longue, and Annie hoped this meant their presence no longer interested her.

"What time is it?" Liz asked.

"Just five o'clock."

"So, what's happening back at your place right now?"

"Lisa, bless her heart, will have just finished feeding the horses, and they're all happily munching hay in their stalls. How about you?"

"My husband is pulling out a frozen lamb chop and figuring out how to defrost it in the microwave. He'll give up trying and decide to broil it rock solid. There's an HBO sports special on that he'll watch while he eats the chop and drips beans, which he's eating out of a can, all over the counter."

"Wow! You really know your husband well."

"Actually, I just talked to him. The part about

dripping beans over the counter came from years of seeing it happen."

Annie laughed. It was nice to talk to a normal human being, especially when the subject wasn't always about dressage. There was another normal human being she wanted to connect with. She felt as if she hadn't talked to Marcus in ages and vowed to try to reach him tonight. Annie knew that at five o'clock, Marcus would still be at his office and probably wouldn't leave for several hours. He'd told her he considered the hours after everyone else had left his most productive time.

"What are your plans for Sammy tomorrow? Does he get a day off, or are you and Patricia going to work some more?"

Annie never received an answer. At that moment, the patio doors opened again, and Amy and Tabitha, clad entirely appropriately for getting their bodies wet, came out, chattering away. Tabitha walked to the shallow end and cautiously dipped her toe in, but Amy walked straight into the pool.

"C'mon, Tabitha! It's great! Practically bathwater!"

Annie saw Tabitha frown.

"I don't know. There might be chemicals in there."

"Of course there are! That's to keep the bad stuff out! It's solar heated, for heaven's sake. You're practically swimming in a mountain lake."

Tabitha took two more hesitant steps into the water. Her indecision roused Gwendolyn, who stirred from her immobile position and propped one side of her face up with her hand.

"Honestly, Tabitha. Don't be such a baby. If you don't go in in the next five seconds, I'm going to push you in."

Tabitha squealed and rushed forward into the water, her eyes tightly shut.

"See? It's not so bad." Gwendolyn turned over and resumed her tanning position.

"By the way, have any of you seen Nicole?" Her voice was muffled somewhat by the beach towel underneath her.

Annie and Liz tensed at the same time.

"Not for a while." Liz's response was technically true.

"Well, if you do see her, would you tell her I need to talk to her about something?"

"Sure."

Liz glanced at Annie, with a glint of amusement in her eyes. Since Nicole deigned to talk to no one she didn't have to, Annie knew chances were slim to none that Liz would have the opportunity to pass on Gwendolyn's message. And Nicole sure wasn't going to talk to her right now—of that, she was certain.

But here Annie was wrong. Once more, the patio door slid open, and Nicole's angry face appeared, pointed straight at her.

"How dare you! You know nothing at all about what I do or how I train my horse! Who the hell do you think you are to judge me?"

Nicole was dressed in a short red cocktail dress and very high heels. She would have looked extremely pretty if her face weren't so twisted in anger. It made her eyes bulge and her chin jut out. Annie had never noticed Nicole's rather marked jawline before. Perhaps Douglas would have that fixed for her after the marriage. Annie willed herself not to reply.

"As for you," Nicole snapped at Tabitha. "Stay out

of my tack chest. I saw you looking in it earlier. Keep your dirty little mitts out of my stuff, you hear?"

Tabitha looked astounded.

"I didn't go near your tack chest today," she exclaimed. "I never go near your stuff. I don't know what you're talking about."

"I think you do. I'm warning you. There's a surveillance camera back there. If I find anything missing, we'll all know who did it."

Nicole slammed the patio door again and walked with short angry steps toward the entrance.

Silence reigned for a few seconds, then Tabitha wailed, "What is she talking about? Why is she accusing me?"

No one answered. Instead, Annie did a head count on the patio, and asked no one in particular, "Where's Lucy?"

No one knew.

Lucy, it turned out, had been down at the stables all afternoon, faithfully attending to Prince's care. As Annie went upstairs to change for dinner, she saw Lucy walking toward the house, twenty feet ahead of the tuk-tuk that had managed to fit in all three trainers and Miriam. The foursome in the small vehicle looked to be in serious discussion. Annie would not have been surprised if Lucy had been asked to go ahead for reasons other than there was no more room for passengers. She had a very good idea the group was discussing Nicole's treatment of her horse. Lucy certainly must have heard Nicole's angry harangue even if she didn't know the reason for it. It had been too loud to ignore.

Hollis proved to be an accomplished actor during the ritual cocktail hour. His game face was spot on, and in a few minutes, he had also managed to jolly the somber trainers into sharing his mood. Annie wasn't sure who else had picked up on the fact that something was amiss in their small world although the sly look on Gwendolyn's face made her suspect that she at least knew something was up after Nicole's outburst. And she obviously had taken Nicole's absence from the festivities as her cue to hold forth without fear of being upstaged. The only other person absent was Tabitha, who had spoken briefly to Hollis and apparently been given permission to skip the before-dinner social hour. Annie wondered if she was examining her body for a chemical reaction after her five-minute dip in the pool.

"I understand you brought three of Hilda's horses with you." Gwendolyn addressed Patricia with only a soupçon of snootiness.

"Yes, they've been staying at our rehab and training center for the past six months, just waiting to find new good homes."

"I remember several of them," Gwendolyn mused. "One of them was an incredible Warmblood Hilda had brought over from Denmark. I think she called him Victory. All dressage bloodlines on the dam's side and an elite jumping stallion on the other. Do you remember what happened to him?"

"He's actually one of the ones we brought with us." Patricia gave Gwendolyn a warm smile Annie was sure she did not feel. "He's been a bit difficult to place because he is so pedigreed and talented. Frankly, there aren't many people qualified to ride him. I can't be sure, but I suspect he's trained to fourth level. Would you like to meet him?

Gwendolyn smiled broadly. "Super. Perhaps when Marcus arrives. After all, it is his horse now. I'd like his opinion, as well."

Annie seethed from where she was sitting but decided to sip her martini rather than speak.

"Of course," Patricia said smoothly. "I'm sure Marcus will be happy to see you ride him. Although be aware that I don't think Victory had any dressage training when he was at Colbert Farms. I understand that Hilda was more into jumping."

Gwendolyn gave an exaggerated sigh.

"It's true, although believe me, I tried to change her mind several times. She simply liked the thrill of the jumps. If the British hadn't outlawed fox hunting, I'm convinced she would have flown over every season just to be in the pack when someone yelled 'Tally Ho!'"

Patricia smiled again, this time a bit less warmly.

"Yes, well that's one equine sport that I believe has passed its prime. Still, England does offer marvelous cross-country courses, many of them on private lands."

"Never appealed to me. I just got the dressage bug early and never looked back. But Hilda, well, she wouldn't miss the Rolex if her life depended on it."

Gwendolyn turned toward Annie.

"Do you know that's where Marcus and Hilda first started dating, after years and years and years of not seeing each other?"

Annie finished the last of the martini she was

holding. It was simply remarkable how Gwendolyn could turn any conversation into one about Marcus.

"I had no idea."

"Oh! Well then, let me tell you. Hilda was there as usual, and Marcus was practically dragged there by one of his entrepreneur clients who happened to be based in Lexington. They met in the tent serving G and Ts. Can you imagine?"

"I'm sure it was a surprise for both of them. Although I'm sure Hilda was much more into the show than Marcus was."

"Isn't that the truth! Tell me, have you been able to interest Marcus in any of your local horse shows? You must have a rodeo where you live, all the way out in the country."

"Not yet. But thanks for the suggestion."

"Did you ever ride in a rodeo, Annie?"

The question came from Lucy, who was steadfastly sticking to her belief that Annie was the direct descendant, if not the reincarnation, of Annie Oakley. She inwardly sighed.

"I barrel raced as a teenager, when I was active in 4-H."

"How exciting!"

"It really was," Annie said grudgingly. She remembered the thrill of entering the ring at a full-speed gallop, slowing only to make three rapid turns around three strategically placed barrels, and trying to leave the arena even faster than when she came in.

"Do you still race?"

"No, I gave it up when I was a senior in high school. It can be a dangerous sport for both horse and rider. I saw my best friend lose her balance on a turn and crash into a barrel. She spent six months in the hospital and had to relearn how to walk. And frankly,

I didn't think I was doing the horse any favors. There are a lot of ligament injuries in horses that barrel race professionally, just like the one you were afraid Prince might have had. It didn't seem fair to subject the horse to the sport long term. We had our fun, then he was retired."

Lucy nodded. "Just like Charlotte Dujardin and Blueberry," she said dreamily. Gwendolyn snorted.

"Who's Charlotte Dujardin?" The name was unfamiliar to Annie.

The face of every woman in the room fell on her, some showing disbelief, others pity, and in Gwendolyn's case, scorn.

"She's an elite British dressage rider, Annie," Patricia told her gently. "The best ever to compete in the Olympics. Almost a year ago, she retired her performance horse, saying he deserved a rest. He's a Dutch Warmblood named Valegro, but his stable name is Blueberry. His farewell performance was televised live on the Beeb in 2016."

"I see."

The only person who memorialized Annie's last performance as a barrel racer was her mother, who was sitting in the crowd with a Kodak Instamatic. She wondered if the photo even existed now.

"Where's Tabitha?" Harriett finally seemed to notice that one of her students, if not her star one, was missing.

"She said she had something to attend to at the barn that couldn't wait," Hollis said. "Under the circumstances, I didn't think I should deny her request."

Everyone in the room knew what that meant. Annie had seen Tabitha's habit of going from calm to hysterical in about six seconds. If something was bothering her, it was easier to give in as well as give her a wide berth until the immediate crisis had passed. Annie only hoped Tabitha wasn't returning property she had actually stolen from Nicole's tack trunk.

A tuxedoed waiter came onto the patio to announce that dinner would be served in five minutes. It was everyone's cue to drink up, freshen up, or do whatever needed doing. Annie instinctively knew that Chef Gustav would not be amused by any latecomers to the table.

She felt Miriam's cool, thin hand on her arm as she stood up to deposit her martini glass on a tray.

"Do you have a few moments to talk? I'd like to fill you in on what's been happening, and, for obvious reasons, I'd like to keep this among ourselves."

"Of course."

Miriam led Annie to a quiet corner, far away from the rest of the crowd and the pool.

"As you can imagine, Nicole was quite upset at your seeing her with Andy. She thought you had no right to be, as she put it, 'spying on her.'"

Annie felt blood rush into her face. She was instantly angry.

"I wasn't 'spying on her.' I heard a horse in distress and went to investigate. What I saw told me the reason for his distress. I came and told you. End of story."

"I know, Annie. I realize you had only the horse's best interests at heart and acted accordingly. And there was strong evidence that Nicole was misusing her aids and applying far too aggressive force."

"I should say so."

Miriam sighed. "The problem is that dressage riders are allowed to use hyperflexion with their horses. It's called LDR, or low, deep, and round. The hard job is knowing when the line has been crossed."

"Miriam, I'm not a dressage rider. But I do know when a horse has no control over his own flexion and is being forced into an unnatural position. And that just seems wrong to me."

"The fact that Nicole was found using hyperflexion in a place where she knew no one would see her certainly adds strength to your story." She sighed again. "I've discussed it with all three trainers. We have no authority to report this incident to either the technical delegate or to Judge Bennett."

Annie's eyes flashed. She stared at Miriam, silently asking her to explain.

"If a witness from a governing body had seen it, we would have instantly known whether Nicole's use was reasonable or not. Since no such person saw it, we have no recourse except to give her the benefit of the doubt."

Annie felt her heart begin to pound in her chest. She couldn't believe Nicole was going to get away with her outrageous treatment of her horse.

"In other words, she'll be allowed to ride on Saturday."

"Yes, Annie. Nicole's been severely reprimanded. She's been told not to use hyperflexion again on her horse without one of the trainers present, and to only train and ride her horse where she's in eyesight of a trainer."

Annie said nothing. There was nothing that she could say. She had no voice in the matter.

"She's also been strongly advised not to discuss this

episode with you and to behave civilly to you at all times. If she doesn't, I want you to tell me immediately."

"I'm not going to bother you if that occurs, Miriam. I can take care of myself. I'll only come to you if I think she's abusing her horse again. The horse can't speak for himself. In fact, he couldn't even *see* for himself this afternoon."

Annie felt tears welling up, a reaction that often happened when she had no place to put her anger. It irritated her to no end every time it happened.

"I want you to tell me. Now, let's go in to dinner and try to put all of this behind us. It's probably good that Nicole's off with her young man tonight. Hopefully, she'll enjoy a good dinner and several glasses of wine and come back in a better frame of mind."

Annie smiled and nodded. She held little hope of that happening. Nicole looked like the type of woman who held a grudge until she got revenge. And even then, she probably hung on to the grudge.

Tabitha appeared in the dining room just as the waiters had finished serving the first course. Her soup bowl was at her usual place; Hollis had insisted. But Tabitha didn't sit down. She stared wildly around the table, looking at each person accusingly.

"Which one of you has stolen Jackson's rhythm beads?"

No one said a word. The words sounded preposterous. What was the woman talking about? Was she referring to the clanking necklace of small stones she'd seen around the Friesian's neck?

"I know one of you took it. I went back to make

sure Nicole was full of—was wrong about my taking anything from her tack chest. I thought she might be trying to set me up. But now I can't find Jackson's beads anywhere! You all know how important they are to me. Which one of you took them?"

Tabitha's sentence ended in a high screech. Hollis immediately rose and quickly led her out of the room. Annie saw the woman uncontrollably shaking.

A short silence followed, broken by the sound of Miriam clinking her wineglass with her sterling silver knife. She raised the glass and spoke gaily, as if nothing of consequence had just occurred.

"Chin chin, everyone. And *bon appétit!*"

Chapter Nine

The day that had started with minor bickering had evolved into a major skirmish on several fronts. Nicole was furious at her. Tabitha was furious with everyone. Throughout dinner, Gwendolyn behaved like an army spy, trying to find out what the trainers knew and weren't saying. Annie still felt resentment toward all of them for what she considered giving Nicole a pass. She knew it was a decision based on the rules, but still felt that her own opinion had been diminished.

She declined Liz and Patricia's offer to go for a leisurely walk around the property after dinner. Tonight, she felt as world-weary as Patricia had the previous night. And she wanted to talk to Marcus in the worst way. Gwendolyn's insistence on sharing the halcyon days of the Marcus-Hilda romance had stirred an unnamed fear in Annie's heart. She needed to be reassured, and badly.

She made a point of thanking Chef Gustav for yet another magnificent dinner. It seemed the least she could do, especially since everyone else had rushed off after coffee without a thought for the person who had prepared it. She omitted telling the beaming chef that as wonderful as the breast of duck had tasted, the rancor of recent events had succeeded in dampening even her appetite.

She took a shower, checked her e-mail, then her voice mail, and found one message. It was not from Marcus. It was from recently promoted Undersheriff Kim Williams, who wanted her to know that the opening celebration of Alex's Place had brought in more than twenty thousand dollars in donations. This was good news, indeed. Annie had reviewed the construction costs along with other trustees at the last board meeting for Alex's Place, and the invoices seemed shockingly high. But then, Travis Latham was determined to spare no expense at "doing the thing right," as he put it. A few dollars to offset the cash both Travis and Marcus were constantly shoveling out would be most welcome.

She then talked briefly with Lisa, who assured her that the horses, dogs, sheep, and one cat were doing fine. Glancing at her watch, she saw that it was nine o'clock. Marcus should be home by now. She punched in his cell number and held her breath until he answered.

"Annie! I was hoping to hear from you tonight. How are things in Southern California?"

"Oh, all right, I guess."

"That doesn't sound very promising. What's going on?"

"Where do you want me to begin?"

"The beginning is usually good."

"Well, the good news is, or rather was, that Patricia

lined up a prospective buyer for Beau Geste even before I arrived yesterday."

"Excellent news! I had a feeling the show would generate some interest."

"Well, it did. The woman was absolutely taken with the horse, the letter of agreement was signed, and all we were waiting for was the vet check, our home visit, and of course the money."

"But something went wrong."

Annie found her throat had an enormous lump in it.

"Terribly wrong. The buyer died in a car accident just a quarter mile from the Darbys'. It happened a few minutes after she left us. And she was so happy."

Annie swallowed hard. She was not going to cry. She hadn't when she'd heard the news and wondered why Betsy's accident was affecting her so much now.

There was a short silence, then Marcus spoke.

"Did you see it happen?"

"Thankfully, no. Patricia and I were up at the house having drinks with the rest of the women when Hollis told us. We made a taped statement to the police, but it looks like just a freak one-car accident. The woman's husband is a doctor, so he'll know if she might have crashed because of a medical condition."

"How horrible. For everyone."

"Yes, although only one rider here seems to have actually known her." She sighed. "And today, I saw her being exceptionally cruel to her horse—in my eyes, anyway, and I reported her. Now she hates me, I feel like a rat, but I'm still furious at what I saw her do."

"Spare me the details. I trust you."

"Oh, and by the way, she knows you."

"She does?"

"Actually, two women here know you. Your name apparently is legion among dressage riders throughout the world."

"Who are these mysterious women?"

"Well, the one I royally ticked off is Nicole Anne Forrester. She's engaged to a guy who supposedly handles your investments. A Douglas something. I don't know his last name."

Marcus laughed. "Doug Kenyan. We went to business school together. Yes, he handles some of my money, and I'd heard he was getting married. It's his third. What's his latest bride like, other than a horse abuser?"

"Well, that about pretty much sums it up. She's snooty, ignores the rest of us, doesn't take criticism well, and is very proud of the rock on her fourth finger of her left hand."

"Maybe I should warn Douglas. She sounds like trouble."

"Well, don't bring up my name. She already loathes me and I'm sure is looking for revenge. I'm thinking of hiring a taster to make sure I'm not poisoned at dinner. Although that is one wonderful part about being here. The chef is incredible."

"I look forward to sampling his creations."

"And it's been great getting to know Liz and Patricia better, just as you predicted. I'm learning a lot about dressage, and you're right, all I have to do is enjoy watching everyone else work."

"So, why are you sounding less like your usual perky self?"

"I am not perky."

"Okay, ebullient."

"I'm not that, either. I don't know . . . it's just some of the people here are so caught up in their own thing."

"Such as the other woman I'm supposed to know?"

"She's in a league all her own. Gwendolyn. I've forgotten her last name. She said she had dinner with you a few days ago." *With your mother,* Annie silently added.

"Gwen? Gwen's down there with you?"

Well, that certainly didn't sound too reassuring.

"Yes." Annie bit her lip, so she wouldn't ask the thousand questions she wanted answered.

"She said she was going to a dressage show. I had no idea it was the same one."

Annie patiently waited to be told Gwendolyn was nothing to him. No way could Marcus be in love with her, or even like her, for that matter. No man could possibly tolerate the woman unless he just wanted her money. And that was something she knew Marcus didn't need.

"Well, give her my best, will you?"

Give her my best? Annie began to feel the telltale signs of anger rising in her once more. It had happened too many times already today. She couldn't help what she next blurted out.

"Marcus, is something going on between the two of you?"

"Annie, whatever do you mean?"

"As soon as we met, she made a big point of telling me she knew you. And that she'd dined with you and your mother the day you returned from the Peninsula."

There. It was all out. Annie waited to see how Marcus would deal with that loaded statement.

"She's right, she did dine with us last Monday. What of it?"

"Her implication was that it was more than just a friendly dinner."

"Why? What did she say?"

Annie wracked her brain, trying to remember Gwendolyn's exact words.

"I can't remember exactly. Just that she'd recently had dinner with you and your mother. It was the way she said it that got me. She also made a point of telling me how you and Hilda first met at the Rolex. And what a great rider Hilda was."

And how little I know about her world, horses and otherwise, Annie thought to herself.

"Annie. You haven't told me anything that isn't true. Hilda and I did meet at some fancy horse show in Lexington. It probably was the Rolex. She *was* a great rider. At least, she won a lot of ribbons. But you know what our relationship was like. I've poured my heart out to you about our marital issues. Why should it become an issue now? Hilda's not in my life anymore. She's not in anyone's life. She died a horrible death. Why bring all this up now?"

The conversation was quickly heading somewhere Annie didn't want it to go.

"This isn't about Hilda, Marcus. I know her death was tragic, and of course it shouldn't have happened." *In case you've forgotten, I was the one who found her body,* she wanted to add, but didn't. "But Gwendolyn is always comparing Hilda and herself with me, and in her eyes, I come up way short. And she definitely is trying to imply that she has a close relationship with you. To be honest, I think she'd like nothing more than to have me out of the picture and have you all for herself."

"Annie, I've known Gwen for twenty years. She was one of Hilda's closest friends. She knows you and I are together. If's she's sharing bits and pieces of the past with you now, it's just her way of trying to connect because I'm the one person you have in common. It's unfair for you to put a spin on what she says and assume she means something that just isn't there. I think you're overreacting. Frankly, I would have thought you to show more maturity than what you're exhibiting now. This is way out of line."

There was nothing more to say. Things had not gone as Annie had expected. She'd assumed that Marcus would commiserate with how awful Gwendolyn behaved and assure her he loved only her and no one else, especially not that loathsome cow. Instead, he had defended the woman and blamed Annie for "overreacting."

"I think we should end this conversation," she said stiffly. "Let me know if you still intend to try to come here this weekend."

She didn't wait for his answer. She ended the call. And then she burst into tears.

An hour later, Annie emerged from her room, calmer but with a much heavier heart than she could remember—not since those horrible days last spring when Marcus had disappeared, and she thought he might be dead. Now, he might as well be dead, at least in her life. She was still reeling from his words. She couldn't believe that he had not offered her the support she'd asked for, or she'd thought she'd asked for.

She held fast to her small piece of anger toward him. His refusal to see things from her perspective was the only thing that kept her from crying now.

As she walked down the hallway, she heard Amy and Lucy talking quietly in one of their rooms, and from an open upstairs window, gales of laughter far off in the distance, probably from one of the trainers' cottages. Annie listened and recognized Gwendolyn's mocking laugh. It must be Harriett's cottage. Who else would she deign to hang with?

Walking down the staircase to the main floor, she saw Melissa heading off once again to the stables. There was no sign of Tabitha, and presumably Nicole was still at dinner with her fiancé. Even the kitchen was dark and silent.

She needed to go to the gym and work off some of her anger, so she quietly opened the front door to start her walk there. It was ten o'clock, and the sun had long set. She wished she had a flashlight. Perhaps the Darbys had installed ground lights on the path to the sports pavilion. It would be just like them put in lights for the infrequent guest who liked to work out at night.

"Annie? Is that you?"

She started, unaware that anyone else was in the open foyer. She looked toward where the voice had spoken and saw Hollis sitting in a wingback chair in the back of the living room. A single reading lamp illuminated his body. His legs were crossed, one knee supporting his overturned open book.

Just as she started to approach him, he clapped his hands, puzzling Annie for a half second, until the overhead lights miraculously came on.

"Now that's impressive."

"We put it in just to impress our guests. Actually, it makes life easier for Miriam, so she doesn't have to walk to every single light switch in the house."

"What are you reading?"

"Oh, just an old Agatha Christie. I've read them all once, but most of them so long ago that I can pick up one now, and it's like reading it for the first time."

He flipped the book over and glanced at the title.

"This is a Hercule Poirot mystery, one of my favorite characters in the Christie collection. I always wanted to play Poirot, but was told I didn't look Gallic enough. I did have the pleasure of playing Sherlock Holmes once. Another rotten film. It didn't follow the canon. It was just a made-up story that didn't do justice to Arthur Conan Doyle's genius for plot. I believe Holmes stopped the Nazis from invading England or something like that."

"I always suspected Winston Churchill didn't act alone."

Hollis laughed, and the sound of it made Annie smile for the first time in hours.

"This has been quite an exciting twenty-four hours for you, hasn't it? One motor-vehicle accident, one horse injury, a kerfuffle with a rider whom I believe was clearly out of line, and it's not even Friday yet."

She was glad Hollis had called out to her. He'd already made her feel better, particularly his comment that Nicole was "clearly out of line."

"Can I persuade you to have a cognac with me on the back terrace? It's well-known for its medicinal benefits in ensuring a good night's sleep. I'd offer you a cigar to go with it, but my doctor made me give them up years ago."

"I'd love to. And as I recall, Winston Churchill's

doctor often gave him the same advice, and Churchill always ignored it. Look how long he lived."

Annie followed Hollis outside to the back terrace, which was a small, sweet pavilion tucked into the rear garden. Hollis poured two generous portions of Courvoisier into large snifters and handed one to Annie. She was seated in an antique Mission rocking chair. Hollis settled into a matching one a moment later.

"This is where Miriam and I come when even we've been exhausted by our guests. It's close enough to the main patio so we can hear any scurrilous remarks they may make when they think they're alone. But it's hidden enough that, so far, no one's discovered it. Now you know about it, and I'm afraid if you tell anyone, well, you know the consequences."

His tone was humorous, but Annie replied quite seriously.

"I feel honored that you'd share your private place with me. Girl Scout's honor I won't tell a soul."

"I knew I could trust you."

A minute passed without talking, except for an occasional tree frog making its presence known in the distance. Annie took a sip of her cognac, and thought if she finished the snifter, she'd definitely sleep the sleep of the innocent that night.

"Have you and Miriam been tempted to come out here recently?" It was the most delicate way she could think of to say what she really meant.

"You mean, have our current guests driven us out here yet? Well, Tabitha's behavior tonight certainly tested our mettle."

"How is she doing now?"

"Better, I think. I sat her down and tried to convince her that her precious beads were somewhere in the tack room and that she'd undoubtedly find them first thing in the morning."

"Did she believe you?"

Hollis paused. "I think not. I thought I saw her scurrying back to look for them a few hours ago. Have you seen her since dinner?"

Annie shook her head. "I got the full effect of her horse charms this afternoon, though. Her poor Friesian was covered in them from mane to hoof. It's hard to believe she actually believes they improve their performance."

"The placebo effect can work wonders."

"Too bad. I mean, there are enough variables in professional competition without having to worry about whether your horse has the right good-luck charm attached to its bridle."

"The irony is that Tabitha's horse can't wear most of them into the ring. Judges frown on horse bling. You've seen what riders wear. A flash of unexpected color and the judge might be predisposed to knock off a few points just because she disapproves of the rider's bridle adornment. It probably hurts Tabitha's scores more than helps."

Another few moments passed, and Annie ventured on another topic.

"Is there any update on Betsy Gilchrist's accident? I went out to the place where her car crashed today. I couldn't find anything to explain why her car hit the tree. Not that I'm a professional or anything."

"I took a good look around last night after the police and ambulance had left," Hollis admitted. "I'm not a professional, either. But I'll be damned if I can think of any reason for the car to go off the road."

"What was she driving?"

"A late model Mercedes-Benz. A convertible. That didn't help."

"No, I'm sure it didn't. I feel so sorry for her husband."

"And their two grown children. I spoke only briefly with him—somehow I felt that I should offer my condolences since his wife had just been on our property—and he said she hadn't any health issues that would cause her to lose consciousness. He said he'd just have to wait for the autopsy. Of course, people do drop dead from heart attacks and brain aneurysms every day. I suppose that's what he's expecting to find."

Annie did not want to dwell on Betsy Gilchrist's death. She was curious to know what caused it, but any more conversation just seemed ghoulish. Hollis apparently felt the same.

"Annie, I know you've been stung more than a few times by the rather callous remarks of Gwendolyn, and I had hoped that I could shed some light on her background to put her behavior in perspective."

Not another attempt to placate me, Annie thought. *If Hollis tries to explain away Gwendolyn's bad manners because of a troubled childhood, I'll implode.*

Something about Annie's body language must have clued Hollis into what she was thinking because he quickly added, "I'm not going to try to justify how she's acted around you—and the others, I should add. I just want you to understand why she's become the tough, brittle woman you see at the dining-room table several times a day."

Fair enough, she thought. *Fire away.* She took another sip of cognac. Its medicinal powers already were making her feel quite mellow.

"Gwendolyn is the daughter of old family friends, and we've known her since she was a little girl. It's not a stretch to say she is the ultimate trust-fund baby. Nothing was too expensive to indulge little Gwen. She had her first Shetland pony at three and instantly fell in love with horses and riding."

So far, none of this was news to Annie.

"I'm not surprised. She also knows the family of my boyfriend, Marcus Colbert, and I know they're an old San Francisco family, too." Annie hoped she could still call Marcus her boyfriend.

"Yes, they're all part of the same clique— memberships in several of the most time-honored business and social clubs. Compared to Gwendolyn's family, Miriam and I are part of the nouveau riche, who've been thoughtfully invited to join the inner circle. Both of us grew up poor as church mice. But a career in Hollywood, especially when we were there, gives one a certain cachet, and somehow we made the A-list."

"Who wouldn't want you and Miriam at their party? Miriam positively sparkles in a crowd. And everyone is drawn to you. You're the kind of people no one can resist."

Hollis smiled. "At the risk of sounding arrogant, I daresay you're right. We're both notorious extroverts and thrive on attention. But back to Gwendolyn. She wasn't a very pretty child, not like her two older sisters, nor an outstanding student. The only thing she did well was ride, and that was through a lot of hard work. You'd think she would have had an idyllic childhood, even with these minor handicaps, but upper-class girls have a nasty habit of ferreting out the weak and making their lives miserable."

"Unfortunately, I don't think that's confined to just girls from rich families."

"You are undoubtedly correct. In any event, Gwendolyn compensated for the cruelty she experienced at school by developing a hard shell. She also learned how to give back as good as she got. But deep down, Gwendolyn is still very much that plain, chubby little girl who was always the last to be asked to dance."

"Hollis, we all have tough childhoods in some form or another. Gwendolyn didn't have to choose this route. Look at Lucy. She obviously comes from a privileged background and is never going to be the belle of the ball, but wealth has turned her into an insecure, emotionally fragile young woman. It's not an ideal outcome, but she doesn't go around biting the heads off other people. If anything, she empathizes too much."

"Yes, but Lucy's family is still intact, and there's not a whiff of public scandal surrounding it."

Annie looked at Hollis.

"Gwendolyn's parents divorced when she was a teenager. It was fairly acrimonious, but nothing out of the ordinary. Her father had a mistress, wanted a divorce, and he got it. He paid heavily for breaking up his family, but Gwendolyn, her siblings, and their mother came out with most of the fortune, and life went on pretty much as usual.

"Gwendolyn's father, however, resented giving away so much of his wealth to his first family and got involved in a number of financial schemes not precisely on the up-and-up. Gwendolyn only had one boyfriend in college, who did the expected thing and proposed. A week before the wedding, Gwendolyn's father was indicted for tax fraud. Her fiancé left her flat. Of course, at this point, announcements had gone out, caterers had been hired, and gifts were pouring in. It was a terrible mess, and as you can imagine, quite humiliating for the poor girl. Her father was tried, convicted, and given a ten-year sentence in federal prison. I can't imagine a more terrible time in her life than that period. All the stares and whispers behind her back drove her into a deep depression."

"But all this happened years ago. Haven't people forgotten about her father's bad acts by now?"

"Not really. Not in her crowd, anyway, although she does have a few staunch friends. And over the years, friends, family, everyone in her circle has tried to introduce her to other men, but nothing's ever come of them, and Gwendolyn is convinced it's because of her father's criminal past. When her best friend Hilda got engaged to Marcus, she simply gave up trying to find a new relationship."

"Not quite," Annie said ominously. "I don't mean to be cavalier about Hilda's death, but I think Gwendolyn's taken it as an opportunity to step in where Hilda left off."

"Perhaps she has. Which makes your relationship with Marcus that much more infuriating. As I understand it, your meeting was rather like love at first sight, wasn't it?"

"More like lust at first sight. But yes, we clicked right away, despite our obvious differences."

"You made it look so easy, and for Gwendolyn, it's always been so hard. First, Nicole snares a very eligible bachelor, and now, if what you say is true, you've just whisked away the only possible prospect she's had in years."

"You know, I don't think she's an unattractive woman at all. I mean, once she wipes that smirk off her face. She's tall, slender, and not at all pudgy, and has great bone structure. I don't see how she could have been as plain as you've described her as a child."

"Well, my dear, if I commented on that, I'd be betraying information that people in my profession work very hard to protect from the outside world."

Annie chuckled. "What ever happened to Gwendolyn's father? He must be out of prison by now."

"He died a few years after he went in. Suicide was the official verdict, but the story's a bit muddled, and no one knows for sure what really happened."

Hollis got up and went to the small cart of liqueurs behind him.

"And that, my dear, is Gwendolyn's story. I hope it helps you understand a little better why she acts the way she does. Now, what do you say to a touch more Courvoisier before toddling off to bed?"

Annie didn't feel much more compassion for Gwendolyn after talking to Hollis, but she did appreciate his efforts to explain why bitterness seemed to be at the core of everything she said and did. Annie had little sympathy for people with money, never having had much herself, and bad-luck stories had never held much water for her. Her father had left when she was twelve, her mother had died when she was twenty-two, and frankly, before Marcus came along, her dating life often had been as nonexistent as Gwendolyn's.

Did she appear as tough as Gwendolyn? Had she developed a "hard shell," too? She hoped not. She decided to ask her friends sometime. Most had no difficulty telling her exactly what they thought.

She yawned as she walked back to her room, closed her eyes at the same time, and in her somnambulant state, nearly missed the strange item wound around Tabitha's doorknob. It was a thin, supple leather strap, bound up neatly, with one long grassy stalk woven in. A tag was attached to one end. Had someone left a gift for Tabitha? Annie stopped to look more closely. It was not, quite the opposite. It was the leather necklace, or rhythm beads, as Tabitha had called them. Annie had seen it draped over her Friesian's neck just earlier today. She recognized the copper color of the strap. But all the stones had been removed.

Annie carefully removed the denuded necklace and note from Tabitha's door and retreated to her own room. She unwound the strap. All that was left were tiny indentations where the stones had been set. She sniffed the grassy strand. Rosemary. Annie knew the scent well; the herb grew like crazy in the Pacific Northwest, wanted or not. Opening the note, she read, "REMEMBER TO QUIT WHILE YOU'RE AHEAD." The words were written in block letters and made with a felt pen.

Quit while you're ahead? Now what the hell was that supposed to mean?

Chapter Ten

Sometime during the night, the weather had changed, and along with it, the mood of the riders around the breakfast table the next morning. Blue sky had given way to gray clouds, and the gloom that prevailed during the morning meal was as palpable as the fine mist now gently falling on the green lawns and pastures below them.

Annie had not expected to hear from Marcus, but she was still disheartened when she checked her phone upon awakening and saw no attempt on his part to reach her. She collected her breakfast from the buffet and sat down with barely a nod to Liz or Patricia. She was still deeply disturbed at finding the mutilated rhythm beads and after glancing at Tabitha, was glad she'd removed them before the intended recipient had discovered them.

Tabitha looked awful. Huge bags hung under her eyes, and her blotched face matched the now muted clouds in the sky outside. Annie wondered if the woman had slept a wink, or if she'd spent the entire night looking for her precious rhythm beads in the stables. Whoever placed the stripped leather strap on her door must have known she was out when they'd left it—or, if Tabitha had been inside, completely brazen.

Annie turned to look at Nicole, who was doing her best to freeze Annie out of her line of vision. But here, Annie was in good company. Nicole showed no interest in making eye contact with anyone, including Hollis, who seemed aware that he, too, was on Nicole's do-not-contact list.

"Did you enjoy your night out with Douglas?" he politely inquired.

Nicole glanced up quickly, unaware that her disdain-for-the-world look had vanished, replaced by sheer smugness.

"It was super! Douglas took me to an incredible new restaurant on the Strip. He even arranged for a private tour of the kitchen. The food was unbelievable. It made us rather sad we'd already hired our caterer."

"I'm so glad you had a good time. And I'm sure your original choice of caterer will do an outstanding job."

Nicole looked doubtful, but her smug mien remained in place for the rest of the meal.

As usual, Gwendolyn was sitting across from Nicole. Annie thought she looked positively subdued this morning. She wondered if Nicole's impending marriage really was that upsetting to her, a knife in an old wound that reminded her of a wedding that should have taken place but never did. At least Gwendolyn wasn't making her usual snide remarks to the less resilient souls around the table.

But then, no one was talking much at all. Both Lucy and Amy looked a little green about the gills. Annie knew the source of Lucy's stress. She was still awaiting the verdict on the state of Prince's hoof, which would determine whether or not he would be sound by tomorrow. For Amy, the realization that she would be riding in front of Judge Bennett in a little more than twenty-four hours had finally sunk in. Even Liz seemed quiet and restrained. The reality of why they were all here must be hitting home. Only the three trainers behaved as they normally did. Annie overheard snippets of conversation about the order in which their students would ride and details about the event that did not interest Annie in the least. What interested her was finding out which of the women around the table wanted Tabitha to fail so badly that they had resorted to destroying the object in which she held the most faith. It was an intentionally cruel act, and Annie was resolved to find the person responsible.

The group dispersed quickly. Tabitha mumbled something about looking for her rhythm beads, shooting a particularly nasty look at Nicole as she left the table. Annie felt a pang of guilt, but only because she knew the truth, not because she was hiding the evidence. Nicole ignored the look and wordlessly departed a few seconds later, followed by Gwendolyn.

Annie was tired of the sullen silence that had pervaded the room.

"I'll join you at the stables in a bit," she told Patricia and Liz, then picked up her plate to take to the kitchen.

"It's time we all got to work," declared Harriett.

Her edict roused everyone else at the table to move, and Annie watched with amusement as everyone—even Hollis—followed her example, carrying their dishes into the kitchen and depositing them by the sink.

Chef Gustav now seemed accustomed to his guests making this small gesture. He nodded cheerfully, made several short bows, and waved them good-bye with his white towel.

"*Travail bien!*" he called after them.

Annie went in search of Hollis, who seemed to have vanished as soon as he'd left the kitchen. She hated to bother him, but she had to share last night's discovery with her hosts; it was only right that they know what had occurred. But Hollis was not in any of the common areas, nor on the patio. Annie wondered whether he was seeing to his wife, who had never appeared before noon since Annie had arrived. Other than knock on the door of their upstairs suite, which she was not going to do, she had no other way to find him. She didn't even have Hollis and Miriam's phone number.

She returned to the kitchen to consult with the only person she could think of.

"Mademoiselle Annie! What brings you back? Are you hungry for a second *petit déjeuner, peut-être*?"

"*Non, mon ami*. I'm looking for Monsieur Darby. Do you know where I might find him?"

"I do not know. Monsieur Darby keeps his own business. But when I see him I will tell him you are searching for him."

"*Merci*, Chef Gustav. *Merci beaucoup*."

She walked past the dining room and the door to the library, the one room Annie had never seen anyone enter. As she started for the spiral staircase leading up to her room, she heard a familiar voice, talking softly but insistently. *Had it come from the living room?* Looking around carefully, she saw no one. It had to have come through the seldom-used library. She tiptoed back and stood next to the shut door. If anyone came down the stairs or out of the kitchen, they would see her eavesdropping, but it couldn't be helped. She had to know what urgent information Gwendolyn was conveying, and to whom.

"You know it's only a matter of time. The police will find out and want to question you." Gwendolyn's voice was barely audible, but the menace behind her words came through loud and clear.

"I don't know what you're talking about." Nicole spat out the words. "And if you even think about repeating what you've just told me to anyone, trust me, you'll regret it."

"Shhh! Keep your voice down! Unless you want everyone to know. Is that what you want, Nicole? Do you really want everyone to know——?"

Gwendolyn's sentence ended in a gasp. Then Nicole spoke again.

"Listen, you little minx. I'm telling you this only once, so listen good."

Well, Annie automatically corrected Nicole in her head. *Listen well.*

"I had nothing to do with Betsy's death. Nothing, do you hear? Everything you say is a lie! You're trying to meddle in something that's none of your business. So, keep your opinions to yourself, or I'm warning you, you'll be sorry."

Annie heard another gasp, and realized Gwendolyn was gasping for breath. Then she spoke.

"Now I'm warning *you*. Lay your hands on me again,

and I'll tell the police everything I know. Then your precious Douglas will know the truth about the kind of woman he's marrying. *If* he still wants to marry you, that is. If I were him, I sure wouldn't."

"Yes, well, you do know a bit about broken engagements, don't you?"

Gwendolyn gave a curdled shriek and Annie could tell from the noise that an all-out catfight was under way. It was definitely time to vamoose. She didn't care who won. In fact, she wanted them to pound each other. She just hoped they didn't destroy any of the leather-bound books the Darbys had so lovingly collected and placed in the room no one used anymore.

She tiptoed up to her room. As she turned the corner of the staircase, she heard Chef Gustav's heavy footsteps in the hallway.

"*Mon Dieu!* What is going on?"

Thank heavens the library books, at least, would remain intact.

Marcus still had not called or texted her. Annie sighed, grabbed the one sweater she had packed, and headed off for the stables. As she opened the wide front door, her peripheral vision detected nothing. Perhaps both women had been hauled off in straitjackets to the nearest hospital for observation. It was a pleasant thought. She looked up at the sky, a familiar gray hue, and fondly thought of home.

The quiet, peaceful equestrian grounds had been transformed into a frenzy of activity. Despite the mist, sprinklers were on full tilt in the dressage arena and warm-up ring. She started on the path toward the stables and noticed even the pastures were getting a good soak. Workmen were heading in all directions. She saw a trolley wheeling out a covered booth, fully enclosed except for the front, and a door in the rear. Annie was certain this is where the judge and scribe would preside. The portable stadium tiers she'd seen wrestled into the back of a pickup truck yesterday were now set up on the side of the dressage arena, ready for spectators and auditors. Unknown people seemed to be walking everywhere at once, some dressed in breeches, others in ordinary clothes. It hit Annie that the small insular group in which she'd existed the past few days was about to explode, as competing riders, trainers, grooms, and show personnel flowed into the stable area and rings. Four horse trailers were already parked on the side of the barn, and small lines had accumulated in front of several tables near the stable office, each covered with a pristine white tablecloth. The atmosphere had changed, too. It was charged with an excitement she hadn't felt since her arrival. It was nearly show time, and Annie felt herself caught up in the enthusiasm.

She noticed Tabitha on her Friesian in the ring closest to the stables. She wondered if this is what the trainers had been discussing that morning at breakfast—which student would ride when, and where. Annie doubted anyone would have the luxury of an entire ring to themselves in a few hours. So much was going on, and space was now at a premium. The line of horse trailers had steadily increased in the fifteen minutes it had taken her to reach the ring in which Tabitha was riding.

"Send him forward!" Annie heard Harriett's impatient voice before she saw her. "You need more energy.

And keep your lower legs quieter. You look like a jumping jack up there."

Tabitha nudged her horse, but he was having none of it. From her vantage point of fifty feet away, she could see how frustrated the rider was and how hard she was trying. Unfortunately, her frustration seemed to make her Friesian more intransigent.

"Get off and let me show you." Harriett strode to the center of the ring and gestured for Tabitha to dismount. As soon as Tabitha had jumped off, the trainer took the reins and swung effortlessly into the saddle.

"Now watch me and pay attention. You're somewhere else this morning. Get back on track, or you'll never get a passable score tomorrow."

The Friesian took off at a trot, and for the next few minutes, Annie admiringly watched Harriett put the horse through its paces. It was an impeccable performance, she thought. So this is what dressage is supposed to look like. Annie was beginning to see what all the fuss was about. The challenge, she suspected, was getting to the point where the rider made the horse look easy to ride. It had to take years of dedicated practice.

"If he's having difficulty, do something different," Harriett called out to Tabitha while executing a perfect circle. "Lower the bar. Raise the bar. Slow down or speed up. But do something to get his attention. Then go back to what you originally were asking him to do."

Tabitha nodded from the sidelines. She looked thoroughly humiliated. Jackson did not have a single item of bling on his body. And he was performing beautifully. Annie wondered if his owner would make the connection and realize it was skill, not stones, that made the difference.

Glancing behind her, she saw Melissa working with Amy in the warm-up ring. Lucy's friend was the much better rider of the two, but Annie decided to forgo watching them to see Liz at work. She had yet to really see Patricia's star pupil in action. And she wanted to be in a place where she could sit and think at the same time about the bitter conversation between the two dressage divas. She had a pretty good idea what it all meant, but a bit of reflection might clarify the implications in Gwendolyn's words.

She climbed to the middle row on the spectator tier and waved discreetly to Patricia, who was fiddling with one of Liz's stirrups while Liz sat in the saddle, her leg bent over the knee roll. As she waited for Liz to resume riding, she thought about Gwendolyn's opening gambit.

Nicole knew Betsy Gilchrist more than she'd originally let on to Annie, that was a given. Now it was clear that Gwendolyn had known the woman, as well. And she'd had made it clear that once the police knew about Nicole's connection with the dead woman, they'd want to talk to her about Betsy's death. Well, that was entirely reasonable. The police usually wanted to talk to anyone who was familiar with the deceased. But Nicole's response had implied that Gwendolyn believed she was involved in Betsy's death, something she'd adamantly denied. Although there was something Nicole was keeping from Gwendolyn. What was it?

Did Nicole, in fact, kill Betsy Gilchrist? Annie couldn't see the stylish diva rigging Betsy's car, the most obvious method of ensuring her crash. Mechanical engineering just didn't seem a likely part of Nicole's skill set. Nicole wouldn't risk chipping her nail polish, not to mention the colossal ring adorning one finger, to loosen the brakes, drain the oil, or do whatever it took to make the car unsafe to drive, would she? But you never knew.

So where had Nicole been on Wednesday afternoon? Annie's memory of that day was hazy when it came to the movements of the other guests, most of whom she hadn't met yet. She'd had her memorable introduction to Gwendolyn and Lucy on the front steps of the Darby house minutes after she'd arrived. Presumably, the two women had then gone down to the stables, while she and Patricia had used the Mercedes convertible to get there. Whom had she seen while Patricia prepared to meet with Betsy Gilchrist? Annie thought hard, trying to recall anyone else in the stables at the same time. She drew a blank. She couldn't even remember who had been riding in the other rings when they'd brought out Beau Geste for a trial run. Perhaps no one had. It had been late in the day, and the other riders might well have finished their sessions with their trainers and were up at the house in anticipation of cocktail hour.

Who had been present at that event was just as much a blur. She remembered seeing Patricia and Liz as well as Gwendolyn out on the patio. And, of course, Miriam and Hollis. But the whole encounter had been so daunting she'd not focused on individual faces, just the room of elegantly dressed women.

Then she remembered—she'd counted eight women as she'd approached the patio. That meant Nicole had to have been in attendance. She mentally recounted who should have been there. Six riders, one trainer, plus Miriam. Was that right? If Harriett and Melissa had been in the crowd, then the group would have been at least one rider short. Two, if not all three trainers were present; although Hollis had introduced both Melissa and Harriett on Thursday as "now taking their meals with us." Surely they wouldn't have shown up for the Wednesday evening cocktail hour and then not stayed for dinner. But she couldn't be sure.

She'd have to ask Liz, who was at both the cocktail hour and following dinner. And perhaps Chef Gustav would remember the number of people who had enjoyed the delicious raspberry iced tea he'd sent down to the stables. Although she'd have to be careful how she asked the question. Along with her hosts, the chef was one person whose good opinion she always wanted. The thought of upsetting the person responsible for her excellent meals was painful to contemplate.

Liz was now riding on the rail at a trot. She looked less stressed than she had at breakfast, and Sammy didn't look as if he had a tense bone in his body.

"Super!" Patricia called out to her student. "Working canter left lead, please, and keep his hind legs under him!"

Liz looked terrific on her Warmblood. As she cantered past the spectator seats, Annie concluded it was far more likely that Nicole was simply having an affair with Dr. Gilchrist than responsible for his wife's death. A home wrecker she could visualize. But killing someone might muss Nicole's hair, plus Annie didn't think the diva had the stomach for it. Although perhaps in her rage this morning Gwendolyn had managed to yank out a chunk by the roots. Well, Annie would know by lunchtime. She settled in and watched Sammy and Liz practice their test, looking more and more as if they'd always been meant for each other.

Two hours later, Annie was itching to go back to her room to see if Marcus had communicated with her yet. She'd deliberately left her phone in her room. She didn't want to be pegged as one of those irritating people who constantly look at their device, and she knew that's what she would have been doing this morning. Excusing herself, she walked out of the stables as Tabitha and Amy brought their horses in. Predictably, Tabitha was prattling on about the lost rhythm beads.

"I know exactly where I left them yesterday afternoon," she told Amy. "I *always* put them in the same place in my tack chest. And I checked with the office manager. There are no surveillance cameras in the tack room, just by the stalls and in the aisles. So, Nicole was lying."

Tabitha sounded peevish and put out. Annie felt for her, knowing the fate of the necklace, but simply gave her a sympathetic nod as she passed by. She didn't know whom she pitied more—Tabitha for her loss or Amy for having to endure Tabitha's unending tale of woe.

A red Audi entered the main gates at a slow crawl and Annie saw the driver pause after entering, as if unsure of where to go. No one else was on the pathway leading to the house, so Annie trotted over to see if she could help, mindful that her knowledge of the event was probably the least of anyone here.

"Hi, I'm looking for Hollis Darby. I'm Brianna Bowen, the technical delegate for the show on Saturday. Do you know where I can find him?"

Annie had no idea what a technical delegate did at a dressage show. She knew this was not the time to ask but contented herself with knowing at least what one looked like. Short hair definitely was the current style in Southern California. Brianna's was jet-black and spiky on top, probably kept in place with an expensive hair product. She was petite, along the lines of Miriam's small frame, and dressed in slim black leggings and a flowing silklike blouse with sleeves just beyond the elbow. Annie noticed she was wearing black high-top Converse sneakers, unlike the thick dressage boots everyone else around here seemed to favor. She looked as if she'd just stepped out of an ad in *Vanity Fair*, modeling clothes most people would never think of wearing and certainly couldn't afford. A fresh citrusy scent filled the car interior.

"He's usually up at the main house," Annie explained. "I'm going there now. There's a place to park in the back. It's pretty close to the time they serve luncheon, so I expect we'll find him inside."

"Super. Do you mind hopping in and showing me exactly where to park? I haven't been here before and don't want to make a mistake."

"Sure. I'm Annie Carson, by the way, a friend of one of the trainers and riders."

"Nice to meet you."

The two women shook hands. Annie got into the car and pointed out the parking-lot entrance on the north side. As before, nearly every available space was taken, but Brianna managed to squeeze into a spot at the very end.

"Are you staying here?" Annie was curious where the technical delegate would be housed, since the judge and scribe had been sequestered.

"Yes, in one of the guest cottages. Mr. Darby said just to check in with him when I arrived."

"Let's go find him."

"Wait a sec. Has the judge arrived yet?"

"You mean Judge Bennett? I don't know. I know she's supposed to be here sometime this afternoon to check out the grounds, but she's not staying here. She's being put up at a hotel."

"Okay, thanks."

Brianna seemed relieved. That seemed odd. Annie assumed that in her role as technical delegate, Brianna would be working closely with the judge and all the other show officials.

"Why? Are you not supposed to talk to the judge, like the riders?"

Brianna looked at her. She seemed a bit confused by Annie's question.

"No, not at all. Although we often don't have a lot of interaction since we're involved in different aspects of the show. I was just curious."

"You'll have to excuse me. I know next to nothing about dressage, and this is my first show. I'm a bit overwhelmed by all the different rules and regulations. I often ask questions that must seem ridiculous to you."

Brianna smiled. "I'm trying to figure out the lay of the land here, myself."

They began to walk up the circular driveway leading to the house entrance.

"Do you know the judge?" Annie asked. She wondered if Brianna's concern about encountering her was based on her own bad experience. Everyone who'd interacted with Judge Bennett seemed to have had one.

"Oh, we've met," Brianna said vaguely. "She judges a lot of shows in the area."

Her answer seemed to merit no response, so Annie was quiet as they walked up the front steps. The door was opened before Annie could reach for the knob. Hollis stood there, looking as debonair as he'd looked when he'd greeted Annie for the first time.

"Annie, I see you've brought our latest guest with you. I'm Hollis Darby. You must be Brianna Bowen, our technical delegate. Please do come inside and have lunch with us. You can settle into your cottage afterward."

"Thanks, Mr. Darby, but I really should start getting organized for tomorrow. If it's all right with you, I'll skip lunch and get right to work."

"Please call me Hollis, and of course, you can do anything you want. You won't object if we have a tray of food brought to you, will you? Good. Then why don't you stay here with Annie, and I'll get one of our staff to show the way and bring your luggage along."

"Super."

Annie and Brianna stood on the step. Annie wasn't quite sure what to say, if anything. She didn't know the protocol well enough.

"Um, Annie, you wouldn't happen to know if the judge is bringing anyone with her to the event, do you?"

"You mean besides the scribe?" Annie felt quite proud of herself remembering this. She reminded herself to ask Patricia exactly what the scribe did.

"Yes."

"I really don't know. But I don't think so. Hollis didn't mention anyone else coming with her."

of the house sounded, and both unconsciously
ed at their watches.

nie cleared her throat. "So that leaves our other
ect." She didn't want to say Gwendolyn's name.
ehow, that would have sounded too accusatory.
es, Gwen. I have no idea where she was last night.
ou?"

heard her laughing someplace outdoors toward
ports pavilion around ten o'clock. I was coming
f my room to go downstairs. Right before I saw

he probably was in Harriett's cottage. Well, I
ose I can ask both of them how long they were
her last night although it would be damned un-
ortable."

nie was silent. She was weighing in her mind
her or not to tell Hollis about the conversation
l overheard between the two suspects in the li-
. To her relief, Hollis beat her to it.

don't suppose you've heard about the contre-
s between Gwen and Nicole earlier this morning."
nie shook her head, her eyes wide-eyed on Hollis.
ay was she going to admit that she was snooping
d the library to hear exactly that.

ustav found them face-to-face in what may have
a physical fight a few seconds before. Both de-
d to divulge the nature of their disagreement.
ustav said both looked a bit disheveled and, how
e put it? '*Les dames se comportent comme des chats!*'"
chuckled, then quickly grew sober.

don't like what's happening, Annie. It's as if poor
Gilchrist's death has sparked an avalanche of
eelings among our group. Everyone's cross with

"Thanks. Oh, here he is."

Hollis came back with one of the tuxedoed waiters,
the same one, Annie realized, who had delivered the
raspberry iced tea two days before.

"Brianna, this is Jorge, who will show you to your
cottage and collect your things."

Jorge and Brianna disappeared around the corner
to get the luggage from the Audi. Hollis turned to
Annie.

"I hear you've been trying to hunt me down."

"I have. There's something I have to share with you."

"That sounds ominous. Well, we've got another fifteen minutes before the luncheon gong sounds. Will
that give us enough time?"

"It should be fine."

"How about we meet on the private terrace, now
that you know the secret password?"

"Sounds great. Let me just get something out of my
room first."

"I'll see you there."

Annie bounded to her room to retrieve the leather
strap and note. She couldn't help glancing once more
at her phone to see if Marcus had left a message. He
had. He'd texted a half hour before:

"If you still want me, I'll be there on Sunday afternoon. Yea or nay?"

If she hadn't been staying in such a posh place, she
would have been dancing around her room, shrieking
with joy and relief. Instead, she demurely typed back,
"Yea. And yay!"

Chapter Eleven

FRIDAY AFTERNOON, OCTOBER 13

"Maybe I should have left it hanging there," Annie told Hollis. "But I was afraid of how Tabitha might react if she found it."

Hollis rocked back and forth in his Mission chair, idly fingering the stalk of dried rosemary Annie had handed to him. He seemed lost in thought.

"No, you did the right thing," Hollis finally replied. He sighed heavily.

The overcast sky of this morning had largely dissipated, and Annie was glad to see the sun triumphantly reassert its rightful place in the sky. She wished her conversation were going as cheerily as the weather.

"I'm assuming Tabitha filled you in on Nicole's accusations at the pool."

"Yes, she told me about them after we'd left the dining room for our little chat. She said Nicole's remarks were pretty vicious."

"They were. The accusations seemed to come out of nowhere. Tabitha was completely blindsided."

"It's hard to believe that Nicole would accuse

Tabitha of stealing from her tack simpl[y]
to do the same to her gear."

"I agree. But frankly, Hollis, there a[re]
guests I can think of who are capable of [do]
thing like this."

Hollis sighed again. "I'd like to think no o[ne]
But I'm not going to argue the point."

"When did Nicole return home? Do you k[now]

"I don't. But it was after I retired, which wa[s]
after I said good night to you. One of our w[indows]
overlooks the private parking area, and I notice[d]
Nicole's Jag was still gone. So, I think we can [rule]
her out."

"Is it there now?"

Hollis looked at her. "Why would that matter?[”]

"Well, what if Nicole decided to leave her c[ar in]
town, and her fiancé drove her home? What [I'm]
saying is if it's there now, then I agree, she like[ly re]
turned after I'd found the strap. If not . . .”

Her host looked at her admiringly. "My, m[y, you]
really are a detective. Let's go look, shall we?"

They rose and walked to the corner of the [room]
where they could see a portion of the parking [lot.]
There was Nicole's green Jaguar, gleaming in t[he sun.]
It appeared not to have a speck of dust on it.

"I guess we can rule out Nicole." Annie sig[hed.]

"You sound so disappointed, Annie." Hollis [looked]
amused. "Unless, of course, her fiancé retu[rned the]
Jaguar under cover of darkness and with a [friend or]
ate who could drive him home."

Annie laughed. "Now you're being the [detective.]
One with a vivid imagination."

They returned to the pavilion. The g[uests]

each other, and now poor Tabitha's miserable rhythm beads have been destroyed by one of us."

"This is what happens when you invite Jessica Fletcher to one of your affairs."

Hollis laughed. "Nonsense, Annie. It would have occurred anyway. I'm just happy you're here to help. By the way, you do recognize the significance of the rosemary stalk, don't you?"

"I'm afraid not. I thought it was curious."

Hollis struck a melodramatic pose, and spoke in a high voice. "'There's rosemary, that's for remembrance. Pray you, love, remember.'"

Annie's eyes widened. "Ophelia? The speech from *Hamlet*, when she goes mad?"

"Very good! I got to play Hamlet once or twice. This was before Hollywood came calling. Never made a sou on the performances."

"So, we're looking for a Shakespearean scholar as our culprit? I'm afraid that does rule out Nicole."

"Don't be catty, Annie. But if you see anyone bearing columbines, let me know. That's for disloyalty. And worse."

Lunch was a mercifully civil affair. Miriam's rare appearance at the table at this hour made an appreciable difference in everyone's behavior. Annie was disappointed to see that neither Gwendolyn nor Nicole showed any signs of battle scars and that Nicole's manicured nails were intact. When Lucy tentatively asked Tabitha if she'd found Jackson's rhythm beads, Annie tensed, but the reply was polite and with no tinge of hysteria. Tabitha had not found the beads, but she was going to continue to look after lunch. Annie avoided looking at Hollis and snared another piece of asparagus instead.

Another reason for the relative calm around the table was because Hollis dominated the conversation. There was much that everyone needed to know about the next few days, he told the group, and that pronouncement got everyone's attention.

"As you know, the show arena is now off-limits, and the other contestants have first priority on the schooling arenas this afternoon. Please stay away from the areas that we're preparing for use tomorrow. Our barn staff and many volunteers are working hard to make sure everything goes as smoothly as possible. The best thing we can do for them right now is give them a wide girth, no pun intended."

A ripple of polite laughter went around the table.

"While you're free to hack around the property, I'm sure each of your horses could use a bit of a breather and will appreciate an afternoon off. I do realize you'll all want to hand-graze to get them out of their stalls, and you're welcome to do so whenever you'd like."

Tabitha and Nicole looked a bit doubtful, but everyone else nodded. Annie was relieved. If none of the trainers was working with her students, Nicole would be unable to ride. It was the surest way Annie knew to keep the Andalusian free from Nicole's tyrannical training methods.

"You also should know that our technical delegate, Brianna Bowen, has arrived. She's staying in the south cottage. However, she's quite busy getting the show organized, and so you may not have a chance to meet her until tomorrow.

"Finally, Lucy, if I may be so bold to ask, what's the verdict on Prince?"

Lucy glanced at Melissa and smiled tremulously. "His abscess is gone, and both Melissa and the vet say I can ride him tomorrow."

For the first time, Lucy received a round of support from her fellow riders. Cries of "Super" and "Good!" and other encouraging comments followed her announcement, and Lucy blushed, making her look quite pretty. It seemed that in the final hour, the small band of dressage riders were beginning to bond. Then again, Annie remembered that each rider really was competing with only herself and her horse, so was it too much to ask that they shore each other up?

"That brings me to the subject of grooming. Nicole, I know you have your own groom—"

"Yes, he's arriving this afternoon. I appreciate the offer of using yours, Hollis, but Andy won't let anyone except Miguel clip his ears and bridle path."

Harriett looked at Nicole. "You should train your horse to accept any professional who works on him."

Nicole smiled at Harriett. It was a deprecating smile. "Whatever you say, Harriett."

Annie was certain that Nicole would have had a lot more to say if the three trainers hadn't thoroughly chastised her yesterday.

"Good, good," Hollis said briskly. "Miguel will be staying in one of the double-wides out back, Nicole. I believe you can point him to the right one. Now, those of you who have signed up for a groom will be sharing Ann Corbett. She'll be here in a few hours, and you can talk to her about any idiosyncrasies your horses may have. Otherwise, be assured that she'll be hard at work throughout the night making sure your horses are absolutely clean and gorgeous by the time you greet them early tomorrow morning. Ann will leave a bill for each of you tacked on your horse's stall door, and it would be nice if you could pay her promptly. And remember, tips are always welcome."

Annie was speechless. She couldn't imagine paying someone else to groom her horse. When she'd attended shows as a teenager, she'd always taken care of this task herself. Nor had she seen anyone else hand it off to a total stranger. Sure, maybe a friend or family member would come by and help, but the job of grooming was never given to a paid professional. The grooming process for dressage horses must be far more elaborate than she could even imagine. She wondered which, if any women around the table, would tackle the job herself.

When Hollis was finished, Patricia stood and took the floor.

"Attention, ladies! I know that Hollis and Miriam have a long-standing tradition of feting the show judge the night before the event, so what do you say we give Chef Gustav a night off, and we have a ladies' night in town? Liz and Melissa already are in. What say the rest of you?"

A buzz of conversation ensued, and Patricia continued to speak over the noise.

"I know it's the night before the show, but honestly, it'll just be a quick dinner out. We'll be back in plenty of time to kiss our darlings good night and make sure all their creature comforts are met. And it would be a great time to kick back before the big day!"

"Impossible," Harriett muttered. "Too much to do. You, too, Gwen and Tabitha. You need to concentrate on your tests tomorrow."

"I need to look for my rhythm beads," Tabitha muttered.

"No, you do not," Harriett said firmly.

"So sorry, I have to wash my hair," was Gwendolyn's blithe reply, her hand rippling through her close-cropped spikes.

"Douglas and I have an art opening to attend. Quite impossible to get out of."

Annie noticed that Nicole's turndown did nothing to impact the enthusiasm of the rest of the group.

"It sounds like it will be super fun," Amy said. "C'mon, Lucy, let's go. We'll be back in time to make sure Prince is doing all right." Lucy nodded. She still seemed on the fence.

"You'll come, won't you, Annie?" Liz turned to her, asking with her eyes for her to say yes.

Annie's heart sank. The last thing she wanted to do was go out on the town, even if it was only an hour or two. She wasn't a party animal by nature, and the thought of having to spend more time telling Lucy about her cowgirl life was mind-numbing. But there was no way out of it. She had no excuse. Marcus's arrival was still a day away.

"Of course," she said simply.

Fortunately, her reprieve was quick in coming. After lunch, Miriam took her aside.

"Annie, I know you've probably got your heart set on going out with your friends, but Hollis and I wondered if you would mind having dinner with us, instead. It turns out Judge Bennett's scribe won't be arriving until late, and we'd love a fourth at dinner, and you're such an interesting person to talk with. Would it be much of a hardship to stay in?"

Annie gave her a broad smile. "I'd be happy to join you."

"That's wonderful. I'll tell Chef Gustav now. He'll be delighted to know that he's only preparing one dinner tonight. So thoughtful of Patricia to think of making his life easier at this busy time."

"It's too bad the technical delegate can't join us. I met her this morning, and she seems absolutely charming."

Annie couldn't put her finger on it, but Miriam's face underwent a subtle change.

"Yes, isn't she? Brianna seems like a very nice young woman but terribly busy right now, I understand. I'm sure she'll be joining us for dinner on Saturday."

Annie looked at Miriam, unable to read any specific emotion. But it had been evident that Brianna was trying to avoid contact with the judge, and now Miriam appeared to be endorsing that decision. Annie couldn't fathom why this should be since there didn't seem to be any rule prohibiting them from talking to each other. It was odd.

Annie took Hollis's words about steering clear of the workers down at the stables to heart. She was curious about the entourage of women arriving with their horses and spent an enjoyable hour on the patio watching the procession of trailers roll in, followed by the careful unloading of each gorgeous horse inside each one. Walking by, Miriam noticed her interest and had suggested she enjoy the pool while she surveyed the arrival of contestants. When Annie confessed she'd omitted bringing a bathing suit with her, her host quickly showed her a cupboard filled with one-piece suits from L.L. Bean in various sizes, all still packaged in plastic.

"You're not the first guest to forget a bathing suit. Enjoy yourself." Miriam then handed Annie a pair of binoculars, along with a wink. "Sometimes it's more fun to see what's happening from a distance."

Annie was now dressed in her new suit and enjoying her use of the binoculars very much from her private vantage point. There seemed to be a lot of paperwork for participants in a dressage event. Patricia earlier had told her that every horse had to have a CVI, or certificate of vet inspection, and a certified Coggins test no more than six months old. Annie thought she wouldn't be surprised if the owners also had to bring along proof of the horse's pedigree and identity. She was beginning to understand just how highly regulated the dressage world was.

As she watched riders lug big, unwieldy tack chests into the stable, Annie wondered where they all would sleep tonight. Probably in nearby hotels, she thought, the same as Judge Bennett and her scribe. She scoured the crowds for anyone who had a distinct judicial bearing, but too many people were swarming around for her to keep track of whom she'd already seen. Well, she'd meet Judge Bennett this evening. She was looking forward to getting to know the woman so many other women feared or heartily disliked. Annie anticipated very interesting dinner conversation.

She glided through the water, happy to be totally alone for once. She was deliriously happy that Marcus would be joining her and spent several minutes pondering his sudden change in attitude. "If you'll have me" definitely implied that he'd changed his opinion of what she'd told him. But she would not pry. She

would not ask him why he'd backed down from his
original stance or even ask for an apology. Oh, no.
She would remain sweetly silent about their last conversation. Knowing Marcus, he'd be back on the road
Monday morning, and she wanted to make every
minute with him count—and fight-free.

"Now, what about this horse you're so anxious to
buy?" Harriett's unmistakable voice filled the air.
Annie was floating on her back and her ears were
halfway in the water. But what she'd heard gave her a
legitimate reason to eavesdrop. After all, they were discussing a horse she was trying to sell. She carefully
made her way to the shallow end, where she could
stand up and hear better. The sound seemed to be
coming from behind her, near the parking area.

"He's a drop-dead-gorgeous Warmblood Hilda
brought over from Denmark. Stellar pedigree, and
when I saw him, he was showing fourth level. Hilda
wasted him trying to make him into a hunter. But I
still think he'd be an excellent dressage horse for me,
particularly as I move into FEI levels."

"How long ago did you see him?"

"Oh, heavens. Five, six years ago. Hilda had recently moved to Washington and had just finished
building her equestrian estate."

"Well, let's take a look at him, then. As Patricia said,
if you're really serious about this, you can ride him on
Sunday. Although I must say, Gwendolyn, there's nothing wrong with Martinique. He's young but is eager to
learn. You could take him to FEI just as well, and more
easily, too. Your horse is trained in dressage. The other
horse is rusty, at best."

"Oh, I have my reasons for wanting this horse."

"I'm sure you do. Just make sure they're the right ones."

Gwendolyn gave a low, conspiratorial laugh.

"They are. The plan is to cruise through this test with Martinique. Then I'll sell him and buy Victory."

"Stop being so smug. With Judge Bennett in the booth, you're not likely to cruise through this or any other test. I've seen her eliminate a rider for just wearing a stock tie without a jacket. She once eliminated a student for supposedly talking to his horse because she couldn't tell the difference between a human voice and a squeaky saddle."

"Oh, Harriett. She can't be all that bad."

"She is, and more. What's worse is that she's not even a competent rider herself."

"C'mon. She wouldn't have an 'S' behind her title if she wasn't a damn good dressage rider."

"The only reason she can judge FEI levels is that she bought the horses who could do the work. If you choose to do that, I can't stop you, although I think you're going in the opposite direction with this new horse you're thinking of buying. But with a judge, it's different."

"Oh, that's not the only deep-dark secret Judge Bennett keeps hidden in her personal tack chest."

It was a new voice—Nicole's. Annie wished she could see the speakers. She felt certain that Gwendolyn's face had either gone bright red or ashen, depending on who had prevailed at their fisticuffs a few hours ago.

Annie heard the sound of feet shifting on gravel, confirming her guess that the conversation was taking place near the parked cars.

"Whatever do you mean, Nicole?" Gwendolyn's voice was icy.

"Just that. This is a very difficult time for Judge Bennett." Nicole's voice dripped with false sincerity. "Her husband filed for divorce two weeks ago. It's pretty nasty, from what I hear. Another woman."

Harriett tsk-tsked. "Her husband's a film producer, isn't he? He's probably around beautiful women all day long. What did she expect?"

Nicole snickered. "Apparently not this."

Annie heard a car door open and shut and the sound of Nicole's Jaguar roaring to life. She dove underneath the water as the car peeled past the patio and down the driveway. She was pretty sure Nicole couldn't have seen her in the pool even if she'd looked in her direction but wasn't taking any chances.

From the parking lot, she heard Gwendolyn give an unladylike cackle.

"So, Judge Bennett is being dumped?"

"Don't be so flippant. If her husband is in love with another woman, she's going to be in a foul mood. Which means she'll be even tougher than usual."

Yes, this was going to be an interesting dinner party, indeed.

Chapter Twelve

"I'm so sorry you won't be able to join us, Annie." Patricia looked genuinely disappointed that she wouldn't be joining the rest of the gang.

"It's fine, really. I'm happy to be the fourth at the table, particularly since you'll all be dying to know what I've learned about the judge afterward."

"True," Liz said eagerly. "We have dibs on you."

"But do tell me what I'm missing. You know whatever Chef Gustav serves will be mouthwatering good."

"Well, we're starting at a martini bar on the south side of town and working our way up to an Asian fusion place that's just opened to rave reviews."

"Sounds yummy."

"Oh, and then a stop at the local ice cream shop, apparently one of the original eateries in the valley that has withstood the advance of commerce."

"I should hope so. If Wolf were here, I'd make you bring back a vanilla cone just for him." Wolf was Annie's Blue Heeler and boon companion.

"Oh, I miss my critters," Patricia said.

"So do I. But remember, in a few days we'll be back with them, along with the wind, rain, and creeping darkness."

There was a collective groan. No one liked to see daylight inch away on the Olympic Peninsula, culminating in late December at the winter equinox, the shortest day of the year. For months, the sun would rise long after Annie had jumped out of the bed and set long before her workday was over.

"So, we should all enjoy ourselves. Oh, and Liz, I have a question for you."

"Shoot. Is it about dressage? If so, you'd better ask the professional standing next to me."

"Actually, it's a simple math problem."

"Definitely better ask Patricia."

"As it turns out, you're the only one who can solve it."

"I hate math questions. But go ahead."

"The first night I was here, last Wednesday, when Patricia and I were called away from the house, do you remember how many people came to the cocktail hour? We left too soon for me to take notice."

"What a funny question! Everyone, I assume. Hold on, let me think." Liz tilted her head à la the Scarecrow in *The Wizard of Oz*. "Okay, I think I remember where everyone was seated. Here goes. Hollis was at the bar as usual. Miriam was sitting down nearby, and you were next to her, at least until Hollis had to answer the door. Lucy and Amy were sitting near the back of the pool, the shallow side. I remember they talked between themselves most of the time. Gwendolyn was in back of you, Annie. I remembered she was throwing invisible daggers at the back of your head."

"Not surprised. Your recall is excellent. Who else?"

"Let me think again. Patricia was with me until, well, you know. We were standing close to Hollis, and looking for a place to sit down although I think most of the lounge chairs were taken. Where was Harriett? Oh, she wasn't there. She and Melissa didn't start taking meals with us until the next day, Thursday at lunch."

"Which leaves Tabitha and Nicole," Annie said encouragingly.

"Tabitha was . . . oh, yes, she was a bit to the left of Gwendolyn, who was doing her best to annoy her. Nicole was . . ." Liz stopped. "Nicole wasn't there when both of you left. She came in late. Now I remember. I thought it extremely rude of her to show up midway through cocktails, but Miriam, being the perfect hostess, just said she was glad to see her and made her a drink."

"What was her excuse? Did she give one?"

"I think something about talking to her fiancé on the phone. She didn't exactly announce her late arrival to the group. I just happened to be standing near Miriam and overheard a bit of what she said when she came in. And that was all. There's something about the woman that makes you want to walk in the opposite direction as soon as you share airspace, so that's what I did. I went over to talk to Lucy and Amy, right up until dinner."

Nicole hadn't been at cocktail hour the entire time. Maybe Gwendolyn's suspicions weren't so preposterous after all.

"How did she look?"

"Annie, now you're venturing beyond simple addition. I don't know. She looked like Nicole. Dressed and made up to the nines, nose slightly tilted in the air, eyes averted from the rest of us commoners. You know. She looked like Nicole."

"Not upset? Worried? Out of breath? Nothing out of place?"

"Good heavens, Annie!" Patricia was looking at her with a curious gleam in her eye. "Are you detecting again? What is she accused of? You don't seriously think she's involved in Betsy's death, do you?"

"I admit, it doesn't sound likely," Annie replied. "Tell me, do either of you remember seeing her down at the stables that afternoon?"

"I wasn't there. After lunch, I was off to pick you up at the airport, remember?" Patricia reminded her.

"Of course. How about you, Liz?"

"We worked in the morning right up until lunch, too. I confess I took most of the afternoon off. I checked on Sammy around three, but then spent the rest of the day out by the pool. I didn't want to be a nuisance while you were showing your first potential customer the horses."

Annie smiled at Liz. "As if. One last question, then I'm done. Did everyone who was present at cocktails also trail into dinner that night?"

"A resounding yes. The only people missing at the table that night were you and Patricia. And dinner was wonderful, by the way."

"I know. I got the remnants later that night; and then, just like Nicole, got my own private tour of the kitchen."

The three women laughed hysterically.

As Annie dressed that night, she wondered if her friend Luann had been right. Maybe she should have taken a look at one more adorable cocktail dress. She was now wearing the one she'd worn the first night. By Sunday evening, she'd be wearing it again—*l'horreur*!

Miriam had informed her earlier that tonight's cocktails and dinner would be served in their suite, which had its own dining area. Annie felt as if she were about to enter the inner sanctum. She managed to put on mascara without smudging it on her eyelids and was gratified to see that no blush was necessary. Mother Nature was doing the job very nicely, and it had only been forty-eight hours since she had arrived.

She rang the doorbell on the second-floor suite but heard nothing from inside. She was just about to ring it again when the door opened. Hollis ushered her in, and Annie saw a small sitting area in front of her, in a room that had nearly floor-to-ceiling artwork on every side.

Miriam got up from her chair, using her cane.

"Annie, how nice of you to join us this evening. Let me introduce you to Judge Jean Bennett, who will be officiating tomorrow. Jean, this is Annie Carson, a friend of our good friend Patricia Winters and now a good friend of ours, as well."

Annie blushed slightly at Miriam's kind words. She held out her hand.

"A pleasure to meet you, Annie. Please call me Jean."

Judge Bennett didn't look like a crabby judge who found fault with riders at every step. She was a large woman who knew how to dress to hide her girth and still look stylish and attractive. Her long brown hair was in a soft bun, and diamond earrings dangled from each earlobe. Her handshake was warm and firm but not bone breaking, as Annie had halfway expected. She had a delicious smile that curved up one side of the face a bit more than the other, and her lips were adorned with bright red lipstick.

"Please sit down, Annie," Hollis encouraged her. "May I bring you your usual?"

She happily nodded her assent and sat in a chair opposite the divan on which Judge Bennett and Miriam were perched. A plate of canapés sat in front of her, and included what looked like tiny cream puffs filled with something delectable. The judge saw her eyeing them.

"They're cream puffs with lox, one of my favorites. Chef Gustav is kind enough to always remember to make them when I'm here. Try one, and tell me what you think."

Annie dutifully picked up one of the small puffs and placed it in her mouth. The melding flavors of cheese, chives, and salmon filled her senses, and she forgot for a moment she was eating alone in front of several important people. She unconsciously reached for another puff as soon as she'd swallowed the first.

Judge Bennett laughed. "I see that you approve."

Annie nodded, embarrassed by what she had just done, and quickly swallowed.

"All the food has been so wonderful here. I keep meaning to get to the gym but never quite make it. I'm not riding, so there's no excuse for the gluttony you just observed."

"Oh, you're still young. You can eat all you want and not pack on a pound. I'm now reaching the age where I have to worry what one piece of chocolate cake will do to my thighs."

Since this was obviously true, Annie simply smiled. She gratefully accepted the martini glass Hollis had placed in her hand. So far, Judge Bennett was turning out to be a thoroughly normal person. Empathetic, even.

"Miriam tells me you train horses back in Washington State."

"Yes, I'm a Western rider, and so that's the discipline I use with all my horses. But I've enjoyed getting to know a bit about dressage this week. I'm amazed at the level of skill to which riders advance with their horses. It's sometimes made me feel that I still have a lot to learn about my craft."

"I'm glad to hear you say that, Annie," Miriam chimed in. "Not that I expect you to go home and change into a student of dressage. But I'm glad you appreciate what we're trying to do. So many people think dressage is just a sport for women who want to control their horses."

"Which is antithetical to the whole idea," Judge Bennett said warmly.

"Yes," Miriam agreed. "The ultimate purpose of dressage is the harmonious development of the physique and ability of the horse."

"What a beautiful sentiment!" Annie exclaimed.

"Thank you. As usual, the line is not my own. It's from the U.S. Equestrian Federation rulebook. But notice it says nothing about the rider. It's all about the horse."

"I've seen that in the way the trainers have worked with their students." Annie thought back to the session she'd observed with Liz on Sammy. "The horses really are star athletes. Although I imagine their riders have to be in pretty good shape, themselves."

"Yes and no." Judge Bennett put down her glass of red wine and folded her hands together. "Of course, all riders should have good physical strength and excellent balance. But riders who pump iron often have problems in the ring. Their strength can work against them and the horse's looseness and suppleness, two things we work hard to achieve."

"Interesting. A friend told me the Greeks were the first to develop the training methods modern-day dressage is modeled after."

"She's right. In the very beginning, the objective was to control warhorses in battle to soldiers' best advantage. Are you familiar with the term 'piaffe,' Annie?"

"Two days ago, I would have said no. But I believe that's when a horse appears to be dancing in place, almost floating in air."

"The popular tale is that horses were trained to perform the piaffe in order to stomp on a fallen enemy."

Annie smiled. "That makes sense."

Judge Bennett turned to Miriam. "She didn't blanch. Most women look as if they'll faint when I tell that story."

"She's very tough, our Annie," said Hollis. "I would have no hesitation sending her out to battle on her horse, dressage training or no."

Annie had consumed more than half her martini, and Hollis's words caused her to inwardly swoon just a bit. She realized she was blushing and reached for a handful of nuts just as Miriam began to speak.

"I have no truck with women who swoon," her hostess said, not aware that the guest opposite her had been in danger of doing precisely that. "When I began studying with Harriett, most of the dressage riders were men. We women had to work hard to be noticed and respected in the ring."

This caught Annie's attention. "Really? I assumed that dressage has always been a female-dominated sport."

"Quite the opposite," Hollis told her. "Up until the mid-1940s, most dressage riders in this country came out of the U.S. Cavalry. It was only after World War II, when the Army disbanded the unit, that women got into the game."

"And when Lis Hartel won the silver medal at the 1952 Summer Olympics, the invisible barrier was gone forever," Miriam added.

"You'll still find a lot of male dressage riders in Europe," Judge Bennett told Annie. "Dressage riding is part of their culture, one that goes back generations. Here, young men are expected to excel in contact sports. It's really too bad."

A soft knock on the door announced the arrival of dinner, which was delivered in a series of trays. Two waiters stood back unobtrusively, waiting to serve the first course.

"Ah! *Soupe à l'oignon.* My favorite. Chef Gustav never forgets."

The four sat down before steaming bowls of soup, covered with a crust of melted cheese on a slice of baguette. Annie quietly inhaled the scent rising before her. It smelled wonderful.

"I take it Margaret will be arriving later this evening?"

Hollis inquired after the wine had been poured and approved.

"That girl!" For the first time, Annie saw the judge react with real irritation. "She was supposed to drive up with me today, then canceled, and now, she tells me she won't be able to get here until tomorrow morning."

"How frustrating for you."

"Yes, I must find another scribe to work with locally. Margaret's done this once before. She showed up less than five minutes before the first horse was scheduled to enter the ring. I can't tolerate a scribe who plays fast-and-loose with showtimes."

Annie's ears perked up. Finally, this was her chance to learn what this arcane role actually was.

"I've been meaning to ask," she began. "What exactly does the scribe do? When I hear the word, I think of a monk copying a religious tract in the bowels of a monastery."

Miriam laughed. "She's the right-hand person for the judge. Indispensable, wouldn't you say, Jean?"

"The good ones are. Is this your first dressage show, Annie?"

"It is."

"Do you have a copy of the day sheet yet?"

"I don't even know what the day sheet is."

"Miriam, you must get one to Annie before she leaves tonight. The day sheet tells the order in which the riders appear before me, along with the name of their horse and the level at which they're testing. It's a very tight schedule. Tests take less than ten minutes to perform, and we work hard to stay on time. Miriam's right, the scribe is literally my right-hand person, who takes down my comments, scores, and any errors I note during each test. It's her job to make sure each rider appears in order and that everything I say is recorded accurately. My former scribe was wonderful, but she decided to have a child, and so that relationship ended. I've been trying out Margaret, but frankly, I don't think our working relationship will extend beyond this weekend."

"Let's hope Margaret arrives in good time tomorrow." Hollis was excellent at placating distressed guests. Annie murmured her thanks to the judge and returned to her soup. She was not going to leave a spoonful if she could help it.

Sole meunière was served next, and Judge Bennett again expressed her delight at Chef Gustav's prescience to serve one of her favorite dishes.

"Do you have many guests staying with you this week?"

Miriam gave a quick glance at Hollis.

"Oh, our usual roundup. I believe you know many of our riders. Lucy Cartwright was afraid she wouldn't be able to test—her horse developed a sudden abscess although thankfully that's been resolved."

"Good. I hope Lucy's performance has improved since her last disaster in the ring."

"She's been working very hard, Jean. If she can control her nerves, I think she'll do just fine."

"Who are the other riders? Anyone else I know? And who's the technical delegate for this show?"

Annie noticed another quick glance between husband and wife before Miriam replied.

"Several riders have appeared before you before. I'm sure they remember you if not the other way around. In fact, I believe Gwendolyn Smythe is the only one you haven't seen before."

"And Liz," added Annie. "She's from the Pacific Northwest, and a relative newcomer to dressage, although her horse has some prior training."

"Yes, our guests are presenting at a variety of different levels, from training level one all the way to Prix St.-Georges."

"I noticed Nicole Anne Forrester's name on the day sheet. I hope she's improved. I can't forget the image of her maneuvering her horse around corners as if she were driving a Mack truck."

Annie reached for her water so she wouldn't laugh.

"Now, Jean, Nicole's also improved immensely since you last saw her. Promise me you won't let her prior performances affect your opinion now."

"Wouldn't dream of it."

Hollis spoke up. "So how are things at the university? Students keeping you busy? Any internecine battles with the evil administrators?

"Hollis, I do believe you're trying to change the subject. You always were such a diplomat. I think you missed your calling."

"Ah, but I've played the role of diplomat in several films. That's better than the real thing."

Dinner ended at nine o'clock, and by the time cognac and coffee had been served, Annie was beat. When Hollis rang for Jorge to take away the last dishes, Annie excused herself, citing an early morning, although she knew the judge would probably be rising even before she did. She gratefully accepted a copy of the day sheet and made her departure. Fortunately, she didn't have far to go—just up another flight of stairs to her own bedroom. She flopped on top of her bed and vowed that was the last formal dinner party she would attend for the remainder of the year, superlative food or not.

She was up a minute later after realizing that the dress she was wearing would probably be back in service a few days hence. Wishing Marcus were there to help, she struggled out of the slim dress and hung it up, looking for any telltale spots that might be difficult to get out later. Thankfully, she found none, and got into her sweats and a T-shirt in preparation for bed.

Yet she found her mind still swirling as she recalled the conversations over dinner. She'd found the judge intelligent and entertaining but definitely with a critical edge to her that might make less confident dressage students cringe. Annie understood that the judge had to firmly abide by the rules, but she didn't seem to have a lot of leeway in her feelings concerning tight corners and late scribes. And then there was the interesting news about Nicole's late entrance at the cocktail hour on Wednesday. Had she really been talking to her fiancé—or had she been ensuring the death of Betsy Gilchrist?

She found sleep impossible. Putting on the one pair of sneakers she'd packed, she tiptoed down the stairs to take a quick stroll around the grounds. Perhaps the fresh air would make her bed more inviting.

This time, the living room was dark and silent, and Annie hoped the alarm had not been set, assuming the Darbys had one for their vast house. But she hadn't heard Patricia, Liz, and the other women enter, and she was certain the house would not be shut down until their arrival. Nicole also hadn't returned from traipsing around an art gallery, most likely still hanging on the arm of her precious Douglas.

The outdoor light came on, flooding the circular driveway. Annie decided to walk to the right, past the kitchen, and near the path she knew led to the tennis courts and other exercise venues. It was immensely quiet. The tall incense cedars gently swayed from some far-off breeze, and the moon shone brightly overhead. She had no qualms about walking alone or without a flashlight. The illumination from above was more than enough to guide her way.

She turned at the fork in the path to begin a brisk walk around the sports pavilion but abruptly stopped. Somewhere amid the giant trees surrounding her, two people were speaking. She assumed they had to be guests in the house, and pressed back against the stucco wall closest to her to find out who was in an intimate conversation. If it were Lucy and Amy, she could join them. If it were Nicole giving her fiancé a last lingering kiss, she would remain frozen to her spot. That was one image she had no desire to see.

It was neither. She quickly recognized the voice of the woman she'd just said good night to, and that of a woman she'd only met this afternoon. Judge Bennett and Brianna Bowen were in deep conversation. The technical delegate who seemed so concerned about not encountering the judge was now talking to her urgently, only twenty steps away from Annie's hiding place.

"You're not being fair!" Annie heard Brianna tearfully tell the judge.

"I have no choice, Brie," came the tired reply. "The divorce is way too messy. If I remain your thesis adviser, you'll be thrown in the dirt, too. I can't do that to you. And you don't want it either, trust me."

"But don't you see what that does to me? Where am I going to find another adviser now? Christ, I'm supposed to be defending in a month. How could you do this to me? Will you at least find someone else who can substitute for you?"

"Brie, I can't even be on your thesis committee anymore. Look, I'm fighting for my career, too. If this gets out more than it already has, I'm possibly looking at disciplinary action that could strip my tenure status."

"Oh, you've always thought about yourself first," came Brianna's bitter reply. "All the time we've been together, that's all you've thought about. What will this do to your marriage, your career, your freakin' dog, for that matter. Who will walk Caruthers if I'm not home in time because you're spending time with me? But this is my life, too, Jean. If you fail me now, I don't know what I'll do."

"I've tried and tried to think of a way, really I have. But if I'm involved at any level in getting your thesis approved and published, it will come back to bite both of us. Jim is not about to show either of us any mercy. We have to keep our heads low and just go it alone for now. It's just the way it has to be."

"You never used to be like this. You used to love me."

"I still do, Brie! I just can't be with you right now. And I can't help you. I'm sorry. I wish I could, but I can't."

There was silence, and Annie held her breath as she continued to let the wall prop her up. She was glad her sweats and T-shirt were dark-colored but wished she was barefoot instead of wearing bright turquoise athletic shoes. Her heart hammered in her chest. She was hearing a very private conversation— one that she very much wished she'd never come across.

"Fine." Brianna's pleading tone had changed to one of stone. "I guess there's not much point in talking anymore. You've made yourself clear. From now on, I'm on my own."

"I hope someday things will change."

"They've already changed. But don't bother chasing me again. I won't be there. And you'd better hope you don't see me in your rearview mirror. You might regret it."

"What's that supposed to mean?"

"Nothing. I'm leaving. Good-bye."

Annie watched Brianna run away from the trees and toward her cottage. A minute later, she saw Judge Bennett leave the canopy of the trees and slowly walk out and away from Annie, toward the private parking lot. Only when she saw the judge's Prius silently approach the front gates of the estate did she move from her place of concealment. She walked noiselessly back to the front of the house and let herself in, gently shutting the front door.

She knew sleep would not come easily to her tonight. Nor to the women she'd just overheard.

Chapter Thirteen

Annie awakened to the sound of a long, persistent buzz from her phone. She grabbed it, thinking someone must be calling her. But it was simply the alarm. She'd set it two days ago but had never needed the reminder. Today she did. The time on the screen showed seven thirty, hours later than when she usually arose. What could have kept her in bed this long? The uncomfortable scene between Brianna and the judge flooded back into her consciousness, and she groaned. It had taken forever to drift off to sleep last night, and when it finally came, troubling dreams kept jarring her awake.

She showered and dressed in record time and would have raced down the stairs if she hadn't worried about encountering one of her hosts. The dining room was nearly deserted. There were signs that many other people had breakfasted before her, but the only person who now remained at the table was the one Annie least wanted to see—Nicole.

Apparently, Annie's rank on Nicole's social register

was similarly low. The diva swiftly rose and swept out of the room without a glance at where Annie was standing by the buffet.

"Best of luck today," Annie lamely called after her.

"Luck's got nothing to do with it," was the reply, then Annie heard the front door slam.

She quickly ate her solitary breakfast and took her dishes out to the kitchen. Chef Gustav seemed to be six places at once, observing a rolled pastry crust here, tasting the sauce on the gas stovetop there, and all the while issuing orders to his waitstaff who were patiently lined up, waiting to do his bidding. Annie saw a row of thermoses on the counter, each with a Darby Farms logo on it. She wondered if they were filled with coffee and, if so, she could snag one for herself.

As if he'd read her mind, the chef gestured with his arm as he bustled by. "Take! Take!" he said genially, then shouted to the other end of the kitchen, "*Non!* That is not the knife to filet the fish! Give it to me before you butcher it!" Annie watched him snatch the offending cutlery out of the hand of an astonished young man, who then meekly looked over the chef's shoulder as the small Frenchman deftly separated fish from bone with the correct blade.

Chef Gustav next raced back to the stove, grabbed a mitt, and peered inside the oven.

"Who is supposed to be watching the tarts?" he bellowed to no one and everyone at once. "One more second, and they would have been ruined!" He carefully removed a sheet of perfectly bronzed tart shells and placed them on the counter. Then he turned to her and spoke in his normal, pleasant voice.

"Mademoiselle Annie, are you well? You are late for

the *petit déjeuner*. Everyone else has eaten and gone many hours before."

"I'm fine," Annie stammered back. "I just overslept. And I can see you're busy. Is there anything I can do to help?"

"*Non, mon amie.* I am merely upset because my best sous chef has not shown up, and now I find I am a waiter short. In a few hours, I must serve luncheon to fifteen guests and also prepare for an afternoon tea. But do not worry. Chef Gustav does not fail! Not once has a guest not been served an exceptional meal. Today it will be no different."

"I'm confident of that. And if I truly can't help, I'll leave you to it."

"Take your carafe of coffee. And please, tell your friends they are welcome to help themselves to their own if they desire."

"Thank you, Chef Gustav. I hope your morning improves."

The chef sighed. "It can only be so. *Adieu, Mademoiselle.* Now you must go and watch all the pretty horses."

That was one way of putting it, Annie thought as she set off for the stables a few minutes later. If she'd been in Chef Gustav's predicament, she would have phoned the nearest pizzeria for takeout.

The transformation that had begun the day before was now complete, and Annie took a moment to take in the view before she wended her way to the stables. "Wend" was the operative word today. The population had increased tenfold from yesterday, and now hummed with riders dressed in white breeches, dark cutaway coats, and cream-colored vests. The entire west side of the barn was filled with horse trailers parked back-to-back. She saw several riders on their horses in the warm-up ring, all deeply concentrating on their walk, trot, or canter. The spectator tier was already full, and dozens more observers milled around the front of the stable. Annie noticed a new table set up at the far end of the show ring, a large sign on top touting the services of a videographer. For a fee that was far from modest, riders could have their test recorded for posterity. The cameraman was fiddling with a large camera mounted on a tripod.

Annie looked at where he was aiming the camera and saw the judge's booth. She could just make out Judge Bennett seated inside. She tried to see if the scribe was beside her, but the angle was too sharp to know for sure. For the scribe's sake, she hoped the judge's right-hand assistant was ensconced in the booth and sharpening her pencil.

Annie wondered where Liz and Patricia were in the midst of this teeming activity. According to the day sheet Annie had quickly scanned, Liz was the second rider to test this morning. *She must be in the warm-up ring,* Annie thought, and headed in that direction.

She saw Brianna talking to two women dressed in regular breeches by the warm-up ring. Annie noticed one of them had a name tag designating her as a volunteer. Today, Brianna had heightened the haute couture look with leggings, black boots that nearly reached her thighs, and a long, silk blouse that draped in front. Annie couldn't hear what she was saying, but from the response of the women, Brianna was conveying information in a no-nonsense, take-charge kind of way. Annie walked by the small group and stopped by the fence line, resting her arms on the top rail as she searched for her friends inside the ring.

"Annie? Is that you?"

Brianna walked over to her, smiling. If Annie hadn't been privy to her highly wrought encounter with the judge a few hours before, she would have never suspected one had occurred.

"How are you?"

"Fine. Just looking for my friend. I notice she's the second to ride this morning."

"Liz Faraday on Sammy?

"Yes, very good! Do you have all the riders' and horses' names memorized in order?"

Brianna laughed. "Almost. I certainly have the volunteers' names memorized. I'm depending a lot on them today."

"How are things going so far?"

"Pretty well. Aside from missing a scribe."

Well, that wasn't good news. Judge Bennett probably was doing a major slow burn in the booth as they spoke.

An ancient Honda Civic pulled into the stables and jerked to a halt, the driver looking for a place to park that wasn't there.

"Oh, that must be Margaret now. Damn her hide! She's very, very late. I must fly, Annie, and get her parked and in the booth. Judge Bennett already is fit to be tied."

I'll bet, Annie thought, and watched Brianna trot over to the car and point with her right arm where a small car still might fit in.

She saw Melissa in front of the barn, Amy and Lucy by her side and dressed in full dressage regalia. She waved over to them, receiving three enthusiastic waves in return. Glancing down at the day sheet, she saw that Lucy wasn't scheduled to ride her test until close to eleven thirty, with Amy following her. That still gave them hours to sweat, or, Annie hoped, to take deep, calming breaths and try to relax. As tough as it was to be among the first riders, Liz might prefer her position. At least the anxiety would soon be over, and she could cheer on everyone else without worrying about her own time in the ring. Annie pointed to her chest, then to the warm-up ring. Three heads bobbed up and down. She had made her point, that she wanted to wish Liz good luck while there was still time. The day sheet stated she was on at precisely 9:08, now a mere seventeen minutes away.

She spotted Liz on Sammy's back at the back of the ring. Liz was trotting very slowly, posting as she did so. Patricia was outside the ring, her lips moving, although Annie could not hear what she was saying.

She threaded her way through the crowd of other onlookers to where Patricia stood.

"That's excellent, I think you're good to go. Let's give Sammy a rest. Walk him on a loose rein."

She was speaking in her ordinary voice. Annie had no idea how Liz could have heard her. Then she saw Patricia remove a small earpiece. *Of course,* Annie thought. Liz and Patricia were speaking on Bluetooth headsets. How clever of them.

"How was girls' night out?"

"Super. We stayed out two hours later than we'd promised ourselves. I hope there's time for another one before we leave. How was dinner with the judge?"

"Interesting. She didn't come across like a fiend in human form. Just very strict and by-the-book. I'm sure she's got her list of pet peeves for riders, but I doubt Liz is going to trigger any."

"I hope not. She's worked so hard to be here. And we really should be heading toward the front of the ring. I've got to remove Sammy's brushing boots before we enter."

"We? You get to go in, too?"

"I'm reading Liz's test to her as she performs. It's allowed, and I don't want to put any more stress on Liz and Sammy right now than they already feel."

"Sammy looks pretty relaxed."

"I don't think this is his first time in the ring. But it is for Liz."

"Good point. I'll let you two gather your thoughts and find you later."

She waved both arms over her head, and yelled to Liz, "You both look beautiful! Good luck! Remember to have fun!"

It was what Annie's 4-H mentor had always told her right before she entered a competition ring. She'd liked being reminded that fun was on the agenda, too.

Annie managed to squeeze into a corner seat on the top row of the spectator tiers without stepping on anyone's foot or spilling their coffee. She put her own carafe underneath her and glanced at her watch. It was now five minutes to nine. She looked over at the warm-up arena, where the first rider, a young woman of about twenty-five, was sitting perfectly erect on her horse. She saw the rider hand her whip to a volunteer, while another volunteer removed the final wrap from the horse's rear leg.

The bang of a door against its hinges brought her attention back to the ring in front of her. The scribe had emerged from the back of the booth and now was running quickly toward the main house. Was everything all right? It was so close to start time, and Annie knew the judge was a stickler for staying on schedule.

Two women seated below her quietly chuckled to each other.

"Looks like someone forgot the Lady Grey tea."

"Not good. I'd hate to be in that scribe's shoes right now."

So that was it. The scribe not only was expected to take down every comment the judge uttered, she also was expected to fetch the judge's morning beverage. The crowd settled down to wait, but Annie thought that Judge Bennett looked none too pleased—her arms were folded in front of her, and her expression was positively steely. Annie nervously glanced at her watch again. It was now two minutes to nine. She looked over at the first rider sitting patiently on her horse. It was too difficult to gauge what the woman was feeling, but she certainly looked calm and confident.

At one minute to nine, the scribe had still not returned, but Judge Bennett was not going to wait any longer. She lifted a small golden bell on the table in front of her and rang it for two long seconds, the high, tinkling sound resonating throughout the arena. Annie assumed it was the cue for the rider to enter the ring, and she was right. A trainer or perhaps a friend was walking away from the horse and the rider began to adjust her reins. Now Annie saw the scribe hurrying back behind the warm-up ring, a Darby Farms thermos clutched against her chest. Seconds later, the scribe entered the booth and Annie watched her shakily pour a cup of steaming liquid from the thermos into a mug. She noticed Judge Bennett failed to acknowledge the scribe's presence, but she did take a deep swallow from her now-filled mug.

That crisis averted, Annie turned her attention to the horse and rider, who were entering the arena at a trot. The horse turned squarely into the arena and continued to trot toward the judge's booth. Halfway down the arena on the centerline, the horse halted. Annie watched the rider put her right arm out at an angle, palm backward, and slightly lower her head. This, she knew, was the rider's obligatory opening salute to the judge.

Judge Bennett stood up slowly and acknowledged the salute with a short nod. Something seemed a bit off. The judge appeared to have difficulty standing. Both of her hands were flat on the table, and Annie wondered if she was using them to push herself upright. Suddenly, the judge swayed. A few people in the audience murmured their concern and she abruptly righted herself. Annie noticed the judge still looked none too steady on her feet and continued to grasp the table for support. Now the rider brought her arm back to her side, which gave Annie a clear and unobstructed view of the far end of the ring. She watched in disbelief as the judge crumpled to the floor and disappeared from view. It was like looking at a marionette onstage whose wires had suddenly been cut. One moment, Jean Bennett had been standing. The next, she was not.

* * *

At first, no one moved. But the scribe was now standing, her hands near her face. For a few seconds, she seemed frozen to her spot, but then she bent toward the floor and gave a shrill scream. The sound galvanized the crowd. Everyone in the spectator section rose as if on cue, craning their heads for a better look, turning only to ask their neighbor if they'd seen what had just happened.

Annie had no desire to be in what would soon be a crush of people clambering to get down. She glanced to the right and gauged the distance. It was a good eight feet to the ground, slightly less if she could hook her feet on one of the extended slats. She decided to try. The worst would be a turned ankle, and Annie liked to think that at age forty-four, she was still agile enough to jump. She landed feet-first in the dirt, creating a puff of dust that slowly settled over her clothing. With all the attention elsewhere, no one had noticed her unorthodox exit.

She ran toward the dressage arena and saw Brianna running from the opposite side, closest to the barn office. They reached the booth at the same time. The scribe was screaming hysterically, and Brianna abruptly pushed her out the rear door.

"Call the show medic! And get a blanket and water! Now!"

Judge Bennett was sprawled on the floor in a tangled mess of arms and legs. Her face was bright red, and her eyes were wide open and staring, although Annie didn't think she was still conscious.

"We have to move her," she told Brianna, looking her full in the face. She was aware that she was speaking to the judge's lover, or ex-lover, and possibly the person who had caused Jean Bennett's suffering now.

Brianna nodded, and they each grasped a set of the judge's limbs, Annie taking her arms, and Brianna her feet and legs. Annie was struck by how cold and clammy Judge Bennett's arms felt on her own skin. As the two women began gently maneuvering her out of the booth and onto the grass, the judge's head lolled back, and Annie quickly tucked her elbows in to lend support. Annie wished she could feel for a pulse but knew this would only be possible after the woman was stretched out.

Margaret ran up, her arms full of saddle pads.

"It's all I could find," she panted. "The medic is right behind me. But people are starting to come inside the arena. What should I do?"

Brianna looked at the scribe, her exasperation evident. "Stay here with Annie," she told her. "I'll be back as soon as I can."

Annie already had packed several of the pads under the judge's head and was now taking her pulse. It was weak and erratic. This was not good. She heard Margaret whimpering beside her. This was unacceptable.

"Margaret, I want you to round up all the volunteers. They've got name tags, so it shouldn't be hard. Ask them to come into the ring and make sure no one else gets in. Can you do that?"

The scribe numbly nodded, one hand over her mouth. She stumbled off, and Annie turned back to the judge. She was not moving, and her breath seemed as sporadic as her pulse. She wished an EMT would arrive and whisk the judge off to the nearest hospital. She knew that without immediate medical assistance, Judge Bennett's survival was very much in question.

The show medic, Liz, and Patricia all suddenly appeared at the same time. Liz spoke first.

"We had to fight our way to get here, but when I told them I was an ER RN, they finally let us through."

Annie nodded gratefully and spoke to the young medic beside Liz.

"Thank God you're here. This doesn't look good. She's cold, clammy, low pulse, shallow breaths, sporadic heartbeat, and you can see her face for yourself."

The medic immediately crouched down and pulled down the lower lid of one of the judge's wide, unseeing eyes. The pupil was enlarged and a deep black.

"I'm calling a paramedic. In the meantime, we need the respiratory emergency kit. Can you get it from the office?"

"I'm on my way."

"And someone's going to have to do something to quell the crowds, Patricia added. "Someone needs to tell them the event's been canceled and to stay calm."

Annie had already started to jog toward the office. She stopped and yelled back, "You do it. Everyone pays attention to an English accent."

Patricia gave her a patronizing gaze but obediently got up and jogged over to join Annie.

"Where's the sound system?"

"I don't know. Maybe they'll know at the office."

Just as earlier this morning, people milled about everywhere, but now they did so with no particular purpose. Yet no one was panicking or was making a fuss, and Annie concluded that was one saving grace about a dressage crowd—they were calm in a crisis. It was just that there were so many of them, and at the moment, they were maddeningly in the way. At least the riders knew what to do. Most of them were leading their horses into the barn as if nothing unusual had happened.

She found Brianna inside the office, talking on a landline. Patricia had already gone off on her own path in search of the sound system and a mike.

"I don't know," Brianna said into the mouthpiece. "She was fine this morning. She just suddenly collapsed. How far away is the ambulance now?" The confident voice Annie had heard a few minutes ago was now tremulous and shaky. She grabbed Brianna's arm. Brianna whirled around, then relaxed when she realized who wanted her attention.

"Just one moment," she said to the entity on the other line, and then put her hand over the phone, mouthing "9-1-1" to Annie, who was fully aware of that fact.

"Where's the respiratory emergency kit?"

"I don't know. I haven't seen it. Maybe up at the main house."

That made sense, considering Miriam's health issues. Although Annie thought there should be one at the stables, as well.

"Have you contacted the Darbys?"

"I asked one of the volunteers to go up and tell Hollis. I haven't talked to him yet."

"Listen, Brianna, I don't know how long it takes for the local fire department to get here, but the medic has to act fast. Can you help me find the kit and ask Hollis what medical equipment he has in the house?"

Brianna nodded. Through the window, Annie was immensely relieved to see the familiar red trucks roll through the front gates. Help had arrived at last.

"Never mind. Reinforcements are here," she said

simply, and ran out to guide the medic truck and ambulance to where the judge had been laid. As she ran
to the gates, she heard Patricia's voice emanating
from a large speaker over the crowd.

"May I have your attention, please? Judge Bennett
has been taken ill, so unfortunately we will have to
cancel the show today. Medical aid has just arrived.
Please do not leave the premises until the ambulance
has left. We want a clear path, and if you try to drive
out now, you will be obstructing their exit path."

There was a pause, then a rush of shouted questions.

"This is all I can tell you at this time. One of our
volunteers will call you later today with more information. We will let you know when the event will be
rescheduled. In the meantime, please attend to your
horses, and we'll try to get you on the road as soon as
we can."

Annie had been correct. There was nothing like a
patrician British accent to get people to settle down
and shut up.

She stood aside as four burly men exited the two
vehicles bearing a stretcher, blankets, and, thankfully,
a bag-valve mask. Liz was talking to one of them in a
low voice. Annie knew she was filling him in on the
judge's vital signs and symptoms. She continued to
stand back anxiously as the medics went to work.

"Assist ventilations."

The medics surrounded the judge, and Annie was
unable to see what they were doing or the judge's
condition. Three long minutes passed. Annie realized
that Brianna and Patricia were now beside her. They

all stood back and silently watched the crew, knowing better than to ask questions or disturb their concentration.

Then two of the men stood up, carrying the judge on the stretcher. Judge Bennett's face was still covered with the mask, but her eyes were shut. The blotchy red spots on her face were gone, replaced with an ashen pallor that Annie recognized far too well. The lead medic, whose name tag read, M. FISHER, approached the small group of women.

"I'm so sorry. I'm afraid your friend didn't make it. I'm going to need information about the deceased from one of you. Is there someplace we can go and talk?"

Brianna gasped, then let out a long, guttural cry that went on and on. It reminded Annie of a wounded animal in the throes of dying, and for a moment, she thought Briana would collapse just as her lover had. She put an arm around the woman's waist and lowered her gently to the ground, as Brianna moaned, "She's dead! I've killed her! It's all my fault!"

Chapter Fourteen

Patricia and Liz volunteered to stay with the vans until they began their long, slow journey around the crowd and out to the waiting road. A glass of cold water had done much to restore Brianna to her normal state. There were no more hysterical outbursts, and after refusing any assistance from the medics, Brianna quietly walked over to the office to deal with the hundred riders who would want to know what was going on, when the show would be rescheduled, and voice a million other questions that Annie knew the technical delegate would be unable to answer.

Margaret Woods was an entirely different matter. When she learned Judge Bennett would not be able to scold her ever again, she began to sob loudly, and Liz persuaded a medic to provide a chill pill. The scribe was now curled up on one of the unused saddle pads, still awake but quiet at last.

Still using her best British voice, Patricia had commissioned Annie to break the news to Hollis, and Annie agreed without argument. In theory, a volunteer was supposed to have already made contact with the Darbys, but even if that hadn't occurred, it would be a miracle if Hollis and Miriam didn't know by now that something had gone dreadfully wrong with the scheduled show. She trudged up to the house, dreading the task ahead of her. She wondered where all the other houseguests were in the swarm of people below. Except for her brief glimpse of Melissa and her students, she hadn't seen anyone else in the stables all morning. But then, she had been occupied with a medical emergency most of the time.

She walked over the crest of the small rise leading up from the pastures and saw two black-and-white patrol vehicles parked in the circular driveway. She was frankly relieved the Darbys already knew the worst, and she hadn't had to deliver the news. She thought about simply turning around and heading back to the stables, but quickly nixed the idea. She had seen the judge collapse, and she had been present when the judge had died. If the Darbys wanted to know precisely what happened, it was her job to deliver the facts as she'd seen them. If they didn't want to hear the nitty-gritty details, she was sure the police would.

She opened the front door and heard Chef Gustav's voice from the kitchen, agitated and upset, beyond the tone he reserved for waiters and kitchen staff who managed to annoy him. The memory of Margaret Woods scuttling back from the kitchen with the gray thermos flashed through her mind, and she quickened her own step to see if the source of his distress was, as the chef described them, the local gendarmes.

"I have told you twice already! I make the tea this morning at six o'clock on the dot. No one comes to pick it up, so at seven o'clock I discard it and make another, fresher pot. There it sits, along with all the other thermoses, until Mademoiselle Woods flies in the door to grab one off the tray. I hand the one I have prepared to her, and that is it. *La fin!* What more can I tell you?"

Again, Annie felt at a crossroads. Should she enter, or would she be intruding on a confidential police interview? Well, if her presence bothered anyone, she'd simply retreat. She felt for the little Frenchman inside the kitchen. This was the second time he was getting grilled by the police in as many days. Surely the Lady Grey tea he'd prepared hadn't caused Judge Bennett's sudden collapse. But if it hadn't, what else could have caused it? As much as Annie did not want to believe in coincidences, she had a sinking feeling that a tampered beverage might very well be behind the judge's death. If so, that made it just as likely that Betsy Gilchrist had also died from a tampered beverage. Yet neither she nor Patricia had suffered ill effects. It was all too confusing. She sighed and knocked quietly on one of the swinging kitchen doors.

Deputy Collins opened the door. If possible, he looked even more handsome than he had three days ago when he had casually told her that he probably wouldn't have need to contact her again.

"Ms. Carson, what a pleasant surprise. You're one of the people I want to talk to this morning."

"May I come in?"

"Why not? Mr. Raymond mentioned that you were in the kitchen this morning. I'd like you to corroborate that, if you don't mind."

"Mr. Raymond? I don't know anyone by that name."

"The chef."

"Oh, you mean Chef Gustav. Yes, I'd be happy to."

Annie stepped into the kitchen and saw Hollis and Miriam sitting at the white kitchen table. Chef Gustav was by the stove. Nearby cupboard doors were flung open, and Annie noticed an array of loose teas arranged in mason jars inside one of them.

"Ah! Mademoiselle Annie! You will tell the police what happened. Then they will believe me!"

She gave the chef a quick smile she hoped was reassuring, then looked at her hosts, who for the first time looked haggard and truth be known, close to looking what Annie suspected were their fairly elevated ages.

"Sit down, won't you?"

Annie pulled up a chair at the table and folded her hands.

"What do you want to know?"

"Just what time you were in the kitchen this morning, and what you observed."

Was she doomed to spend the rest of her life repeating boring stories of where she'd been and with whom? Annie related in as few words as she could how she had come into the kitchen after breakfast, talked briefly to the overworked and harried chef, and saw the row of thermoses prepared for guests.

"Chef Gustav told me to take one, which I did. He also told me to tell the others that they were welcome to grab their own if they wanted."

"Where's your thermos now?"

Annie realized she'd forgotten all about stowing this item.

"It's still down at the stables. I didn't drink out of it.

I didn't really have time. I got down there just a few minutes before the show began."

"Tell us where it is if you don't mind."

"Not at all. It should still be under my seat on the highest tier."

As Annie continued to answer Deputy Collins's questions, she realized she was not helping Chef Gustav's story at all. If anything, she was a hindrance. No, she hadn't seen the special tray on which the thermos of tea for the judge had been put. But then, she hadn't had a clear view of the kitchen. It had been filled with people, working on every available counter space. And she'd only been in the kitchen a few minutes, if that. No, she hadn't seen any other guest enter the kitchen that morning, but as she'd said, she was the last one to arrive in the dining room. The only other guest still in the house was Nicole, who, if the slammed front door was any indication, had left a minute after Annie had entered the dining room. She now wished she hadn't heard the front door slam. She'd much rather have turned the dressage diva into a viable suspect.

"Right. Well, Ms. Carson, we'll want to talk to you further, but I think I have what I need for now."

He looked at his left wrist, on which there was a large watch, and spoke.

"Look for thermos, last row, spectator stand. Should have the Darby Farms logo on it."

A voice came back. "Copy."

"What, you've replaced your squawk-boxes with talking smart watches now?"

Deputy Collins grinned. "New regulation equipment as of last year."

"Does anyone ever tell you they remind them of Dick Tracy?"

"All the time."

Deputy Collins left the room although Annie knew it would be many hours before he left the property. He and his fellow officers now had the daunting task of taking statements from everyone who had witnessed the judge's collapse that morning. She did not envy them.

Miriam and Hollis tried to reassure Chef Gustav that the police would certainly not be stupid enough to cast suspicion on him, and to please, please proceed as usual and to give Deputy Collins not one more thought. Annie wasn't sure that was the right advice. She believed with all her heart that the chef had nothing to do with either the judge's or Betsy Gilchrist's deaths. She wasn't so sure about the Darbys' guests, all of whom had access to the kitchen, night and day.

Annie had offered to return to the stables to help the show staff, but Miriam had asked her to stay, and she'd looked so fragile and woebegone that Annie hadn't the heart to say no. They decided to retreat to the patio, and all chose chairs with umbrellas. The sun was high in the sky and certainly in the eighties. Annie thought about the tumult going on below them. She felt for the riders. She was now fully aware of the preparation time and cost it took to put on a dressage event, and while she was sure the Darbys would be more than financially fair to the people who had signed up, there was nothing they could do about the riders' missed opportunities to test and hopefully advance in their training.

"I know it sounds cruel, but I suppose we could try to find another judge," Miriam said. "That is, if there are enough riders who could return tomorrow. I suppose we should try that route."

"As a matter of fact, our technical delegate already has suggested that," her husband answered. Miriam looked at Hollis in disbelief.

"Brianna came up with that idea?"

"She did, indeed. She phoned me about a half hour ago, asking if she could query riders about that possibility. I said she could. As tragic as Jean's death is, there's not much point sitting shiva for the rest of the weekend if some good can still come out of it. Of course, we'd have to get the police's permission. The stables may be a crime scene and off-limits longer than just today."

"Oh, that would be a shame. I suppose I should say that Jean Bennett would want the show to go on, but I honestly don't know how she'd feel."

Annie said nothing. She had a feeling that Judge Bennett would be quite gratified if everyone sat around and mourned her death for a day or two. Dressage professionals did not seem to be lacking in ego.

"You do realize that the police are getting a search warrant right now for the kitchen area, at least."

Annie said this as nicely as she could. But the fact was that the police's departure was only temporary. They'd be back, looking for more evidence, as soon as they got the required stamp of approval from the court.

Hollis sighed. "Deputy Collins told me as much. I

told him not to bother, that the kitchen was at his disposal whenever he wanted it. He promised not to ransack the place. I think he was a bit intimidated by Chef Gustav's temper, or at least respects what he does in the kitchen. Collins did warn me, although perhaps that's not quite the right word, that a Detective Wollcott would be here later today to interview everyone in the house."

Miriam uttered a small moan.

"Honestly, Hollis, is that necessary? Can't you tell the police that everyone will give them a written statement and be done with it? Do they really have to harass our guests, too?"

She put a thin hand over her eyes and sighed. Annie raised her eyes and met Hollis's gaze halfway across the patio. She knew what they were both thinking. One of the guests in the house was a cold-blooded killer, twice over. And if the police didn't find out who it was, the killer might go on killing.

By one o'clock, all the guests had returned, and luncheon was served, this time without the anticipatory sound of the gong. Melissa told the Darbys that the scribe would not be joining them, as she was still groggy from the tranquilizer she'd been given. Melissa explained that the tranquilizer seemed to be affecting Margaret's short-term memory. At first, Margaret had been eager to tell her story. She'd told Melissa all she'd done was rush up to the kitchen, pick up the thermos on the tray the chef had pointed to, and flee. The only thing Melissa remembered hearing the chef say was that he hoped the tea was still hot and not cold.

He'd sounded a little put out that she was so late picking it up.

He wasn't the only one, Annie thought.

"But now she seems obsessed with the idea that somehow she had something to do with the judge's death." Melissa rolled her eyes just a tad. "Under the circumstances, I thought it was better that we send down food rather than have her join us. I was afraid she'd continue to harp on that ridiculous idea at the table."

Miriam assured her she had made the right decision. No mention was made of Brianna's absence from the luncheon table although Annie assumed that the Darbys had intuited that she had her hands full at the stables and would send down lunch for her, as well.

Chef Gustav delivered on his promise. The lunch was truly exceptional, although appetites were small to nonexistent. Whether by coincidence or design, the only beverage offered was sparkling water, and it was served direct from the green glass bottle. No one, it seemed, wanted to talk about how the judge had died. Instead, the main topic of discussion was what to do now that Judge Bennett was permanently out of the picture. Hollis and Miriam were not dining with them, and Annie dreaded the direction the conversation might take without their calming presence.

Harriett was livid. It was as if the minor detail of a felled judge was standing in their way of the more important issue—her students' ability to test.

"Of course the show must go on tomorrow," she angrily told the group. "What other choice is there? Gwendolyn and Tabitha have worked too hard to let this opportunity slip by simply because the judge is no longer available."

"She's not unavailable," Amy said in a shocked voice. "She's *dead.*"

"It's the same thing," Harriett firmly replied.

"No, it's *not.*" Amy muttered this under her breath, but her words were audible to everyone in the room.

"So sad. But at least *you* got what you wanted." Gwendolyn pointedly looked at Lucy.

How typical, Annie thought. The woman simply could not resist the opportunity to attack the most vulnerable person in the room.

Lucy dropped her fork with a clatter. "What are you talking about? I told you, Prince is perfectly sound. I was planning to ride today."

"Yes, but are you sure you wanted to? Now you'll get to ride in front of someone else. And you did want that, didn't you?"

"Gwendolyn, stop right now." For the first time, Annie heard Melissa speak in a heated tone of voice. "Lucy is as disappointed as the rest of you, and I resent your implying otherwise."

"Well, Judge Bennett's unexpected . . . departure did save her from a miserable score." Nicole seemed intent on exhibiting her own mean streak following Gwendolyn's attack on Lucy.

"Stop it, both of you! We've just lost a respected dressage judge, and all you can think of is how many points she might have scraped off your scores." Now Patricia was up in arms.

"Besides, how is it even possible to find another judge on such short notice?" Melissa asked.

"I've told Brianna that she must find a replacement

by tonight and I expect her to find a way to make it happen." As usual, Harriett put a lid on the discussion.

Tabitha and Liz were silent. Annie wondered how they felt about competing the next day if a judge could even be secured at the last moment. Seeing a judge die could put anyone off her stride. She wondered if they really might prefer to table their tests until the memory of seeing the judge suddenly collapse in her booth had been muted by time and perhaps a change of venue. It would be perfectly understandable if they needed time to process what had occurred today.

Hollis and Brianna came into the dining room as the lunch dishes were being taken away. Brianna looked exhausted, but she was in control of her emotions.

"The majority of the riders have told us they'd be willing to return tomorrow if another judge can be found," she announced to the group. "So that's what I'm trying to do right now."

"Super news," Harriett said approvingly. Brianna ignored her.

"Margaret is still very shaken, and is resting in my cottage right now. I'm hoping we also can find a replacement scribe, because frankly, I don't think she's up for the job."

"As if she ever was," sniffed Gwendolyn.

Brianna went on as if Gwendolyn had never spoken.

"As you know, the police are investigating the death of Judge Bennett. I've talked to them at length, and they'll want to talk to everyone who's staying here at the house."

"Well, that eliminates the trainers," Harriett said, with no little satisfaction. "We're all staying in cottages."

"I'm afraid you're not off the hook," Hollis said gravely. "Everyone who's a guest of ours will have to talk to the police. I'm afraid there's no way around it. The fact is, Harriett, the police believe Jean's death is murder, not an accident. I know many of you were off the premises when the judge had dinner here last night, but as I recall, you and your students remained on the property. I believe it was at your request."

Harriett did not look happy. Hollis looked out at the entire table of women.

"So please do not leave the house until the detectives have had a chance to talk with all of you. Afterward, you're free to go down to the stables or do anything else that you want—unless the police decide to place some restrictions on our movements, which I doubt will happen."

No one said anything, and in the sudden silence, Annie looked around the table. Nicole and Gwendolyn were scowling, which did nothing for either one's complexion. Harriett looked disgruntled but resigned to her fate. Lucy and Amy seemed a bit apprehensive, an understandable reaction, Annie thought. Her gaze turned to Brianna, who was staring impassively at all of them. She wondered what the technical delegate was thinking and feeling right now. Did she regret the words that had flown out of her mouth the moment she realized Judge Bennett was dead? Had she shared them with the police? If not, that would be unwise, since she, Patricia, and Liz had all heard her utter them, and if asked, Annie would tell the truth, as she knew her friends would.

But the real question was, were the words true? Had Judge Bennett looked in the proverbial rearview mirror and seen her jilted lover coming after her? If so, then perhaps there were two killers, not one killer, staying on the Darby estate. Because if Brianna killed the judge, who killed Betsy Gilchrist?

Chapter Fifteen

It seemed like a good time to call Marcus.

"Not another death," he said morosely. Annie had shared the news about the judge's collapse as dispassionately as she could, but it still sounded awful.

"I'm afraid so. We're all hanging around, waiting to talk to a detective. I've already spoken to one deputy, the same guy who interviewed me about Betsy Gilchrist."

She saw no reason to add that Deputy Collins was unquestionably the most drop-dead-gorgeous cop she'd ever laid eyes on. It was an empirical observation that did not need to be shared.

"You're not a suspect, are you?" He sounded a bit anxious.

"No, nor am I likely to be. The poor chef is the one who's on the hot seat. It looks like beverages from his kitchen may have been tampered with. It's very unfair. Most of the time, that kitchen is going like gangbusters, but the chef has been kind enough to let us use it whenever he's not. Anyone could slip in at night and poison the well."

"You weren't kidding about getting a taster. Is, ah, anyone upset at you at the moment?"

She was determined not to mention Gwendolyn's name.

"Nicole is still furious at me, but she's not likely to pour me a drink unless it's over my head."

"As long as it's not acid, you should survive. Tell me, how many people are staying at the Darbys'?"

"Quite a few. Nine or ten, I imagine, and more if you count the trainers staying in the cottages."

"And one of you is a killer? This is beginning to sound like an Agatha Christie reality show."

"Tell me about it. But I hope you've eliminated me from the lineup."

"Oh, yes. And Patricia. And Liz. That leaves only seven or eight."

"Not to mention the maids, groundskeepers, and all the show personnel and volunteers. If you go outside our little group, the list of suspects is pretty much endless."

"Are you sure you don't need an attorney? It's a lot easier to round up someone in LA than it is in eastern Washington."

Marcus had insisted on securing one for Annie last summer, and in retrospect, she was very glad he had. Although of course back then, she'd actually been a suspect.

"Nope. I just need you. Oh, and the show staff is trying to find another judge and scribe now. If they can, then the show will take place tomorrow. I thought it only fair to warn you. I know we'd both hoped to have some time alone."

"I'm a big boy. You won't be riding, so you can hold my hand and tell me what's going on in the arena."

"Hardly. But holding your hand sounds lovely."

Annie felt palpable relief that the misunderstanding of a few nights ago was a thing of the past. She was still curious as to why Marcus had changed his perspective so quickly, but she'd find out soon enough. The important thing was that they were tight once more. Sixteen hours agonizing over the state of the relationship had been long enough.

She'd heard no sound of a doorbell or any kind of activity on the main floor during her conversation, so decided to check in with Undersheriff Kim Williams back home. She wanted to get Kim's take on the events. She got it in spades.

"It sure sounds like poisoning to me, Annie. True, I'm just going off what you've told me and without reading the autopsies. But I'm thinking both the raspberry iced tea and Lady Grey are fairly aromatic. It wouldn't be out of reach to add a poison that didn't have a strong taste or smell."

"I can vouch for the iced tea—aromatic and yummy. And I assume Lady Grey is a special blend with its own fragrance. What kind of poison are we talking about?"

"Oh, the mind boggles. Cyanide, arsenic, any number of street drugs, indigenous plants such as belladonna. Even a household product like turpentine will cause the symptoms you saw with the judge."

"Since when did you become an expert on poisons?"

"They do teach us something at the academy. And I took a course on the subject a couple of years ago. Fascinating. You'd be amazed at how deadly substances can become when taken the wrong way or in excess. I'm not just talking about alcohol. Nature can be hazardous to your health."

"I'll bear that in mind the next time I'm traipsing through a field of flowers."

"Do that. And if that chef of yours serves you quail for dinner one night, make sure the bird hasn't been around hemlock."

"What? You mean the stuff that killed Socrates?"

"The quail's immune to the seeds. But we aren't. Eat a quail that's been feasting on hemlock seeds, and it'll be the last breath you ever take without an intubation tube."

"You really know how to cheer up a gal, don't you?"

"Well, you asked. Anyway, I'm sure the teas are being analyzed now by the local crime lab."

"No one's consulted me, but I assume so. I expect this second death has made both a high priority."

"Keep me informed. And try to stay out of trouble. You're not a suspect, are you?"

"You're the second person to ask me that today. I'm beginning to take it personally."

By midafternoon, the detective still had not shown up. Annie had run out of people to talk to back home, and everyone seemed to be keeping their own counsel in their rooms. She wandered down to the library to find a book that would take her mind off the impending interview, first looking around the room for any remaining signs of Gwendolyn and Nicole's row.

There were none that she could see, but then, the room looked freshly vacuumed and dusted. She moved on to the books. It was an impressive collection. On the side by a fireplace that looked as if it was used as seldom as the library, she noticed a vast set of tomes on history, philosophy, and world religions. If it had been designed to impress, it had succeeded. She turned to the wall behind the sitting area. Here were rows and rows of well-thumbed mysteries. She saw dozens of books by Agatha Christie, several more by Dorothy Sayers, and a complete set of Sue Grafton's series.

She'd just chosen a book at random when the doorbell ominously rang—or at least, that's what it sounded like to Annie in her current mental state. She quickly shelved the book, waited a moment, and walked out to the foyer. Hollis was already at the front door. He appeared to have come out of nowhere, but then she remembered the silent elevator at the end of the hall that whisked the couple back and forth from their suite.

"Annie, come and meet Detective Wollcott. This is Annie Carson, one of our guests. She arrived last Wednesday."

She shook hands with the detective. Although not as handsome as Deputy Collins, he had his own style of charm. Detective Wollcott was in his late fifties and had thick salt-and-pepper hair. He looked intelligent and reasonably kind, his eyes looked at her with interest, and she suspected that he listened well. Another deputy stood by him, carrying a large leather bag. Apparently, the other man held too lowly a position to merit any introduction.

"I'm familiar with your name," Detective Wollcott

told her. "I understand you'd met both of the women who died."

"That sounds so macabre. But yes, I met Betsy Gilchrist on Wednesday and Judge Bennett last evening."

"Which makes you the only houseguest who met both victims."

Now wait a minute, she thought. If he was implying that somehow made her a suspect, she was going to be more than a tad ticked. But she tabled her emotion.

"What you say is true," she replied simply.

"That should put you in a good position to help us since you saw both shortly before they were poisoned."

That was better. Although Annie wondered if his you'll-be-such-a-help approach was merely a ploy to make her think she was above suspicion when she really was not. Then she realized he'd said the women had been poisoned.

"Are you sure that poison is what caused their deaths?"

"Looks that way. We've turned up the heat on the crime lab and coroner and have a preliminary report from the latter on the Gilchrist death. I can't tell you more, but I'm sure you can connect the dots. But please keep this information to yourself. I've told Mr. and Mrs. Darby, and they've assured me you can be trusted."

"Absolutely."

"Good. Where are we meeting with the guests, Mr. Darby?"

"Please, call me Hollis. I thought we'd convene in the library. It's quite private, and with the door closed, no one will be able to hear our conversation. Although other than the women staying here, there aren't many people left to overhear you. I'll go fetch our guests now."

Annie followed Detective Wollcott into the library and watched his deputy set up a video camera at one end on the room and arrange seats so that the camera lens would take in the entire group. *Much better than taking notes,* Annie thought. She knew if he'd been in Washington, he'd have to get everyone's permission to film the interview before he could proceed, and wondered if the same was true here.

When the deputy was done arranging chairs, she chose the one closest to the collection of mystery books, which gave her a clear view of the room and door. Guests began to trickle in, all looking uncertain of what to do, although Annie thought the semi-circle of chairs made it obvious. She caught Patricia's eye as she entered with Liz, and nodded over to where she was seated. Alas, Lucy was standing in front of Patricia and took the nod as directed toward her. She smiled and quickly walked over and claimed her space next to Annie. Patricia and Liz gave her "oh well" shrugs and sat to the back of them, along with Amy.

The last to arrive was Nicole, whose hurried and distracted entrance made clear her displeasure at having her busy schedule disrupted. The downside to her timing was that she was forced to take the last seat, which was front and center. Nicole looked none too happy at being in the fishbowl spot, but she had no choice. She frowned as she sat down to emphasize that the meeting was intruding on her valuable time.

After introducing himself, as well as identifying his deputy as Michael Watts, Detective Wollcott explained the format of the meeting.

"We don't often interview witnesses together," he

explained, "but in the interest of time, I've decided to do so with all of you. If any of you offers up an interesting observation that might help us find Judge Bennett's killer, I'll follow up privately."

Hollis had already described the judge's death as murder, but somehow Detective Wollcott's statement seemed more provocative. Annie looked at the group to gauge their reaction. She'd heard Lucy's sharp intake of breath, and she could sense that Amy, sitting behind them, also was rattled. Tabitha looked absolutely in shock, wide-eyed and unblinking. The rest of the group was silent. Nicole looked at her nails.

"We've already spoken to many of the show personnel, including Brianna Bowen, the steward, and—"

"Technical delegate. Brianna is a technical delegate, not a steward."

Annie was amused to hear Gwendolyn's clear voice correcting the detective, who, she noticed, also looked amused.

"Thank you, Ms. . . ."

"Smythe. I'm Gwendolyn Smythe, Smythe with a *y* and an *e* on the end."

"Thank you, Ms. Smythe. As I was saying, we've interviewed Ms. Bowen, the technical delegate, and the judge's scribe, Margaret Woods. Both of them agreed to being videotaped. It's our preferred way of conducting interviews these days because it leaves such little room for error or for doubt about what was said. But we'll need permission from each of you before we begin our questions. Does anyone here have any objection to being filmed on camera for this interview?"

Detective Wollcott looked around. Several people were shaking their heads, confirming it was fine with them. No one said a word.

"Fine. Then we'll let Deputy Watts get the camera going. We always start the process by asking each of you to say and spell your name, and state for the record that you agree to be audio- and video-recorded. Which means I'm afraid you'll have to repeat yourself, Ms. Smythe."

Once these preliminaries were done, Detective Wollcott continued.

"As you know, Judge Bennett took ill shortly after the start of the dressage show this morning. We're in the process of taking statements from everyone who was present at the event when this occurred. I want to confirm that you all know that the stables are off-limits to all of you at the moment."

Heads nodded throughout the room.

"Good. When we're done with our work, you'll be free to use them again. In the meantime, if there's anyone you know who was at the stables but may have left before Judge Bennett took ill, please give me their names now."

"My groom," Nicole said. "He left around seven forty-five this morning. He was supposed to return around one thirty. I was scheduled to ride an hour later. Will your men have let him in?"

There was nothing particularly off-putting about the words, but the way Nicole expressed them made it clear that she would be extremely upset if her groom had not been given access to the stables.

"I'm sorry, Ms.—I'm doubly sorry, I've already forgotten your last name."

"Forrester. Nicole Anne Forrester. Maybe we should all have put on name tags to make your job easier."

"What an excellent suggestion. And I'm sorry, Ms. Forrester, but I'm afraid the grounds have been off-limits since nine thirty this morning. So, unless he returned before then—"

"He didn't. And now I have no one looking after my horse."

Detective Wollcott paused. He was sizing her up, Annie thought, and just realized he's got his hands full with this one. He gave an almost inaudible sigh.

"I know this must be a great inconvenience for all of you, but it's only temporary. We're hoping to have the scene cleared by six o'clock. You can call your groom and assure him of that."

Nicole abruptly stood up and turned as if to leave to make the call at once.

"I meant," Detective Wollcott said gently, "you should feel free to call him when our meeting is over. At the moment, I'd prefer that no one leave the room."

Nicole slowly sat down again, her angry eyes on the detective.

"Why don't we start with you, Ms. Forrester? If you could just give us a brief account of your movements today, starting from the time you awakened."

Nicole looked if she'd been asked to disrobe in front of a crowd of strangers.

"What time did you get up?" the detective asked encouragingly.

Nicole scrunched in her chair, as if she couldn't get comfortable. "Six o'clock," she finally answered.

"Very good. And did you go down for breakfast?"

"Not then. I was in my room until about seven. Then I left for the stables. I talked with Miguel, my groom, reviewed what he'd done, then talked briefly with Brianna, the technical delegate, as well as the barn manager. There have been issues with Andy's feed the past few days. No one seems to be able to get it right."

"How did you get to the stables?"

"I took my Jaguar. It was parked out in back."

"And the license plate is . . ."

Nicole looked at the detective as if he'd gone mad, but reeled off the tag numbers and letters.

"I drove back to the house an hour later and went to the breakfast room. That woman"—Nicole pointed to Annie—"came in just as I was leaving. Then I went to my room and stayed there until Hollis knocked on my door to tell me the judge had died, and the show had been called off."

"What time was this?"

"Oh, I don't know. About ten thirty, I think."

"Why didn't you return to the stables after breakfast?"

Nicole smiled at the detective as if he were a small, ignorant child.

"I told you. My test wasn't until midafternoon. There was no reason to be down at the stables hours before I had to ride. I was one of the few riders riding an FEI level test. Prix St.-Georges, to be precise. FEI tests are usually scheduled later in the day, when the show has the biggest crowd."

Annie knew most of the other women in the room could have throttled Nicole right about now. It wasn't just because she'd admitted she had no interest in seeing her fellow riders perform. It was because she was so certain that everyone was dying to see her oh-so-special ride. The woman was completely insufferable.

"Did you have any contact with Judge Bennett?"

"No, of course not."

Detective Wollcott looked sharply at her, as if he didn't trust the veracity of her answer.

"None of us would." Again, Nicole used the same patronizing voice reserved for people who aren't very bright. "It's in the rules. We shouldn't have any contact with the show judge before we ride."

The detective smiled. "That's good to know. If everyone had followed that rule, perhaps we wouldn't be here right now, discussing Judge Bennett's death."

Annie felt she had to speak up even though she knew Hollis already had told him about her presence at dinner last night.

"I'm not a competitor, so not restricted by those rules. I saw the judge last night at dinner. I also saw her this morning, in the judge's booth."

"Did you observe the scribe bringing her tea?"

"I did. I saw her leave for the house and return, then pour out a cup of tea. She was cutting it pretty close to the wire. The judge had already rung her bell, and the first rider was gearing up to enter the ring."

"Is there anything in that sequence you've just described that seemed out of place, or odd?"

She looked at Detective Wollcott, and said firmly, "No, there was nothing I saw that was odd about the way the scribe obtained the tea for the judge, other than being late."

She could have added, "But there are a lot of other odd things I could tell you about." Such as the two people who had been poisoned for no apparent reason. The destruction of one rider's personal gear, delivered with a nasty note that made no sense. Or Gwendolyn and Nicole's argument over something that Nicole knew or did that may or may not have pertained to Betsy Gilchrist's death. Not to mention

Brianna's emotional outburst with Jean Bennett hours before the judge's death.

Everything was just too damn odd. Including the new fact that Nicole claimed to have stayed in her room after breakfast for nearly two solid hours before Hollis had knocked on her door. But Annie was sure she'd heard the front door slam moments after Nicole had made her departure from the dining room. If Nicole hadn't slammed the door, who did?

The detective looked back at her and nodded. Annie felt better. She would inform the police of all the strange conversations and happenings and would let them sort it out. She had no intention of saying anything now. Not when she knew the killer, or killers, were in the room with her at that very moment.

Chapter Sixteen

"Shall we move on?" Detective Wollcott smiled at Lucy as he sat down next to her.

"Okay," Lucy said faintly. Her cheeks were bright red. Annie tried to give her an encouraging glance.

"I set my alarm for six o'clock," she began in a nearly inaudible voice.

"Excuse me one moment. It's Ms. Cartwright, isn't it? You'll have to speak up. The microphone on the camera can't pick up your soft voice. Can you do that? Or we could get a microphone for you."

Detective Wollcott's suggestion that her delivery could be amplified pulled Lucy out of her shell. She sat up, cleared her throat, and began again in a much stronger voice.

"Amy and I had both agreed to get to the stables by seven," she started again. "So, we both set our alarms for six and met in the dining room around six thirty."

"Amy? Rather, Ms. Litchfield? Can you confirm this?"

"Yes, everything Lucy's said is true. And I was with

her almost the entire morning. So, I'm just going to say the same thing."

"Very good. Then you need speak up only if you want to correct anything that Ms. Cartwright says, or to tell us about when your paths diverged."

Lucy glanced back at her friend, looking a bit cheated at having drawn the short end of the stick in regard to talking. But she turned back, looked at the detective, and continued.

"When we got to the dining room, Tabitha was already there. She was just finishing her breakfast and left about five minutes later."

"Thank you for clarifying. Did you talk about anything with Ms. Rawlins during those few minutes she was with you?"

"Not really. It was too early to talk. And I think we were all thinking about our performances today."

"Quite understandable."

Detective Wollcott's empathetic interjections were doing the job. Annie could feel Lucy begin to relax beside her.

"Breakfast didn't take very long, and we got down to the stables at seven, like we'd planned. We walked."

She paused, looking up at the detective, who merely smiled and nodded to continue.

"Melissa, our trainer, was already there. She was with my horse, Prince. Prince had had a hoof issue, and we wanted to make sure I'd be able to ride."

"How was Prince?"

"Just fine." Lucy emphasized the two words and stole a quick look at Gwendolyn, who was looking down as if she found something fascinating about her lap.

"Prince was groomed already, and after checking on him, I was really there to help Amy groom Schumann. That's her horse's name. Neither of us was scheduled to ride until almost eleven thirty, but it takes a while to get button braids done."

"How on earth do you create button braids, if I may ask?"

"They're quite difficult, actually," Lucy confided to the detective. "Especially the way Amy wanted them, tight and close together. Each one has to be braided, then folded over, then folded over again into a button. We used yarn to keep the braid in place, then tiny rubber bands to make them into buttons."

"And the horse doesn't mind?"

"Oh, no. I think they know that when their manes are braided, they're going to compete. They get super excited."

"Funny. When my six-year-old granddaughter gets her hair braided, she knows she's going to school, and the reaction isn't quite the same."

No one laughed, although Lucy gave Detective Wollcott a smile that seemed truly genuine.

"We were nearly finished with the mane around the time the show started, so Melissa, Amy, and I went outside to take a break and see the first few riders test. We didn't want to miss seeing Liz and Sammy. They were scheduled to compete right after the first rider."

"How nice of you to support your fellow riders, Ms. Cartwright. One question before we move on. Did you see anyone in this room now at the stables when you were there this morning? I'm talking about the period before the show began."

Lucy looked around. "Not really. When we got to

the stables, we went straight to our horses' stalls. They're next to each other. Anyway, we braided Schumann in his stall, so we wouldn't have seen anyone if they had come in. And some of the other riders' stalls are at the other end of the building."

Detective Wollcott nodded thoughtfully.

"We did see a few people once we were outside. We looked especially for Liz, since she was about to ride. We could see her in the warm-up ring with Patricia. We were too far away to make contact, but we could see her. And then we saw Annie, right by the warm-up ring. We all waved, and Annie went over to say hi to Liz."

"Anyone else? Ms. Smythe? Ms. Forrester? Or any of the trainers?"

Lucy shook her head.

"Let's see, I'm missing someone." Detective Wollcott consulted a list in his hand. "Ah, yes, of course. Did you see Ms. Rawlins again, after she'd left the breakfast room?"

Lucy thought for a moment. "Not then. I saw her afterward, after the ambulance had left and we were all wondering what happened. But not before."

"Thank you, Ms. Cartwright. You've been very thorough and clear. Ms. Litchfield, do you have anything to add? No? Well, if either of you thinks of anything you might have missed, you will let me know, won't you?"

"Excuse me, Detective? There's just one thing. Remember, Lucy, we needed sharper scissors, and Melissa said she had a pair in her cottage."

Lucy's face turned a brilliant red. "Oh, yes," she said softly. "I forgot."

"Did one of you return to fetch the scissors?"

"Yes, Lucy did. Melissa said to take the golf cart. It was parked outside, and no one was using it. You weren't gone long. Only five or ten minutes."

"I can see how that little side trip could have slipped your mind, Ms. Cartwright. Please, just tell us what you did on your short jaunt."

Lucy seemed to have difficulty speaking. In her soft voice, she said, "I drove to Melissa's cottage, found the scissors, and returned."

"And about what time was this, do you think?"

"I don't know."

"I know, Lucy! It was ten after eight. I know because Melissa said something about having less than an hour to finish Schumann's mane, and asked me if I thought that was enough time."

"Did you happen to look at your watch when Lucy returned, Ms. Litchfield?"

Amy looked a bit crestfallen. "No. But honestly, it wasn't very long, just five or ten minutes. She came back with the scissors, and we went back to work."

"And which road did you take, Ms. Cartwright? The footpath or the one used by cars?"

"The footpath. Until you reach the circular drive. Then you have to veer off to get to Melissa's cottage."

"Did you happen to see any other guests on this brief trip?"

Lucy shook her head no. She looked as if she'd used up all her words and could say no more.

Detective Wollcott seemed to sense this.

"Thank you for remembering that little detail. Now, Ms. Phelps, why don't you tell us about your morning."

And so it went for the next two hours. Each woman gave her version of her morning, from sunup, which

Annie learned was when all of them arose, until nine o'clock, when Judge Bennett succumbed to whatever noxious substance had been placed in her tea. It was no surprise that Melissa was the earliest to arise. The woman had worn a path from the house to the stables over the past few days in her dedication to Lucy's horse. And she'd skipped breakfast that morning.

"I didn't sleep very well last night, for some reason," she told the detective, a bit embarrassed over this nocturnal detail. "I gave up around four thirty and read for an hour or so. I wasn't hungry, so just grabbed a thermos from the kitchen and headed over to the stables. I think I got there about five forty-five, more or less. I know I had time to look at Prince myself before the show vet showed up at six. We both agreed that Prince was sound, and Lucy would be able to ride him. I knew Lucy would be thrilled by the news. Prince had already been groomed and was enjoying his breakfast, so I went out to the front room to wait for the girls to arrive. I was eating a donut when they showed up at seven."

Melissa also confirmed she'd consumed the entire thermos of coffee from the kitchen and had suffered no ill effects.

As far as early risers, Tabitha came in a close second. She told Detective Wollcott she'd awakened at five, meditated in her room for an hour, then gone down to breakfast. No one was there, and the breakfast buffet looked untouched. Amy and Lucy had shown up when she was about to leave, and no, nothing of substance was said by any of them, they were all too worried about their upcoming performances. They all wished each other good luck, but that was all she remembered. Tabitha walked to the stables and got there around six thirty. She braided her horse's mane and groomed him, then walked back to the house to take a shower and get dressed. Like Nicole, she wasn't riding until later in the day, although she intended to return to the stables that morning to watch other riders in the ring. She was pretty sure she'd left the stables at eight o'clock, give or take a few minutes.

"Did you happen to see Ms. Cartwright on the golf cart?"

"No. But you can't see the cottages from the main footpath, so she might have been on it someplace where I couldn't see her."

"Yes, of course." The detective then turned to Nicole.

"Wasn't that around the same time you also returned to the house, Ms. Forrester?"

Nicole had been staring out the window, studiously trying to give the impression that she was not listening to a word anyone said.

"More or less."

"Well, let's try to be as precise as we can, shall we? Did you happen to look at your watch before you left, or perhaps when you got back to the house?"

"I left right at eight," she said angrily. "My fiancé phoned me just as I was getting into my car. He always phones me at that time. It's what he does."

"How very romantic of him. Did you see Ms. Rawlins walking to the house at any point?"

"No."

"Really? Wouldn't you have expected to have seen her?"

"Not really. The footpath is on one side, and the road is on the other."

"I saw *you.*" The accusatory tone of Tabitha's words was unmistakable.

"Oh, yes?"

"Yes. I was ahead of you, and watched you drive right by. I don't see how you could have missed me."

"Must have had my eyes on the road."

"Must have."

Detective Wollcott decided it was time to intervene.

"How about back at the house? Did the two of you . . . run into each other there?"

"No." Both women answered at the same time, with the same amount of forcefulness.

"I went straight to my room," Tabitha said. "I needed a shower."

"And I went straight to breakfast," Nicole said brightly. "I didn't."

A soft knock on the library door caused ten sets of eyes to turn toward it. A moment later, Jorge entered with a large tray of cups and saucers.

"Excuse me," he mumbled to the inhabitants of the room. "Chef Gustav asked that I bring in some refreshments."

"Thank you so much," Detective Wollcott said, although he looked a bit critically at the coffee and hot water urns next hauled in. No one went near them.

"Right." The detective walked to the back of the room, where the trainers and Gwendolyn were seated. "Let's move on, shall we?"

"Well, I might as well join the lineup," Gwendolyn said grumpily.

"Excellent, Ms. Smythe. Tell us how you spent your morning."

"It's pretty simple. I got up around six, showered and dressed, then walked over to Harriett's cottage. I got there about seven fifteen. We had coffee, chatted a bit, then drove to the stables in my car, which is a Porsche, by the way, the only one in the lot. I think we got there around seven forty-five?"

Gwendolyn looked inquiringly at her trainer, who nodded, and said, "Seven forty-four, if you want to be accurate."

"Okay, fine. Seven forty-four. Harriett always knows best." She sighed. "Harriett went to my horse's stall first, to check the grooming job on Martinique. I went to the tack room to get a few things, and saw Nicole talking to the stable manager in the aisle, haranguing her about something to do with Andy's feed. I tried to shut her out. It was too early in the morning to hear someone else's argument, and Nicole was quite shrill, even by her standards. When I got to the tack room, Tabitha was rooting around in her tack chest and going on and on about her stupid rhythm beads, which were still missing. Since she'd said it all before, I didn't add to the conversation. I just got what I needed and left."

"Even I could hear Nicole," Harriett told the detective. "She seemed to be obsessed."

"Well, if your horse was receiving the same poor care that mine is getting, you'd have been angry, too!"

"Oh, stop." Gwendolyn told Nicole, trying to look bored. "Andy's on the same feed as everyone else in the stables."

"That's the problem!"

"Getting back to times, Ms. Blechstein, do you recall seeing Ms. Rawlins when you arrived?"

"Yes, Gwendolyn came back from the tack room and mentioned seeing Tabitha inside. I saw her leave a few minutes later, a minute before eight o'clock."

right now, but remember, no one is going down
e stables until you get the all clear from me. So
w would be an excellent time to get this one last
k done."

Annie stood up and stretched. She thought Detec-
e Wollcott had done an admirable job of eliciting
formation out of the group. Handling ten female
gos at once was not for the fainthearted, especially
hen none of the women probably had ever given a
statement to the police before in their lives. She
turned to get in line for her statement form, but
Detective Wollcott was suddenly beside her.

"Ms. Carson? I think your statement can wait a
while. Would you mind coming with me?"

"Did the two of you talk?"

"Only to tell her what I thought of her grooming
job. She said she'd be back in an hour or two to correct her mistakes."

"And the two of you stayed in the stables up until
the time the show was to start?"

"That's correct," Harriett told the detective. "Although we didn't go out to watch. We only went out
when we heard the commotion and realized something had happened."

Gwendolyn looked as if she regretted not seeing
the judge's fatal collapse.

Looking around the room, the detective spotted
Liz and Patricia in the back, on the far side.

"That leaves just the two of you. It's Ms. Winters
and Ms. Faraday, isn't it?"

"I'm sure everyone is tired, so we'll try to be extremely brief." Patricia's clipped British accent was a
welcome relief from the ugly tones Gwendolyn and
Nicole had employed.

"Why don't I start?" Liz asked her trainer, who
nodded. "We'd agreed that whoever was up first would
text the other. That happened to be me. I couldn't
sleep past five, so got up, had a cup of coffee in my
room, and texted Patricia that I was heading over to
the stables. As you've heard, I was the second to ride,
at 9:08, and I still needed to groom my horse. I showered, dressed, and got over to the barn pretty quickly—
I remember it was around six fifteen on my watch. But
Patricia had beaten me to it."

"I didn't have to spend half the time she did dressing," Patricia explained with a smile. "I just threw on
my breeches and headed down to the barn. I walked,
of course. It's so lovely out that time of morning,

before the heat takes over. I arrived a little after six and headed straight for Sammy's stall."

"We both saw Melissa looking at Lucy's horse with the show vet," Liz added. "Prince is stabled a few doors down from mine. But I can't remember seeing anyone else, can you, Patricia?"

Patricia shook her head no. "We had our hands full braiding Sammy's mane and making him beautiful. I knew people were coming and going, and I expect not just from our group. I'd seen a few new trailers when I was walking down to the stables, so other contestants were driving in at that hour, too. At eight fifteen, we brought Sammy over to the warm-up ring, and that's where we were when the show started, or was to have started, I should say."

"Annie came over briefly to wish us luck." Liz flashed her a warm smile. "But aside from Melissa and Annie, I don't recall seeing a single other soul from the house. But this was supposed to be my first test. I had other things on my mind."

"I'm sure you did." Detective Wollcott gave her a small nod and turned to the entire room of women.

"Thank you all for sharing what you remember. I believe I have a much clearer idea of how you all spent the early hours of the morning, and just want to make sure I have a few things right. It appears that when the dressage show began, the only two riders left in the house were Ms. Forrester and Ms. Rawlins. Am I right? Good. Ms. Faraday was on her horse in the warm-up arena, along with her trainer, Ms. Winters. The rest of you were still in the stables or in the vicinity, with the exception of Ms. Carson, who was seated in the spectator tiers."

"Who isn't competing," Gwendolyn loudly broke in.

"Just so. And among all of you, five [...] the dining room at various times. Tha[...] Carson and Ms. Forrester, who saw each [...] and Ms. Cartwright, Ms. Litchfield, and [...] who also all saw each other in passing. Al[...]

The women mentioned nodded in assen[...] Nicole's contribution was barely noticeable[...]

"Good. One last question. Did any of you, [...] you had breakfast or not, happen to go i[...] kitchen this morning? Ms. Phelps, you've alrea[...] us you went in to collect a thermos of coffee. D[...] of the rest of you have reason to visit the kitchen[...] to nine o'clock?

"Amy and I took in our breakfast plates after [...] ate." Lucy spoke up immediately.

"As did I. On my way out, I also picked up a thermo[...] of coffee," Annie added.

"Anyone else? No one else picked up a thermos [...] coffee? All right, then." The detective glanced at [...] watch, then at Deputy Watts. "We're now conclud[...] the group interview of the Darbys' guests at 5:05 [...] and turning off all recording devices. Thank [...] ladies, for your patience and understanding. [...] you go, if you would please pick up a statemer[...] from Deputy Watts over here. I know we've go[...] on tape, but we'd also like for you to write do[...] you've told us for our files."

Nicole and Gwendolyn had already arisen [...] heading for the door. Annie could tell si[...] their respective backs that they were no[...] being restrained further from whateve[...] wanted to do. Detective Wollcott also [...] displeasure.

"I know, it's not how you'd like to be [...]

Chapter Seventeen

"I'm not sure I fully understand how you all managed not to see each other. I mean, the house is crawling with women. Yet everyone seemed to have passed like ships in the night."

Detective Wollcott looked utterly perplexed, and Annie smiled at him.

"It's really not that difficult. Over the past few days, I've often been in the Darbys' home or walking to and from the stables and felt that no one else was about. The estate is quite large. We all have our own private bedroom suites. The place you're most likely to find anyone is at the stables."

"Yes, but even there, no one seems to have run across a fellow rider."

"You have to understand that dressage essentially is a very solitary sport. I understand that on occasion there's some collaboration, but in the main, all these women are competing only with their horse, and that's their primary focus. Especially on the day of a show. It's not surprising that everyone had her head in the clouds."

The detective shook his head. "I'll take your word for it. Anyway, the surveillance cameras will bear out the authenticity of their stories. Most of their stories, anyway. Apparently the cameras don't extend to the bedroom areas or inside the kitchen."

"That's a tough break. Just where you need them most."

Annie was sitting with the detective on the private veranda. Chef Gustav had brought out tea and cookies, and Annie made a point of pouring each of them a cup, desired or not.

"I consider you the observant outsider, Ms. Carson. Did any of these women truly have reason to want Jean Bennett dead?"

"It's Annie, please. And no, I can't think of anyone who actually hated the judge so much that she would try to eliminate her from her role by killing her. She had a reputation as a tough judge, but I'm sure that the majority of dressage judges fit that description."

She paused. Now would be the time to tell the detective about the conversation she had overheard between Brianna and the judge. Unfortunately, the Darbys chose that moment to make an entrance.

"How's the case progressing, Detective? Any new leads?" Hollis helped Miriam into one of the patio chairs, then sat down himself. "I can't tell you how many times I've used that line on a movie set."

Detective Wollcott smiled wryly. "Not as many as I'd like. I'm sure the deaths of the two women are connected, but until we find out what that connection is, it's damned tough to pin down a suspect. How are things progressing in the kitchen?"

Annie had seen two officers enter the kitchen on their way out to the private veranda. She hoped Chef Gustav was nowhere nearby. He would be horrified to see mere mortals, especially ones with badges, pawing their way through every nook and cranny of his beloved kitchen.

"I was only allowed to peek in, but from what I saw, as best as can be expected. I sent the chef out to the garden and told him not to return until I said so. And your men seem to be doing a reasonable job of keeping things tidy."

"Aside from the tea, we're really only looking for some obvious poison on the premises, so it shouldn't take too long. As soon as the crime lab gives us a complete analysis, that is. Then we might be back. Just a heads-up."

"I understand. If I might ask, how are things proceeding at the stables?"

"Nearly done. By the time I finish up with Ms. Carson, I think we'll all be on our way and out of your hair."

"Good. Keeping these women from their horses is proving a bit difficult. Which reminds me. Our show staff is trying mightily to find a replacement judge and scribe, with the hope that the show can take place tomorrow. Do you have any objection?"

"In other words, will the presence of the Sheriff's Office interfere with your entertainment? Barring another murder in the next twenty-four hours, I should think not. Although if police business requires us to talk to anyone on your property, we will be back, dressage show or no. But honestly, Hollis, a well-publicized murder has just occurred on your estate, and the killer may well be residing in your home. Do you really want the potential liability of another murder taking place when the public's around? We don't know who we're dealing with—someone with a grudge, or someone who's just plain crazy. I would be very cautious. Have you thought about bringing in private protection? It wouldn't be a bad idea right now."

"Miriam and I have already discussed that option, and we've agreed to do so, if for no other reason than to keep the media at bay. And I say that with all due irony. I believe it's one of the few times when we haven't wanted the media on our doorstep. But finding a substitute judge who's willing to come in on such short notice is not as easy as it sounds. The show may or may not go on."

"If you decide to do so, I can't stop you. But it just doesn't seem like the right time to put on a horse show. Not if it provokes a killer."

"You have no idea how unhappy a lot of women would be if they didn't have a chance to perform."

"Well, let me know what happens with your search for a replacement. If you do decide to go forward, I'll do my best to send out some plainclothes cops to keep an eye out. No promises, you understand."

"Thank you, Detective. It's gratifying to see our tax dollars at work."

The Darbys made their exit, leaving Detective Wollcott again shaking his head. He looked more perplexed than before.

"What is it about these women and their horses?" he asked Annie.

"It's complicated," she told him. "Just trust me on this. More tea?"

* * *

The tea was delicious, and Annie felt revived by the beverage, not to mention the heavenly madeleine cookies that accompanied it. The detective seemed to relax, as well. He set his cup down and leaned back in his chair.

"Let's get back to the judge. Tell me how each woman felt about her, as far as you know."

Annie thought for a moment. "Well, two of the riders knew her only by reputation. They were to ride in front of her for the first time today. That would be Liz and Gwendolyn. The rest of the women had been judged by her before, and none seemed to think too highly of her scoring, although that could just be sour grapes, of course. Harriett, one of the trainers, apparently has had a particularly bad experience with her, but she certainly never threatened the woman in my presence. She only warned her students about how tough she could be."

She hesitated. Would the detective care about the destroyed rhythm beads? Well, it couldn't hurt to tell him.

"Tabitha mentioned something once about the judge's having put a hex on her horse although I can't believe she was serious. However, she is into some kind of woo-woo mysticism, and has been unreasonably upset about the disappearance of her horse's rhythm beads. What's worse, she doesn't know the half of it."

The detective sat up. "Rhythm beads? What are those?"

"Something you drape over a horse's neck, which, if you believe Tabitha, improves your performance in the ring. She's got lots of stuff like that—charms and amulets that are mostly horse bling and couldn't be worn in front of the judge, anyway. They're not allowed. But Tabitha does takes great stock in them, and when the beads disappeared a few days ago, she went temporarily berserk looking for them."

"Do you think this has anything to do with the judge?"

Annie hesitated. "No. Just one of the guests who is trying to spook Tabitha. And has succeeded."

"How do you know this?"

"I found them. The strap that held the beads was wrapped around Tabitha's bedroom doorknob. All the beads had been taken out. And there was a note that came with it, that said—" Annie tried to visualize the block letters she'd read. "It read 'remember to quit while you're ahead.' Oh, and there was a piece of rosemary wrapped up in the strap. As in rosemary is for remembrance, à la Ophelia."

The detective was staring at her as if she was as mad as Hamlet's sister.

"I'm not making this up," she said simply.

"I wish you were. Go on. When did you find this?"

"Oh . . . it was Thursday, Thursday night. I was heading for bed around eleven and saw them on Tabitha's bedroom door. I took them off and gave them to Hollis the next day. He's the one who made the rosemary connection."

"Who do you think is responsible? You must have an opinion."

When she'd talked to Hollis, Annie had had no problem asserting either Nicole or Gwendolyn had to have been responsible. Now, in front of the detective, she wasn't at all sure she wanted to share what she believed. Detective Wollcott decided to make her job a bit easier.

"Ms. Forrester, I'm guessing, is one suspect. And Ms. Smythe, perhaps? They each seem to be the type of woman who would stoop to something like what you've just described."

"Bingo. Although there's no evidence to suggest either one's guilt, and in fact, Nicole was off on a date with her fiancé that night, and Hollis is sure her car hadn't returned at the time I found the broken necklace."

"So that leaves Ms. Smythe."

"Yes. She was visiting Harriett in her cottage. We don't know what time she came back to the house." She paused again and reminded herself to ask Hollis to tidy up this small detail. "And there's something else you should know about Gwendolyn and Nicole's relationship. Something that might pertain to Betsy Gilchrist's death."

"I'm listening."

As Annie described the contretemps she'd over-heard in the library and the ensuing brawl, she wondered if there was anyone in the house who didn't have a secret they wished kept hidden. It seemed that half the women harbored information about the others that they wouldn't hesitate to use if it bene-fited them.

"Does Hollis know about this, as well?" the detective asked when she was finished.

"He knows something occurred. The chef over-heard the physical fight and stopped it. But he doesn't know why they were arguing. Or, I should say, if he does, he hasn't shared it with me."

"Interesting. What was your take on Ms. Smythe's veiled accusations?"

"My gut tells me Nicole is involved with Betsy's husband, Gwendolyn found out about it, and was threatening to tell Douglas, Nicole's fiancé. But this was before the judge's death. I wasn't taking the poison theory seriously. At least three of us picked up a glass of iced tea on a tray, and only one of us died. Poison didn't make sense. I thought it more likely someone had rigged Betsy's car, and I couldn't visualize Nicole doing that. And I still thought Betsy's death might truly have been accidental."

"It wasn't, believe me. I wish I could tell you more."

"Well, just to make your day complete, there's one more conversation I overheard that you should know about. It happened last night, and Hollis doesn't know about this one, either. Although he may know the circumstances surrounding it."

"You're confusing me. Tell me what you know."

Annie noticed that the detective's agreeable bedside manner, so evident in the library, was missing from their conversation. She wasn't put off by his change in demeanor. Quite the contrary. He was speaking to her like an equal, and that was far more complimentary than being coddled.

"Interesting," he said again after Annie had related what she'd heard in the trees between Brianna and the judge. "Brianna copped to knowing the judge at the university. Said she was an adviser of some sort for her graduate studies. But she didn't mention the romance. You saw the judge collapse, right? I don't suppose you saw Brianna's reaction to that?"

"As a matter of fact, I did," Annie said reluctantly.

"Not at the exact time of the collapse, but a minute or two later. As soon as the judge crumpled to the ground, I ran toward the booth. Brianna was running just as fast from the other direction, and we got there at the same time. We moved the judge out on the lawn and got her settled. Then Brianna left to call 9-1-1. I don't think she fully trusted the skills of the show medic who'd arrived. She did seem a bit inexperienced. This may have been her first real emergency. But while we were fighting to keep the judge alive, Brianna was absolutely professional and together."

"How do we know she called 9-1-1? I thought you stayed with the judge."

"Not for long. Liz is an RN trained in ER procedures. Once she arrived, I took off to find the emergency respiratory kit. It was clear we needed one, and the medic hadn't had the presence of mind to bring it with her. I didn't have the slightest idea where it was, so I ran to the office to ask Brianna. She was on the phone with a 9-1-1 operator then."

"How'd she seem at that point?"

"A bit more emotional. Concerned. But still under control."

"And when was she not under control?"

Annie sighed. She didn't want to share what she'd heard but knew she didn't have a choice.

"When the paramedic told us the judge had died. Brianna was terribly upset. I was afraid she was going to faint. I grabbed her, and she said something about it being all her fault, and that she had killed her."

"Meaning the judge? That she'd killed the judge?"

Annie nodded. "It sounded horrible, but knowing the conversation she'd recently had with the judge,

I took it to mean that she thought she'd stressed out the judge to the point that she collapsed. That she was responsible for her illness."

Detective Wollcott was looking at her, skepticism plainly on his face.

"You'd mentioned that Hollis might know the circumstances. Can you explain what you meant by that?"

"Oh. Well, when I asked if Brianna would be joining us for dinner last night, Miriam was kind of evasive. And I got the feeling during dinner that she and Hollis were trying to keep the judge from knowing that Brianna was on-site. Which is kind of odd, since they were both officials at the show. Although Brianna said the technical delegate and judge often didn't interact with each other very much."

"When did Brianna tell you that?"

"Earlier in the day. I was walking up to the house just when she pulled in. In fact, Brianna specifically asked me if the judge had arrived yet, and I said no, and that she'd be staying off-site. She seemed relieved when I told her that."

"Really."

"Really what? If Brianna intended to kill the judge, wouldn't she have wanted her on the property?"

"Perhaps not yet. Perhaps she wanted time to prepare the poison, and it was better that Jean Bennett not be present until the time came to administer it."

"That's impossible," Annie insisted. "Brianna didn't have time to kill her. First off, she was never in the house. She's staying in one of the cottages. She didn't even eat with us. She was just too damn busy. All her time was spent at the stables getting ready for the show. If she spiked the judge's tea sometime between six and nine this morning, she must have vaporized her way up here."

Plus, she was just too nice to kill Judge Bennett. Yes, she'd said hurtful things last night, but wouldn't anyone under the circumstances? Her academic standing was in jeopardy, all because of the judge's stupid divorce. When Brianna had told her mentor it wasn't fair, she was right.

"You're thinking she's too nice to kill someone."

Annie nodded.

"But yet she warned Judge Bennett she might do something. Threatened her, really."

She shrugged, and with it, shrugged off her reticence to shield others from the detective's scrutiny.

"Who hasn't said something like that to another person in their lifetime? Nicole and Gwendolyn make threats on a daily basis. Brianna says one hateful thing in the heat of the moment, and she becomes the lead suspect."

"You said yourself that Gwendolyn's never met the judge. Nicole assured me that she never spoke to her. I know it's not the way we'd perhaps like the case to go, but the fact is Brianna's the best lead we've got right now. She knew the judge intimately and made a threat against her. We can't change the facts, as much as we might like to."

Annie felt a sick feeling in her stomach. She wished she'd never told the detective about Brianna's reaction to the judge's death. She wished even more that Brianna had never uttered the words.

Chapter Eighteen

By the time cocktail hour rolled around, a mutiny was gathering among many of the riders. They'd spent an entire afternoon sharing everything they'd done that morning in front of all the others, then been subjected to writing it all down for the police's pleasure, and they still hadn't been given clearance to visit their beloved horses.

"This is outrageous!" Harriett told the others, as Hollis handed her a second glass of red wine. "Who is feeding the horses? How do we even know they have water in their stalls?"

"Brianna will be here shortly with an update," Hollis told her. "And she's already told me the horses have been fed. The show volunteers offered to stay and help."

"And has she found a judge yet?"

"She didn't mention it. I'll let you ask her when she arrives."

Even Melissa and Patricia expressed concern about being kept from the horses.

"I doubt they've been groomed," Patricia told the other trainer. "And I suspect all the commotion from the police has them a bit upset. I know we'll all feel a lot better once we've seen them."

Melissa nodded. "I wish the time would hurry up and come."

Brianna showed up just after Jorge announced that dinner would be served in fifteen minutes. Annie had noticed this was the time when Nicole and Gwendolyn usually rushed off to reapply their makeup and perhaps announce on Facebook what they were about to eat, but tonight not one of the women moved from where she was seated. All eyes were on the technical delegate, who looked tired and, yes, sad. Annie wished Detective Wollcott could see Brianna now. Her grief was apparent in her face and in the way she held herself. But she was a true professional. When she spoke, it was with her usual calm confidence and clarity although with a somewhat flat affect.

"I have good news," she began. "We have found a substitute judge who will officiate tomorrow, along with her regular scribe. Her name is Phyllis Hobert. She's an S judge so will be able to judge all levels. All of you will be able to ride tomorrow."

"Thank God!" Harriett exclaimed.

"Super news!" Melissa turned to smile at Amy and Lucy, who returned it somewhat belatedly.

"I'm so happy for you," Patricia told Liz.

Gwendolyn and Nicole said nothing, but they, too, looked pleased.

"Judge Hobert lives in Santa Monica, not too far away, so she'll be driving up tomorrow morning at the crack of dawn. She's agreed to have dinner with us afterward, when you can personally thank her for her great kindness in stepping in and saving the show."

"How is Margaret feeling?" Trust Patricia to inquire about the scribe who had dissolved into a puddle during the most critical time today, Annie thought.

"She's doing better. She's still resting in my cottage, but Hollis has offered to drive her home once the Sheriff's Office has given us permission to open up the property as usual."

"And when will that be?" Nicole demanded. "I've had to significantly change my plans because of their stupid investigation." Annie had a feeling she was referring to her groom, who'd gone off-site and was still unable to return. Nicole would not take kindly to the idea of grooming her own horse tomorrow, if it came to that.

"Yes, how much longer will it be?" The question seemed to come at Brianna from all sides.

"I don't know," she said helplessly. "Soon, I hope. We're all anxious for you to be able to tend to your horses. But please know that they've all been rubbed down and fed for the evening. I'm sorry they'll all have to be groomed again tomorrow. But it can't be helped."

Hollis came up to Brianna and put his hands on her shoulders. At the moment she seemed frail, even tiny.

"We're very grateful for all you've done, Brianna. I know you're exhausted, so I am sending over dinner to your cottage for both you and Margaret. And I hope you're able to take the rest of the night off. Tomorrow will be another long day, but a much happier one, I trust."

Brianna attempted a smile and left the room amid a smattering of clapping and a chorus of thank-yous!

"Miriam is feeling a bit tired, so we won't be joining you for dinner tonight," Hollis addressed the crowd. "But we will see you bright and early tomorrow. For everyone's peace of mind, we've decided that from now on lunch and dinner will be mandatory meals at the house, whether you're staying here or in a cottage. The only exception is Brianna, who keeps very busy hours and can't get away."

There was a short, stunned silence as the enormity of what Hollis had said hit them. Nicole looked as if she was about to protest.

"No more exceptions, I'm afraid," he said, smiling at her. "Although you're welcome to invite Douglas to dine with us. And as I understand it, Marcus Colbert also will be joining us tomorrow for dinner, isn't that right, Annie?"

Annie nodded. She felt a small, selfish smugness at being singled out as the one to confirm the news. She was sure Gwendolyn had not missed Hollis's remark.

"Second, I regret to tell you the kitchen is now off-limits to everyone. Chef Gustav will put out thermoses for you to take with you tomorrow morning, and will also put out drinks and snacks throughout the day. But for the time being, the only people allowed in the kitchen will be authorized personnel. Thank you for understanding.

"Finally, you should know that we've hired extra security around the house and stables for the duration of the weekend. No one will stop you from going anywhere, but you should know that they'll be around and watching out for our safety."

The doorbell rang. Hollis excused himself and walked quickly toward the foyer. He returned a minute later, smiling broadly.

"More good news, ladies," he announced. "I've just been told that the stables are now open to all of you. I know you're longing to go there now, but Chef Gustav has worked quite hard under very trying circumstances to serve an excellent dinner tonight, so please, enjoy the meal he's prepared first. And then you can rush off to your horses. And now, I'll bid you adieu, but I look forward to seeing you all in the morning. Sleep well, and best of luck tomorrow."

Hollis left, heading toward the hall end where the elevator stood, doors open, ready to take him upstairs to the Darbys' suite. Annie was afraid that with his departure the last bit of civility among the group also had disappeared.

Annie's suspicion of how the dinner would progress proved correct. As always, the food was superb. The conversation quickly degenerated into a freefall of barbs and vicious innuendoes.

"We're all suspects, you realize." Nicole opened the gate. "All except me, of course."

"And why not you?" Tabitha demanded.

"I've never been in the bloody kitchen. I try to avoid them."

"Douglas may not be happy to hear that." This was Gwendolyn's contribution. "But then, that may not be the only thing he's unhappy to hear about. Are you bringing him to dinner tomorrow, Nicole?"

Nicole glared at Gwendolyn.

"If I do, I'll at least be glad he doesn't have to see the rest of you carrying out your dishes, like the hired help."

Annie squelched the angry retort she'd wanted to utter. Instead, she said, "You know, there's no evidence that the person who poisoned Judge Bennett even used the kitchen."

"Oh, well, since we now have Nancy Drew on the case, we'll all just have to shut up and listen to her." Gwendolyn's voice was icy. "What exactly did you talk about with Detective Wollcott this afternoon? We all thought you were about to be arrested when you walked off with him."

Annie refused to rise to the bait. Patricia tried to change the subject.

"I do think, as a precaution, we should start locking our doors at night."

"I've been doing that every night." Gwendolyn sounded astonished that at least one other guest had not. "But yes, let's all lock our doors. After all, one of us is apparently a killer."

That stopped the conversation for a few minutes. But not for long.

"Has anyone noticed anything missing from her room?" Tabitha inquired. "I mean you all know someone stole my rhythm beads. Has anyone else noticed anything missing?"

"Stop obsessing about those beads, Tabitha." Harriett had run out of patience for her student's ongoing quest to recover them. "It's too bad the thief didn't take all the bling you're accumulated for that horse. Then maybe you'd spend your time on what's really important, which is your performance tomorrow."

No one knew what to say. After a brief silence, Gwendolyn decided to respond to Tabitha's initial question.

"As you know, I lock my door, so no, nothing of mine is missing. But frankly, I wasn't aware that any of the rest of you had anything worth stealing."

"Not all of us are as lucky as you, Gwendolyn," Tabitha shot back. "Some of us have to work for a living so we can support ourselves. You should try it sometime. It can be rewarding."

"Rewarding? Sitting in a cubicle all day long reading law? Oh, spare me, Tabitha. You call that rewarding? I call it sitting around waiting to die."

Annie noticed that Gwendolyn had referenced death twice in as many minutes. As Detective Wollcott would say, interesting. A waiter entered discreetly and refilled everyone's wineglass. Most were empty.

"Perhaps we could discuss how we're going to get ready for tomorrow rather than jump down each other's throats," Melissa suggested. "Does anyone know if Ann Corbett will be able to groom tonight?"

No one did. If she were not, then there would be a lot of women up as early as Melissa tomorrow morning making button braids in their horses' manes.

The women practically flew from the table as soon as dessert plates were removed. Annie noticed that Liz and Patricia seemed to be the only exceptions. She joined them outside on the patio by the pool.

"Why aren't you rushing off like everyone else?"

"We thought we'd wait until the hubbub dies down a bit. There's bound to be a lot of yelling about how no one's taken good enough care of her horse."

"Very diplomatically put, Liz," Annie told her.

"Anyway, it's nice to have a chance to relax for a moment. I feel as if we've barely spent time with you. How are you holding up?"

"Oh, fine. It's just a bit hard to acclimate to all this catty backbiting."

"I should have warned you," Patricia said. "This seems to be a particularly virulent strain of dressage riders. Must be all the sun down here. Usually, we're a much more civilized crowd. Although we are a competitive bunch. None of us ever really stops thinking about how to improve our performance."

"Oh, I don't know. I'm sure Nicole spends a lot of time obsessing about the color of the flowers at her wedding and who on the A-list to invite. And I know Gwendolyn spends all her spare time scheming to get Marcus away from my tentacles."

"Have a glass of wine. We snared a bottle from the sideboard."

Annie gratefully accepted the glass. "I feel just by talking about them I'm stooping to their level. But it's hard not to be a bit resentful of women who can so easily afford the best horses, the best trainers, not to mention the entry fees."

"Which should make us more sympathetic to those of us who don't have those privileges," Liz said. "You should talk to Amy sometime. She worked her way through law school and barely makes enough money as a law clerk to buy her horse hay. Tabitha works for a cutthroat law firm with a very intact glass ceiling. As an RN, I make decent money, but I also have elderly parents to support. It's taken a long time for me to be able to afford a dressage horse of my own."

"I'm so glad you have Sammy in your life. The two of you are such a superb pair."

"Aren't they?" Patricia looked approvingly at her student. "Considering the short time you've been working together, your progress has been incredible."

"Thanks, both of you. But getting back to the other riders. Lucy comes from a privileged background yet doesn't show it."

"Well, she does have a fabulous Hanoverian, although truth be told, he's a bit too much horse for her, I'm afraid." Patricia shook her head. "But in her other life, you're right, you'd never know that she's a Boston Brahmin. Do you know she donates her legal services to several nonprofits for displaced women and victims of domestic violence?"

"I had no idea." Annie was astonished. "And yet in the few short days I've been here, I've watched her absorb insult after insult from Gwendolyn and Nicole. Kind of ironic that she's able to stand up for others but not for herself."

"Ironic, but not too surprising, really," Patricia told her. "I think it's sometimes easier to help others than it is to improve ourselves. And for the record, as horrible as the snottiest guests are, it's hard to think of any of them killing Judge Bennett."

"Maybe none of the houseguests did," Liz said. "I talked with Chef Gustav today, and he was so busy with his skeleton crew that almost anyone could have walked in and spiked the judge's tea."

Annie was silent. Now that she knew that Betsy Gilchrist's death was officially a homicide, she was convinced that one of the houseguests *was* responsible. She just didn't know which one.

"Er, Annie? Can I talk to you about something?"

Liz's summons brought her out of her private thoughts. She looked at Liz, who to her surprise, looked a bit guilty.

"I forgot one little part of my narrative when Detective Wollcott was going around the group today. Would you mind telling me if you think it's important?"

"Forgot? Or didn't want to say in front of everyone else?" Annie asked quietly.

"Oh, all right. Didn't want to say. I was going to tag the detective afterward, but he grabbed you right away, and I didn't have the chance. Could you tell him for me?"

"If it's important, I'm sure he'll want to hear it from you. But he gave me his card. We can call him together. What didn't you feel comfortable sharing in front of everyone?"

"You know when Gwendolyn told us she'd walked over to Harriett's cottage this morning, I think she said around seven fifteen?"

Annie slowly nodded. "I remember. She said she got up around six."

"Well, I saw her out back when I was leaving for the stables. That would have been around the same time."

"What? You mean she was outside the same time she said she got out of bed?"

"Pretty much. And she was dressed. Ready to go."

"What was she doing? And where were you?"

"Still in my bedroom. I was about to go downstairs. I looked out the back window, just glanced, really, and saw her walking around the corner toward the kitchen. Like she'd gone to her car, forgotten something, and was going to go back inside. At least, that's what I thought at the time."

Annie stared at Liz, her heart pounding. Then to her own embarrassment, her excitement faded. As much as she would have loved for Gwendolyn to be the killer, the facts she was privy to didn't quite jibe with what Liz saw.

"I think you definitely have to tell Wollcott. Although that's exactly what you may have seen, Gwendolyn going inside because she forgot something. Chef Gustav told me he had the judge's tea ready at six, but when no one picked it up, he tossed it and made a fresh batch. If Gwendolyn did spike the first thermos, the contents were discarded. The poison had to be in the second batch, the one made around seven. And by then, Gwendolyn was at Harriett's, having coffee."

"Yes, but what if Chef Gustav didn't rinse the thermos thoroughly, and some remnants of the poison remained?"

Annie paused. "Good point. I mean, why would the killer know that the chef was going to replace the first batch of tea with another? It makes sense that whoever did it would have spiked the tea that was made first."

"Yes," Liz said doubtfully, "And I know you said the kitchen was hopping, Annie. And that's my problem. I still don't understand how *anyone* could have poisoned the tea. Honestly, don't you think someone in the kitchen would have seen a guest creep in, unscrew a thermos, pour a vial of poison or whatever into it, then seal it again?"

They were all silent. The scenario Liz had described did sound pretty ludicrous.

"I don't know how the police can be so certain," Liz finally declared. "It's like the iced tea that everyone seems to think killed Betsy Gilchrist. How would anyone know which one she was going to pick? If Jorge was the killer, which I don't believe for an instant, even he couldn't predict which glass she'd choose. What was he going to do if she picked the wrong one? Say, excuse me, Mademoiselle, this iced tea, the one laced with arsenic, tastes so much finer?"

They all laughed.

"Liz, it's nearly gone past nine o'clock. We'd better get down to the stables if we're going to tuck Sammy in tonight."

"Ready whenever you are. Hopefully the atmosphere is quiet and peaceful by now."

Annie bade the two women good night but stayed out on the patio, thinking. It occurred to her that she'd never even considered her hosts as potential suspects, only their houseguests. Should she? Ridiculous. Miriam was too frail, Both of them obviously had been quite fond of the late judge. Besides, they were just too damn decent to kill anyone, at least off stage. It was time to have another talk with Chef Gustav. She *knew* he was innocent of any wrongdoing. But she suspected he still had a lot more to say.

Chapter Nineteen

Then she remembered. The kitchen was officially off-limits, with no exceptions. She knew Chef Gustav would still be embroiled in kitchen affairs, prepping for tomorrow and overseeing the cleanup. How could she get him alone?

She peered through the window on the upper side of the swinging doors. There he was, rolling out a piecrust, and talking behind his back to a young man who was chopping a massive pile of onions into tiny bits. The knife he was wielding moved so quickly, the blade was nearly a blur.

Annie hated to bother the overworked chef, but too many questions were crowding into her brain to be ignored. She tapped on the window. The sound of running water inside rendered her timid knock mute. She tapped again, loudly this time. Chef Gustav looked up, and she waved to him. A smile creased his face and he motioned for her to come in. She shook her head no, trying to look as sad as she felt at being banned from this place, the room of wonderful aromas.

The chef looked puzzled, but put down his rolling pin, dusted his hands on his coat, and waddled over to the door.

"What is it, Mademoiselle Annie? Anything you want is here. You need only come in and ask."

"I'm sorry, Chef Gustav, but Hollis told us that the kitchen is now off-limits. I'm sure he has your best interests at heart. But I do want to talk to you. Do you think you'll have any time tonight?"

"Off-limits? Ridiculous! I am the one who chooses who will enter and who will not. Come in and make yourself comfortable!" The chef opened the door and gestured for her to enter.

"No, I really can't. Only authorized personnel can come in. It wouldn't be right to ignore Hollis's directive. But I can come back later."

"Authorized personnel? What does he mean?"

"I think he means only people who work for you."

"*Bien sûr!* Mademoiselle Annie, how would you like a job washing mushrooms?"

She smiled. "I'd love it."

At Chef Gustav's instruction, she donned a white coat two sizes too big and rolled up the sleeves. She then joined the chef, who was now putting the piecrust into a large tart pan. Annie was amazed at how easily he flipped the perfect elastic circle into the pan without it breaking apart. Annie had tried to do this in her youth and had never succeeded. All her piecrusts were patched together with stray bits of floury dough. The chef pulled a large bowl of mushrooms toward them.

"Now. Watch me closely. Take the brush and lightly scrub the top, *comme ça*, until it is clean, but not too much is shaved off. With the knife, remove the very end of the stem; and then place the mushroom in this bowl, the one filled with water and lemon slices. That will keep them fresh. Do you think you can do that?"

Annie nodded. She could tell from his one tiny slice that the knife he'd handed her was wickedly sharp. After nearly three glasses of wine, she hoped she'd finish the job with all her fingers intact. She picked up the first mushroom and began to work.

"So, what is it you wish to ask me?"

"Well, I'm curious. Did your missing waitperson ever show up today? And your sous chef?"

"The sous chef, *oui*. His car ran out of petrol, and he was very late. The *imbécile*! I tell him, fill up *la voiture* before you depart in the morning but these young men, they never listen. Yet he is a very good sous chef; *très bon*. So, I scold him and let him get to work."

The chef's backward glance revealed the young man dicing onions now with very bright red cheeks. *Aha,* Annie thought. His identity is a secret no longer.

"But the waiter." Chef Gustav clicked his tongue. "He remains at large. He does not answer his phone, and so his absence is *un mystère*. One of the other waiters has agreed to check his home to see if he is all right. He is a good boy, and I am a bit worried about him."

"Has he worked for you long?"

"All my staff has been with me many, many years. I inspire much *fidélité*," he replied with not a trace of modesty in his voice.

"I'm sure you do. Tell me, were the police polite to you today?" What she really wanted to know was what they might have hauled away.

The chef shrugged. "They are gendarmes and not polite by nature. But they do not do too much damage to my kitchen. And aside from the *thé*, they take nothing with them."

That question was answered.

"And since Madame Bennett is no longer with us, her special flavor of tea is not needed. It is sad, but so very true."

"I thought it was Lady Grey tea."

"It was! But with my special addition, just to her specifications. Madame Bennett has been a friend of the Darbys for many years, and I have learned exactly what she likes to eat and drink. I have always kept a canister of her special *thé* in my cupboard, for just those occasions when she is here."

"You mean it's more than just Lady Grey?"

"*Mais oui, Mademoiselle*. And much, much better."

"Chef Gustav, is this something only you can do, alone? Or is there anyone else you would have entrusted to make the judge's tea?"

"Ah, now you are beginning to sound like the gendarmes, only you are much prettier. I will tell you what I tell them. It is a process, making this tea. One job I give to the staff, but only a small one, you understand. The mixture is my own creation, and only I can do it, because, *naturellement*, it is all in my head."

"Of course. But would you mind sharing the process with me? The steps you do, and the steps you give to your staff?"

"Yes. But only because I know you are trying to help, Mademoiselle Annie."

The chef toddled over to the cupboards below the ones filled with loose tea and pulled out a large, round, stainless steel container.

"This is how it begins. I put the *thé* in cheesecloth, then in the pan. I then give it to my staff, who take it to the garden, fill with springwater, and let it bake in the sun for one entire day. Now we have the makings of the *thé*. It goes in my refrigerator, not the one here, the bigger one in the pantry, and when it comes the time to make hot *thé* for Madam Bennett, I gently heat in a saucepan on the stove and transfer to the thermos. I then place the thermos on the tray, and it is picked up."

"But today, Margaret was late, and you had to make a whole new thermos up for her."

"*Exactement!* After an hour, I notice no one has come by, and the *thé* will be getting cold. So, I repeat the process in the saucepan and set the new thermos on the tray."

"New thermos? You mean you didn't just wash out the old one and fill it up again?"

"*Non*. Every dish that is used in the kitchen, no matter how slightly, must go in the dishwasher. And it is no trouble. We have dozens of thermoses. It is easy to grab a new one, whenever one is needed."

The chef opened a small cupboard that appeared to be built into the wall. Annie noticed this cupboard opened with a small china knob, the old-fashioned kind that she'd seen in older houses, instead of the modern handles on the other cupboards in the kitchen. She peered inside the cubicle and saw a half dozen gleaming thermoses, each with the Darby Farms logo.

"Wow. You do have a lot."

"And not only here. Monsieur Hollis orders them by the box, to give to his guests as a small gift of the house. If you go to the pantry, you will see many more, some on the shelves, some still in the case."

"You've found an interesting place to keep them.

What was this cupboard used for? It looks as if it's an original part of the house."

"It was once a dumbwaiter, Mademoiselle. It used to be that dishes were carried from here to upstairs by means of a pulley, then delivered back to the kitchen the same way. It is most charming, is it not? But no longer in use. Still, the space is good, and so that is where the thermoses are stored."

Annie had heard about these devices but never seen one. She stuck her head in and tried to find evidence of the pulley system.

"You cannot see the pulleys. I believe they have been cut away, many years before."

Annie nodded and looked at the chef.

"Too bad. What an ingenious idea."

"*D'accord.* But now we use the elevator, and much more food can go into that."

Annie saw his point.

"Chef Gustav?" It was the voice of the sous chef, who now placed the chopped onions in a large bin in the refrigerator. "I believe that's everything. If it's okay with you, I'll take off now, but I'll be back at five tomorrow morning."

"*Très bien.* And make sure that *voiture* of yours is filled with petrol!"

"It will be, I promise! See you tomorrow."

"*Bonne nuit.* And safe travels home."

Chef Gustav turned to Annie. "Now we are alone. And your mushrooms are clean and put away. Are your questions done, too? Or do you have more?"

"Just a few, if you have the time."

"*Mais oui,* but let us enjoy a sip of Armagnac while we continue our conversation."

He pulled a dusty bottle from a nearby shelf, along with two small brandy snifters.

"Shouldn't we go outside? Officially, I'm no longer your employee."

"If anyone comes, I shall say I am reviewing your work."

"How am I doing so far?"

"*Pas mal,* not bad. But you need to learn how to better handle the knife. It is one of the most important tools in the kitchen."

Annie smiled. "I look forward to the lesson."

They sat down at the white table, and the chef deftly poured a small amount of dark liquid into each glass. Annie noticed an XO on the bottle.

"What's that stand for?"

"Not poison, I assure you. It means the brandy has rested in an oak barrel for six long years. There are many kinds of Armagnac, but this is one of the best."

He raised his glass for a toast.

"To the memory of Madame Bennett!"

Annie raised her own glass, and they each took a delicate sip. The flavor was intense. But somehow it reminded her of home and her Northwest forests, and although the earthy, fiery taste startled her at first, she'd found, with each successive sip, that it really was the most remarkable beverage she'd ever tasted.

For the first several minutes, Annie was content to let the chef regale her with stories of his childhood in Gascony, where, as a boy, he had watched local farmers create small batches of Armagnac and occasionally was rewarded with a soupçon of the stuff himself.

She gently brought him back to the subject at hand—the mysterious deaths of two women, seemingly because of something they'd ingested from his kitchen.

"Chef Gustav, I know you didn't poison anyone. And frankly, I think the police realize this, too, and they're looking for someone who had access to your kitchen. Not long, just for the brief moment in time it would take to put something noxious into a thermos."

"Let us hope so. I have been with the Darbys for ten years and not once have I poisoned anyone!" His eyebrows knitted together in sudden anger, and Annie knew she should leave the topic of his own liability.

"Let's go back to the raspberry iced tea Jorge brought down to the stables. Was that prepared the same way as Judge Bennett's tea?"

Talking about food preparation had a calming effect. The chef settled back in his chair and took a small sip from his snifter.

"*Non*, that was much simpler. It is a black tea I mix with a few herbs and fresh raspberry juice and a dash of sugar. We always have it on hand in the refrigerator and it is always offered to guests wherever they might be, by the pool, or the tennis court, or on this day, with the horses. There was nothing strange about this errand. It is one Jorge performs nearly every day if guests are present."

Annie nodded. "Did you pour the tea yourself? Do you remember?"

"*Non*, this would not be necessary. Jorge would do this task, but Mademoiselle Annie, Jorge is above reproach."

"I'm sure he is. Have the police questioned him?"

"*Bien sûr.* But he was so nervous that the gendarmes must have seen that he was innocent."

I hope so. "And how did he bring the tea to the stables? Surely, he must not have walked that distance with a tray."

"*Absolument pas!* The ice would have melted. We use a small *voiture* Monsieur Hollis has given us to transport food to other locations when necessary. One with *air conditionné.*"

Annie sighed and looked at her snifter. It was almost empty, and she had enjoyed every last drop.

"I guess it boils down to who else was in the kitchen at those critical times, both Wednesday afternoon and early Saturday morning. Which guests, I mean."

"That is difficult to answer. We are so busy, and the guests are welcome, although not so much when we are preparing a meal. Most of the guests know this and stay away at those times."

"And I'm afraid I've made my question even more difficult to answer, now that most of us bring our plates to the kitchen after breakfast. Well, let's start from the other end. Is there anyone in our group who hasn't visited the kitchen? I mean, when you've been here?"

The chef thought for a moment. "Mademoiselle Forrester I have not seen. Nor Mademoiselle Smythe. The others, I believe, have been in the kitchen at one time or another to pick up something or ask a question. And, of course, Mademoiselles Rawlins and Litchfield assisted me one afternoon, as you did tonight."

"And you've seen none of these people do anything that you thought suspicious?"

"Not a one."

"Have any of the guests ever taken anything from the kitchen, besides a bottle of water or a cookie, I mean, anything that really belongs here?"

"Not that I am aware of. Perhaps a wine opener? But I think not even that."

She leaned forward. "Chef Gustav. Remember when you told me someone evil was staying in the house? I assumed you were referring to a guest. But you've told me that none of the people who have been to the kitchen have done anything suspicious in your eyes. Does that mean that one of the two women you've *not* seen in the kitchen is the one you consider evil?"

Chef Gustav carefully finished the last bit of brandy in his snifter.

"I regret that I cannot say anything further. I have my suspicions, but no proof. I will only say this, Mademoiselle Annie. The person I believe is doing these evil things has problems other than teaching her horse merely to go and then stop. I also fear that when it comes to more killings, it will be difficult for her to stop."

Annie waited for him to speak further, but it soon became clear that was all he intended to say.

"Thank you, Chef Gustav. You've been very generous with your time. And I appreciate what you've told me."

She rose from the table and left the kitchen, trying not to show her disappointment. Chef Gustav had been so adamant when he'd first told her evil resided in the house. She was sure he had a specific person in mind then, and she was even surer now. But the way he'd described the killer matched the mind-set of just about every guest in the house—with the exception of killing again. Who didn't have problems beyond training their horse? Instead of homing in on the killer's identity, he'd only expanded the list of suspects.

Still. She had picked up one tidbit of interesting information from the chef. It had given her just an inkling of an idea on how the murders might have occurred. As she climbed the stairs to her room, she vowed she would find out tomorrow whether or not she was right.

Chapter Twenty

Two text messages greeted Annie when she reached her bedroom. One was from Patricia, telling her Ann Corbett had agreed to groom the horses once more, but Liz deserved a break, so she was springing for the groom's fee to work on Sammy tonight.

Good for Patricia, Annie thought. That meant only Amy and Tabitha would have to groom their horses again, unless they, too, had decided to pay this extra fee. Annie doubted that Amy would spend the money; she had Lucy to help. Tabitha did not. She wondered if grooming was a job Tabitha preferred to do alone or if she would appreciate an extra hand. Perhaps she'd offer her services tomorrow. Tabitha had had enough abuse heaped on her this week from Gwendolyn and Nicole, culminating in the theft of her rhythm beads. And anyone who trained under Harriett might welcome the company of a colleague who didn't criticize but merely offered friendly help.

The second message was the one she'd hoped for. Marcus's text read: "Leaving early tomorrow morning.

Should arrive in time for lunch. Don't have seconds without me. XXOO."

Annie glanced at her watch. It was now only a few hours from the time he'd leave his home in San Jose. She fell asleep almost as soon as her head hit the pillow, a smile on her face.

She awakened at dawn, and again her thoughts turned to Marcus. He'd be hitting the road right now, and she couldn't wait to see him. She felt wide awake, having slept soundly, although remnants of hazy dreams flittered through her consciousness. And, of course, now she could not remember a single thing about them. But one thought was firmly embedded in her brain. Today, she had to find out if her theory held water. Her concern that the killer might try again had solidified overnight. Of that, Annie was sure.

Her first stop was the kitchen, where she tapped on the window of one swinging door, this time, insistently. Chef Gustav quickly walked over. The usual smile that lit up his face was gone, replaced by a distinctly somber look.

"What is it?" she asked without preamble.

"My waiter, he has truly vanished. His apartment is empty, his *voiture* is not in his usual space, he gives all the evidence that he has gone to work, but he is nowhere to be found. When the gendarmes arrive, I think I must tell them."

"Oh, Chef Gustav! I'm so sorry. I hope it's just a family emergency."

"*Oui.* But he would tell me. I know this boy."

"Yes, I'm sure you're right. I wanted to warn you not to put out any glasses of iced tea or any other beverage until we've all returned. Can you do that? I know you like to do everything ahead of time, and this makes more work for you."

"If it will stop another death, I will do anything you wish, Mademoiselle Annie. I have a bad feeling about the events of today."

Annie did, too, but she chose not to add her agreement. She did not want to upset the chef any more than he already was about the unexplained disappearance of one of his staff.

"I need to go to the stables now," she told him. "But I'll be back later, hopefully in just an hour or two. There's something I need to do in the house. If you see me around the place, just ignore me."

"You are an impossible person to ignore, Mademoiselle, but I will do my best to avert my eyes. I hope you find what you are looking for."

"I hope so, too."

She turned to leave but heard the chef call her name once more.

"If you cannot make it back, and you need me for any reason, please, call me. Let me give you my number. My telephone is here." He patted a large pocket on his white chef's coat. "I keep it with me at all times. Especially now."

Annie took the number, written on a piece of butcher's paper, and thanked him again. She entered the dining room a few seconds later, surprised to see how full it was. Every woman was present, some sitting at the table, some standing. Everyone looked on edge, far more so than the previous day. Annie found Patricia and looked at her with questioning eyes. Patricia beckoned for her to come over.

"We're being escorted to the stables today," she told Annie. "Hollis has been kind enough to bring out some of his vintage cars for the occasion. We're waiting for him now."

"How lovely." What else could she say? And in truth, she applauded Hollis's concern and the steps he was taking to ensure that today would be, as Patricia said, tickety-boo.

"Is this really necessary?" Gwendolyn's voice seemed more annoying than usual.

"If Hollis says it is, I don't think we should question him," Melissa told her. "It is his house, after all, and we are his guests. If he wants to escort us in style, then I think we should simply be grateful and enjoy the ride."

"Oh, honestly, this has nothing to do with our comfort, and you know it," Nicole replied impatiently. "He's doing it because he doesn't want to give the killer any time alone. Which is one of us, in case anyone's forgotten."

An uncomfortable silence settled over the group. Annie noticed that Gwendolyn's head was down, as if she was avoiding everyone else in the room. She slowly stirred a cup of coffee with a small silver spoon, over and over again.

Lucy walked over to Annie, a set of papers in her hand.

"Would you like a new day sheet? Brianna brought these over late last night, after we'd all gone to bed."

Annie smiled and accepted the sheets. "Thanks, Lucy. Has the lineup changed much?"

"It's a bit smaller than yesterday. But Amy and I are still riding at the same time. Liz is first now. The rider from yesterday couldn't return."

Couldn't or wouldn't? Annie thought. She glanced down at the first page. The number of contestants riding was definitely smaller than those scheduled yesterday, but still, there were possibly forty riders who would compete. Dressage people were a resilient bunch, she thought. The very public death of the show judge was proving insufficient to keep most of them away.

Hollis appeared at the door.

"Ladies, your chariots await you. Take your pick of a Rolls-Royce Silver Cloud, vintage Bentley, and a Packard that's part Woodie. They're a lot older than all of you but still purr like kittens on the open road."

The landscape looked dramatically different this morning. Perhaps it was the prevalence of all the new security. They seemed to be everywhere—at the main gates, checking the ID of each driver who pulled in, and stationed every fifteen feet or so around the stables and arenas. They were trying to be discreet, Annie thought, but still were a visible force. Perhaps it would be enough to deter the killer from acting again today. She feared not. The heightened security presence might only spur her on and make the game more thrilling.

There was no sign of the media, although from the front of the stables she could see one telltale van camped out on the farm across the road. But the only camera she saw inside the estate gates belonged to the same videographer who'd been on the premises the day before. She wondered what he'd managed to capture on video during those opening seconds when the rider entered the ring, and reminded herself to find out. Although she was pretty sure the police already had a copy of whatever he'd managed to get on film.

As the first rider, Liz seemed far more nervous than she'd been the day before, and Annie intuited her presence probably wouldn't help right now. She wished Liz luck and watched as she and Patricia walked Sammy over to the warm-up ring. It was eight o'clock, and there was nothing to do but wait. Annie was itching to go back up to the house to do her private sleuthing, but there wasn't time before her friend would ride. Besides, if she left right now, alone, her departure would be very conspicuous. She knew Hollis's new set of rules required no one to return to the house unless it was in one of his vehicles, and never alone. And that was precisely what she needed to be this morning—alone and undisturbed.

She'd have to bring Hollis into her plan, and before he returned to the house to fetch Miriam. Driving down, he'd told her his wife had insisted on watching the show this morning, come hell or high water.

"Hollis, I think the way you've handled security this morning is just perfect," she began.

"Thank you, Annie. I'm afraid we can't be too careful." He turned to get into the Rolls. She put her hand on his arm, and he turned back.

"I need to get back to the house sometime this morning. There's something . . . something I have to look at."

His eyes lost a bit of their brilliant hue.

"You have a theory?"

"I do. But I need to test it when the rest of the guests are out of the house."

"Miriam should be ready to go in twenty minutes. Will that give you enough time?"

"It should."

"Then hop in."

She quickly slid into the passenger side and tried to slink down. She did not want to be seen by any of the other women right now, even Patricia and Liz.

"I could put you in the boot of the car on the way back, if you'd like," Hollis said as he smoothly drove away from the stables and toward the house. "I did that to a moll in a B movie once."

"Did she manage to escape?"

"I believe she kicked her way out. I'm not sure I'd like you to do that to this beauty."

"I agree. Why don't you let me get back on my own? I'll be less conspicuous that way."

"If you go around the cottages, you should end up just behind the judge's booth."

"Perfect. Although I think this judge is safe today."

"I hope so. And, Annie, you will tell me what you find, won't you?"

"Hollis, you'll be the first to know."

Once inside the house, Annie raced upstairs, taking two steps at a time. Then she groaned. Every door to every guest suite would be locked—isn't that what they'd all agreed to do? Why hadn't she bothered to ask Hollis for a master key, assuming he had one? She bounded downstairs, this time, three steps at a time, and headed for the kitchen.

"Back so soon, Mademoiselle Annie? Is everything all right?"

"Yes, but I need a master key to the rooms. Do you have one, by any chance?"

"No, but I do." It was Hollis's voice, right behind her. "Good heavens, you do make a lot of noise coming downstairs for such a slender thing, don't you? Come along, Annie, and let's let Chef Gustav return to work. I'll be happy to open any door you want."

She grinned at him, happy to have a confederate in this undertaking. She'd committed to trespassing on every single woman's room, if necessary, but the thought of doing so still made her feel a bit guilty. It would be much better to have the master of the house in tow. It made what she was going to do seem legitimate, which it almost was.

"We'll start on the second floor. In Lucy's room."

"Fine. I suggest we take the elevator and preserve the hardwood floor."

Lucy's suite was a mirror image of Annie's own bedroom right next door. The door opened to a large sitting area, followed by a canopied bed in a small nook and a luxuriant bath at the far end. As in Annie's room, Lucy's windows overlooked the path that led to the trainer's cottages and sports pavilion. But unlike Annie's, one of its walls was flush with the far end of the kitchen, one floor underneath.

Even if a maid didn't come in every day, Annie could see that Lucy was a tidy houseguest. Her clothes were organized and hung in the small walk-in closet, and a pile of books about dressage were neatly stacked on the coffee table. Annie walked over to Lucy's bed. A copy of *Dressage 101* by Jane Savoie was on Lucy's bedside table, and Annie found a well-worn copy of her dressage test inside, apparently acting as a bookmark. The book opened to the section on "riding accurate school figures."

"What are we looking for?"

Annie walked from the bed over to the west wall, nearly completely covered by an overstuffed sofa.

"The old dumbwaiter."

"The *what*?"

"There's a dumbwaiter in the kitchen. Chef Gustav showed it to me last night."

Whoops. Annie wasn't supposed to be in the kitchen last night. She could feel her face turning red.

"I was helping the chef with prep work," she said feebly.

"Aha. I wasn't aware of that. Please, do go on." Hollis didn't look completely displeased, but he didn't look altogether benign, either.

She took a deep breath. "I figured out the dumbwaiter must have stopped on both floors, but where? I mean, I'm sure there was a lot of work done on the house when you and Miriam purchased it, but the dumbwaiter took up a good three feet of wall space, and it obviously wasn't removed."

She started to tug at one end of the sofa. It felt as if it weighed about a thousand pounds.

"Here, let me help."

Hollis was in surprisingly good shape. They managed to scoot it back eight inches with just a few coordinated pulls. A door that looked very much like the one Annie had seen in the kitchen was near the floor. It had the same china knob, and was of the same dimensions.

"Chef Gustav thought it wasn't in use anymore, in

fact, thought that the pulleys had been removed. But I wanted to make sure he was right."

"Let's do so."

Annie crouched down and was able to work her hand around and find the knob. She pulled the door open. Hollis was on the other end of the couch, in a place where he was better able to see inside.

"Do you see anything?" She suddenly realized this might be all a wild-goose chase over nothing.

"I do. I think you'd better come around to my side, Annie, so you can see for yourself."

She did, and saw a half dozen gleaming thermoses inside, each with the Darby Farms logo, that looked just like the ones she'd seen last night in the kitchen. Only this time, a mason jar, filled with a milky-white substance, stood front and center.

"I can't believe it. I don't believe it. Lucy wouldn't hurt a fly."

Hollis was staring at her. He looked dumbstruck, as if, for the first time, he wasn't sure of his lines.

"I know it looks bad for Lucy, but it's not proof positive. Let me do a bit more snooping, if I might. I'll join you at the stables when I'm done." She gave a quick laugh. "After all, I can't miss seeing Liz ride."

Hollis glanced at the large Rolex adorning his wrist.

"Good heavens, Miriam will be downstairs waiting for me. All right, Annie, sleuth if you must, but not a word of this to anyone, agreed? Not at the moment."

"Agreed."

He tossed her the master key and left, his footsteps

clattering on the wood floor as loudly as her own a few minutes ago.

Once his footsteps had faded and she heard the front door close, Annie turned back to the small shelf inside the wall. She looked around for something to wrap around her hand and finally grabbed a wash-cloth from Lucy's bathroom. She gingerly picked up the mason jar and set it on the floor. No way was she leaving this behind. Not when she was certain that its contents had already caused two deaths, and possibly were intended for one more.

She managed to wrest the sofa back into position by herself and locked the door. She glanced at her own watch. It was eight thirty on the dot. She didn't have much time to complete the rest of her task.

She tiptoed up to the third floor and jiggled the knob to the bedroom door of the suite above Lucy's. To her surprise, the door swung open. How could that be? Hadn't everyone decided last night that locked doors were now de rigueur? She looked around the suite. This bedroom was far less orderly than the last one she'd entered. Clothes were strewn on the bed, jewelry had been indiscriminately slung over the near-est available chair, and glancing inside the bathroom, she saw barely a spare space left on the counter, clut-tered with lotions, perfumes, and other bottles. On the side tables, Annie saw many glasses she recognized as the same ones she'd seen on the dining-room table. Was it okay to take them upstairs? She'd never asked. Fortunately, the only piece of furniture adorning the same wall as the dumbwaiter in this bedroom was an old-fashioned hutch with long legs. Annie could see the beveled part of the outer door of the dumbwaiter protruding from underneath the hutch's legs.

She still had to move the cumbersome piece of furniture in order to open it, but this proved far easier to nudge than a Victorian sofa. Once this was done, Annie covered her hand with Lucy's washcloth and pulled the same china knob to open the door. She saw two pulley ropes hanging in the air, and gave one a slight tug. It immediately responded. Yup, this was a fully functional dumbwaiter, all right. Hollis and Miriam Darby may not have ever used it, but at least one houseguest, and possibly two, had been taking full advantage of its services.

She sat back on her knees and thought. In general, Annie agreed with Hollis. It was hard to see Lucy plotting the death of the judge. It was a lot easier to see Gwendolyn, whose bedroom she was now in, doing such a thing. But if she were responsible for one, perhaps two deaths, could she really be so stupid as to keep her door unlocked, where anyone could find the means by which she transported poison to a glass or thermos? She couldn't imagine Hilda's best friend making such a significant mistake. Yet criminals had made stupid mistakes before.

There was at least one more room she had to search, but she'd run out of time. Two minutes later, Annie was out the front door and trotting toward the back path Hollis had suggested she take. She strolled into the stables four minutes later. The mason jar was now safely stowed in the locked suitcase in her room, where no one could get it. It was five minutes to nine and time to watch Liz ride. She waved to her friend, who was seated on Sammy in the same spot as the rider had been yesterday morning. Patricia was beside her, waiting to take her own place outside the dressage court as her reader.

"Remember, have fun!" she yelled, and then walked over to where Melissa, Amy, and Lucy were standing to watch the show. A number of heads turned around, curious to see who would give a dressage rider such unorthodox advice.

She didn't care.

Chapter Twenty-one

"You did beautifully!"

"Thanks, Annie. Sammy did it all."

"I find that hard to believe. When will you know your score?"

"Soon, I think. I'm pretty sure a runner sends them over to the office staff on a regular basis."

Liz was standing on the ground next to her horse, looking very happy and immensely relieved that her five minutes in the spotlight were over. Every few seconds, she patted Sammy on the neck and told him how wonderful he was. After a bit of this, Sammy decided to return the compliment and reached down to nuzzle her neck. Annie whipped out her smartphone and made both pose for a picture. She'd seldom seen a horse and rider look so content with each other.

Miriam and Hollis joined the group, and Liz leaned forward to receive hugs from each of her hosts.

"We're so proud of you," Miriam said, and Annie could tell she meant every word.

"I'm just glad it's over. And I'm so glad I had Patricia's

help. I almost forgot my stretchy circle. If she hadn't been reading, I would have completely blown it."

"It's amazing how easy it is to have a brain freeze during a test," Patricia assured her. "But let's not talk about what-ifs. I see Lucy and Amy coming over and don't want to get Lucy's nerves more on edge. She'll be riding the same test in just a few hours."

"You got it. I'll tell her how easy it is."

"Unfortunately, I don't think that will wash," Miriam said sadly. "I believe this is the third time she's ridden this test. And that's just at Darby Farms."

Annie felt her smartphone buzz in her pocket. It was Marcus with a travel update: "Got the wind at my back. New ETA is 11:50. Everything OK?"

She knew the vague "everything OK" question really meant "is everyone still standing, and in particular, you?" She texted back, "Can't wait. Everything's fine," and sent the message on its way. There would be plenty of time to fill him in later. Right now, Annie needed to talk to her hosts and decide on a game plan. She was very much aware that they had information the police would want and evidence that rightfully belonged in their possession. The question was if Hollis would feel the same urgency in delivering what they had and knew. She wasn't sure she did—yet. Not while there was still a bit of sleuthing she needed to do. She began thinking of the best way to broach the subject when she realized Hollis was speaking to her.

"Annie, I need to consult with Gustav about lunch. Because of the tight ride schedule, we're having it delivered to the stables today, and I want to make sure everything's in order. Why don't you and Patricia show Miriam the horses you've brought down from Washington State? I'll be back in two ticks."

Annie was sure this was Hollis's way of telling her
he intended to talk to Chef Gustav himself about the
discovery of the dumbwaiter. She could only imagine
the chef's surprise when he opened the cabinet door
in a few minutes and found two pulleys instead of a
shelf with thermoses arrayed on it. She wished Hollis
had asked her to accompany him but knew it would
appear strange to anyone seeing her get in the car.
She'd already run that risk once today.

Miriam was using her cane this morning. Patricia
gently took her by the arm that was still free.

"I heard you tell the others that you occasionally
still ride. I think I've got just the horse for you, Picante. He's such a sweet, gentle boy, and I believe he
is trained to third level. I definitely could see you
on him."

"Dream on," was Miriam's laughing reply. But the
glint in her eye as she proceeded with Patricia to
the stalls belied what she truly felt. Annie was sure
riding again was a challenge her hostess would be
thrilled to meet head-on. And why not? Annie certainly intended to be riding when she was Miriam's
age, whatever that might be precisely.

Patricia brought out, as she boldly had called him,
"Miriam's new dressage horse," and this time, Annie
noticed, Miriam had not demurred the moniker. To
Annie's annoyance, Gwendolyn seemed to magically
appear beside them, and immediately addressed
Patricia.

"Remember, I want to ride Victory tomorrow. Perhaps around eleven or twelve, sometime before lunch?"

Patricia looked up from where she was adjusting

Picante's halter. The slight irritation Annie noticed on her face disappeared by the time she responded.

"That should be fine, Gwendolyn. I'll have him tacked up by eleven, if that fits."

"Oh, I'll want to use my own saddle. It's the same model Steffen Peters uses."

"Of course."

Gwendolyn turned to Annie. "You don't mind if Marcus watches me ride?"

Annie stifled her desire to stuff a sock down Gwendolyn's throat. "It's not for me to say. Marcus makes his own decisions."

"Oh, I'm sure he'll want to see this." She nimbly turned and walked away.

"Exactly when do you expect Marcus to arrive?" Miriam asked when Gwendolyn was out of earshot.

"His latest ETA was right before noon. Is that all right?" Annie asked anxiously. "I suppose I should have told Chef Gustav he'd be here for lunch."

"Not at all. Gustav always has enough food for several surprise guests. No, I was just wondering how much time I have left to convince Gwendolyn not to make a complete fool of herself."

"I'm sure you'll find a way. I hope so, anyway."

What Annie had really wanted to say was, "Why not just let her?"

Patricia was doing her usual superb sales job, although Annie knew that convincing Miriam she needed a dressage horse was a bit like shooting fish in a barrel. She decided to leave her to it and walked down the main aisle. She saw the heads of Amy and Lucy poking out of Schumann's stall. They had just finished braiding his mane.

"He looks very handsome," Annie observed, and got two smiles in return.

"Yes, he does. You might think about grooming as a new career, Lucy, before you blow another test today."

Annie recognized the voice; she'd just heard it back at Picante's stall. And Miriam was not around to stifle her words. Annie couldn't hold back any longer. She turned to Gwendolyn, who was languidly propped up against a nearby wall, and said what she'd wanted to say the moment she had arrived.

"I'm sick and tired of hearing you tear down every single person you encounter. I realize the concept of supporting fellow riders eludes you, but the least you could do is just shut up when you're around them. Does it bother you that no one likes you, Gwendolyn? It would bother me. But Lucy and I don't have to worry about that because we treat people nicely and actually care about them. Just the way we do with our horses. You, on the other hand, don't even care about developing a relationship with the horse that's working so hard for you. And that is truly unforgiveable. If anyone needs remedial work, it's you. Starting with your brain."

Annie had tried to speak softly but, by the time she was done, realized she was nearly shouting. She stopped abruptly and waited for the fallout. But all Gwendolyn could do was open and close her mouth like a widemouthed bass waiting for someone to drop in the baited hook. Well, she had delivered the bait, and all she could do now was hope Gwendolyn would take it. But she didn't hold out much hope. When Gwendolyn managed to slink away, Annie glanced over at Lucy, who had stopped grooming and was now looking at her with radiant eyes.

"That was super. Just what I wished I had said a long time ago."

"Lucy, you're a fine rider. Your horse adores you. I'm sure you'll do very well today. Don't let people like Gwendolyn get to you. They're just not worth it."

Annie walked off in the direction opposite the one Gwendolyn had taken. She'd just told one potential suspect she was a great person and told off the other. She was pretty sure she'd gotten the order right. But it was time to find Hollis and talk turkey about this new evidence and what to do about it.

But Hollis was nowhere to be found. She did find Tabitha and Harriett outside Jackson's stall, arguing over whether or not a star-studded saddle pad was permissible in the show ring. She veered off before they could see her. This was one topic that was out of her depth, and she had no desire to enter into the fray.

Annie finally spotted Hollis at eleven thirty, the same time that copious amounts of food arrived. Trays and trays were wheeled into a separate room at the back of the office. Annie felt almost guilty that their group was going to dine so sumptuously but not enough to stop from grabbing a wedge of cheese on a passing plate. Between moving furniture and telling off snooty riders, she'd worked up quite an appetite.

Hollis spoke as soon as she approached him.

"Deputy Collins is here today in plainclothes. I've given him the bare bones of what we discovered. He's looking at the dumbwaiter now, and he's none too happy that you've absconded with the mason jar, which is what I assume you did, Annie. He'll want to talk with Lucy and Gwen but has agreed to wait until after the show. All we have to do is make sure neither leaves the grounds. He's assigned two plainclothes deputies to watch them and told me frankly he'd like every guest to have a tail but just doesn't have the men."

Annie nodded at Hollis approvingly. She was so relieved that Hollis had informed the police already and not waited until after the show. And by doing so he'd achieved just what he'd wanted. Hollis's promptness in relaying the new information probably was why Deputy Collins had agreed to put off his interrogation of the two women until after the public had dispersed.

"I moved the mason jar to my suite. I didn't want to take the chance that anyone would use it even though the house is supposed to be off-limits. I'm sorry if that makes Deputy Collins unhappy, but it was my best judgment."

"Let's be honest with each other, Annie. Don't you really mean you didn't want Lucy or Gwendolyn to have access to what we assume is poison?"

"It's not quite that simple."

Annie briefly told him about finding Gwendolyn's door unlocked and the much more public display of the dumbwaiter in her suite.

"The thing is, Gwendolyn made a big point last night at dinner of telling us how she locks her door every night. She was shocked that the rest of us didn't, but we agreed that from now on it would be prudent to do so. If she *is* the killer, it makes no sense that she would leave her door unlocked this morning. It doesn't make sense even if she isn't."

"So, either Gwen hasn't been locking her door as she says she has, or someone's managed to find a duplicate key to get in."

"Looks that way. Which means, in theory, any guest could have accessed the dumbwaiter in Gwendolyn's room. The dumbwaiter isn't hard to get to, not as it is in Lucy's room. All the woman had to do was make sure Gwendolyn was out of the house."

Hollis sighed. "And since our guests have spent most of their days down at the stables, it wouldn't have been difficult to find a time when she knew Gwendolyn was riding and wouldn't return to her room for some time."

"All very true. I'll make sure Deputy Collins gets the mason jar as soon as I can manage it. I may need another clandestine ride back up to the house."

"We'll find a way to do that." Hollis looked a bit pained. "It's still hard to reconcile myself to the idea that one of our guests is a cold-blooded killer. Let's give it a rest. It's nearly time for Lucy to ride. Let's go cheer her on."

Now that the local gendarmes were up to speed, this seemed like an excellent idea. Then she needed to find Deputy Collins and hand over what she'd taken from the dumbwaiter cupboard. It occurred to her that picking up evidence was beginning to become a bad habit. But this had been done for the best of reasons. No one else needed to die.

Annie spotted Lucy's cheering section at once. Amy, Miriam, Patricia, Liz, Tabitha, and Harriett were all standing together in a small circle just beyond the spectator stands. Melissa was talking to Lucy, but when Hollis and Annie joined the group, she began walking over, too.

"She's not reading?" Annie whispered to Patricia.

"No, Lucy said she wanted to do it on her own. And

frankly, she probably does have the test memorized at this point."

Annie looked at Lucy to make eye contact, but Lucy wasn't looking at her supporters, or anyone, for that matter. Her gaze was straight ahead, and Annie realized that somehow Lucy looked different. Perhaps it was the way her chin now seemed to jut out a little, or the way she was seated in the saddle. In any case, Lucy looked composed and calm. But there was something more to her demeanor that Annie had not seen before. What was it? Ah, yes. A sense of determination. Lucy looked determined. As if she wasn't depending on anyone but herself and her horse.

The tinkle of the bell sounded, and Lucy continued to slowly walk Prince in a large circle until he was near the entrance of the ring. She halted, but almost immediately asked Prince to walk again, which in three strides became a trot. Annie could hear Amy and Melissa pull in their breaths as Lucy entered the ring and turned squarely onto the centerline. Halfway down, she halted and made her salute. Annie noticed even Prince seemed to nod a bit in deference to the judge. She heard Melissa and Amy exhale, and turned toward them. Melissa looked very pleased.

"Notice how straight Prince is? Lucy tends to start her halt late and in her rush her horse often ends up crooked. The fact that he's not means she prepared him well for the transition. And that's a very good sign."

Annie nodded. She watched Lucy continue her trot down the centerline and turn left to make her first circle. A few hours before, Annie had watched Liz do the same thing, and had noticed that Liz's circle was a bit more oblong than round, although she had no intention of repeating that observation to her friend. But Lucy's circle seemed spot on. So did the next one. And the next. Nor did Prince's pace seem to vary. The rhythm of his trot was sure and consistent. Annie saw that Prince was now at a walk, but it was no leisurely stroll, but rather a big, bright walk that told Annie the horse, at least, was enjoying his time in the arena. Lucy then urged him into an even, light canter that was beautiful to watch. She led Prince into another circle at this gait, and again, it was good, solid, and round, with no discernible slowdown that Annie could see. Lucy next changed direction and led Prince through another circle at a canter, this one a bit smaller than the first ones, but just as accurate as before. A minute later, she watched Lucy again trot down the centerline and halt. She made her salute, watched the judge return it, then walked Prince out of the arena. Annie realized that throughout Lucy's test, no one within their small group had made a sound. She wasn't sure if anyone had breathed.

Earlier today, she'd expected cheers to ring out as soon as Liz and Sammy had exited the ring, but she now knew that didn't mean Lucy's test was quite over yet. Instead of dismounting, Lucy walked Prince over to a volunteer steward, who'd carefully inspected his mouth, Lucy's blunt spurs, and her whip. Patricia had explained that the steward was making sure riders had used only accepted bits, had not abused their spurs or left marks on their horses, and that the whip was regulation size.

Annie had to content herself with walking over to the proud rider after this exercise was complete, along with everyone else, and instead of whoops and yells, extend her congratulations in a civilized tone of voice.

"You were amazing," Amy said. "What happened?"

Annie realized Lucy could have chosen to take umbrage at this remark, but instead, she good-naturedly replied, "I just decided to ride for myself. For myself and Prince, I mean, and forget that the rest of you were there."

"Thanks a lot," Melissa said, just as good-naturedly.

"You know what I mean. You couldn't be in there with me, telling me what to do any longer. It was time for me to put everything you'd told me into play."

Annie could see Melissa close to tears. She was so proud of her student and what she had just accomplished.

"I can't wait to see your score," she simply told Lucy. "I wouldn't be surprised if you've set a new record at Darby Farms."

Hollis and Miriam were effusive in their praise. Liz and Patricia heaped so many accolades on her that Lucy had to tell them nicely to stop. Even Harriett told Lucy that she'd ridden very well.

"You could learn something by watching those circles," she said sternly to Tabitha. "Did you notice how Lucy didn't counterbend her horse to get him in the corners? She actually used her inside leg!" Tabitha was polite enough to nod and tell Lucy she'd done a great job.

Annie added her own congratulation to the other well-wishers surrounding Lucy and Prince. She was infinitely glad that neither Gwendolyn nor Nicole had been there to try to belittle Lucy's successful test. Although she wondered where they had been keeping themselves, especially Nicole, whom she hadn't seen since she had emerged from the Packard this morning, looking extremely put out for having to take such a luxurious ride down to the stables. She couldn't be back at the house, and there weren't that many places to hide here. As much as she dreaded another encounter with the woman, Annie felt she needed to know her whereabouts. Everyone else was right with her, except Gwendolyn, of course, who was probably off someplace licking her wounds. Nicole was the only truly missing guest. Annie decided she really should make sure she was all right. She wished a plain-clothes deputy were watching her.

A moment later, she lost all interest in finding Nicole or anyone else. Because walking toward her, and looking more handsome than any man had a right to, was Marcus. His face lit up in a wide smile when he spotted her, and Annie abandoned all care for behavior codes at dressage affairs and ran straight to him. He took her in his arms. She searched for his lips, found them, and for one long minute, felt that she could melt into his body forever and never miss her own. Finally, she took him by the hand to lead him to where she had so suddenly left the Darbys and everyone else.

Lucy was still astride Prince. Marcus walked up to her, and said, "Are you the rider who was just in the arena? I don't think I've ever seen a more beautiful performance. Please accept my sincere congratulations."

Lucy's countenance turned bright red from her neck to her forehead. As she stammered out her thanks, Annie realized another would-be paramour of Marcus Colbert likely had just blossomed into being. It really was getting a bit tiresome.

Chapter Twenty-two

Gwendolyn and Nicole were still nowhere in sight, but now that Marcus had arrived, their whereabouts seemed of secondary importance to Annie. After all, where could they go? Both were scheduled to ride this afternoon, and Annie was sure neither woman would willingly give up her opportunity to shine. Besides, it was time for lunch.

Chef Gustav had once again created a feast. Every square inch of the buffet table by the back wall was laden with food, and people eagerly began to build their lunch on the china plates set out for them. Annie was among the foragers but not so far entrenched in the crowd that she couldn't hear Marcus and Hollis talking in the background.

"I can't remember when our paths last crossed," she heard Hollis tell Marcus, "but I'm awfully glad they have now. How have you been?"

"Fine, fine. In survival mode the first half of the

year, but now that I've met Annie, life has been much better."

"Of course. How remiss of me. Miriam and I were so sorry to hear about Hilda. And your troubles, too."

"Hilda's death was a terrible shock. But all that's behind me now, and I'm happy about the way the future is shaping up."

"Well, we've thoroughly enjoyed getting to know Annie and hope we'll see more of both of you now that we're all reacquainted. Shall we join the others at the groaning board?"

Annie smiled as she forked a piece of melon draped with prosciutto onto her plate. She sat down by Amy and Lucy, placed her napkin on the empty seat beside her for Marcus, and began to dig in. She noted Amy was eating very lightly. Her time to ride was fast approaching, and Annie wasn't surprised at her lack of appetite. In comparison, Lucy was devouring everything on her plate. But this was after she'd rubbed down Prince and given him a flake of alfalfa in his stall. Not to mention several kisses.

Annie looked across the room for Marcus and saw Gwendolyn and Nicole at the door. Of course, they would choose to make their entrance at the most opportune time, when nearly everyone was seated and they had a captive audience.

Their clothing reflected the epitome of dressage elegance. Both had shunned the traditional jackets Liz and Lucy had worn in the ring. Nicole had opted for cutaway tails, as well as immaculate white breeches and a stock tie. Gwendolyn was sporting a very short jacket with slit pockets and had what looked like flat nacre pearl buttons down the front. Nicole's helmet nearly lit up the room with its multicolored bling. Gwen's looked like a glittering black moon crater. While Nicole stood back, the better to show off her stunning attire, Gwendolyn rushed to Marcus, flinging her arms around his neck.

"Marcus! When did you arrive? I wasn't sure you were coming!"

If everyone hadn't known better, they might have thought Gwendolyn was Marcus's main squeeze. It certainly looked that way. But everyone had seen Annie's exuberant embrace of the same man a few minutes ago, which had been fully reciprocated. Annie knew she was not the only person who was slightly embarrassed by Gwendolyn's very public display of affection.

Marcus obviously felt the same way. He carefully unwrapped Gwendolyn's arms and held them gently at her side, as if he was afraid they would spring up again if he let them go.

"How nice to see you, Gwen," he said pleasantly. "Are you riding this afternoon?"

"You know I am," Gwendolyn replied warmly. "Remember, I told you all about it at your mother's just a few days ago."

"Ah, yes. I remember you mentioning an upcoming show. I look forward to seeing you in the ring. Have you eaten? I was just about to get some food."

"So, when did you get here, you sly thing? I suppose you drove down in the Spyder."

It occurred to Annie that she had no idea what kind of car—or cars, when it came to it—Marcus owned. She'd only seen him in rental vehicles when he had been visiting her.

Marcus smiled but didn't answer. Somehow, he

managed to slip by Gwendolyn, quickly fill his plate, and slide into the seat waiting for him in remarkably short time. Annie never failed to marvel at the dexterity of such a big, tall guy.

"That was a close call," she murmured to him as he sat down.

Patricia nodded from where she sat on the other side of the table. "A bit too close for comfort."

Marcus smiled again and raised his glass. "Wonderful to see all of you again in sunny California. Have you tried the prawns, Annie? I'm happy to share what I have on my plate. You seem to have done a good job demolishing yours already."

Gwendolyn did not hide her displeasure well. Out of the corner of her eye, Annie saw Gwendolyn eyeing their table, no doubt wondering if she should barge over and take the last seat. To Annie's relief, she swept by Annie and Marcus and sat down with Miriam and Hollis, who were eating alone. Since the couple appeared to be enjoying a private meal, Annie wasn't sure why Gwendolyn thought she'd be welcome there. But Annie didn't dwell on it. Not when Marcus was beside her and keeping her and the rest of the table laughing about all his previous encounters with horses.

"We'll make a rider out of you yet," Patricia told him. She was very fond of Marcus, in a strictly professional way, of course. For a man who barely knew one end of the horse from another, he'd invested thousands and thousands of dollars to ensure the health and continued well-being of a very large herd.

"Perhaps," Marcus replied thoughtfully. "When pigs fly."

The table erupted into laughter once more, and Annie watched Gwendolyn's head snap around in anger. She hoped she'd seen the last of Gwendolyn's flirty ploys. She certainly did not want her ersatz rival's behavior to escalate.

At Annie's suggestion, she and Marcus agreed to sit with the rest of the spectators; it was the safest place to keep him away from Gwendolyn, who should be prepping for her ride in any case.

"I have to leave you for a few moments," she told him once they were seated. "But not for long. Here, take the day sheet. It'll show you the order of riders. Three are guests from the house, starting with Amy, then Tabitha, and after a few others, Gwendolyn."

He nodded and held the sheet upside down, squinting at it as if it made more sense this way. How droll. She turned the paper around properly and gave him a quick kiss on the cheek before leaving.

Finding Deputy Collins in the crowd was something of a challenge now that he wasn't in his usual khaki uniform. She finally spotted him near the judge's booth, talking to Brianna. She would not be happy if he was treating the technical delegate as a suspect and slowed down to see if she could hear any of their conversation. Not for one moment did Annie believe Brianna was responsible for Judge Bennett's death, despite the incriminating words that had flown out of her mouth when she'd learned the news.

But no, Deputy Collins was only talking about security details. She could tell by the way Brianna responded and pointed to various eaves under the stable roof. Brianna's reply to his last question was audible as she walked toward them.

"We're all ready for you. The barn manager has promised to have today's surveillance put on a thumb drive and on her desk by five o'clock for you. The videographer's also agreed to give you a copy of everything he films today. Although he's not too happy that he has to hand it over without his usual compensation."

Deputy Collins grinned. "I'll talk to him and remind him how much we appreciate assistance from civilians."

"I'm not sure 'the heartfelt thanks of a grateful nation' ploy will help much," Brianna replied. "But don't worry about it. He's a fixture at all the local shows and makes enough money, anyway."

She turned slightly and saw Annie.

"Hi, Annie. Can I help you with something?"

"Actually, I'm here to talk to Deputy Collins if you can spare him for a few minutes."

"Sure. I need to get back to the office, anyway. Everything okay?"

"And this won't take long."

Brianna nodded and walked off briskly. Deputy Collins locked his very handsome eyes on her.

"Interesting discovery you made this morning."

"I thought so. Have you had a chance to take a look at it?"

"I have, and it's being examined for fingerprints and anything else we can find as we speak. But we were expecting to find more than a bunch of thermoses. Hollis thought you might have walked off with the key piece of evidence."

As good-looking as Deputy Collins might be, he was beginning to irritate her.

"I sure as hell wasn't going to leave a jar of poison sitting there, just so whoever concocted it could come back at her leisure and slip it to another unsuspecting victim."

"Your intentions are great. But that's why we're here. So, if you find anything, you can tell us, and let us handle it."

He was speaking slowly, as if somehow enunciating each word might make his point clearer. All it did was infuriate Annie.

"I came over to tell you as soon as I could. And to tell you where you can find it. And by the way, I didn't touch it. I do know a few things about how to handle evidence."

"Worked many homicides before?"

She wanted to tell him yes, three to be precise, and that was just this year. Instead, she ignored his question.

"It's in my suitcase, which is now locked and in my bedroom closet. I'm going to watch the next two riders, but then I'll be happy to take you right to it."

"You know, you were taking a big risk handling that jar by yourself. Did it ever occur to you that it might have been a bomb?"

She curtly turned on her heel and stalked off. Honestly, some people were so touchy about letting other people help. So much for *her* civilian assistance.

Annie wished she could share with Marcus everything that she knew, although trying to explain how the presence of an old dumbwaiter in the Darcy mansion pertained to the killer's methodology would be difficult in a very public spectator stand. Particularly if she had to avoid using certain words such as *killer*, *poison*, and *next intended victim*. She decided to wait until the next short break to bring him up to speed. She knew that Marcus would much prefer to hear it all now than watch the dressage show. But the next two riders were both people she really wanted to see perform. She returned to the spectator section and climbed up to join him. Marcus looked at her curiously.

"Who was that man you were talking to?"

"A stuck-up cop who doesn't appreciate my help."

Marcus laughed. "I thought he was asking you for a date."

"Him? I'd rather eat ground glass."

"Whew. For a moment I thought I had a rival."

"Unfortunately, I have to deal with him again after Amy and Tabitha ride. But it'll only be for a short bit."

"If you don't return within ten minutes I'll call the . . . oh, wait. They're already here."

"Very funny."

"You will tell me what this is all about at some point."

She smiled at him.

"I'd love to."

Annie sensed that the people sitting nearest to them were trying to understand their conversation. It was time to change the subject.

"Have you had a chance to look at the day sheet?"

"I've done nothing but stare it since you left. It's all Greek to me."

"Let me see if I can help."

It was a bit like the blind leading the blind, she thought. But at least someone was doing the leading.

Amy entered the arena at precisely one thirty, the first rider on the afternoon schedule. Like the two previous riders, she entered at a trot, but this time the horse's carriage and its gait seemed quite different. Instead of the stretchy neck Sammy and Prince had shown at this pace, Schumann's neck was raised and arched, and his nose was nearly vertical with his poll. There also was an enhanced level of expression in his trot. It seemed to Annie that the horse was somehow more motivated to move forward although he appeared completely at ease as he made small, light steps down the centerline. Energy seemed to surge through his body, from his back onward.

Schumann also knew a lot more dressage moves, she soon realized. She watched him prance down long rails in a lateral direction, one hind foot elegantly stepping beneath the other. And his canter seemed like perfection itself. His strides were shorter than what she'd seen with Prince, but they resulted in light, almost buoyant steps. She applauded enthusiastically as Amy and Schumann left the ring, restraining her urge to whistle.

"Who's next?"

"Tabitha Rawlins. She and Amy are riding the same test, second level test three, which obviously is much more advanced than what you saw Lucy do."

"Right."

She looked at him suspiciously. "You did see Lucy ride, didn't you?"

He grinned. "The last bit. She just looked as if she needed a kind word, way up there on that big horse."

"You were absolutely right. Anyway, it'll be interesting to see how Tabitha performs. Amy trains under Melissa, who's an absolute sweetheart, and Tabitha's trainer is Harriett, who's a bit of a tyrant although Miriam swears by her. Both trainers are excellent riders, just different styles. I'm curious to see how Harriett's training is reflected in Tabitha's ride."

"Tell me what you see. I can guarantee that any subtleties will be lost on me. Which is not to say I won't enjoy the show."

"Of course not." She wondered what he'd rather be doing than what he was now, then blushed.

Annie couldn't quite put her finger on it, but Tabitha's ride was significantly different than Amy's. There were no gaffes, no egregious errors that Annie could see. If anything, Tabitha's transitions from gait to gait seemed more precise, and her execution of each movement was so knowing and immediate that Annie suspected the rider really had spent her evenings memorizing each pattern. She looked for any trace of bling on Jackson but found none. There was no hint of color, nothing jangled, and Annie was relieved that Tabitha seemed to have overcome her superstitions about what her baubles could do. All in all, it was a very clean, even, and meticulous ride. Annie dutifully clapped as Tabitha rode Jackson out of the ring. But something was missing. What was it?

Then it came to Annie. It was heart. When Amy had ridden, it had been clear that her whole heart was in the ride, and with her horse's performance. Tabitha had executed what seemed to be a near flawless ride, but the spirit and intensity Amy had exhibited were just not there.

She stood up and stretched, and Marcus joined her. She glanced at her watch. Sixteen minutes until Gwendolyn's test time. She looked for her over in the warm-up pen. There she was, trotting on her

Warmblood, Martinique, with Harriett close by. The
trainer must have just said something that Gwendolyn
didn't like because Annie saw her abruptly wheel Martinique around so that she no longer faced Harriett.
She saw Harriett raise her hands and drop them, then
walk out of the warm-up ring, shaking her head.
Gwendolyn didn't seem to be getting along with
anyone today.

"Be right back," she said to Marcus, and scrambled
down the spectator tiers and over to where she'd just
espied Deputy Collins. When she reached him, all she
said was "Ready?"

Deputy Collins didn't even give her a verbal response; he merely nodded. Fine, if he wanted to pout,
let him. He motioned her toward a subcompact Ford
that despite its size, still looked to Annie like a minia-
ture cop car. It took two minutes to get to the house,
and not a word was spoken on the way. Annie discreetly
felt the zippered pocket in her breeches. Hollis's
master key was still there. Good. Now all she had to do
was find a way to ditch the deputy for a few minutes to
accomplish her final task.

The house seemed cavernously empty. Perhaps it
was the juxtaposition of coming from a crowded place
that was humming with activity. Whatever it was, Annie
felt as if she and Deputy Collins were the only two
people on the premises. That was fine with her.

She used her own key to get into her bedroom. No
sense in letting Deputy Collins know she had the ability to access every room in the house. She lugged out
her suitcase and deliberately turned her back on him
as she adjusted the combination lock to the code to
open. The lid popped, Annie pried up the top, and

there it was, nestled in a bed of towels, a small mason jar with a milky-white liquid inside. She stepped aside.

"It's all yours."

Deputy Collins stared down at it, as if could explode at any second. He leaned over to take a closer look, and Annie was pretty sure that he sniffed it. Honestly. This was getting boring. Couldn't he just pick it up, put it one of his evidence bags, and leave? She'd make an excuse for sticking around for a few more minutes. She wasn't above using the vague excuse that for reasons of her sex, she needed to use the bathroom.

You could just tell him what you're up to, her Good Angel reminded her.

Forget about it, her Bad Angel scoffed. *He'd just make it into a big production, and all you need is a couple of minutes to do the job.*

"This is not going to be simple," Deputy Collins said the words begrudgingly.

"Oh? Why not?" She'd have liked to tell him she'd managed to pick it up, carry it to her room, and place in her suitcase with no difficulty. But she said nothing more.

"I want to get the explosives squad to remove this. It'll take a while."

"Okay. Well, I'll just scamper off, then."

He nodded absently, his eyes still on the jar.

"And, uh, you will lock my door when you leave, won't you?"

He nodded again without looking at her.

Annie left one heartbeat later, pulling her bedroom door five inches closer to her as she did so. Deputy Collins did not have to see what she was about to do.

* * *

She glanced back one more time as she rounded the spiral staircase and headed up one floor instead of down. The deputy was now talking to his wrist, no doubt gathering forces. She knew she was taking a big chance right now, but she also knew this was likely her only opportunity to find out who had been accessing the dumbwaiter. She wasn't at all convinced it was the occupant of either bedroom she'd been in earlier. Lucy truly wouldn't hurt a fly, and Gwendolyn had more pressing issues to deal with than murder, such as getting Marcus around to her way of thinking.

But the bigger problem still remained. Annie wasn't at all sure which guest she *was* looking for, but a quick tour of each bedroom seemed to be the logical place to start. Which one first? For some unknown reason, her mind kept coming back to the same person. She wasn't sure why, since there was nothing that overtly linked this guest to the murder of Judge Bennett. Still, she couldn't shake the feeling that this woman's bedroom was the one she should investigate first.

She dug out the master key from her pocket and placed it into the keyhole. The door swung open, and she quickly entered, scanning the tables and counters for some clue that would tell her she'd made the right decision to come here.

Like Gwendolyn's bedroom, this one was rather unkempt, with clothes, books, notebooks, and trinkets strewn over chests, chairs, and bookcases. But she found what she'd unconsciously been looking for in a very conspicuous place.

It was on the table where the coffee machine stood, along with a basket filled with coffee, tea bags, and the usual condiments. Should she take it with her? Annie wavered. It would be horrible if it were to go missing before she could inform Detective Wollcott, the only law-enforcement official she intended to tell. But if it did, would her word be enough to convince the detective that she had seen it, just in this place, a few hours before? Probably not.

Yet what were the chances of any guest's returning to the house unless Hollis authorized it? And she could tell him, as well. Of course she would. He needed to know which of the many houseguests he'd so hospitably hosted for the past week had killed one, probably two people.

She decided to risk leaving her found object in situ. Chances were no one would return here before she could make her discovery known, but just as a precaution, she used her cell to snap a quick photo to prove that it had been here when she was. She tiptoed out of the room and locked the door behind here. Lightly running down the stairs, she slipped out the front door and took the same path back to the stables, ar-riving behind the warm-up ring.

She saw Gwendolyn, poised on Martinique by the entrance to the dressage court. Her face was set as if she were ready to go into battle.

"Lots of luck," Annie said under her breath. "You'll need it."

Chapter Twenty-three

The judge's bell rang out as Annie walked briskly toward the spectator booth. Then she stopped. She'd looked up, expecting to see his familiar face, but Marcus was no longer seated there. She looked around, but his equally familiar frame was nowhere in sight. Then she saw Harriett standing by the tiers, and walked over to join her. If she admitted it, Annie was curious to see how Gwendolyn fared in the dressage ring. She might as well get the running commentary from the person who knew her student's riding better than anyone else.

Harriett nodded at her in a not-unfriendly manner. "She is in a state," she said shortly. "I'm not holding my breath."

Annie wondered if Marcus might have played a part in creating that state but simply returned the nod and concentrated on what Gwendolyn was doing in the ring.

This test did not ask for the immediate circles she'd seen before. Instead, she watched Martinique perform the same collected gaits she'd seen in the other rides, but in quick, successive order. When the gaits were against the rail, the horse often seemed to be on a multilane track. Gwendolyn was asking a lot of Martinique, and Annie could see her requests weren't often producing the desired effect.

"She's not preparing well!" Harriett hissed to Annie. "Rushing is the enemy of balance! She knows this!"

The judge's bell jangled, and Annie froze. What did it mean when it rang mid-test? She watched Gwendolyn bring Martinique over to face the judge, then turn in the other direction. Annie looked inquiringly at Harriett.

"She's gone off course," Gwendolyn's trainer said through gritted teeth. "That will cost her in points."

Annie could not keep up with the flow of the test, but even she was aware that Gwendolyn was not connecting with her horse, who seemed stiff, tense, and a tad unsure of where he was next supposed to place his hoof. Each time Gwendolyn passed by at a trot or a canter, her face seemed a shade more rigid and intractable. Neither rider nor horse was enjoying their time in the arena. That much was evident.

Martinique trotted down the centerline one last time and halted. Gwendolyn gave a short salute and turned to exit without even waiting for the judge's recognition. Harriett sighed heavily and began to walk over to the warm-up ring, where Martinique would now be examined by one of the stewards. Annie could think of nothing to say to Harriett that would be helpful, so she simply watched her go and began to look again for Marcus. Could he have gone to the public parking area? She walked past the warm-up pen on her way, studiously avoiding eye contact with Gwendolyn and her trainer.

"Is there anything in those boots of yours or are they hollow?" she heard Harriett sharply remind her student. "Collection is with the seat and leg, not only the reins!"

Even Harriett seemed at her wit's end with Gwendolyn right now. Annie knew she was. Gwendolyn had done nothing but irritate her from the moment they'd met.

Marcus was indeed in the parking lot and smoking a Sherman cigarette, a habit he tried to hide from Annie, usually not very successfully.

"How'd she do?" he asked casually.

"Slightly less than hideous."

"I was afraid of that."

"Why? What happened? I was only gone for ten minutes."

"That was all the time she needed."

Annie fell silent. This ought to be interesting.

Marcus threw his cigarette butt on the gravel, ground it to a pulp, then picked it up and placed it in his pocket.

"That'll just make your clothes stink. Why not try the trash bin over there?"

Marcus looked at her as if advice was not what he most wanted to hear right now but obediently went over and deliberately placed the cigarette remnant in the trash. He walked back and gave Annie a long hug. At last, he released her and held her at arm's length.

"You were right."

"I love hearing those three little words. In what way, Marcus?"

"I told someone close to me about our little spat, expecting to get her full sympathy and support for my position. Instead, I was told I was an ignorant and stupid, stupid man who couldn't see the truth when it was staring me in the face."

"That bad, huh?"

"That bad. I was told even a fool could see that Gwendolyn had been doing her best to get her hooks into me for years, even before—well, as soon as she realized my marriage was on the rocks."

"Aha. And who was this brilliant sage?"

"My mother."

Annie burst into laughter, which didn't stop until Marcus found an excellent way to do so.

When he'd stopped kissing her, Annie told him, "I'd like to meet your mother someday. Not in the way it sounds but because she sounds like such an interesting woman."

"She told me she'd like to meet you, too. In just about the same words. Just be forewarned. She's a lot smarter than I am."

The sound of a sports car in high gear came from behind them, and Annie watched a gold Porsche roar out of the parking lot and toward the front gates.

"I don't think she's supposed to leave," Annie mused. "I wonder if the plainclothes deputy who's supposed to be watching her will be able to stop her."

"He should let her go. She didn't kill anyone, did she, Annie?"

"No. She just tried to make everyone's life miserable. And pretty much succeeded."

"Well, she's not going to make mine that way. I won't repeat what she told me when you'd gone off to do your derring-do, whatever that was. And I tried to tell her the truth as gently as I could."

"But it wasn't enough."

"I'm afraid it never will be."

Annie sighed happily.

"If it's any consolation, you make me as happy as I ever hope to be."

"Same here. I don't suppose there's a refreshment bar around here? I could do with a good bracing drink."

"Let's go look. I'll join you. I'm not riding."

They found Hollis and Miriam in the refreshment area under the shade of a large umbrella, each holding a tall G and T.

"I'll have what they're having," Marcus told a passing waiter. "Annie?"

"In retrospect, I think I'll just have a Pellegrino. I may not be riding, but I do have to talk to a couple of burly policemen this afternoon."

Hollis's eyes immediately locked on hers. "What have you found, Annie?"

"I'll tell you, but first I want to make sure that every one of your guests is still present and accounted for. Gwendolyn just left, or at least, she tried to leave in her car. I don't know if the guy covering her will reel her back in, although I think she's blameless in both deaths. But it's imperative that everyone else remain here, at least until I can talk to Detective Wollcott."

"This sounds ominous."

"It is. I—"

"Hollis!" It was Melissa, running toward them, Amy a few steps behind her. "I can't find Lucy! The test scores for her level are posted, and I wanted her to see them. She scored 75.17! But I can't find her anywhere. Amy's looked, too!"

Hollis frowned. "Unbelievable. The two people the police are supposed to watch seem to have vanished."

"Supposed to watch? Why? Is Lucy in danger?" Amy's anxiety over her friend was palpable.

Everyone seemed to be looking at Annie. She chose her words carefully.

"Not in immediate danger, no. At least, not in my opinion." Turning to Hollis, she said, "But we do need to find her. And quickly. I am afraid that our killer may decide to make one more heroic gesture, even though—"

She stopped. No one except Hollis and Deputy Collins knew she'd discovered a container that looked to contain poison. And, of course, they had no way of knowing whether this was the only one.

"Hollis, when did you tell everyone that you'd be escorting them to the stables today in your cars?"

"Last night. I went down to the stables around nine, right after we'd made the decision. Miriam and I had talked about it and decided it was the sensible thing to do."

Damn! That meant the killer could have secreted the poison on her person and brought it to the stables. So no one was safe. No one who encountered her, that was.

"Did I do something wrong?" Hollis seemed genuinely distressed.

Annie gave him a quick smile. "No, we just have to make sure we know where everyone is from now until I can contact Collins and call Wollcott."

"Liz and Patricia are by the horses for sale," Melissa said. "They're surrounded by people and seem to be fine."

"Great. Can you tell them to stay there and not move until further notice?"

"I'll go." Amy turned and began to run back to the stables.

"And come back here when you're done!" Melissa called after her. Amy didn't turn, but her bobbing head told everyone that she understood.

"Whom else are we missing?" Hollis sounded as if he dreaded the answer.

"Harriett was in the warm-up arena before Gwendolyn took off. She's probably still there with Martinique. Gwendolyn didn't have time to groom him before she hightailed it out of here."

"I'll tell her to—what, Annie?" Melissa asked. "What do I tell her?"

"Tell her to come to the hospitality area and hang with Hollis and Miriam. Just say it's police orders. She'll grumble, but she'll do it."

"Right." Melissa left at a run.

"What can I do?" Marcus asked.

Annie scanned the warm-up area. There was no sign of Nicole, who she knew was due to ride soon.

"Do you remember the woman who came in with Gwendolyn?"

"The one with the Mardi Gras helmet?"

"That's the one. Her name is Nicole, and she'll be riding her test in—" She glanced at her watch. "In forty-two minutes. I would have expected to see her in the warm-up arena by now. She must be with her horse near her stall. I'll go with you, point her out, then let you cover her."

"Do I have to talk to her?"

"Better that you don't. She'll be mentally preparing

for her test and won't appreciate your brilliant wit right now. Just don't let her out of your sight."

"What can we do, Annie?" Miriam's voice expressed the concern that Annie knew all of them felt, an unknown fear that someone else's life was still in danger. And they didn't even know what she knew. She was touched by their faith in her.

"Just gather people in as they arrive. After I point out Nicole, I'll go in search of Lucy. And Tabitha. Have you seen her since she was in the ring?"

"Just briefly," Hollis said. "We watched her ride and congratulated her afterward. She was about to take Jackson back to the stables to groom."

"Great. With luck, she'll still be there. Okay, everyone, with the exception of Patricia and Liz, whom we'll let stay in the stables with potential customers, everyone else agrees to meet here as soon as they get the word. Marcus, you can tell Nicole when her ride is over. Now, let's go, but not at a run. The public is going to get suspicious if too many people start racing around, especially after the events of yesterday."

"True," Miriam agreed. "It's not really done at these kinds of shows."

Marcus grinned and set off with Annie for the stables at a brisk pace.

Andy's stall was at the opposite end of the barn from where Lucy, Amy, and Liz's horses were housed. Annie scanned the aisle and saw with relief the big Andalusian saddled and now being handheld by Nicole outside his stall. Nicole's brilliant, sparkling helmet was a dead giveaway.

"There she is, in the helmet with the rhinestones," Annie told Marcus, pointing with her arm. "Just wander over to that area, look at all the nice horses, and follow her out when she goes into the warm-up ring. She won't leave it, except, of course, to enter the dressage court once the judge rings the bell. I realize her safety seems assured, but I'll still feel better knowing you've got her in your sight at all times."

"Yes, but Annie—"

Annie turned impatiently.

"What if someone does approach her? Who's the bad guy here? Can't you tell me anything?"

"I wish I could. If someone does approach her, just make contact with Nicole as well. That should be enough of a deterrent. Bottom line, she can't be alone with anyone. Does that help?"

"Your wish is my command." Marcus gave her a quick kiss and strode down the aisle. Annie hoped he wouldn't be too conspicuous. He was one of the few spectators she'd seen today who had completely skipped the English riding look and was wearing khakis and boat loafers. And as Nicole's fiancé had pointed out, he was a devilishly good-looking man. Oh, well. Marcus would just have to do.

Annie ran down to Jackson's stall but only found the horse, unsaddled, placidly chomping on a bit of hay. She ducked into the tack room. Several people were poking through their tack chests, but Tabitha was not among them. The rear entrance was just around the corner, so just to make sure, Annie looked around by the hot walkers, wash rack, as well as the huge round pen where she'd seen Nicole misuse her horse a few days ago. Neither Lucy nor Tabitha was visible. All this exertion was catching up with her. She was breathing heavily. Perspiration from her forehead dripped down her face. She unceremoniously wiped it off with one forearm and then reached into her pocket. It was time to bring Detective Wollcott up to speed.

He answered on the first ring, and Annie plunged in.

"It's Annie. I think I've found our killer."

There was a slight pause on the line.

"Who?"

Annie told him. "She's in the bedroom next to Gwendolyn's, which is the one where the dumbwaiter is in almost plain view."

"And?"

"I went into her room today. I just had a feeling I'd find something. And I did."

She paused, and wondered briefly whether her discovery was really the great epiphany she'd thought it was just an hour ago.

"And what did you find, Annie?" Detective Wollcott was being very patient. But at least he wasn't condescending, as Deputy Collins had been.

"It was a traveling immersion heater, the kind that's just a coil and you plug in to heat water. It was right by the coffeemaker, and near an outlet."

"I'm sorry. I'm having difficulty making the connection."

"We know the dumbwaiter in Gwendolyn's room was how she transported the thermos of the tea from the kitchen to her room. Obviously, she must have had a key to Gwendolyn's bedroom to be able to get in. But if Gwendolyn was down at the stables, which is where she is most of the time, it would be easy to retrieve the thermos, go back to her own room to add the poison, then switch the thermos Chef Gustav had prepared with the lethal one."

"So far I'm following you."

"The only problem was that Judge Bennett liked

her Lady Grey tea served hot. Our houseguest couldn't very well go to the kitchen and heat it as the chef did, in a saucepan on the stove. So she used the coil in her room to heat the tea, poured it in the thermos, then took it downstairs to make the switch. That should have been fairly easy. The kitchen was bustling early Saturday morning, Chef Gustav was preoccupied with his missing staff, and guests had been invited to pick up a thermos whenever they wished. It wouldn't have been difficult to walk in with one thermos and walk out with another."

"Interesting. You may be right."

"Well, there's one way to check. There were six thermoses in the dumbwaiter when Hollis and I first looked inside. If one of them is filled with Lady Grey tea, then it's got to be the one Chef Gustav prepared and was swapped out. As you know, Chef Gustav tossed the first batch. I don't know if she knew that, and this was her second poisoned thermos, or if she just waited until after seven to make the switch."

"Where's Deputy Collins now?"

"I left him around one forty-five in the house. He was staring at the mason jar I'd locked in my room. I believe he decided that your explosives team should be involved in its transport from the property."

"Complete overkill. Between that and his Dick Tracy watch, I'm beginning to lose patience with the lad."

"There's more. And this is what's bothering me. Hollis took us down to the stables this morning in his old vintage cars. But he told everyone this was the plan last night, when everyone was down at the stables checking on their horses. So, our killer could have brought the poison with her this morning. No one gave us a pat down when we got here."

"Hell and damnation."

"Yes, and I can't find Lucy or Tabitha. I've asked people to round up every houseguest they see and to congregate at the hospitality bar. Oh, and Gwendolyn left in her Porsche, after her ride. She was in a bit of a huff."

"Over what?"

"Unrequited love."

"Oh, that's all right, then. Wait—weren't she and Lucy supposed to have tails?"

"That's what Hollis told me."

"I'll be there within the half hour. Meanwhile, I'll find out from Collins what's happened to the deputies who were supposed to be covering the two women and why it's taking so damned long to put a jar into evidence. By the way, what's the status of the horse show?"

"It's going well, and only one more rider from the house is still on deck."

"Who's that?"

"Nicole Anne Forrester. But I've asked my boyfriend to keep her in sight. She should be in the warm-up arena now, waiting to ride. So she's safe. It's the other two I'm worried about."

"With good reason. See you in a jiffy. Oh, and Annie?"

"Yes?"

"Good work. Have you ever considered a job in law enforcement?"

"When pigs fly."

"Just thought I'd ask."

* * *

Annie ended the call and walked out through the stables into the entrance area. She peered past the dressage court into the warm-up ring. There was Nicole, slowly trotting her Andalusian in a large circle, her head bowed in deep concentration. Marcus stood a discreet distance away, his arms draped over the top rung of the white fence.

She felt better knowing one more houseguest was safe. If only she could find Lucy and Tabitha. Then she heard the jingle of the judge's bell, and paused. It was Nicole's time to ride.

Chapter Twenty-four

For one fleeting second, Annie was tempted to watch the diva's performance. But the urgency of finding Lucy and Tabitha was far more compelling. She turned back to look again in the stables and nearly ran into Marcus.

"I just saw you by the warm-up arena!"

"Yes, but once the bell rang, I figured it was recess, so I came around to find you. I'd spotted you coming out of the stables."

"Thanks for keeping track of Nicole. I knew it was a long shot that anyone would try to get to her, but still, it was good to know she was covered."

"My pleasure. It was completely humdrum. She preened a bit when she thought no one was watching, led her horse out to the pen, then went into a deep repose on the horse's back."

"What, she fell asleep?"

"Looked like it. As if she were meditating on her upcoming performance. Rather picturesque, actually."

Nicole meditating? Annie couldn't even imagine

such a thing. Whenever she'd seen the woman astride her horse, she was trying to get results, and as Annie had seen, at times had tried rather too much.

Marcus's use of the word *meditate* stirred something in her brain. Where had she heard the word used recently? Oh, yes, it had been during the round-robin interview with Detective Wollcott yesterday, which seemed a long time ago now. In fact, it had been Tabitha who'd used it. She'd said she'd arisen early on Saturday morning and meditated for an hour before going down to breakfast.

Annie suddenly stared at Nicole in the ring. She was cantering Andy down the centerline, the first rider she'd seen start in that gait, and this one was exceptionally precise and elegant.

Then she and Andy began riding on the diagonal, transitioning from what looked like a collected trot to an extended trot and back to the collected trot, the one that Amy had done so well. Annie looked closely at the rider. Nicole and her horse appeared very much at the top of their form today. At letter B, Nicole asked Andy to make a tiny circle, and she watched the Andalusian make very small steps that matched the rhythm of his trot. The performance looked similar to the one Annie had seen Nicole do in practice, but there was some small difference in the way it was performed now. She wished Patricia were by her to point out what that tiny distinction was. If she only knew more about dressage, she'd know. Because right now, what she was thinking seemed totally preposterous.

Marcus was still standing next to her. She glanced over at him and noticed his quizzical gaze.

"Is there something wrong?"

"I'm not sure. I'll know in a minute."

She turned her eyes back to the dressage ring. Andy was cantering around a corner of the arena. His head was lowered, and his front legs produced big and extravagant strides, one after another. Now he was performing a half pass with a gracefulness she did not know a horse could possess. In a few moments, Annie saw the movement she was looking for, the flying lead change. A few seconds later, he did the movement again, changing the direction of his lead in midair. Each was perfection itself. There was no hesitation from his hindquarters; they moved perfectly in sync with his front. As the Andalusian turned at the far corner, Annie took her gaze from the horse to the face underneath the radiantly colored helmet. And then she knew she was right.

Without a word to Marcus, she turned and ran as fast as she could to the office, where Brianna was immersed in paperwork.

"Come with me!" She tugged on Brianna's arm. Startled, Brianna rose from her chair and let Annie quickly lead her into the center aisle of the stables.

"What is it?"

"Nicole. We have to find her. You take the dressing rooms to the left of the office. I'll do the right. If we don't find anything, let's meet in the middle and figure where else to look."

Brianna nodded and ran away from Annie to inspect her designated area. If she thought it was strange that Annie was asking her to find a rider who gave every appearance of performing outside at that very moment, she didn't say so. Annie ran in the opposite direction. A moment later, she heaved open the door to the ladies' restroom and quickly ran her hands through the cotton shower curtains on one side. Nothing. All the stalls were empty. Where else could she look? She yanked open the door to a small linen closet in the back. There lay Nicole, on the floor and on her back, wearing only the skimpiest of lingerie. She was writhing as if in deep pain and clutching her stomach. Annie heard the sound of footsteps approaching her, and Brianna was suddenly behind her, peering over her shoulder.

"I'll call the medic," she said abruptly, and turned to leave.

"Have her bring the respiratory kit this time, and any activated charcoal if it's on hand."

Brianna nodded and was gone. Annie bent down and took Nicole's pulse. It was weak, but not as weak as Judge Bennett's had been, and she was still conscious.

"Nicole! Can you hear me? Nicole!" Annie very gently moved the woman's shoulders to try to get her attention.

Two eyes lolled back at her, wide, dilated, but aware on some level that someone else was now with her. Annie slowly helped Nicole to a sitting position and wrapped a towel around her, then took two more from the closet to place around her head.

"Nicole," she said softly. "We're getting help for you right now. Please try to stay awake. I want you to concentrate on your breathing right now. Can you do that? Let's do it together. Inhale. Exhale. Inhale. Exhale. That's it. You're doing fine."

The show medic banged the door open. Brianna was behind her, holding a bag.

"She's conscious. I think if she can expel the poison herself, she should be all right."

The medic nodded curtly and crouched down beside her. Annie stood up.

"I need to go," she told Brianna, and without waiting for a response, ran out the door and back outside. The first person she saw was Detective Wollcott, who was talking to Marcus in the same spot where she'd left him two minutes earlier. The next thing she noticed was the Andalusian, who was now in the warm-up ring, being inspected by a volunteer steward.

Annie rudely inserted herself between the two men. Thrusting one arm out, she pointed to the rider.

"Arrest her. Arrest Tabitha. She's just tried to kill Nicole."

Many things happened at once.

In her desire to expose Tabitha, Annie had neglected to keep her voice down. In retrospect, that was a mistake. Not only did several bystanders overhear her indictment, but the accused also got the message loud and clear. Andy surged forward, nearly toppling the steward as he bolted away at Tabitha's command. Tabitha headed for the exit gate, but an intelligent volunteer had just finished locking it, and Annie saw another one running to secure the one to the dressage court.

At that moment, Lucy appeared in front of the stables, leading Prince on a rope attached to his halter. His coat was still wet, and he looked exceptionally clean.

Annie ran up to her and grabbed her by the shoulders.

"Lucy! Where have you been?"

She looked surprised. "In back, giving Prince a bath. Why? Did I miss something?"

"But I looked there! We all did!"

Annie glanced in back of her. Tabitha was still in the warm-up ring, wildly looking for an escape route, and the Andalusian was visibly upset. Unlike the polite manner in which the person on his back had asked him to move just a few minutes before, she now was running him into corners, desperately trying to find a way out. No one was foolhardy enough to approach the horse; Annie was sure Tabitha wouldn't hesitate to run anyone down who got in her way. She saw Detective Wollcott talking on his phone as he attempted to climb over the fence, not very successfully. Annie turned back to Lucy, who was trying to explain where she'd been.

"Annie? The ones behind the stable were full. But a nice stall worker showed me the old ones I could use, in that building over there." She pointed in back of her.

"Well, I'm sorry, Lucy, but I may need to borrow your horse."

She handed the lead rope to her without a word.

Annie feverishly tied the end of the rope to the halter and slung it over the Hanoverian's head. She looked for a place to mount. Prince was so incredibly tall. She could jump on just about any horse, but not this one. She glanced over to the warm-up pen again. Now Tabitha was backing Andy up very quickly. The Andalusian's eyes were wide and white around the edges. His mouth was pried open and his chin pulled down from the hard pressure Tabitha was exerting on the reins. Annie heard Detective Wollcott drop heavily on the other side of the fence and watched him run toward the horse and rider.

Marcus was suddenly beside her, cupping his hands. She put one foot in his makeshift mounting block and was on Prince's back a second later. The view was perfect for what she next saw. Tabitha tapped her spurs into Andy's side and made a hard run for the arena fence. They sailed over and landed in the pasture beyond and out into an open field. Detective Wollcott stopped, and she heard him swear. Annie didn't wait to see or hear more. She leaned forward, and Prince took off at a fast canter through the aisle separating the arenas, through the astonished spectators and around the corner of the warm-up pen. Annie had done little jumping in her lifetime, but she instinctively leaned forward to give him his back. Prince practically floated over the four-foot fence separating the Darby property from their neighbor's. He landed lightly and continued to canter, while Annie looked around for a glimpse of Andy. She saw his back far in the distance and almost out of sight. Tabitha was determined to flee, it seemed. She'd driven Andy at a gallop, soaring past the singlewides in back and out into an empty field Annie had never seen before.

Prince's back was quite broad and Annie wished she had a saddle. Her svelte, eat-all-you-want-and-never-gain-a-pound Thoroughbreds were much easier to ride bareback than this massive gelding, but she didn't have a choice. Annie slowed the Hanoverian down to a soft, slow trot to try to get a better look at what lay before her.

She saw two small farmhouses, one on each side of her. By the moss on their roofs and the antiquated farm machinery parked neatly out back, they looked as if they'd been there for generations and owned by the same families. A long slope led to both. If Tabitha really wanted to hide, she'd find an outlying building on one of these old structures, ditch Andy, and take her chances on foot. Riding a beautiful Andalusian down the highway would only draw attention to herself. Even in full dressage regalia, the press would tag her as a modern-day Lady Godiva.

Relief poured through her when she realized the hard knob on her right thigh was the outline of her cell phone. She asked for a halt. Prince stopped on a dime, and Annie had Detective Wollcott's number on redial.

"Where are you?" His voice sounded urgent.

"In a pasture, looking at two farms. She has to be holed up in one. I'm going to scout out the closest one, on the west side."

"We've got the roads blocked. She can't get out, on horseback or otherwise."

"If she's walking by now, she might. But let's hope she isn't thinking that clearly."

"Is there a road back there? One for vehicles?"

"Haven't seen one yet. The farms will have them, of course. I'll let you know when I'm closer. You could always take the tuk-tuk."

"The *what*?"

"The golf cart."

Annie heard sputtering on the other end but decided to ignore it.

She hung up and trotted down to the first farm, keeping her eyes on the horizon just in case Tabitha had decided to go farther afield. She saw nothing but soft, undulating brown hills. Not even a small herd of grazing cows broke up the landscape. Of course, by now, there was nothing to graze on.

As she suspected, the farm had a number of old buildings in back, probably used to store old equipment. She'd seen plenty of these back where she lived. But were any of them big enough to hide a horse? A sudden whinny below gave her the answer. It came from a dilapidated old shack with a sloped roof that had half fallen in. The remnants of an old stile fence surrounded the shack on three sides. An overhang extended from one side of the rotting roof, and Annie wondered if it had once been the area where a farrier had done his work on horses, perhaps mules. The side of the shack facing her was made up of solid boards. Andy and Tabitha had to have entered on the other side. The slope of the roof was tall enough to accommodate a horse, even an Andalusian of Andy's size.

Unfortunately, Prince felt compelled to return Andy's call, and his own sharp whinny emerged seconds after Andy's. Annie not only heard it but felt it reverberate throughout his body. Her cover, such as it had been, was blown.

She walked Prince down the slope. When she was twenty feet from the shack, she halted him again and called out.

"Tabitha? It's Annie. I think we need to talk."

Silence. A breeze fluttered across the pasture, causing a wooden board to creak. Or had a human made that sound?

Annie quietly slid off Prince and hoped sometime in his lifetime he'd learned to be ground tied. She walked ten noiseless paces toward the shack and looked back. Prince seemed content to pick at whatever nubs of grass still remained. She continued walking toward the shack, looking for any sign, any movement that showed Tabitha and Andy were there.

The sound of a chair scraping on the floor coincided with her arrival at the overhang. She paused and heard a long, ragged breath inside.

"I'm not going to take it." It was the voice of a young man, who sounded terrified.

"But you have to. It's for your own good." The female voice sounded so sweet, sweeter than Annie had ever remembered hearing. But she still recognized it as Tabitha's.

In one step, she whipped around the corner, and with one more, she was inside the shack. As she'd suspected, she was in an old abandoned horse barn. Despite the sun outside, it was semi-dark in here. The only light came from the broken-down entrance, and that was a mere two feet wide. Straining her eyes, Annie saw that just two stalls remained along the back, a solid plank of wood attached to thick posts separating them. In one of the former stalls stood Andy, still saddled and looking a bit sweaty, Annie thought, but reasonably okay. In the other sat a young man of about twenty-five. He was vehemently shaking his head back and forth, his stringy blond hair falling over his forehead as he made each violent gesture. He was dressed in a filthy tuxedo and looked exhausted and stressed. She could not see his hands; they were behind his back, and, Annie presumed, tied. A long chain was around one ankle. He could move perhaps twelve feet, Annie thought, but not far enough to get outside the shack.

Tabitha stood over him, holding a small glass high in her right hand. Her back was to Annie, and it took only two strides to reach Tabitha and knock the glass from her hand. Tabitha screamed and put her hands to her face. Then she pulled them away and turned to look at Annie. Annie noticed some of the liquid had fallen on her hands and was on her face.

"You've ruined everything!" she shrieked.

Without thinking, Annie slapped her. Tabitha slumped against the wall and slid down to the floor, sobbing.

Annie quickly untied the young man's hands. She shook Tabitha for the key to the chain, and she handed it over, her hands trembling.

"How long have you been here?" she asked.

The boy shook his head before answering.

"Days. It seems like forever."

"Well, you're safe now."

She pulled out her cell phone and once more pushed redial.

"Everything's under control. Tabitha's here, along with a waiter who's been missing for a few days. We're at the west-side barn, in the old stall."

Annie listened intently for a minute, then smiled.

"Easy. There's a big, beautiful Hanoverian grazing on the hill right above us. Tell Lucy her boy's a hero."

Chapter Twenty-five

"You should have seen Douglas's face when he drove in," Liz told Annie. "He ran all the way to the stables from the parking lot and nearly collapsed when he got there. I actually thought he might have gone into paralytic shock."

They were talking on the patio, waiting for cocktail hour to officially begin. Annie had just emerged from a long conversation with Detective Wollcott. To her extreme satisfaction, he had told her Deputy Collins had retrieved a thermos from the dumbwaiter that contained Judge Bennett's special blend of Lady Grey tea. That pretty much put the lid on Tabitha's perfidy in her book, and she was rewarding herself for her perspicacity now by serenely floating on her back in the pool. Marcus, who had been prescient enough to bring his swim trunks, was splashing the water beside her to make her come out and play. It wasn't working.

"But how could Douglas have known that Nicole had been poisoned? You said he showed up about ten minutes after we found her."

"That's the funny part. He didn't. He was just afraid he'd missed Nicole's ride and had been anticipating her fury."

Patricia finished the story.

"So, when one of the medics pulled him aside, and said, 'I'm sorry, sir, but I'm afraid your fiancé was unable to ride today, she's suffering the ill effects of poison,' he just gasped, 'Oh, thank God!'"

Annie started to laugh and discovered she had inhaled a large amount of water. She stood up, coughing and laughing at the same time, while Marcus gently patted her on the back.

Liz next gave Annie the full medical update. Three ambulances had come and gone since Annie had returned from what Marcus was calling "Mr. Toad's wild ride." The first ambulance had taken Nicole, who, thanks to the activated charcoal, had managed to rid herself of most of the poison. The medics assured her fiancé that she would make a full recovery.

"Did anyone think to take photos?" Annie inquired innocently. Marcus promptly dunked her.

The second ambulance had taken the waiter to the local hospital for observation. He was dehydrated and extremely hungry, but aside from being scared out of his wits by Tabitha's attempt to poison him, also was going to be all right. He was young and strong, and Annie suspected he'd be back on the job by tomorrow. Chef Gustav was overcome with joy when he was told the waiter had been found. At the moment, he was busy concocting a special broth for the young man, as well as the waiter's favorite desserts.

The third ambulance had transported Tabitha to the local hospital as well, but her destination was the psychiatric ward. Detective Wollcott had officially

placed her under arrest for the murders of Betsy
Gilchrist and Jean Bennett and the attempted murders of Nicole Anne Forrester and the waiter, whose
name she learned was Eric Sumner. But she would be
housed in the psych unit for quite some time while
her mental status was evaluated and, with luck, stabi-
lized. Annie doubted Tabitha would ever be declared
competent to stand trial. But perhaps with the right
medications, she would regain some semblance of
sanity. Perhaps.

Annie was enjoying the calm of the pool and the
blessed silence within the house. She hadn't realized
how much adrenaline she'd used up until now, and
lazily went over the final events of Tabitha's capture in
her mind.

Once Deputy Collins and his men had taken over
the crime scene at the shack, Annie had again mounted
Prince, using a stump this time, and gently jogged him
back to Darby Farms. Miraculously, the dressage show
was still going on. It was hard to fathom that even after
all the recent mayhem, there were still fourteen riders
on the day sheet who were determined to ride, and
ride they did. One of them was in the dressage court
when she walked in on Prince, so she dismounted and
quietly walked the Hanoverian back to the stables
and into Lucy's waiting arms.

Annie wasn't sure who Lucy was in awe of the
most—her horse or Annie. In her eyes, both had saved
the day, not to mention the town from the bad guys.
Annie had tried to deflect Lucy's unending praise by
heaping it instead upon her horse.

"Prince was the real hero today. Did you see the way
he took that fence? You might think about renaming

him Snowman," she told her. Lucy looked as if she might seriously consider her suggestion.

The gong for cocktail hour sounded, and Annie reluctantly got out of the pool. The only silver lining, she thought, was that neither Gwendolyn nor Nicole would be in attendance at this ritual gathering. Gwendolyn had been pulled over by a deputy shortly after she'd made her own dash off the Darby farm. She'd been asked to park and lock her Porsche and step into the back of the deputy's patrol vehicle. According to Detective Wollcott, Gwendolyn was not particularly cooperative, and it was only until the deputy politely told her he would arrest her for obstruction of justice that she sullenly got in the backseat and put on her seat belt. After Tabitha's arrest, Detective Wollcott had given Gwendolyn permission to leave once more, but Annie had missed seeing her departure. Liz had told her she'd had Jorge bring down her bags and ordered the barn manager to see to her horse's transport back to the Bay Area. Any talk about riding and perhaps acquiring Victory had been abandoned.

"Just as well," Patricia had told her. "I'd already decided that was one sale that simply could not go through."

Annie had wholeheartedly agreed.

Hollis and Miriam made sure that conversation during both the cocktail hour and following dinner was light, bordering on the frivolous, and with no mention of Tabitha or her arrest. Joining them was Phyllis Hobert, the judge who had stepped in, her scribe, and Brianna, whose volunteers had convinced her that they could wrap things up just fine without her. Hollis informed the group that Douglas Kenyan, who had intended to join them, was now at Nicole's side at the local hospital, and he had been assured that Nicole would be fine. This opened the door for everyone to relive the highlights of the day that they wanted to remember.

Patricia was ecstatic about the serious interest two women had shown that afternoon in Beau Geste and Victory. Picante was spoken for, Miriam had informed her, and arched eyebrows from Hollis or no, the decision was final.

"I really think both horse and rider pairings will be excellent," she told Marcus over dinner. "And if you don't object, I'd like to stay on a day or two to see the sales go through."

"By all means," Marcus said. "And try to convince Annie to stay, as well. I have to return to work tomorrow and won't be around to keep her out of trouble. Ouch!"

Annie had kicked him under the table. And as much as she had enjoyed the Darbys' kind hospitality, she had no intention of changing her airline ticket, which put her on a plane tomorrow morning. She missed her animals, all of them, and it was time to return home.

"I hope you're right about these horses." Harriett was still dubious about their futures in competitive dressage. "If they don't have the movement, temperament, and conformation for the work, these women will be disappointed."

"I believe the women are convinced on all counts," Patricia said politely. "And you rode Picante this afternoon. Don't you think he and Miriam will make a perfect pair?"

"You have promised to school us," Miriam gently added.

"He *is* a horse with a lot of potential," Harriett grudgingly admitted. "But you'll have to work hard, Miriam."

"Harriett, is there any other way to work?" Miriam's sweetly spoken reply apparently did not warrant a response.

All the riders around the table were more than content with their test scores, and Lucy was over the moon with hers. It seemed even she couldn't quite believe what she had pulled off, and naturally, credited Annie's impromptu pep talk as the source of her success in the ring. This was more than a bit embarrassing to Annie, who knew that without Melissa's patient, thorough coaching, Lucy never would have ridden as well as she had. If Annie had played any part in this, it was only to give Lucy a nudge to realize and act on all she'd learned. Annie intended to make sure Melissa knew how she felt about Lucy's fulsome praise, although the trainer did not seem at all upset about Lucy's lopsided division of credit.

Liz, who'd received a score of 68, was thrilled at simply receiving a score that she felt enabled her to start showing first level. She and Patricia already were plotting when they would start work back on the Peninsula. Annie knew that thermal underwear and down vests would soon be part of their riding attire. One had to be a dedicated rider to ignore sleeting rain and cold, damp weather, even if the lesson was conducted inside a covered arena.

After dinner, the group dispersed. Amy and Lucy were heading back to Boston the next day and went off to pack. Their plane would leave just about the time the commercial transport came for their horses, although the latter would arrive in Boston two days later.

"Next time, let's fly them, so we don't have to be separated from them for so long," Lucy told her friend.

Amy smiled. "Maybe. But let me finish out my year clerking and land a job with a law firm first. I promise to use all my signing money on Schumann."

"Of course!" Lucy seemed astounded at the idea that it would be spent on anything else.

At eight o'clock, the front doorbell chimed, and Detective Wollcott was ushered in. Hollis had warned Annie of his impending visit, and that he intended to update them on the case. She was eager to hear everything the detective had to report. The issue of how Tabitha had managed to poison three, almost four people was largely answered in her own mind. But the issue of why she had done it still hung in the air, with a large question mark beside it.

Annie took Marcus with her as she joined Hollis and Miriam on the veranda. Detective Wollcott made no objection to Marcus's presence. Before the informal meeting began, Hollis offered everyone a glass of brandy or cognac from his private stock, then, ignoring Miriam's reproachful gaze, pulled out a box of cigars. Miriam and Annie declined, but Marcus and the detective seemed extraordinarily happy to accept one from the fragrant container.

When everyone was settled, all expectant eyes fell on the detective.

"I had a chance to go over Deputy Collins's initial

reports before I got here," he told the group. "It seems Ms. Rawlins was eager to talk on her ride to the hospital."

"Did Deputy Collins go with her?" Annie asked.

"Oh, yes. We weren't going to let her out of police custody for one second. And as soon as the medics told us none of the poison had penetrated her system and she was compos mentis—well, at least enough to understand her Miranda rights—we read them to her."

"And she waived them?"

"Completely. Even after Collins asked if she was sure she didn't want an attorney present. She was happy to talk."

No one said anything. If anyone thought it odd that Tabitha, a tax attorney, had waived her rights, they didn't express their opinion. No one, it appeared, wanted to impede the flow of information about to come out of the detective's mouth.

"I think she truly is legally insane," he began. "A typical killer wouldn't take what Ms. Rawlins saw as tangible reasons to kill another human being. But she told Collins that Judge Bennett had put a hex on her horse, and that convinced her the judge had to die."

"What! She actually *meant* that when she said it?" Annie couldn't believe it.

"That's what she told Collins. She'd intended to kill her as soon as she learned the judge would be offici-ating, and since she'd stayed at your place before, Hollis, she managed to plot it out rather carefully beforehand."

Hollis put a hand over his face. "We had no idea."

"Of course you didn't. No sane person would ever suspect that one of their houseguests would kill a competition judge, or anyone else, for that matter, for such an idiotic reason."

"How did she know about the dumbwaiter?"

"She'd stayed in the room, the one Ms. Smythe occupied this time, before. She'd hoped she'd stay in it again, and had quite the quarrel with Ms. Smythe over it when she realized she'd been assigned one room over. Ms. Smythe wouldn't budge, so Ms. Rawlins took it upon herself to steal the extra key. Apparently duplicates of all the room keys are hung in the pantry."

"That's right," Miriam said. "Sometimes guests take food and drink up, and the kitchen staff have to retrieve it. And, of course, if guests choose to lock their doors, the maids have to have keys to be able to clean."

"Tabitha also helped Chef Gustav out on at least one occasion," Annie remembered. "And there might have been more times she was in the kitchen."

"Yes, she had ample opportunity to take an empty thermos, which I understand are stored in the pantry. She told Collins that on Thursday, the day she and Ms. Litchfield helped the chef, she'd offered to go out to get something out of the garden. She swooped up the tea where it was baking in the sun, then hid the thermos in the dumbwaiter, where she could retrieve it whenever Gwendolyn was out of her room. Annie figured out how she'd heated the tea on Saturday, and the rest is, well, you know the outcome."

Annie frowned slightly. "One thing I haven't understood is why the dumbwaiter was resting on the same level as Lucy's bedroom when Hollis and I found it, instead of her own."

"Oh, that was just a bit of insurance. Ms. Rawlins said she deliberately left it there on Saturday, so that if anyone had discovered the dumbwaiter's criminal use, it would look as if Lucy was the culprit."

"Really!" Miriam was incensed. "That was a bit below the belt."

"What was really below the belt was trying out her concoction on Betsy Gilchrist first," the detective said drily. "Although quite frankly, any of you could have been the victim instead. The poison Ms. Rawlins put in the iced tea was just a test run, so to speak. She wanted to know how potent it was and if it really could cause a person's death."

That statement stunned everyone into a temporary silence.

"You mean she put the poison in a glass at random? And then waited to see who reacted to it?" Marcus seemed to find this difficult to take in.

"That's about the size of it. Except one of the waiters saw her put something in the glass, and when she didn't take it, offered it to her, thinking she'd just put in some kind of fake sweetener. She had to backtrack, and as we know, still managed to poison one of the iced-tea drinks, but she was concerned that the waiter who watched her might put two and two together after Mrs. Gilchrist's death. That was Eric Sumner, the gentleman you discovered, Annie."

"How did she manage to get him off the property and into that shack?" Annie had been wondering this ever since she saw the bedraggled waiter in the abandoned stall.

"Oh, the usual way. Feminine wiles. She started to show a romantic interest in the young man and suggested they go for a walk in the country, luring him there with a bottle of wine. Then she locked him inside and left him to his own devices, such as they were."

"The poor fellow!" Miriam shook her head.

"Yes, she left him with only the bottle of wine, which didn't do much to help his dehydrated state. She told Collins she intended to free him eventually, but what you saw, Annie, puts the lie to that."

Annie remembered Tabitha's voice, so sweet and alluring, as she tried to force the waiter to drink her poison.

"What *was* the poison?" Marcus asked.

"One of nature's own. *Convallaria majalis*," the detective said, drawing out each syllable, "commonly known as lily of the valley. It grows everywhere in this region, and the entire plant is quite toxic if ingested, from stem to flower. Reaction time is immediate, and the cause of death usually heart failure, although there are several unpleasant symptoms to live through before that occurs."

"Oh my heavens," Miriam said. "I grow it in my garden. We make sure there's nothing like that in the horse pastures, of course, along with tansy ragwort and other noxious weeds, but I never imagined growing that pretty belled flower would cause the death of two people."

"Don't feel too bad, Mrs. Darby," the detective consoled her. "We always think of nature as benevolent, but it has countless ways of poisoning us. It's impossible to know them all."

Just what Undersheriff Kim Williams had told her, Annie recalled.

"Did you ever really consider Chef Gustav a viable suspect?" she asked.

The detective shook his head.

"Not really. He had no motive to kill Judge Bennett. On the contrary—for years, he'd served her favorite food and beverages in this home with the sole intent of making her happy. And another staff member told us about the fuss he'd made over Mrs. Bennett's tea not being picked up and discarding it to make another thermos."

"I don't suppose this same waitperson saw Tabitha come in and swap it out." Annie wasn't holding her breath.

"Unfortunately, no. As you've said, it was a very busy morning, and the only person in the kitchen who was getting undivided attention was the chef. Anyone who happened to wander in and get a thermos, or in this case, swap a thermos, was left alone and largely ignored. No, I thought all along it had to be one of the guests staying here. The problem was, which bloody one?"

"There were so many to choose from," Annie mused.

"Honestly, Annie, if you think I deliberately choose my houseguests on their capacity to commit murder . . ."

"Hollis, I didn't mean to imply—"

"I'm just joking with you, Annie. But I agree, many of their stories did seem to imply that they might have been involved."

"Yes, indeed. To start with, Ms. Cartwright conveniently forgot to mention that she'd returned to the estate early Saturday morning to retrieve some grooming tool."

"Honestly, I think she did just forget," Miriam told the detective.

"She's a shy little thing, and it's entirely possible.

Later, another houseguest informed me she'd seen Ms. Smythe outside the house at the hour she told us she had arisen. And that Ms. Smythe was in the vicinity of the kitchen."

This had to have come from Liz. Annie was glad that her friend had found time to share this tidbit with the detective.

"Yes, what was that all about?" Annie asked.

"Before she left today, Ms. Smythe admitted to me that she'd lied, but it was for the silliest of reasons. She said she needed more time to study her test, which she'd left in her car, and didn't want the others to know about it."

Now that is silly, Annie thought. And any extra cramming certainly hadn't helped much.

"And then, of course, there was Brianna's incriminating statement after she learned the judge had died," Annie reminded the detective.

"Yes, that was quite intriguing, especially after you told me about the row she'd had with the judge the night before."

Hollis and Miriam looked distinctly guilty.

"You knew, Annie?" Miriam asked sadly.

"I found out. It wasn't something I particularly wanted or needed to know, but I felt I had to tell Detective Wollcott."

"Well, in the light of all that's happened, we're considering Ms. Bowen's outburst nothing more something that was said in the heat of the moment but has no basis in truth."

"As I might have mentioned once or twice," Annie reminded him.

"As you might have done."

Annie took this as a positive statement. "You've explained how Mrs. Gilchrist came to be a victim, and why the judge was singled out. But why did Tabitha target Nicole at the very end?"

"Fortunately, I can and will explain that. It's all very recent information, obtained from Nicole's hospital bedside, where I understand her fiancé is now."

Miriam and Hollis nodded.

"As soon as she was out of the woods, we spoke with her. I wish she had been more forthcoming before. If she had, we might have been able to arrest Tabitha without all the fuss this afternoon."

Typical, Annie thought, then said bluntly, "She destroyed Tabitha's rhythm beads, didn't she?"

The detective nodded. "Yes, and we have the evidence."

"Do tell." Hollis leaned forward.

"As you know, we've been examining the surveillance tapes from the stables for the past twenty-four hours. Ms. Forrester's Jaguar is seen pulling up in front at about ten o'clock on Thursday night. She parks, goes into the front entrance, returns about seven minutes later, then mysteriously parks her car in the public parking area, not at the house. I assume she walked the rest of the way back to the house, put the destroyed beads on Ms. Rawlins's door, and returned her own car to the parking lot early the next morning. We're still reviewing that portion of the tape to confirm when the car left."

"I've been meaning to put in surveillance cameras in our own parking area," Hollis said ruefully.

"Well, we had enough to confront her, and she immediately admitted to it."

"But why did she do it?"

"She'd seen Ms. Rawlins interacting with the waiter, and suspected she was somehow involved in the poisoning of Mrs. Gilchrist. That's why she left the note, "Quit while you're ahead." She wanted to scare Ms. Rawlins, if it was true. Instead, she merely set herself up to be murdered a few days later."

So Nicole did know a thing or two about Shakespearean plays. Annie wouldn't have thought so.

"The door slam." She was determined to have the detective answer every question while he was on the hot seat. "If that wasn't Nicole I heard, who was it?"

"It was Tabitha, coming back from the kitchen after making the thermos switch. She came up from the stables primarily to accomplish this final act. As long as the scribe hadn't shown up, she knew she still had time. Unfortunately, Ms. Forrester saw her coming in as she was leaving the dining area. And that, in Ms. Rawlins's mind, absolutely sealed Ms. Forrester's fate."

Everyone sat in silence for a few minutes, absorbing all they'd been told. Finally, Miriam spoke.

"You know, the thing that still puzzles me is how Tabitha managed to pull off such a magnificent performance of Prix St.-Georges. It's way beyond the level at which she'd studied with Harriett. True, Andy probably knows the movements in his sleep, but still, it amazes me that she could perform so well the first time out, and at a dressage show, no less."

"You've got me on that one, Miriam," the detective conceded. "I don't know enough about horses or dressage or whatever it is you do to answer that. But she did tell Deputy Collins something that might help answer your question. She said that someone named Charlotte never performed pea-offs on a blueberry before a performance, so she didn't have to prepare Andy, either. Does that make any sense?"

"She's talking about Charlotte Dujardin, an elite British dressage rider," Annie informed him. "Blueberry is the name of her horse. And, by the way, it's pronounced piaffe."

"Aha."

"I seem to recall promising you a nice, relaxing weekend when you first arrived," Hollis told Annie after the detective had left.

"Actually, it has been. You've both been such wonderful hosts, and I'm amazed by everything you've done, and continue to do, here. I think it was only when Lucy and Tabitha both went missing that I felt the worst. I was terrified that something had happened to Lucy."

"Yes, I'm actually glad you weren't able to tell us then what you knew about . . . Tabitha." Miriam's voice trembled just a bit. "I'm not sure I would have been able to handle it."

Hollis put his arm around his wife. "I just hope this experience hasn't deterred you from returning. With Marcus, I hope."

"I'd—" Annie glanced at Marcus. "We'd love to. I can't wait to see you riding Picante—after a few lessons with Harriett, of course. And it would be super if we could ride together on your trails."

Did she just say super?

Miriam smiled and grasped one of Annie's hands.

"So, what do you think about all this? Will you take up dressage with Patricia now, or go back to your Western riding and never give dressage a second thought?"

"Seriously? I'm a Western rider and always will be. But I don't think I'll ever look at the riding discipline the same way again. I've learned too much not to take notice of what dressage teaches riders about their horses and how it works with the horses to get the best from them."

"I'm delighted to hear that, Annie. Well, we'll let the two of you get some sleep. I know it's an early morning for you both. Oh, and you may see Brianna about before you leave tomorrow. We've offered to put her up for the next few weeks so she can concentrate on her thesis. She's defending in November, and we want her to be as absolutely prepared as possible."

"How kind of you. I'm sure she'll appreciate the chance to concentrate on her work, and in such a beautiful setting. What's her thesis on, if I might ask?"

"The role horses play in the novels of Jane Austen. It's actually quite fascinating. I've got her latest draft by my bedside now."

There was one more person Annie had to see before retiring

"I'll be back in just a minute," she explained to the others. "I just want to thank Chef Gustav one last time for all his excellent meals."

She knocked on the kitchen window, and the chef motioned for her to enter.

"Mademoiselle Annie! You are leaving us tomorrow, I understand. It has been most enjoyable to have you here. We shall see you again, I hope, in the not too distant future?"

"I hope so! How is Eric doing?"

"He is *très bien*, thanks be to God."

Annie paused. "Chef Gustav, you knew it was Tabitha all along, didn't you?"

"I had my suspicions, *oui*."

"How did you know?"

"She was disturbed in the head, one could see that readily. I knew she had been in the kitchen while I was not, and just not to find food or to help herself to a glass of wine. But that was only one small thing. I could tell that she trusted no one. On the contrary, I believe Mademoiselle Tabitha thought everyone was her adversary. And when one thinks that—" The chef shrugged. "It is only a matter of time when you must strike out at the fabled dragon, *n'est-ce pa*?"

"You are right, Chef Gustav. You are absolutely right."

Annie returned to the veranda. It was getting late, and she could see that their hosts were beyond tired. She caught Marcus's eye and they soon said good night to the couple and walked upstairs. As Annie put the key into the lock of her suite, Marcus put his arms around her waist and with his chin, began to nuzzle her hair.

"So, what is it about women and their horses?"

"It's complicated," she murmured back, and leaned back for a kiss. "Trust me on this."

ACKNOWLEDGMENTS

When I first got the idea of writing a mystery set in the world of dressage, I imagined it would be a bit of a lark. This thought proved utterly delusional. I soon realized that unless I had a professional dressage person lurking behind my shoulder at every page turn, I'd be lost. Enter Rebecca Parker Black, who teaches dressage on Bainbridge Island and is a USDF bronze, silver, and gold medalist. Rebecca had pity on my ignorance and took me under her wing. She spent countless hours explaining dressage terms, its history and philosophy, and then showed me what it all looks like in the ring. She guided me through probable and improbable scenarios that I had constructed, offered brilliant solutions, and remembered every fictional horse's name better than I did. Her exquisite and thoughtful editing and suggestions are reflected on every page, and her contributions are what ensure this book's authenticity. With Rebecca's help, this mystery turned out to be more than a lark to write. It was really, really fun.

I also want to thank Janet Grunbok, another stellar dressage rider and instructor who owns Whitethorn Farm on Bainbridge. Janet persuaded me to attend a master class by Charlotte Dujardin, which was eye-opening, and also was kind enough to let me to watch her instruct others and answer my many questions. Thanks to dressage student Gale Yee, who graciously accompanied me to a dressage show in Southern California. Finally, I want to include Sara Petersen and Cindy Daniels of Woodside Stables in Kingston, Washington, in these acknowledgments. Overlook the fact that they are dedicated hunter/jumpers. For several months, they've been teaching this old dog new tricks under English saddle, and their sage instruction, given so patiently, no matter how oft repeated, on how to ride so your horse doesn't think you're a complete idiot is found on many pages of this book.

My thanks once more go to Paige Wheeler of Creative Media for taking such good care of me, to Robert Schwager and Ken Kagan for their eagle-eyed editing, and to Fern Michaels, who started me on this path and will always be my heroine.

If you enjoyed *Runaway Murder*,
be sure not to miss LEIGH HEARON's

UNBRIDLED MURDER

A CARSON STABLES MYSTERY

After horse trainer and rancher Annie Carson visits
a feedlot in eastern Washington, she is determined
to save as many horses from slaughter as possible
before hightailing it back home—until she discovers
the sleazy owner seemingly trampled in his corral.
With the fate of the feedlot herd in her hands,
Annie must navigate unfamiliar territory while
trying to track down a killer and solve an
increasingly tangled mystery. But unfortunately for
Annie, returning to the Olympic Peninsula alive
will be trickier than she ever imagined.

Turn the page for a special look!

A Kensington mass market and e-book on sale now.

Chapter One

Annie's face was infused with damp sweat. The bright fluorescent light overhead nearly blinded her, and it took all her willpower not to twist and squirm from its pitiless gaze. She scrunched her eyes and tried to breathe evenly. She vowed that she would not speak or cry out in pain, no matter what happened.

"Relax."

The word floated above her, and Annie wanted to kick the speaker. She didn't, and the speaker continued, in a gentle, soothing tone.

"If you squeeze your eyes like that, I can't do my job. And you do want beautiful eyebrows, don't you?"

Did she? Annie had never given much thought to her eyebrows. But apparently, her girlfriends had, and they had pretty much demanded that she *do something about them* before she saw that *fabulously handsome man again.*

Lisa Brunswell, one of Annie's newest friends and her very first stable assistant, was the most adamant. It probably was her age, Annie thought. Lisa was at least two decades younger than she was, the time when things like waxed eyebrows and silky-smooth skin still mattered. Annie was about to turn forty-four, and aside from slapping on a bit of moisturizer before bed— when she remembered—she didn't really think about her face. Her horses had never complained about her looks.

But then Marcus Colbert had entered her life, and everything had changed. Deliciously so.

And now here she was, lying on a massage table with her knees propped up and her hair pulled back into a plump white towel, and feeling extremely vulnerable. She'd felt more courage when she'd encountered a black bear on her property last autumn.

"Your skin might be a little red after the procedure, so we're doing the eyebrows first," the voice continued. "But by the time I've finished with your facial, you'll look perfectly normal. Radiant, in fact. Now, hold still, please. And relax the eyes. That's it."

Annie breathed out and thought, not for the first time, that Marcus had seemed to like her just fine when he had first met her. She'd been wearing dusty cowboy boots and faded jeans.

Two hours later, Annie had to admit she looked remarkably better than any time in recent memory. Her skin *was* glowing, and somehow her green eyes looked more vibrant when unruly eyebrows didn't take center stage. She'd initially squawked at the stylist's insistence on trimming her long, dark brown hair and could barely watch as four inches of it languidly slipped to the salon floor. But looking at herself in the mirror thirty minutes later, she realized the shorter length gave her hair more bounce and shape.

She felt beautiful but had no time to revel in her new stunning self. Annie was meeting Marcus at Port Chester's one French restaurant in two short hours, and she still had to go home to change and check on the horses before making the half-hour drive to the county's most populated—nearly nine thousand at the last census—metropolis.

She ducked out of the salon while stylists from every booth were still oohing and aahing about her transformation. Rushing straight into the sunlit world, Annie didn't see Deputy Tony Elizalde approach until he tapped her on her arm. Predictably, she shrieked, and reached into her saddlebag purse for her never-used can of Mace.

"Relax, Annie. It's me, Tony. Glad I caught you. Boy, you look different."

He was the second person who'd told her to relax today, and she was already tired of it.

"Try calling out my name next time. I respond to words."

"Didn't have time. You burst out of that salon like your hair was on fire. Looks nice, by the way. What's the hurry?"

As if Annie were going to say anything about her date with Marcus. She'd endured enough snide remarks from Tony about her budding relationship to share any new information now.

"Nothing. What's up?"

"I got a call from a buddy in eastern Washington this morning about a lead on some fine horses for sale."

"Thanks, I have all I can handle at the moment."

"Not you, Annie! For Travis's new farm, Alex's Place."

She squinted at Tony, who was standing right in front of the sun. "I thought we'd decided at the last board meeting that we were going to look for horses at our local rescue centers."

"We did, which is why I want to talk to you now. This is an opportunity to acquire good horses for all the right reasons. But it'll take time to explain. And my keen detecting mind tells me you don't have a lot of that right now."

"You got that right, Deputy. I'm booked for the rest of the day. But stop by the farm tomorrow, if that works."

"Will do. Morning okay?"

"Ah . . . let's make it early afternoon."

"Roger that."

Annie nodded at Tony, climbed into her F-250, and started to make an illegal U-turn to head out of town. Glancing in the rearview mirror, she saw Tony still looking at her, his hands on his hips, his expression amused. And curious. Well, he'd just have to stay curious, Annie thought. Although she had to admit she was a bit curious herself about Tony's new lead on adoptable horses. Her friend, Travis Latham, had recently acquired property to build a working farm for boys at risk. Tony and Annie, both members of the nonprofit board overseeing the project, had been tasked with acquiring horses.

Checking on her own horses was pretty much pro forma tonight. As she pulled into her stables, she saw Lisa's yellow VW bug already parked by the tack room and heard her friend humming inside. Annie nudged the door open and slithered inside.

"Wow! You cleaned up good!"

Annie grinned back at her friend, who was stuffing two massive flakes of Timothy into Trooper's hayrack. Trooper was a Thoroughbred and required more hay each day than her youngest horse, a fourteen-hand Saddlebred, consumed practically all week.

"Well, I did have a lot of help."

"And they sure knew what they were doing. You look incredible, Annie! Marcus is going to think he's met a totally new woman!"

Fat chance of that, Annie thought. Miracle workers might enhance her exterior, but she doubted anyone could change her personality, which had been described as stubborn, willful, and annoyingly averse to accepting advice. And those were her friends' opinions. At least everyone stipulated to her fine sense of humor.

"Are you set for tonight?" Annie asked anxiously. Lisa had been Annie's right-hand stable hand for nearly two months now and knew the horses' schedules, needs, and personalities almost as well as she did. But this was the first time Lisa was going to spend the night in her farmhouse, alone, unless you counted the dogs, Sasha and Wolf, and Max the kitten.

"Absolutely. The dogs and I are looking forward to staying up late watching zombie movies and eating all your popcorn. And I don't have to be back at my place until ten a.m. tomorrow, so I've got plenty of time to feed, muck, and make sure everything's set for tomorrow night."

Annie truly relaxed for the first time that day. She was certain everything would be fine and wondered why it had taken her so long to realize that, as her mother used to say, "many hands make light work." For fifteen years, as long as Annie had owned Carson Stables, she'd summarily dismissed any suggestion of bringing help on board, even while her herd grew, and her horse-training business became a demanding year-round job. When Sheriff Dan Stetson, a friend from high school and now a close colleague, had convinced her to invest in a flock of sheep to bring in wool income, she'd still managed to do everything herself. After all, she'd had her horses' help with herding and maintaining the flock's fence line.

But with the arrival of Trooper, her newest horse and a gift from Marcus, plus a sudden surge in income when Marcus had asked for her help in divesting his late wife's equine estate, there seemed no reason *not* to bring in someone to share the workload. Meeting Lisa a few months ago had been fortuitous, indeed.

"Thanks, Lisa. Well, I've got to go—I still have to dress." Annie grabbed her purse and started to jog toward her farmhouse, fifty feet away.

"Go for it, girl! What are you wearing? Something slinky and easy to slip out of, I hope! And don't forget your makeup!"

Laughter was the only answer her new stable hand was going to get.